# Valley
# of the
# Shadow

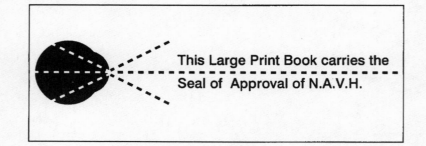

# Valley
# of the
# Shadow

## Stephanie Grace Whitson

**Thorndike Press • Waterville, Maine**

Published in 2004 by arrangement with Thomas Nelson, Inc.

Thorndike Press® Large Print Christian Fiction.

The tree indicium is a trademark of Thorndike Press.

The text of this Large Print edition is unabridged.
Other aspects of the book may vary from the original edition.

Set in 16 pt. Plantin by Elena Picard.

Printed in the United States on permanent paper.

**Library of Congress Cataloging-in-Publication Data**

Whitson, Stephanie Grace.
    Valley of the shadow / Stephanie Grace Whitson.
        p. cm.
    ISBN 0-7862-6359-8 (lg. print : hc : alk. paper)
        1. Women missionaries — Fiction.  2. Dakota Indians — Fiction.  3. Minnesota — Fiction.  4. Large type books.
    I. Title.
    PS3573.H555V3 2004
        813'.54—dc22                                        2004041217

For Robert, My Warrior

Yea, though I walk through the
valley of the shadow of death,
I will fear no evil: for thou art with me;
thy rod and thy staff they comfort me.
— Psalm 23:4 (KJV)

As the Founder/CEO of NAVH, the only national health agency solely devoted to those who, although not totally blind, have an eye disease which could lead to serious visual impairment, I am pleased to recognize Thorndike Press* as one of the leading publishers in the large print field.

Founded in 1954 in San Francisco to prepare large print textbooks for partially seeing children, NAVH became the pioneer and standard setting agency in the preparation of large type.

Today, those publishers who meet our standards carry the prestigious "Seal of Approval" indicating high quality large print. We are delighted that Thorndike Press is one of the publishers whose titles meet these standards. We are also pleased to recognize the significant contribution Thorndike Press is making in this important and growing field.

Lorraine H. Marchi, L.H.D.
Founder/CEO
NAVH

* Thorndike Press encompasses the following imprints: Thorndike, Wheeler, Walker and Large Print Press.

# Acknowledgments

In 1837 Mary Ann Longley Riggs, the daughter of a veteran of the War of 1812, the granddaughter of a man who served under General Washington in the Revolutionary War, set up housekeeping in an eighteen-by-ten-foot room on the second story of a log cabin on a bluff overlooking Lac Qui Parle, Minnesota. Of her eight earthly children, six became missionaries to the Sioux. A seventh, daughter Isabella, served with her husband in Kalgan, China. Only "the day of the Lord" will reveal how many spiritual children Mary Riggs bore during her time on this earth.

Mary and Stephen Riggs were caught up in the events of the 1862 Minnesota Sioux Uprising during which dozens of Dakota men and women risked their lives to save white missionaries and settlers.

What follows is a fictional account that seeks to honor two groups: Mary Riggs and her co-laborers in Christ, and the Dakota Sioux such as John Otherday, Lorenzo Lawrence, Paul Mazakutemane, Simon Anawangami, and Taopi. All knew the meaning of "he who wishes to save his life must lose it" in a way that I, a spoiled white American living in the twenty-first century, will probably never experience.

Today, visitors to southwestern Minnesota can stand on the parade ground of Fort Ridgely. They can visit the Lower Sioux Agency. They can admire the breathtaking view from the very spot where Mary and Stephen Riggs lived. And if they listen very carefully, and let their imaginations wander just a bit, they may even be able to hear the echoes of long-ago laughter as a young boy named Alfred Riggs coasts down the hill, past the cabin, past the mission church . . . across the trail . . . and onto the iced-over river. Of such imaginings are borne books like the one you hold in your hand.

Thank you for reading my story. May we all be challenged to apply Galatians 3:28 in our lives.

*There is neither Jew nor Greek, there is neither slave nor free, there is neither male nor female; for you are all one in Christ Jesus. (NKJV)*

# *One*

Therefore pray the Lord of the harvest
to send out laborers into His harvest.
— LUKE 10:2 (NKJV)

How he had managed to get that beautiful
Ellen Leighton to marry him was beyond the
realm of logic for anyone who knew Simon
Dane. Never, people said, were two young
people more unsuited for one another.

Even though she was only seventeen,
Ellen Leighton was the very definition of a
lady. Why, hadn't her own grandfather
fought under General Washington himself?
And wasn't it her grandfather on her
mother's side who had had a commission
from King George? Certainly Ellen's parents had nothing approaching marriage to
the likes of Reverend Simon Dane in mind
when they sent their daughter to be educated at Miss Bartlett's finishing school in
Ipswich. Ellen had gone reluctantly, but
came home a vision of manners and grace
that made the entire village proud. She

poured tea like royalty. And those gray eyes! Well, any young man upon whom those eyes alighted felt a thrill down to his elegant riding boots.

And so, when the practically middle-aged and almost homely Reverend Simon Dane arrived to temporarily fill the pulpit at Christ's Church, imagine everyone's amazement when Ellen Leighton looked upon him with something more than passing kindness.

"He has a mind, Mother," Ellen had explained firmly. "A girl can't always be a girl. I enjoy flirting as much as anyone, but when it comes to marriage, I want a man with a mind; someone I can talk to late into the night, for all those long years after youthful passions fade."

"Ellen!" Mrs. Leighton scolded, blushing.

Ellen's gray eyes crinkled up at the corners. "It's all right, Mother. You needn't act so shocked. Miss Bartlett's gave me a very thorough education in every manner of life." Her peach-colored lips parted in an almost impish grin. "And what Miss Bartlett omitted from daily lessons, the laundress made certain to cover. Honestly, Mother," Ellen said, sighing, "I don't see what all the fuss was about, anyway. Didn't

God create it in the first place and pronounce it good?"

"Of course He did, dear. But that does not negate the fact that well-bred young ladies do not discuss such things."

Ellen arched one eyebrow as she reasoned. "All I was trying to say was that I crave the attention of a man who can discuss something besides the weather, last week's ball, and whether or not I'll let him kiss me." She looked out the window. "Reverend Dane doesn't act as if he cares nearly as much about kissing as he does about the fifth point of Calvinism." She murmured, "I like that."

Mrs. Leighton sighed, clicked her tongue against the roof of her mouth, and returned to her needlework. Ellen finished her tea while poring over the last chapters of Edwards's *Life of David Brainerd.* Her young heart swelled with admiration for the missionary who died so young yet gave so much in service to Christ among the Indians.

That Sabbath, as Reverend Dane stood in the pulpit gazing over the waiting congregation, he thought he saw Ellen Leighton smile at him. He cleared his throat and lowered his eyes to the open Bible on the pulpit before him. He appeared to pray for a moment. When he

11

looked up and sought out the third pew on the left again, his suspicions were confirmed. It was undeniable. Miss Leighton had favored him with a smile. Gripping the pulpit firmly, the reverend denied himself the pleasure of looking toward the third pew on the left while he delivered his sermon in an unusually halting voice.

On Monday, Reverend Dane accepted an invitation to tea at the Leighton home. On Wednesday, he dined with the family and escorted Miss Leighton to choir practice. After choir practice, he blundered through asking Miss Leighton's permission to ask her father's permission to call. By the following Sunday, it was common knowledge that Ellen Leighton and Reverend Dane were practically engaged . . . and never, they said, were two young people more unsuited for one another.

For his part, Simon could not believe his good fortune. Never had he dared to imagine anyone as lovely as Ellen Leighton looking his way. While he did his best to dress neatly and was always exemplary in personal grooming, Simon could not ignore the fact that the face looking back at him out of the mirror was not really attractive. He was only twenty-eight, but already his hairline was beginning to recede. What little hair he had atop his rather narrow head grew out of his scalp in bunches, leaving irregular spaces of bare scalp exposed. To compensate for his loss, Simon left the strands of dull brown hair above his forehead exceedingly long, oiling and combing them straight back from his already-too-high forehead. In profile, his face was something like that of a hawk, except that Simon lacked the noble eye to balance the mildly hooked nose. His eyes were small, the iris forming a copper-tinted circle around the pupil, which gave him a perpetual expression of intense concentration — or disapproval, depending on whether one was inclined to like or dislike the Reverend Dane.

Simon had received his "call" to the ministry after facing the unavoidable reality that he did not have a mind for law. Having no mind for law, he determined to prove that he had a mind for theology and surprised himself by doing rather well at seminary. He spent hours poring over musty theology books and was always ready to argue the major points of some minor doctrinal issue.

Unfortunately, his readiness to debate made Simon essentially unfit as a minister. He inevitably alienated his deacons with protracted sermonettes at every meeting. In the all-knowing spirit of youth, Reverend Dane was eager to share the wisdom his seminary degree had imparted, even though it drove his deacons to distraction. Most churches endured the Reverend Dane in their pulpit for only a few months before the governing board contacted the church authorities to suggest that young Reverend Dane might be . . . ah . . . more suited to service elsewhere. Thus Reverend Simon Dane "rode the circuit" in a region of the United States where circuit riders were no longer necessary.

It always started well, this pastoring of flocks. Looking at the sheep, he saw their willingness to follow and be taught. He promised himself that this time things would be different. He would learn to shepherd. But when the sheep began to bleat and show their weaknesses, Simon inevitably felt himself pull back. He did *not* want to visit with Mr. Garvey about his lack of discretion with the downstairs maid. And who did Mr. Talbot think he was, sitting so piously in the fourth pew on the right, when everyone knew he'd spent Saturday night getting drunk and had gone home to beat his wife? Time and time again, Simon's congregations transformed themselves from sheep willingly following their shepherd into foul, hell-bent sinners. Time and time again, Simon grew to hate them for it. Were not the redeemed called to be holy? How could they stand the sin in their midst? More important, how could he stand before them week after week, pretending that they were as worthy as he?

But Simon was doubly blessed when Ellen Leighton favored him. The deacons' patience with him had not yet worn out, and he had not yet begun to hate his congregation. Ellen's attentions threw him so far off course that he forgot entirely to hate the flock, in spite of the fact that he was forced one evening to take the bell-ringer aside and speak to him about a late night at the local tavern.

One Sabbath not long after he began calling on Ellen, Reverend Dane was relieved of his pulpit by a visiting pastor. Reverend Stephen Riggs of the American Board of Commissioners for Foreign Missions delivered an impassioned plea for workers among the Dakota Sioux in the Far West. "We bring them the Word of Life," he said, "the Gospel of Salvation through faith in Jesus Christ our Lord, as contained in the Bible. We seek not to preach Christ to them only, that they might have life, but to engraft His living words into their living thoughts, so that they might grow into His spirit more and more. To put God's thoughts into their speech, and to teach them to read in their own tongue the wonderful works of God. That is what we have undertaken."

As he contemplated the "fields white unto harvest," Simon's heart was softened. He envisioned a congregation with no preconceived notions of what a pastor should be and thought that such a group might overlook his shortcomings. Surely, Simon thought, the poor ignorant savages of the west would rise up and call him blessed. As they followed his leading and sought his wisdom, they would learn to admire him. Perhaps, Simon dared to think, they would even love him.

A congregation with no prior knowledge of the Scriptures would not be quite so accountable for its failings. Perhaps, Simon thought, he would grow to love them. Simon determined to go. He shared the notion with Ellen.

"You'll need a wife to help you," she said matter-of-factly.

Simon stared at her in disbelief. Finally he half-stammered, "Dare I — would you —"

"I would," Ellen said.

When Simon mustered the courage to reach towards her, Ellen slipped her hand beneath his and smiled.

He dared to look at her, his heart pounding furiously in response to the warmth in her gray eyes. "I'll speak to Dr. Riggs," he croaked. Squeezing her hand, half amazed when she did not withdraw it, he added, almost in a question, "— and to your father?"

When Ellen nodded, Simon clasped her hand to his heart, thrilled by the silken smoothness of her skin. Blushing, he stood up and bolted for the door.

They were married in less than a month. While Simon gathered up credentials and applied for acceptance as a missionary of the American Board, Ellen prepared for a lifetime in the wilderness. Her friends held sewing bees and quilting bees, teasing Ellen about her new husband, alluding slyly to the groom's blush every time he saw his bride. When this happened, Ellen regarded them with a peaceful smile, holding the secrets of their private life apart from prying questions.

Simon and Ellen Dane had been among the Dakota for eight years when the Far

West became the state of Minnesota. They approved when the six thousand Dakota Sioux in the area sold twenty-eight million acres of their hunting grounds to the United States government and agreed to live on a reservation 150 miles long and 20 miles wide in return for cash annuities amounting to about nine dollars a year each. Pointing to the reservation's fertile bottomlands along the Minnesota River as proof that the Dakota had been treated well, the Danes and other missionaries reasoned that a million acres of well-watered soil was more than enough to support a farming population of six thousand. And concentrating the Dakota into one fertile valley could only help the missionaries in their well-intentioned quest to transform heathen savages into civilized Christian farmers.

By the time Ellen and Simon had been among the Dakota for ten years, two bustling villages had sprung up south of their small mission. The northernmost, called the Upper or Yellow Medicine Agency, was only about thirty miles away and boasted a dozen or so buildings on high ground overlooking the junction of the Yellow Medicine and Minnesota Rivers. Several traders' stores clustered in the valley below the agency attracted commerce from surrounding settlers and natives. Seven chiefs positioned their villages near the Upper Agency, among them Simon Anawangami and John Otherday, who were among the first Dakota to convert to Christianity and become farmers. Two mission stations, called Hazelwood and Pajutazee, served the Dakota living near the Upper Agency and they provided boarding schools and churches as well as agricultural training for a growing flock of Christian Dakota.

Thirty miles farther downriver from the Upper Agency was the Lower or Redwood Agency. The nine chiefs whose villages populated the river valley around the Lower Agency were among the most resistant to change. Even so, one of the most respected chiefs, named Little Crow, had recently cut his hair shoulder length and was living in a two-story board house instead of a tepee.

In spite of what the missionaries considered to be progress, grave problems remained. Nine out of ten Dakota did not want to become farmers. They witnessed the frenzy of white settlers flooding into the Dakota's former hunting grounds with a growing sense of outrage. If white men were so eager to have their lands, then they had been cheated by a government not willing to pay what the land was really worth. As the white population of the state exploded, game became more scarce, and for the Dakota who refused to farm, hunger became an almost constant companion.

Dishonest traders absconded with much of the annuities due the Dakota. They hovered about the agent's residence whenever annuities were to be distributed, producing records they claimed to be proof for what they were owed for goods bought on credit. Illiterate Dakota were at their mercy, often having their annuity barely touch their palms before a trader claimed it. Simon once watched in horror as an elderly Dakota man who was accosted by a trader quickly swallowed the coins in his hand. "I owe nothing!" he shouted. "You will not have what is mine!"

Haunted by the realization that not one of the Dakota living near their remote Renville Mission had converted to Christianity, Simon Dane faced the tenth anniversary of his marriage to Ellen and their ministry among the Dakota with something less than enthusiasm. While the mission workers to the south interpreted for the Dakota, helped negotiate with traders and the agents, and operated boarding schools, Renville Mission was dying. Simon had been unable to convince any Dakota to bring him their children, so there was no school. Even Sabbath attendance had begun to dwindle. Surely, Simon thought, God would smile on his labors soon. Surely there would be an end to the spiritual drought at Renville Mission.

While her husband concerned himself with what he considered to be greater matters than family life, Ellen Dane faced her tenth anniversary with a hidden hurt. While she and Simon had become friends, they were rarely intimate in any sense of the word. Ellen reminded herself over, and over, and over again that she had married Simon for his mind, not for passion. She had not been disappointed.

Her children were Ellen Dane's salvation. By 1860 the Danes had a son, eleven, and a daughter, seven. Aaron had his mother's golden hair and silken complexion and his father's brown eyes. Margaret, named for Ellen's mother but called Meg, was fair-skinned, redheaded, and boisterous to the point of insolence. While Aaron spent his days trying to please his father, Meg seemed to have a gift for calling out Simon's indignance. His sister's lack of tact, combined with his own sensitivity, placed Aaron in the role of protector and peacemaker. With Aaron and Meg, Ellen formed an almost subversive triumvirate, a threesome sharing love and encouragement in the face of Simon's almost bitter stoicism. With the arrival of her children, Ellen had learned to be content. And if she ever regretted the lack of passion in her life, no one — least of all her husband — ever knew it.

# Two

Honor your father and your mother, that your days may be long upon the land which the LORD your God is giving you.

— EXODUS 20:12 (NKJV)

"I won't go and you can't make me!" Eighteen-year-old Geneviève LaCroix stamped one small, moccasined foot on the board floor of her father's cabin.

"*Attends, ma petite.*" Her father removed his pipe from his mouth. Holding up one hand in a vain attempt to silence his daughter's outburst, he leaned forward in his chair.

Gen covered her ears. "I don't *want* to listen!" Her pale eyes pooled with angry tears. She clamped her lips together, willing her chin to stop trembling. "Nothing you can say will convince me to leave you!" She whirled away from her father and crossed the room to where a pot of stew bubbled on the stove. Snatching a wooden spoon she began to stir the concoction, sloshing broth over the edge of the pot. It slid down to the hot stovetop, sending the faint aroma of burned food into the air. Gen's voice trembled with anger. "Can you imagine an entire summer without my stew and corn bread? What would you eat?" she spat out. "Jerky and crackers!"

"I managed for many years on my own before I met your mother," Etienne protested gently.

"Mama told me how well you managed." Gen slapped the lid back on the pot. "When you took off your buffalo robe, she wondered how you managed to carry the weight of it, you were so thin." Gen turned and faced her father, shaking the wooden spoon at him. "Mama said you would likely have starved and been eaten by wolves if you hadn't stumbled into the Dakota camp that night."

Etienne's blue eyes searched his daughter's face. He sighed and shrugged. "It was a hard winter. I was very young. Inexperienced." He nodded. "Finding the Dakota camp probably saved my life." He raised one eyebrow. "But that was over twenty years ago. Look around you, *ma petite.* What do you see? A well-stocked trading post. The largest cabin between here and Renville Mission, miles to the south." He tapped his pipe on the edge of the table, spilling ashes on the floor. He looked up at his daughter and grinned. "*En tout cas,* jerky and crackers are not so bad."

Gen retrieved a broom from near the door, grumbling as she swept up the spilled ashes. The waist-length dark braid that trailed down her back fell over one shoulder as she bent to collect the ashes on a wooden dust pan. "Perhaps not, but there is the danger of your drowning in pipe ashes and unwashed dishes with no one here to clean up after you."

Etienne laid his pipe on the table and stood up. He was not a tall man, and yet he towered over his daughter. Feigning anger that he did not feel, he put a hand on each of her shoulders and shook her gently. "The world is changing, Geneviève. Our Dakota friends no longer roam at will. They have a reservation. They are expected to become farmers." He shook his head sadly. "That means the end for old traders like me. Settlement means no more buffalo, fewer pelts. We may not like it, but we must change in order to survive."

Gen opened her mouth to argue, but Etienne laid a finger across her lips. "*At-*

*tends. Attends à moi.*" He tapped the tip of her nose as he said, "I admit that life would be easier for me if you stay. But that is no reason to deny you what is available just a few miles away. I am not asking you to go so far as those new agencies. Renville Mission is a quiet little place. There is a nice cabin, a barn, a little church — all nestled high on a hill overlooking Lac Qui Parle. Why," Etienne said, smiling, "from atop that hill you can almost see all the way home." He continued, "There is only one missionary and his family. The reverend is solemn, but he is not unkind, and his wife is a good woman. They have two children. You won't be lonely."

"I'm not lonely now," Gen said defensively.

Etienne used his last weapon in the battle of words. "You cannot ask me to face your mother in the next life with no good reason for why I allowed her cherished daughter to remain untaught and ignorant, when a good education and promising future were within my reach." He lifted his daughter's chin and peered into her blue eyes. "You must not ask me to do that."

Gen closed her eyes against the tears that threatened to resurface. Her father pulled her close, enveloping her in the familiar scent of cured leather and pipe tobacco that always made her feel safe and protected.

Finally, after all their months of bickering, Papa had done it. He had found the one argument that she could not resist. Mama had been gone for several years now, but Gen could still hear her voice. *Someday someone is going to call you a stupid squaw. When they do, you must remember who you are. You are the daughter of a French nobleman. Your father speaks four languages. He has studied at schools most whites could never hope to enter. He chose his way of life, not because he had no other choices, but because he loved it. Because he loved* me. *You are the granddaughter of a Dakota warrior who earned an entire headdress of eagle feathers in battle. He was respected by his people and loved by his children. Never forget these things. Carry them always. Remember that they can* call *you a stupid squaw, but you do not have* to *be* one. *When the time comes for you to learn more, I want you to take it.*

Etienne felt his daughter's shoulders slump almost imperceptibly. He heard her sigh. The china-doll chin with the slight dimple burrowed into his chest as she began to cry. This was not anger, the fa-

27

ther knew. This was resignation and a recognition of the sweet sadness that was part of growing up. Holding her close, he kissed the top of her head. "I shall come to visit you often, *ma petite*. It will not be so bad. You will see."

Gen started awake and sat bolt upright. She shivered slightly, hoping a late frost hadn't harmed her tender garden plants. Still half asleep, she reached for her clothes hanging on the hook just within reach beside the bedpost and slid out of bed, pulling her skirt over her head, thinking of the day's work. She would plant turnips today and perhaps turn the earth in front of the cabin. She wanted to try transplanting wildflowers from the prairie to a narrow bed along the porch — *no*. Gen stood still in the darkness, remembering she wouldn't be gardening today. This was the *Day*. Today she and Papa began the journey south to the mission station. They would already be on the familiar trail when the rising sun painted the ripples on the surface of the Minnesota River orange and pink. By sundown they would climb the hill to Renville Mission. And then Papa would leave her with strangers and come back home.

The straw in her mattress rustled softly as Gen sat back down. While she slipped into her blouse, she squinted against the dark, trying to make out the familiar outline of every item in the loft. Where would she awaken the next morning, she wondered. Would she have a bed, or only a mattress on the floor? Would there be a rag rug to shield her bare feet from the cold when she got up? Would the missionary's children like her? After loosely braiding her thick, dark hair Gen slipped back between the covers, overwhelmed with dread, her breath sending visible clouds of moisture into the cold air.

She could remember only one other morning in her life when she had felt such dread — that morning four years ago when an awful silence testified to her mother's absence and sent her scurrying back beneath the covers. She and Papa had buried Good Song Woman the day before, standing together in the rain, their heads bowed as they contemplated the gaping hole in the earth at the bottom of which lay a bundle lovingly wrapped in a red blanket.

Listening in the dark that morning, Gen had quickly found the silence in the cabin too awful to bear and hurried to fill it with the sounds of morning. Without taking time to dress, she scurried quickly down the ladder from her loft-room, her long flannel nightgown trailing behind her. She built a fire in the stove, ground coffee, mixed biscuit batter, and fried salt pork with an unusual amount of clanging and clatter.

Etienne stumbled into the room. *"Ma chère?"* he called softly. Rubbing the sleep from his eyes, he caught sight of his diminutive daughter bent over the table rolling out biscuit dough. He caught his breath, half sobbed, and sat down opposite her, his head in his hands.

Gen stopped rolling out the biscuits. "It's all right, Papa. I am here." She poured a huge mug of thick, black coffee and set it before her father, laying her hand on his shoulder. "Drink your coffee. You'll feel better. We'll have biscuits soon."

Etienne slurped his coffee obediently. He ate six biscuits before stumbling outside to tend his horses.

For weeks, Etienne and his daughter worked feverishly. There was a massive garden to tend and clothes to be mended. There was water to be hauled in from the well, a cow to milk, livestock to feed. It was fall and a constant stream of Dakota came through the stockade gate to trade for winter provisions, to recount their exploits from the recent buffalo hunt, to express their anger against the chiefs who signed a treaty confining them to a narrow strip of land along the Minnesota River. In a misguided attempt to save the other from pain, Etienne and Gen avoided mentioning Good Song Woman. As the weeks passed, Etienne allowed himself to believe that he and his daughter were past the worst of the grief. But then, one evening after supper, he found Gen huddled in the corner of the barn, crying.

*"Qu'est-ce que c'est, ma petite?"*

Gen looked up at him, tears streaming down her cheeks. "I'm . . . so sorry, Papa," she whispered brokenly. She scrubbed the tears off both her cheeks with open hands. "I work and I work and I work to forget. But everywhere I look . . . everything I do . . . reminds me of her." Gen sobbed. "I miss her — so much —" She buried her face in her hands.

Etienne slid down the wall and settled beside his daughter. Putting one arm about her shoulders, he opened his mouth to speak, but his words disappeared in a sob. Father and daughter finally released the emotions of the past few weeks. Etienne reminisced about meeting Good Song Woman. He told stories Gen had never heard, mixing laughter with tears. Finally, he sighed and leaned against the barn wall, holding his daughter's hand.

Gen said quietly, "I thought it would hurt too much to talk about her. I didn't want to make you cry."

Etienne nodded. "Yes. It has been the same with me. But it does not make things better, does it? It only makes the sadness deepen." Etienne stood up, pulling Gen to her feet. *"Vas-y, ma petite."* They walked to the cabin arm-in-arm and began a new phase of grieving, reminding one another of Good Song Woman, sharing her memory aloud, healing together, stopping long enough to cry sometimes, but always working, always together.

Now, four years later, contemplating life away from her father, life among strangers, Gen shivered in the dark. Rubbing briskly at her midsection, she tried to will away the tightness there. She finally climbed down the ladder to begin her morning kitchen ritual, surprised to see that her father had already built a fire in the stove and set a pot of water on for coffee. She hurried to make biscuits and was just rolling them out when Etienne came in the front door.

Looking up at him, she gulped before saying in a trembling voice, "Breakfast should be ready soon."

Etienne lifted his chin towards the loft. "You are packed?"

Gen nodded and looked down at the biscuit dough on the table. "On the bed."

While Gen finished cutting out biscuits and slid them into the oven, Etienne retrieved her bundle. He set it on the table before heading for his room at the back of the cabin, returning with a small wooden trunk on his shoulder. "I think you should have this," he said gruffly, setting the trunk on the floor. He held out the narrow beaded necklace that Good Song Woman had worn. It was decorated with small shells and red and blue trade beads — and the key to her trunk. "Take whatever you might use." He cleared his throat and headed for the door. "I'll get Whiskey ready. He can haul the trunk out on a travois. Just like the old days." Grabbing his coffee, Etienne headed for the door.

Gen approached her mother's little trunk with reverence. She ran her hand across the top, tracing the star-shaped design made by brass tacks in the lid. Finally, she put the key in the lock and opened it, slipped the necklace over her head, and lifted the lid to reveal an almost-new gray calico dress. Gen held it up to herself, realizing how much she had grown since her mother's death. The dress would fit.

Beaded moccasins and leggings lay beneath the calico dress. Gen lifted them out, once again marveling at the softness of the skins. Next came the treasure, Good Song Woman's Dakota-style wedding dress. Deep blue trade beads interrupted by three huge geometric designs covered the entire yoke of the dress. At the lower edge of the blue field of beads ran a narrow red border dotted with small eight-pointed stars worked in two colors of porcupine quills. She closed her eyes, imagining the deep rows of fringe along the hem and sleeves of the dress swaying in the breeze as her mother and father stood before old Chief Enehah and made their promises. Returning the dress to the bottom of the trunk, she wondered if she would be married in the traditional Dakota way, or if being at the mission would change that too.

The image of a wild, young Dakota brave named Red Thunder flashed in her mind. He had shown an unusual interest in her of late. He had a bad reputation, but he was handsome in a fierce, almost frightening way. Two eagle feathers dangled from his scalp lock, trophies from battles with the Chippewa to the north. He never tired of telling war stories, and when he moved he had a way of tossing his head that called attention to the feathers. When he was angry, the long scar across his forehead changed from a pale line to a dark red gash. Once when he saw her looking at it, he touched it and smiled, calling it a gift from a she-bear. The scar had been prominent often recently, as Red Thunder boasted of the day when the white farmers would be driven from the country and the Dakota would once again roam the Big Woods at will. He was big-boned, and taller than most Dakota, and when he spoke of fighting the invading white farmers, the savage light in his eyes made Gen catch her breath with a mixture of admiration and fear. She felt a strange kinship with the emotions that ruled Red Thunder. She understood wanting to rebel against the way things were.

Etienne was not impressed with Red Thunder's boasts and ordered him to stay away from Geneviève LaCroix. Red Thunder kept his distance — barely. But he still managed to catch Gen's attention when he was at the trading post, smiling knowingly when he caught her eye, holding her gaze until she blushed furiously and turned away.

Gen pushed thoughts of Red Thunder from her mind and returned her mother's belongings to the bottom of the trunk, layering her own things on top. At the last minute, she climbed the ladder to the loft and took the wool comforter off her bed, adding it to the trunk. In the tray, alongside the gray calico dress, she put the books Etienne had used to school his daughter. She smiled, wondering what the missionaries would think about a half-breed student who could quote Molière and Shakespeare. Etienne had told her that his old priest in St. Louis had been horrified by Etienne's familiarity with the theater. Gen closed the lid of her trunk just as her father came back inside.

"Good," he said gruffly. "It's time we got started."

An awkward silence reigned as father and daughter sat across from one another, gulping coffee to which Gen had added hot milk and sugar. Etienne finally hauled the trunk outside and strapped it to the travois. To keep from bursting into tears, Gen grabbed Whiskey's halter and headed across the open ground between the cabin and the stockade gate. She heard the heavy gate scrape across the earth as Etienne closed the only opening that admitted visitors to the trading post known as Fort LaCroix. When he finally caught up with her and took Whiskey's lead, Gen paused and looked back. Only the roof of the cabin was visible above the stockade fence that surrounded the compound. Just outside the gate and a little way up a hill, a white wooden cross shone through the predawn gloom. Gen touched her hand to her heart. After standing quietly for a moment, she turned and trotted up the path after her father.

# Three

The robbery of the wicked shall destroy them.

— PROVERBS 21:7 (KJV)

He needed a horse. His two friends needed horses. And they would have them before the sun rose. Crouching behind a patch of tall grass, Red Thunder peered through the darkness at the homesteader's cabin. The trader's whiskey he had drunk last night was bad, and things were not quite in focus, but even with the firewater eating at his belly, Red Thunder knew he was worth ten white settlers. He scurried across open ground towards the barn. Once there, he raised his hand to his mouth and hooted towards where his friends Two Stars and Otter waited a few rods away behind a massive tree.

Two Stars reached for the piece of jerky he had tucked in the bright blue scarf wrapped around his waist. Barely stepping out from behind the tree where he was hiding, he made an odd clicking sound against the roof of his mouth. From where he lay in the dirt beside his master's cabin, a brindle-colored bulldog rose to all fours, the beginnings of a growl sounding low in his throat. The dog inched forward, every muscle tense. He lifted his pushed-in snout to the wind just in time to catch the scent of something dropping at his feet. He snuffled in the dust before licking up a tiny morsel of jerky. Another morsel dropped from the sky. The dog was eager now, wagging his tail as he followed a trail of jerky away from the house. He hesitated briefly when he finally caught the scent of a stranger, but lean rations overcame his reluctance when the stranger tempted him with a huge piece of dried meat.

The dog had no time to finish his treat. In one quick movement Two Stars grabbed the stocky little animal and lifted it off the ground, his huge hands encircling the animal's thick neck, squeezing tighter and tighter. The dog struggled briefly, then hung limp and still.

Two Stars tossed the body behind a bunch of prairie grass behind him. When it was apparent that no one in the cabin was the wiser, he ducked down and moved noiselessly along the homesteader's split rail fence towards the barn. When he was close to the barn, he put a hand up to his mouth, hooted softly, and followed Red Thunder inside. Otter lumbered in moments later, waving a dead rooster in the air like a banner. While Otter tied the rooster to his belt by its feet, Red Thunder and Two Stars took three halters down off their nails inside the barn door. A huge bay threw its head over one stall. Two Stars moved toward it, holding out his hand, talking softly. After rolling its eyes momentarily, the bay tossed its head and thrust its soft muzzle into Two Stars's hand to accept the offering of a dried apple.

Otter and Red Thunder were not quite so patient, but they still managed to get halters on two other horses before Otter went to the back of the barn and opened a huge door to clear the way for his friends' dash for the narrow band of trees that ran along the edge of the farmer's property. The squeaking of a pulley rolling along the door track made the three braves look nervously towards the house.

Red Thunder hiccupped softly. When it appeared all was well, he smiled and scratched the side of his nose. His first attempt to mount the leggy dun gelding he had chosen was unsuccessful. Otter and

Two Stars watched with a combination of amusement and worry. The dog was gone, the rooster wouldn't crow, but every moment risked the homesteader's hearing something. Most whites were stupid, but you never knew when one would prove a little more alert than the rest. The dun gelding was snorting and whirling around, and he had kicked one of the stalls more than once before Red Thunder finally succeeding in scrambling up onto its back.

Red Thunder swore as he gathered the leads to the gelding's halter. He felt foolish, but what bothered him more was the fact that Two Stars was taking the bay. The three had been watching the homestead carefully for a few days, and they all knew the bay was the best horse. They had wrestled for him, Red Thunder certain he could win over his wiry friend. But Two Stars took less than five minutes to best his heavier and less athletic opponent. Otter, larger than either of his friends, had not cared to wrestle, saying the spotted white mare was fine for him and he would save his energy for another contest against a real enemy.

With a last look of admiration at the bay, Red Thunder motioned for Otter and Two Stars to mount and lead the way outside.

Just then the door nearest the house flew open. Silhouetted against the moonlight stood one of the hugest men Two Stars had ever seen, holding a rifle.

"Get off my horses!" the man bellowed, screaming epithets and firing wildly.

With a shout, Two Stars kneed the bay. The horse snorted and reared, almost unseating Two Stars. With a high-pitched war cry, Otter lashed his mare forward. In the chaos, no one was certain what was happening. While the three Dakota braves tried to stay astride their terrified mounts, the homesteader pulled a pistol from his belt and fired again. Noise, smoke, and the smell of burning gunpowder terrified the horses. They whirled about for what seemed an eternity before Otter finally succeeded in forcing his mare through the door. Two Stars was close behind. The two hunkered down over their horses' withers as they crashed through the band of trees and onto the open prairie.

They had put a few miles between themselves and the homestead before Otter slowed the white mare, turning around to call out, "Did you see Red Thunder? Did he come behind us?"

Two Stars grabbed a handful of the bay's thick, black mane, trying to remain conscious while blood poured from a shoulder wound.

Swearing softly, Otter pulled up the white mare, who had begun to limp. Sliding to the ground, he ran to his friend's aid just in time to break Two Stars's fall. The bay sidestepped nervously, and for a moment Otter feared he would lose both horses. He managed to calm them down and turned to his friend, who was crawling towards a rivulet of water that wound its way through the tall grass towards Hawk Creek.

Deftly untying the knots that had created reins from halter leads, Otter wrapped the long leads around his wide midsection, tethering the horses to himself. His arms free, he bent to help Two Stars up. Together, they stumbled towards the brook where Two Stars plunged his shoulder into the water.

While the horses drank noisily on either side of them, Otter examined the wound. "No bullet," he said tersely. "Much blood."

Two Stars nodded, coughing as he lay on his back and stared up at the sky. His eyes rolled back in his head, and he slipped into unconsciousness. An ever-growing stain of red colored the dry prairie grass beneath him.

Otter jerked the bandanna from around his own head and pushed it against the wound. Two Stars moaned and tried to get up. He fought briefly against his friend's attempts to unwind the long scarf around his waist, but finally sank back onto the earth and submitted. Otter had just managed a suitable bandage with Two Stars's sash when a rifle shot split the air. He dove to the earth and peered between the white mare's legs.

A black dot in the distance was coming closer. Red Thunder had said there was no bravery in the big white man's heart. He had bragged about taking bread while the homesteader stood by smiling, letting Red Thunder do as he wished. However amenable the homesteader had seemed to kitchen raids, Red Thunder was obviously wrong about the man being a coward. Another shot rang out.

Otter swore under his breath. He loosed the twine holding the rooster to his belt and tossed the bird aside. Bending over, he jerked Two Stars up, and with one Herculean move he managed to slide the brave across the bay's broad back facedown, head on one side, feet on the other.

Untying the ropes from around his midsection, Otter slipped one end of the bay's lead through the opposite side of the halter and hoisted his considerable bulk up behind Two Stars. He leaned over and slapped the white mare on the rump, letting out a piercing war cry. The mare snorted and tossed her head, moving into an uneven trot as she headed for home.

With a glance behind him, Otter saw the homesteader turn aside to retrieve the mare. Then he kneed the bay fiercely, sending the horse plunging through the narrow stream. In seconds they were galloping across the open prairie, the bay's powerful stride chewing up the earth, putting more and more distance between them and the lone homesteader. Otter guided the horse behind a copse of young trees and stopped, dismayed to see that the homesteader had apparently decided to let his mare find her own way home. He still followed. The early morning sun glinted off his rifle barrel.

Even though whiskey gave him a raging headache, Otter was beginning to wish he had gotten drunk with Red Thunder the night before. Then he would have been too sick to get up this morning, too sick to travel miles and miles before dawn to steal a lame horse. The sun was getting hot. A thin coating of white froth began to lather the bay's shoulders, soaking into Two Stars's red vest. They galloped southwest towards the river. Otter no longer dared to look behind him to see if the white man was still there. The bay chewed up the distance, breathing hard, but still willing to go on.

Topping a rise, they headed down into a lush valley. Out of sight of the white man, Otter pulled the bay up, picking his way along the bank of the river. Finally he slid off the horse, pulled Two Stars onto his shoulders, and stumbled through a plum thicket towards the spot where Red Thunder always secreted his canoe in a stand of tall reeds.

Otter dumped Two Stars into the canoe and raced back to where the bay stood, noisily sucking up the river's clear, cold water. The horse ignored Otter until the brave jerked his halter off and waved his arms crazily. Then, with a snort, the horse twisted its head around in the direction they had come, moving easily back up the path, pausing here and there to graze, taking his time about finding his way home.

Otter hurried back to the canoe. After checking to see that Two Stars was still breathing, he shoved the canoe into the water. Hugging the shoreline, he waded along, pushing the canoe against the current towards Pajutazee and Cloudman's village far upstream. It would be hours before night offered cover for the two fleeing thieves. Otter glanced behind him, wondering if regaining the bay would be enough to make the farmer stop giving chase.

Captain John Willets was having his beard trimmed by Fort Ridgely's finest barber when Abner Marsh rode up to the sutler's and strode inside. Never a man for wasting words, Abner said, "Killed me a Injun' yesterday. Chased two of his friends near twenty miles before I turned back. Figured you'd wanta come get the evidence before we ride out to find the two I missed." Abner spat tobacco juice, missing the spittoon in the corner.

Back at the Marsh homestead, the captain and his men dismounted and tied their horses to the corral fence before walking into the barn. Inside Abner put his foot up on the shoulder of a befeathered form that lay sprawled in the middle of the walkway between the stalls. "He's been around before. Scared the missus to death, rummaging through the kitchen. Don't know why they can't stick on the reservation where they belong."

47

The captain crouched down and peered at the face. "That's Red Thunder. Belongs to Chief Shakopee's band up near Redwood Agency." The captain stood up, grimacing and flexing his back. "Sure was a long way from home, wasn't he? Been in trouble before. Guess that's over now. You got any idea who the other two were?"

"Injuns," Abner said gruffly. "Long, dark hair. Feathers." He shrugged. "They all look alike to me."

The captain suppressed a sigh. He walked down the row of stalls, pausing long enough to admire the bay gelding beside the white mare. "You got all three horses back?"

Abner nodded. "White mare's lame. They musta let the bay go, thinkin' I'd lay off 'em if I got my horses back."

Willets said slowly, "Since you got your horses and since you can't really give a good description —"

"Red vest," Abner said suddenly. "One of 'em had a bright red vest." He patted his expansive chest. "And a blue sash tied around his middle."

The captain tried to look interested. "Anything else?"

Abner thought for a moment, squinting his eyes at the roof timbers while he concentrated. Finally he shook his head. "Nope. That's it."

"I can't promise —" the captain began.

Abner shrugged. He kicked the body in the dust halfheartedly. "Guess they already paid sumpin' for their trouble." He grinned. "Who knows? Maybe I clipped the others before they ran off." The smile disappeared from his face as he nodded towards his cabin. "Thinkin' 'bout the missus and my two girls up yonder in the house, guess I come off easy. Could'a been worse." He shrugged. "I know you can't call out the whole regiment just because three young bucks caused trouble. Guess we can call it good." He jerked his head towards the body. "What do I do with that?"

Abner Marsh loaned the captain his rangy dun gelding to transport Red Thunder's body back to the fort. A messenger was sent to Chief Shakopee's camp. When no one came to claim the body, the chaplain dug a shallow grave just outside the fort burying ground and rolled Red Thunder into it.

It wasn't long before the word was out that if you went near the Marsh home, you'd better be careful because they had three of the biggest, meanest dogs between Fort Ridgely and Minneapolis.

# Four

Be swift to hear, slow to speak, slow to wrath.

— JAMES 1:19 (NKJV)

Gen sat alone on the steps that led up to the little adobe-brick mission church. It had been several weeks since she and Papa made the trek from Fort LaCroix to Renville Mission. They had followed an ancient trail through the woods, camping one night on the prairie, and then finally descending the bluffs and coming alongside the place where the Minnesota River widened, taking on the appearance and name of a lake — Lac Qui Parle, the talking waters. When they reached the place where the lake once again narrowed to a discernible river, they paused and looked up the hill towards Renville Mission. Etienne had said, "It will take time, but you will eventually come to see that I was right to bring you here. Someday you will thank me, Geneviève." He had lifted her up onto Whiskey's back and led the horse across the river, impervious to the thigh-deep rushing water.

When Gen jumped down from the horse, Etienne had taken her arm and headed up the path towards the large log cabin above them. "Someday," he had said, "you will look back on this day with joy."

As she watched the eastern sky blush pink with morning light, Gen thought back to what her papa had said, pondering how wrong he had been. *If only he had known,* Gen thought. *If he had known, he would never have made me promise to stay here until fall.*

The Danes' huge white dog, Koda, loped down the path from the cabin. Shoving his head between Gen's elbow and her body he whined softly, bathing her hands with kisses. She patted the broad head, glad for the dog's warmth as he sprawled across her lap.

Light from the rising sun illuminated the valley below, painting the river pale orange and sending a blush of light across the landscape and up the hill to the mission buildings. Splotches of light shining through the tree branches dappled the path between the church and the cabin and gilded the peeling face of the barn.

"Papa meant well, Koda. But he was wrong. I won't ever be happy here. I won't ever belong." She bit her lower lip and nodded towards the river. "I could find my way home. It isn't far. You know that trail that leads up the opposite side of the river? You just follow it alongside the Lac Qui Parle. Then about three miles upstream you take the west fork and then you come to where a little creek branches off to the north, and at the head of that creek is home." Gen murmured, "Papa's probably just getting up. He'll eat a cold breakfast without me there." She sighed and leaned her head against the dog's massive skull, letting a few tears slide down her cheeks. "Reverend Dane would probably be glad to be rid of me."

Perhaps the reverend didn't mean to make her feel so inept, but Gen had been with them for weeks now, and it seemed that nothing she did was right. She must not wear her hair in braids. It had to be "done up." Her moccasins had to be exchanged for hard leather shoes that pinched and rubbed blisters. Even though it was warm, her bare legs had to be covered with cotton hose that wouldn't stay up and were forever getting holes in them. The reverend didn't like fry bread. He didn't want her to fish. And gathering wood wasn't "women's work." Dakota women always gathered wood for the family. But the reverend seemed to think everything Dakota was pagan. He demanded that Gen change it all.

And that wasn't the end of it. The reverend informed her that her papa, although well meaning, was a *papist*. Gen didn't quite know what that meant, but the way the reverend said it, she could tell he felt it something almost worse than being Dakota. He made it clear without words that he felt that he and Mrs. Dane had rescued Gen from a terrible fate. But Gen didn't feel in need of being rescued, and the longer she stayed with the missionaries, the more she resented the reverend's superior attitude to everything Dakota, everything French.

All her feelings of hurt and anger had come to a head last night. Thinking to help Mrs. Dane by entertaining the children for a while, Gen had settled in the rocker with Aaron and Meg at her feet. "I will tell you the 'Legend of the Head of Gold,' which was told to me by my mother's brother Walking Elk when I was a little girl," Gen began.

Reverend Dane was sitting at his desk, writing one of his endless sermons of many words, and he didn't even look up when he said, "Geneviève. It is too late for story-telling." He looked up from his papers and stared out the window a moment. Without looking at Gen he said, "And my lamp needs oil."

Gen retorted, "Why don't you say what you're really thinking? It's a *Dakota* story. Everything *Dakota* is bad."

The reverend turned to look at her with raised eyebrows. "I didn't mean —"

Gen interrupted. "Oh, yes, you did! You think everything Dakota should be done away with!" She began to cry and blurted out defensively, "What do you know about it, anyway? All you do is stare at your stupid books all day long. You read books and more books and you ignore the living people around you!" She jumped up and stomped her foot. "You don't know what it's like, having to change everything. *Everything!*" She hurried across the room, snatching the lamp off the reverend's desk. The beautiful amber-colored shade with black silhouettes was upset, and before Gen could catch it, it was on the floor in pieces. Her anger shattered with the glass.

Mrs. Dane came and knelt down to pick up the pieces. And then she began to cry. Gen would never forget beautiful, patient Mrs. Dane, kneeling on the floor crying, gathering shards of glass in her apron, spreading them on the table, spending what seemed like hours trying to re-create the shade from dozens of impossibly jagged pieces. Gen had meekly filled the lamp base with oil and hurried the children off to bed. When she finally came back downstairs, the reverend and Mrs. Dane had gone to bed as well.

Looking over her shoulder up the hill towards the cabin, Gen saw a wisp of smoke rise from the chimney. Mrs. Dane was up. Gen had already made coffee before coming down to the church, thinking as she did it, *One-half cup, finely ground — with just a pinch of cinnamon — just the way Reverend Dane likes it.* She hoped the coffee combined with the rising dough and the stack of firewood would be apology enough.

Shoving Koda off her lap, Gen got up and trudged up the hill. Inside the cabin Mrs. Dane was standing at the stove, her back to the door.

"I am sorry about the lamp, Mrs. Dane. I should have been more careful." Gen began to place a tin plate and cup at each place around the rough-hewn wooden plank that served as a table.

Mrs. Dane turned the last griddle cake

on the stove. "Don't worry about it," she said softly. She smiled, reaching back to tuck a wisp of blonde hair back up into the roll that encircled her head. "I know you didn't mean it." She shrugged lightly as she finished pouring the last of the batter onto the griddle. "My husband reminded me last night that we are to be storing up treasures in *heaven*, not clinging to the things on earth."

The reverend came out of the bedroom and headed outside and down the hill to the little church for his customary morning prayer vigil. When he had left, Mrs. Dane poured two cups of coffee. Motioning for Gen to sit down at the table, she said, "You've been with us nearly two months now, Gen, and I'd like it very much if you would call me Ellen." She smiled when Gen looked surprised. "I'm not so very much older than you, you know. I'm only twenty-seven. Nine years' difference hardly makes me ancient, does it?"

Meg and Aaron came downstairs. Ellen sent them to the spring for water, adding, "And then you can go on down to the barn and milk Maizy. Gen and I need to have a grown-up talk."

When they had gone, Mrs. Dane continued. "I want you to know that I am very grateful that you have stayed with us." She reached across the table and patted Gen's hand. "And — I'd like to ask you to try to be more patient with my husband." She looked up at the ceiling for a moment, pursing her lips and frowning slightly. "Last night you said that Simon doesn't know what it's like to have to change everything. You were wrong about that."

She studied the tabletop, smiling and shaking her head. "You cannot imagine what hopeless misfits we were when we first came here . . . so eager, so completely lacking in basic skills." She looked up at Gen. "I had never in my life milked a cow or grown a garden. I had never made clothing or baked a loaf of bread."

"You didn't know how to bake *bread?*"

Ellen shook her head, laughing. "We could have used the first dozen or so loaves of bread I made when we were building the church. They were hard as bricks." She explained, "My family had servants to do the cooking and the gardening. I had a dressmaker too. I was only expected to complete my education at Miss Bartlett's finishing school, get married, produce children . . . and create beautiful needlework in my leisure time." She looked at Gen and said with fervor, "Which was exactly why I was so determined to leave. I wanted my life to count for God." She sighed. "You cannot imagine how refreshing it was to be courted by a young man who had more on his mind than —" Ellen stopped. "— well, the usual things."

Gen could not conjure up a picture of a young Reverend Dane, let alone Reverend Dane courting a girl. She suppressed a smile.

Ellen laughed softly and shook her head. "I know I have provided more than one evening of entertainment around Dakota campfires. They literally roared with laughter every time I attempted to speak." She added, "I'm afraid I wasn't always very gracious about being the butt of their humor." She rested her chin in her hand, concluding almost wistfully, "It was hard to be so stupid. I think I would have given up and begged Simon to take me home if it were not for one called Gray Woman. She was always kind and patient. And she never laughed."

The reverend's footsteps sounded on the porch. Mrs. Dane stood up. "You'll meet Gray Woman today. She promised to come for a sewing class. She may even bring one or two friends with her."

After breakfast, Gen and Mrs. Dane

gathered up the mending basket and their sewing kits and climbed the steep path that wound around the back of the cabin and up the hill behind them. Aaron carried Meg on his back, galloping by Gen on their way up the steep incline, his shaggy brown hair blowing back from his face. Gen smiled to herself. The joy in his warm brown eyes was contagious. It was good to see Aaron, always too serious and bent on acting as much like his father as possible, having fun.

At the crest of the hill, beneath a lone cottonwood tree, stood the ten-by-fourteen-foot cabin that had served the Danes during their first few years in Minnesota. When their growing family demanded larger quarters, friends from Yellow Medicine had come north, camping alongside the river for a week while Simon and several other men built a larger cabin and a barn. The tiny one-room cabin atop the hill had been converted to a schoolroom.

Three Dakota women sat in a small circle on the earth just outside the school. When Mrs. Dane and Gen crested the hill, two of the women stood up, helping their third very pregnant companion to her feet.

Ellen lapsed into Dakota, introducing the older of the three women first. "Gen, this is my friend Gray Woman. The one I told you about."

Gray Woman's leathery face folded into a smile that revealed a missing front tooth.

Ellen put her hand on Gen's shoulder. "Etienne LaCroix from up past Lac Qui Parle has brought us his daughter, Gray Woman. This is Geneviève."

At mention of Etienne, Gray Woman's face lit up with recognition. She had a husky, almost hoarse voice, but it was tinged with sadness as she said, "You are the daughter of Good Song Woman?" When Gen nodded, Gray Woman stepped towards her. Reaching up she held Gen's face in her time-worn hands and studied it, turning it from side to side as she nodded. "Yes, yes, I see. You have your mother's mouth. Her nose. But," Gray Woman concluded, dropping her hands, "your father gave you his blue eyes." She nodded, smiling wistfully. "I remember the night many winters ago when a starving young Frenchman stumbled into our camp."

"You knew my mother?"

Gray Woman nodded and reached out to squeeze Gen's hand. Without releasing Gen's hand, she turned to introduce her friends, both years younger than she. "This is Wing," she said, motioning to the ill-kempt woman who stood, shoulders slumped, a little behind her pregnant friend.

Wing nodded and glanced briefly at Ellen and Gen, but she did not speak. Gray Woman passed over her without further comment.

"And this," Gray Woman said, patting the protruding abdomen of her pregnant companion, "is White Fawn, who is soon to bear the child of Blue Wolf." When Gray Woman spoke Blue Wolf's name, the smile disappeared from her eyes. She said quietly, "He is a foolish boy who leaves his wife to run after the other blanket Indians and cause trouble down at the agency." Gray Woman patted White Fawn's abdomen affectionately. "I am taking her with me to John Otherday's village where the young men are sensible and there will be no trouble with the agent." Gray Woman changed the subject. "Perhaps you know my son," she said to Gen. "He comes to Broken Pipe's trading post sometimes. His name is Two Stars."

Gen thought for a moment and shook her head. "I don't think so."

"Like Blue Wolf he does not choose wisely. He has a friend, Red Thunder." Gray Woman reached up and drew a line

61

across her forehead with her finger. "His face is marked here. He says a she-bear did it, but I know the truth. A Chippewa slashed his head with a broken bottle one night when Red Thunder was drunk."

Gen swallowed hard. "I remember Red Thunder."

Gray Woman's dark brown eyes narrowed as she studied Gen carefully. "Yes," she said. "I see that you know him. And I see that you think of him as do many other young women." Gray Woman looked at Wing, who blushed. She raised her hand and shook a finger at both the girls. "And I tell you not to be a fool. Keep away from Red Thunder."

Gen smiled nervously and nodded while Wing only stared at the ground. "My father agrees with your opinion of Red Thunder," Gen said. "He told him to stay away from Fort LaCroix."

Gray Woman nodded. "Broken Pipe is a wise man. He was wise enough to choose Good Song Woman for a wife. And he is wise enough to choose a husband for you. Be a good daughter. Listen to your father." Gray Woman shook her shoulders in a mock shudder. "Red Thunder will bring trouble upon those around him someday."

Sensing that White Fawn was growing

tired of standing, Ellen reached into her sewing basket and pulled out a large, pieced quilt top. "This was in the very bottom of the barrel sent up from Yellow Medicine last week. We'll put it together today." She sent Aaron and Meg back down the hill to help the reverend, then led the way up the stairs and into the cabin-turned-schoolhouse. "Sit there," she said to White Fawn, indicating an armchair at the head of the table at the front of the room. She handed her a skein of yarn and some large-eyed needles. "You can thread some needles for us while we get the quilt ready."

White Fawn sank into the chair with a sigh of relief and reached behind her to press on her lower back.

Ellen spread a plain piece of calico on the table. Then, reaching into the basket, she extracted a thin, old blanket. "This is almost used up," she commented. "And it will be perfect as a filler for our comforter." The women laid the blanket atop the calico, leaning across the table to smooth it out. Finally, the donated quilt top was laid over the filler and the backing.

"You see," Mrs. Dane said as she worked, "we begin in the center and work our way out to the edges, putting the knots

63

about this far apart." Placing the tip of her little finger on the knot she had just tied, she stretched her left hand across the surface of the quilt, inserting the needle and thread again just where the tip of her thumb touched the quilt.

Gray Woman reached across the table to spread out a huge left hand next to Mrs. Dane's. "Use my hand," she joked. "We finish sooner."

As soon as the comforter was tied, Gray Woman and Gen each began at opposite corners of the quilt, sewing a length of woven tape along the edge. The other two Dakota women followed, folding the binding tape to the back of the comforter and sewing it down to enclose the raw edges.

Mrs. Dane held the finished comforter out to White Fawn. "For when the little one comes."

White Fawn, who was in her last month of pregnancy, smiled shyly and accepted the gift.

At noon the women descended the hill to eat lunch outside on the cabin's broad front porch. Gen went inside to put her sewing basket away.

"I can't!" Meg's voice shouted from upstairs.

"Can too!" Aaron retorted. "I showed you how yesterday. Now it's your turn to make the bed. Father said I'm growing up to be a man. Men don't make beds!"

"Aarrroonnnnnnnnn," Meg whined.

"Miss Meg," Gen called up the stairs, "what's the matter?"

Aaron appeared at the top of the stairs. "I showed her and showed her, Gen. She just doesn't want to do it."

"Guess what?" Gen called up the stairs. "I'm making bread pudding for dessert! But you can't come down until the bed's made. You know that's your father's rule. And he'd be very angry if he knew you didn't do it right away this morning."

Meg pursed her lips. "Oh, all *right!*" She spun around and nearly bumped into Aaron. "Will you get out of my way so I can do my chores? Don't you have something else to do while I do the *woman's* work?" She swept by him, ignoring Aaron's triumphant smile as he clomped down the stairs.

By the time Gen had made the promised bread pudding, Gray Woman and her friends were preparing to leave.

"I'll pray for Two Stars, my friend," Mrs. Dane was saying. "And for Red Thunder and Killing Ghost. Tell Bad Eagle my husband will come to visit him tomorrow. Perhaps he will come with you for the service on the Sabbath." She turned to Wing and White Fawn. "And you come too. Please. One last time before you leave for John Otherday's village."

Watching them go, Mrs. Dane sighed. "They have such a hard life. Gray Woman's husband Bad Eagle drinks. Now it appears Two Stars may bring her grief too." She folded her arms and leaned against the porch railing. "Gray Woman was always so proud of her son." She sighed. "It seems that mothers everywhere have the same worries. Always the same."

She nodded down the hill towards the church. "Bad Eagle has never come. Not once." Mrs. Dane took a deep breath and brightened. "Ah, well. Work always makes me feel better. Let's get to the laundry. It wouldn't do for Reverend Many Words to appear in his pulpit on Sunday with a soiled collar."

# Five

If any of you lacks wisdom, let him ask of God.

— JAMES 1:5 (NKJV)

Simon Dane knelt beside the front bench that served as a pew inside his mission church, his head in his hands. Something must be done, of course. Anyone could see that. The Dakota were leaving the area in droves. Every day they stopped by the mission wanting bread, wanting to say good-bye, wanting a blessing. Even their friends Gray Woman and White Fawn had gone. That morning he had preached to his family. Not one native had come to celebrate the Sabbath.

Simon rose from his knees and sat on the bench in the darkened church, his shoulders hunched, his head bowed. He could not even pretend to pray anymore. He had risen in the night and come down to the church, but he did not pray. What was there to say? *God, I have failed.* Certainly God knew that. He must be sick of hearing it by now.

But more was wrong than a dwindling congregation. The reverend sighed. If only Etienne LaCroix had kept his promise to come to visit. Then they could have sent Geneviève home with no regrets. He did not need those pale eyes following his every move anymore. She thought him impervious to her criticisms, to her watching. But he was not. Daily he felt her anger and resentment wash over him like a cold rush of spring water.

Her outburst and angry lecture on the Dakota the night she broke Ellen's lamp had been especially painful. Simon admitted to himself that part of what Geneviève had said was probably right. Perhaps he *did* need to learn more about the Dakota people. But it was too late now. They were gone. What could he do?

It was a warm spring night. Even so, Simon shivered and rubbed his forearms with long, bony fingers. He looked around him at the empty room bathed in moonlight, remembering how it had once been a refuge for him. He had come here faithfully each morning for ten years, just as Dr. Riggs had suggested, to pray and meditate upon the work of each day. It seemed a very long time ago that he had been so young and energetic. And optimistic.

A field mouse emerged from a corner of the room and moved into the moonlight streaming in one of the windows. It sniffed the floor carefully before skittering across the room and disappearing inside the pump organ.

Simon rubbed his forehead and shoved a thin strand of hair back atop his head. He fingered the edges of his Bible. Finally, he stood up and went to the pump organ, running his hand along the ivory keyboard before he turned around and stepped behind the lectern. Opening his Bible and laying it before him, he grasped both sides of the lectern and looked over the empty room, trying to imagine Dakota faces in the moonlight. He could not. The only thing that emerged from the darkness was emptiness — silent testimony to the truth. Ten years of his life and nothing to show for it. Not one convert to Christianity at Renville Mission, while, off to the south, Hazelwood and Pajutazee Missions thrived with dozens of children attending school and church pews filled every Sabbath.

Simon stood at the lectern, his head bowed, his mind racing, trying to conjure sufficient words to move the Almighty to help him resurrect his dead mission. *Where did I go wrong, God? Why don't the people come? I study for hours to present fine sermons. Why won't they listen?*

The oblique rectangle of moonlight shining on the floor moved and captured the mouse who had crept out of the organ and sat up, washing its whiskers. But God did not speak. Leaving his Bible open on the lectern, Simon went back outside. After standing on the church stoop for a moment surveying the landscape, he climbed the hill to the cabin. Behind him, inside the church, the mouse scratched its way up to where his Bible lay on the lectern. After sniffing the edges of the pages tentatively, the tiny creature began to nibble away at the Gospel of Luke.

"It will be all right, Simon." Ellen Dane reached out and put her hand on her husband's shoulder.

"I didn't mean to wake you, my dear."

The carefully controlled voice nearly broke Ellen's heart. When, oh when, dear God in heaven, would he ever learn to trust her with his feelings? "You didn't wake me, Simon. Surely you don't think I could fall asleep when I know you are in turmoil."

He did not turn over to look at her. Instead, he remained on his right side, facing the wall. She felt his body stiffen. "Is it so evident?"

Ellen looked at her husband's back. Raising herself on one elbow, she touched his shoulder again, pulling gently to try to get him to lie back. He resisted, and so she simply kept her hand on his shoulder. "You cannot think that after a decade with you I would be so blind to your feelings, Simon. I am discouraged too. But you must remember that Gen's words were motivated by her own worry for her father . . . and her homesickness. But remember what it was like when we first came here. We have grown and learned. God will show you the way. I am certain of it." Ellen bit her lip, wondering if it was wrong to speak so confidently when she did not feel confident at all. Gently, she presented the solution she had been pondering all evening. "Do you think that perhaps a visit to Dr. Riggs would be an encouragement to you, dear? The children and I would be fine. Especially now that we have Gen to keep us company."

At mention of Dr. Riggs, Simon lay back. "I cannot see how discussing the dismal failure of Renville Mission with my

71

superiors could prove an encouragement." His voice was not angry. It was, Ellen realized with a chill, completely emotionless. She had never seen him so dejected. She wanted to comfort him, to make things better.

"Dr. Riggs has never been anything but encouraging. We have made friends with Gray Woman and White Fawn. Wing listened carefully when I read the Shepherd's Psalm after lunch last week. Who knows when the seed we have sown in their lives will bear fruit? And Aaron and Meg are living proof that our years here have *not* been a failure."

Simon looked at his wife. The half-light coming in the window opposite the bed made the golden hair that cascaded across one shoulder glow. Something deep inside him stirred. He tried to suppress it. "Yes, my dear. As the Scriptures say, 'children are a blessing of the Lord.' And you have worked diligently with those women. I daresay that the time will come when they will enter the kingdom. But they are women, and if God is to do a great work among these people, the men must be won as well. Bad Eagle is always drunk. And Two Stars and Otter only laughed when I invited them to services this past week."

He sighed and patted her hand. "But thank you for trying to make me feel better."

"You cannot know what God may do, Simon. Two Stars and Otter are young. Many forces pull at them. Don't give up the battle —"

"I have lost the battle," Simon said. "Two Stars and Otter have gone off with that coward Red Thunder and will likely never be heard of again." His voice dipped sadly as he turned on his side again, away from Ellen. "Gone away — just like all of them. Every last one. Gone."

Ellen waited quietly for him to recover. He had been discouraged before. If she waited, she knew that Simon would begin to think aloud, to reason away his depression. When he did not speak again, she thought he had fallen asleep. But then she felt the mattress tremble. Simon was not sleeping . . . he was crying. The thought overwhelmed her. Never, in all their years of marriage, had Simon ever given in to such human weakness. Or, she thought, if he had, he had certainly hidden it from her. She was at a complete loss to know what to do.

Finally, she moved closer to him, slipped her arm beneath his and around his waist, whispered again, "It will be all right, Simon. I am here. We have Aaron and Meg. Those are two little souls that we have won for the kingdom. Who knows but what they will do great things for the Lord . . ." She felt him relax a little. "Two souls we created, in partnership with God."

Simon lay back and pulled her close with one arm. She felt his breathing alter slightly, and her own heart began to beat a little faster. She knew well the battle that was going on inside of him . . . the battle not to give in to what he believed were "baser emotions."

He patted her shoulder awkwardly and moved as if to push her gently away, but then he slipped out from her embrace and, rising on one elbow, looked down at her, questioning.

She didn't give him another chance, but took his free hand and drew it towards her, pressing it to her waist, inviting him. And for a few moments in the night, the Reverend Simon Dane came down from his pedestal and became a mere mortal.

# Six

A friend loves at all times,
And a brother is born for adversity.
                    — PROVERBS 17:17 (NKJV)

Otter paddled furiously against the current, heading towards the bright star in the evening sky, away from the soldiers' fort, away from the agencies. At first he had planned to stop at Cloudman's village, thinking that, as the northernmost of the reservation villages, its distance from the fort would provide protection from whatever the homesteader might do. The medicine man at Cloudman's village would know how to help Two Stars, and then they could decide where to go. But the longer Otter thought, the more afraid he was to let Cloudman's village know about Two Stars's injury.

The problem, as usual, was Red Thunder. If Red Thunder had done more than just try to steal horses — if he had harmed the white woman or her children — the soldiers from Fort Ridgely would be after them by now. Red Thunder had boasted of their plans, and it would not take long for someone in Shakopee's camp down by the Lower Agency to connect Two Stars and Otter to Red Thunder. Not one brave would risk the fury of the white man's army to protect them. They would tell what they knew, and the soldiers would not give up until all three of them had been caught and hanged.

Otter decided he must go past Cloudman's village, up to where the river formed the talking waters, on to Broken Pipe's trading post. The trader the whites called LaCroix hated the changes brought on by the treaties and the flood of whites just as much as the Dakota did. In some ways, Broken Pipe was more Dakota than white. He would not ask questions, and he would know how to treat Two Stars's wound. They could spend the summer with him. With all the blanket Indians moving south to be near the agencies, only Standing Buffalo's people would frequent the fort. Standing Buffalo's people had as little to do as possible with the agency Indians. There was little chance of seeing anyone they knew until it was time for the fall buffalo hunt, and by then Two Stars would be well. And as for Broken Pipe, Otter felt confident that if he was ever questioned about Red Thunder and stolen horses, he would shrug, light his pipe, and say nothing.

It was unusually cool for spring, but in spite of the cold, Two Stars's face was wet with sweat. Earlier in the day he had begun to shiver, muttering about creatures chasing him. Once, he sat up and nearly catapulted himself out of the canoe. It took all of Otter's considerable strength and wisdom to convince his friend to lie back and be quiet. Now he lay still, but fresh blood was oozing from the shoulder wound.

Otter paddled until it was dark, finally bringing the canoe to shore just where the river widened into the lake of talking waters. A full moon cast a light so bright that the hill leading up to the missionary's house was dappled with dark shadows from the trees. The sky was clear. Otter wrapped himself around Two Stars in a vain attempt to make him stop shivering. Together they waited, Two Stars's head hanging low, his chin resting on Otter's forearm, his breath coming in short gasps.

The moonlight revealed a small figure going from the barn to the house, trailed by a big white dog. Otter hesitated. He had not expected a dog. He waited long after the lights inside the big house went out. He tried to cool his friend's face with the icy river water. Soaking his bandanna, he dripped liquid into Two Stars's mouth. He crouched on his haunches, waiting, willing the missionary's boy to keep the white dog inside.

Finally, when the night was half over and the dog had not reappeared, Otter dragged his friend out of the canoe and laid him on the riverbank. Two Stars was unconscious, his breath coming in shallow gasps. Otter frowned, looking up the hill, wondering if the missionary would have medicine to help his friend, worrying what Two Stars might say while the craziness ruled his brain. Two Stars moaned. Otter realized his own shirt was damp with his friend's blood. There was nothing else he could do. He would have to take his chances with the dog. He watched the sky, waiting for a bank of clouds to rise up from the horizon. After what seemed like hours, the clouds passed before the moon. For a few moments, the brightness of the landscape dimmed. Otter knelt beside his friend and pulled him across his shoulders. Barely able to stand beneath the dead weight, Otter staggered up the narrow path towards the missionary's barn. He went inside, laying his friend on a clean mound of straw just inside the door. As he had hoped, a she-cow peered at him between two boards. When they came to take the cow's milk early in the morning they would find Two Stars.

Otter found two thin blankets stuffed beneath the seat of the farm wagon and covered Two Stars. With a last glance at his friend, he opened the barn door and fled down the hill. His arms were too weary to continue paddling upstream, but his legs were young and strong. If he ran all night he could be at Broken Pipe's the next day.

Something grabbed her ankle. Gen froze, her eyes wide with fright. Looking down, she saw dark eyes colored with a terrifying madness staring up at her through the pre-dawn light. She dropped the milking pail, instinctively trying to free herself. The grip on her ankle grew tighter, and the Indian brave muttered something she could not understand but took as a threat.

Koda flung himself through the barn door and at the stranger. His teeth bared, he slashed at the Indian, opening a wide gash from elbow to wrist.

The Indian let out a cry of pain mixed

with rage. Letting go of Gen's ankle he raised his arm to protect his face. He tried to get up, but as suddenly as he had grabbed Gen, he fell back on the straw, unconscious, the white dog atop him.

"Koda!" Gen shouted. "Koda, no —"

Koda backed off instantly, lowering his haunches to the earth and sitting, sphinxlike, ears alert, watching the stranger. When the enemy didn't move, he shifted his alert black eyes to Gen, whining softly and beating his tail in the dust.

"Watch him," Gen ordered, grateful when the dog obeyed and stayed put as she backed out of the barn and ran to the house.

"Ellen!" she whispered hoarsely, shaking her friend awake.

"In the barn — Indian — hurt — grabbed my ankle — Koda bit him — bleeding —"

Gen was only halfway through her first sentence when Ellen leaped out of bed and began to rummage in the trunk in the corner, producing scissors, muslin for bandages — and, from the depths of the trunk, a gun. She checked to see if it was loaded, spinning the chamber expertly. At Gen's amazed expression she smiled. "My brother used to take me along for target practice. Before Simon and I left for the west, he gave me this. I didn't want it, but he insisted. Now I'm glad."

"Mother," Aaron called from upstairs. "What's the matter?"

Ellen went to the base of the stairs. At the top she could see only Aaron's and Meg's faces as they rubbed their eyes sleepily.

"Nothing's the matter. A Dakota brave slept in the barn last night. He's hurt. Gen and I are going out to the barn to see if we can convince him to come into the house and let us help him. You stay upstairs."

Aaron frowned. "Father wouldn't like you going out there alone."

"Your father wouldn't want me to leave a wounded man alone in our barn, either. And besides, I'm not alone. I have Gen." Ellen hesitated before showing Aaron the gun. "And I have your uncle Elliot's gun. We'll be fine. Stay in here with your sister." She glanced towards the fireplace. "Get the fire going."

Aaron nodded and headed down the stairs.

Ellen turned to Gen. "Now let's see what we can do." Hiding the gun in the folds of her nightgown, Ellen led the way to the barn where Koda sat, ears alert, watching the unconscious Indian.

Ellen dropped the gun and sank to her knees beside the unconscious brave. "It's Two Stars — Gray Woman's son." She felt his forehead.

"Is it the cholera?" Gen half-whispered the dreaded word.

Ellen shook her head. "I don't think so."

"Is he —" Gen wanted to know.

Ellen shook her head. "No. Just unconscious. All this blood can't be from his arm." She lifted the edge of his vest. "Oh —"

Gen leaned over and looked. A small dark hole just beneath the brave's right collarbone was oozing dark blood. His entire chest beneath the vest was smeared with it.

"Help me get his vest off," Ellen ordered. She cut the vest and rolled the brave onto his side to look at his back. "At least the bullet went through." She shivered. "I wouldn't relish the idea of trying to dig a bullet out." She tore a strip of cotton from the hem of her gown and wrapped Two Stars's forearm. While she worked she murmured, "We've got to get him inside."

"Two Stars," Ellen spoke in Dakota. "You must wake up and help us. We are only two women, and we cannot carry you, but you must come with us for medicine to help your wounds."

Two Stars stirred. Without opening his eyes, he lifted his forearm off the straw but seemed unable to do more. Ellen leaned down next to him and pulled his arm across her neck. She struggled to pull him upright. "Please, Lord," she gasped, "somehow —"

Suddenly, with a growl of pain, Two Stars pushed himself up off the straw and staggered for the door. Gen and Ellen chased after him, ducking beneath his arms and trying to support him.

"This way," Ellen said, pressing against the brave's side and guiding him up the slight incline towards the cabin.

Two Stars plunged ahead, miraculously reaching the porch before collapsing at the cabin door. The two women rolled him onto an old comforter and, with Meg and Aaron's help, dragged him across to the fireplace.

Koda, who had apparently realized the intruder was a friend, now circled him cautiously, whining, wagging his tail, licking his face, trying in vain to get the man to move.

"Bring me the sewing basket, Meg,"

Ellen ordered. "Aaron, we need more bandages. Go into the bedroom and get the muslin we were going to use for Meg's quilt. Cut strips this wide —" She held up her hands to show him. She looked up at Gen. "I don't want to move him any more than we have to. We'll have to cut his clothes off."

"He stinks," Meg said, moving to the opposite end of the table.

"This first," Ellen said, preparing to cut the bear claw necklace away.

Gen stilled her hand. "Wait. Don't cut it." She bent close, fighting off the nausea that threatened as the smells of blood and unwashed body wafted into the room.

"I won't cut it unless I have to, but we have to get his clothing off. I can't stand the smell. You get water and soap." She fumbled with the necklace, finally getting it off without cutting it, and tossed it up on the table where it landed with a clatter.

Aaron had finished cutting muslin strips when Ellen ordered him and his sister upstairs with a ridiculous order that they "go back to sleep." The children were halfway up the stairs when they paused to watch their mother cut away Two Stars's leggings. She glared up at them, scissors poised in midair. At her unspoken warning, the two scampered the rest of the way upstairs. When she heard their door close, Ellen returned to her work.

"It's like peeling an onion," Gen whispered, rubbing her nose with the back of her hand.

"Yes," Ellen agreed, "complete with the watering eyes."

Two Stars began to mutter, trying to fight them off. Ellen laid a hand on his shin. He kicked at her, narrowly missing her face. When she tried again, he kicked more savagely. She dodged and sat back, a look of dismay on her face.

Gen spoke up. "Can't we just leave him — let him sleep for a while?" She knew the answer. They stared at one another for a moment when Gen had an idea. Standing up, she retrieved a second bowl of water and another strip of muslin. She sat down at Two Stars's side, her back to Ellen, and began to sing a Dakota lullaby. As she did, she reached beneath Two Stars's head and, lifting it, began to unwrap the bandanna around his head.

He grabbed her wrist, pulling her hand away. His eyes were open, dark pools of pain and questions.

She smiled at him and began to speak in Dakota. "Let us help you, Two Stars. I am

Geneviève, Broken Pipe's daughter. Do you know Broken Pipe up at Fort LaCroix? You have come to Renville Mission. We know your mother, Gray Woman. She comes to the little church sometimes. Reverend Dane has gone to Hazelwood, but his wife and children are here, and we will help you." Gen worked as she talked, speaking in a rhythm that blended well with the lullaby.

Two Stars dropped his hand and let her continue to unwrap the bandanna. She dipped a scrap of muslin into warm water and began to dab gently at his face. "Mrs. Dane is trying to help you. Please . . . do not fight us." Without turning around, Gen urged Ellen to try again. "I'll stay where he can see me. I'll keep singing." She had positioned herself so that her back was to most of Two Stars's prone body. Her cheeks burned when she heard Mrs. Dane's scissors cutting away what remained of Two Stars's blood-stained, filthy clothing.

Sometime during the long moments before Mrs. Dane said, "He hasn't been hurt anywhere else. It's just the arm and the wound in the shoulder," Two Stars fell back into unconsciousness. He was impervious to the sewing of the gash on his arm, the cleansing of his wound that produced a rivulet of yellow-green liquid mixed with fresh blood. He sucked in air in shallow gasps punctuated by coughs.

Ellen fed the last bit of Two Stars's clothing to the flames. Exhausted, she sat down at the table, resting her head in her hands. She saw a new problem. The floor where the clothing had been piled was littered with tiny creatures.

Ellen moaned. "Lice." She started to get up, but Gen stilled her hand. "I'll do it."

Gen killed the lice before scrubbing the floor between Two Stars and the door, and all around him, with lye. Finally, she dismantled one of the kerosene lamps and poured some of the liquid in a red enamel bowl. She sat cross-legged at Two Stars's head, massaging kerosene into his long hair all the way to the scalp. Her back began to cramp with weariness long before she had finished. "If we dared cut his hair this would be easier — but he'd never forgive us." She worked for what seemed like hours, combing and massaging until she was confident every intruder was dead. Finally, she and Ellen washed the long, black hair with lye soap.

When Aaron finally mustered the courage to sneak back downstairs both women were asleep, his mother in the rocker, Gen seated with her back against the fireplace. Light from the morning sun spilled in through a window and cast a golden glow across the prone figure of the sleeping Indian.

# Seven

The stranger who dwells among you
shall be to you as one born among you,
and you shall love him as yourself; for
you were strangers in the land of Egypt:
I am the LORD your God.
— LEVITICUS 19:34 (NKJV)

He lived in a colorless dream peopled by disembodied voices that hovered above him. When he thought to lift his hand to remove the stones holding his eyes shut, he discovered that some unknown thing held his arms to his sides. Just when he thought he could summon strength to fight the forces holding him down, he felt strangely lighter and slipped farther into the gray world of his dream until he was lost in the darkness. At times he felt as though he were burning. He concentrated on the sensation and realized he must be near a fire, but the stones kept his eyes closed so that he could not be certain.

After a time he recognized two separate

voices swirling in the air around him. They were feminine, and although he had no energy for listening, he knew from the cadence of their talk that they were not both Dakota. Smaller voices scampered through the strange dream once and almost lifted him into their world before he slipped back into the darkness.

When the stones finally fell from his eyelids so that he could open them, he saw the women and learned that the smaller voices were a boy and a girl. He saw their white faces and wanted nothing to do with them, but he could not speak to tell them to leave him alone. He could not even make his eyes tell them, it seemed, for when they saw him looking at them they chattered happily to one another. He closed his eyes and slipped away again.

When he returned from the valley of shadows, Two Stars watched more carefully. The white woman had gray eyes. He found strength to watch and listen and realized that she was the one deciding what they did to him. Her voice was soothing and calm. Like his mother's. Her hair was the color of the homesteader's fields just before the corn was harvested. The hatred he had for whites in general could not be summoned for this woman who spoke gently while she spread foul-smelling medicine on his chest.

The other one was younger. Unlike the Mother-one, she was dark. She made the same soothing sounds as the Mother-one, but it was her eyes that drew him in. They were great oval pools of sky-light, above which soared feathery dark brows shaped like a bird's wing in flight. When he had strength to watch her move about, he thought she moved with the quiet rhythm of his people. She offered him spoonfuls of hot liquid, and he sucked it in, surprised to realize he was hungry.

He climbed out of the valley of shadows more often. With each bowl of liquid from Blue Eyes he became more aware. One morning he woke unusually early to see Blue Eyes come in the cabin door and tiptoe across to the fireplace. She coaxed the fire back to life and then knelt on the hearth, raking her fingers through her damp, unbraided hair, waiting for it to dry. After a few moments, she separated the still-damp dark mane of hair into three sections, braided it into a long rope, then wrapped the rope about her head, making it stay in place with some odd-shaped things she took from her apron packet.

Her cheeks colored when she realized he

was watching her. When his eyes fell on the beadwork necklace around her neck, she reached up to touch it, but said nothing until he put the question in his eyes and she understood. "My mother's." She gave him more broth. While she fed him she hummed to herself. He recognized the song.

Mother-one tended his wounds. He remembered the dog slashing his arm. But there was another hurt, a larger one, that seemed to penetrate his entire right side. He thought it began near his heart. He reached towards it once, when Mother-one had taken the white bandages away. He could not remember what had happened there.

"You were shot," she said in Dakota. "We don't know how. Someone left you in our barn. You have been unconscious for many, many days. But you are better now." She smiled. "Try to rest, Two Stars. I know your mother. Gray Woman is my friend."

At his look of surprise, Mother-one nodded. "I recognized you by your red vest and the bear claw necklace. Gray Woman often boasted about your hunting. She is very proud of you." She laid a hand on his good shoulder. "Rest now. We will take care of you as long as you need us." It was the first time he had looked into a white's eyes and seen nothing but kindness. He fell into a natural, healing sleep.

He had been in the valley of shadows again, but now he felt completely awake. His shoulder did not hurt. And yet he sensed that something was wrong. But now the dog was gone. The one they called Koda had taken to sleeping next to him. Peering through the darkness, Two Stars could see him across the room. He was acting strangely, circling the same place on the floor, whining softly. Two Stars realized the dog was near the place where the floor lifted. Beneath it, the missionaries had what must be a huge hole filled with food. He had been with them many days now and had often seen the boy Aaron carry sacks of food out of the hole to help the women with their cooking. He lifted his head and whispered to the dog. Koda stopped circling long enough to look at him and wag his tail. Then, he scratched at the floor.

A faint aroma crept across the floor like a cooking fire —

"Fire! Fire!" He thought he was shouting at the top of his lungs, but no one heard him. How could they not hear when he spent all of his strength calling them? He grabbed the tin of water sitting next to him on the floor and flung it across the room towards where Mother-one slept. Finally, she stumbled towards him, concern on her face, but when her bare feet touched the place where the floor could be raised, she drew back. She pulled back the rug that covered the door and hesitated briefly before lifting it. A brilliant streak of yellow light shot into the room accompanied by smoke. Mother-one slammed the door back in place and screamed, "Gen! Aaron! Meg! Fire! In the cellar! Get out! Get out!"

Blue Eyes stumbled down the stairs, followed by the young girl they called Meg. The yellow-haired boy Aaron followed, clutching a blanket.

"To the church!" Mother-one ordered. "Take this!" She ran to her room and returned with a pile of blankets before pulling the door open and sending the children outside.

Two Stars tried to leap up to help the women, but all his strength was spent only getting to his knees. He watched helplessly while they shoved and pushed things out of the room, onto the porch, away from the cabin. There was an ominous sound of crackling, and then part of the floor gave way. Flames leaped up at the base of the stairs.

"Stop!" Two Stars shouted, as Blue Eyes leaped across the flames and scurried up the stairs. Miraculously, she made it. Through the window he could see things falling past the front window of the house, hear the frantic hurrying of her footsteps overhead as she rushed to save things.

Smoke was filling the room. Two Stars began to cough. Covering his mouth with a corner of his blanket, he tried to crawl towards the back door, but his wounded arm would not bear his weight and he could not stand. A huge beam from the ceiling fell across the room, blocking his way. The flames were coming perilously close. It was hard to breathe. He could feel the heat on his face. Hunkering down on the floor, he gasped for breath, waiting for the inevitable.

But then, a slight figure came through the front door. Pulling a blanket over her head, Blue Eyes charged through the flames, prodding him, trying to lift him up, crying with frustration, coughing.

"Get out!" he muttered. "Let me go."

"I won't!" she shouted back at him. Her

eyes were panic-stricken, but she stood in the middle of the burning room, resolute, trying to help him up even though it was obvious that she was too small and they would never make it.

The fire crackled and roared and they were both coughing helplessly when Mother-one appeared. The stairs fell to the floor, sending a shower of embers about them. Mother-one screamed and beat out the smoking embers around them. Together, the women pushed Two Stars down on his pallet, and with the impossible strength of the terrified, they dragged him around the hole in the floor, across the flames, and through the front door. The pallet protected him as they pulled him down the porch stairs and partway down the hill, away from the cabin. Meg and Aaron joined them, and together they easily moved the wounded brave downhill to the church.

Collapsing to the earth beside him, the four watched the cabin burn. Flames shone through the windows, leaping off the floor like dancers, licking at the table and chairs barely visible through the smoke, then encircling the windows and finally climbing higher and higher until the walls and the roof were one great mass of wicked yellow light glowing against the dark sky. Finally, in one horrible, heartrending crash, the roof fell in.

The five onlookers sat in stunned silence. When the flames were only small fingers of light, Mother-one turned to Two Stars. "Are you hurt?"

He shook his head. "Only weak like a woman," he muttered bitterly.

She laughed and he realized how stupid he must sound, talking about their weakness when he owed his life to women.

Moonlight illuminated Mother-one's face. She looked past him, tears filling her eyes as she gazed at the empty place on the hillside where her life had been. The children snuggled close, crying softly.

It was not long before Mother-one took charge again. Looking about her at the belongings scattered on the ground, she said quietly, "We have enough blankets to sleep the rest of the night. There will be much to do tomorrow."

Two Stars could see the weariness etched in the women's faces as they gathered blankets and went inside the church. They emerged in a moment and helped him inside. Aaron and Meg had already fallen asleep on a pallet in one corner. Two Stars sank down willingly on a pile of blankets opposite them. When he coughed, Blue Eyes came to his side, feeling his forehead, worrying aloud about a fever. Even though she was clumsy with fatigue, she trudged up the hill to bring back a bucket of fresh water, to hold his head, to give him a drink.

"You must sleep now," he said gruffly. *"Tanyan waun."*

She did not argue, but joined the other whites on the pallet near the door.

When their even breathing sounded in soft whistles and snores, Koda pushed his way through the crack in the church door. He sniffed each sleeping form, wagging his tail happily before curling up beside Two Stars and, with a deep sigh, falling asleep.

Two Stars lay awake long into the night, contemplating the mystery of these strange people who would risk their lives to save a Dakota man who hated whites.

# Eight

The LORD gave, and the LORD has
    taken away;
Blessed be the name of the LORD.
                    — JOB 1:21 (NKJV)

Clutching a blanket around her shoulders,
Gen crept outside and settled on the porch
of the adobe-brick church. A full moon had
transformed the landscape into a surreal,
blue-white universe, decorated with a silver
ribbon of river. Inside the church behind
her, everyone was asleep. The reverend had
come home today, panic-stricken as he raced
his horse up the hill, clutching his wife to
him, barely able to let go of his children. As
she watched the emotional reunion from the
hillside near the ruins of the cabin, Gen had
felt the pain of Etienne's absence and her
homesickness sharpened. She had managed
to keep it hidden all day, but now as she
stared at the landscape below her, she let the
tears flow.

An owl hooted. Gen looked up at the

moon. Somewhere, far to the north, Papa might be looking at that moon. Perhaps he was thinking of her. She expected the thought to comfort her, but instead it brought a different kind of pain — the reminder that she had been at the mission for over two months and Etienne had not kept his promise to visit. She had worked so hard to learn exactly the things that he wanted her to learn, but he had not bothered to come and see. It left a wound of disappointment deep inside her.

After the reverend's return, they had all gone up to the smoldering remains of the cabin and begun to pick carefully through things along the edges of the debris. Gen had righted her mother's overturned trunk and retrieved the contents. Only the white antelope-skin wedding dress was missing. She didn't find it until right before sundown, when she climbed the hill to get fresh water for their meager supper. Koda must have chewed on it for hours.

As she cried, Gen stroked the remaining fragment of Good Song Woman's elaborate beadwork. Behind her, Ellen opened the church door and whispered her name. Shivering from the cool night air, she sat down and huddled next to Gen. After a moment she reached out to trace a beaded design on the remnant of hide with her finger. "Was this in your trunk?" she asked.

Gen nodded. "Koda must have dragged it away — and —" Her voice lowered. "It was my mother's." She choked back tears.

Ellen held her and let her cry.

After a few minutes Gen took a deep breath and pointed up at the moon. "Papa said to watch the moon when I felt lonely. He said he would look at it every night and think of me. He said it would help." Gen looked down at the dress in her lap and shook her head. "It used to help. But it doesn't anymore." Her voice wavered and she bit her lip, half-whispering, "I just don't understand why he hasn't come."

Ellen put an arm around her shoulders. "It's hard to be lonely." She sighed quietly. "I thought I would die of loneliness when we first came to Minnesota. I rarely heard from home. In those days we had to wait for a kindhearted soul to bring our mail from Fort Snelling. Sometimes six weeks would go by before we heard a word. On the worst nights, I used to slip out of bed and go outside and cry. Like you, I would look up at the moon and think of my mother and father and hope that they were looking at that same moon, thinking of me. It helped somehow."

Gen grumbled, "At least you knew your parents cared. They wrote you letters. And you knew why they didn't come. They couldn't. It's too far." She added, "Papa said he chose Renville Mission for the very reason that it is close enough for him to come and visit often."

Ellen nudged her. "Didn't you tell me he usually goes on a spring hunt with Cloudman's people?"

Gen nodded. "But he doesn't *have* to go. He could come to see me instead. If he wanted to."

"Perhaps he has missed you so much he didn't trust himself to come. Perhaps he was afraid he would be tempted to take you away before you had learned what he sent you to learn. You know your papa loves you, Gen." Ellen patted her knee. "You must have faith that he is doing what is best for you, even though you do not understand." She pointed up the hill. "Everyone comes to a point in their lives when they are challenged to see beyond what *is* and trust that God knows best."

Gen retorted angrily. "Don't ask me to believe that being deserted by my papa is something God is doing *for* me!" She shook her head. "I'm sorry, Ellen. I don't mean to hurt you. If thinking about things

102

that way helps you, then I am glad for you. I don't argue that God *is,* but I don't think of Him the same way you do — not if you're saying that God controls a plan for us that includes bad things like —"

"— like fires?" Ellen completed Gen's sentence for her. "Yes. I do believe that. I think God concerns Himself with every tiny aspect of every day. And somehow, even the bad things that happen are part of His plan."

"That doesn't make sense!"

Ellen nodded. "Real faith doesn't always make logical sense." She sighed, rubbing her arms briskly. "For Christians there is always a space between what we can and cannot understand. Faith is what helps us live in that space and still believe that what God says is true. The challenge for me is to accept by faith a better way — a better reality."

"Which is?" Gen asked.

"In this case, I'm learning a whole new aspect of the promise that I have an eternal house, not made with hands, in heaven. If I focus on my real home in heaven, losing this one isn't so terrible."

"*My* real home is Fort LaCroix," Gen blurted out.

"Yes," Ellen said sadly. "I know." She

patted Gen's hand. "Your papa loves you, Geneviève. But not nearly as much as the Lord Jesus loves you. I will pray that they *both* come to you soon." With a last hug, Ellen stood up and went back inside to bed. She prayed for Gen and Etienne before falling asleep.

Had she known, she would have also prayed for Two Stars, who had lain awake listening carefully as Mother-one spoke mysteries. He thought her foolish in her thinking about God. And yet he lay awake long past the time when her breathing was slow and even, long past the time when Blue Eyes came inside and fell asleep, contemplating the idea of a God who used burning houses and loneliness to teach His children.

Over a cold breakfast of stale bread and fresh milk, the reverend asked again, "Doesn't anyone have an idea of what could have started the fire?"

They sat quietly. Only Aaron didn't look up. Finally, he whispered, "It was me, Father. I did it." Burying his face in his hands, he burst into tears and let out a flood of words. "Mother wanted me to go get some cornmeal and I was scared 'cause last time I was down there I saw a big rat.

So this time when I went down, I took a candle instead of the lamp so I could burn him if he jumped at me." Aaron shuddered. "And I saw him too. He was sitting on the churn and he just looked at me and looked. And I thought he was going to jump at me, so I grabbed the sack of cornmeal and I threw the candle at him and I ran up the stairs as fast as I could." He drew in a big breath and let it out. Finally, he looked up at his father, tears washing a clear trail through the soot on his cheeks. "I stopped at the top of the stairs and I looked and the candle was out." He repeated it plaintively. "It *was*, Father. It was out. There wasn't a flicker. Not even a flicker." His voice was small as he finished with a sob, "But I guess it wasn't really out . . . or maybe it was just the hot wax . . . or it landed on the straw —" He stopped and gulped. "I didn't mean it . . . I just — couldn't — face — that big old rat —"

Reverend Dane looked at his son. The boy's eyes sought the floor and stayed there. Everyone held his breath. Reverend Dane closed his eyes for a moment. Then he slid off his bench and went to his boy and hugged him. "It isn't a sin to be afraid, Son. I should have shot that rat — or poisoned him — before I left."

Aaron wrapped his arms around his father's waist. "But I made it all burn up, Father." He choked on the words, crying harder. "All of your books and all of your important papers."

The reverend sat down and pulled Aaron into his lap. The boy's long legs draped over his father's bony knees, nearly reaching the floor. "You listen to me, Son. There is nothing — do you hear me? — *nothing* more important than the *people* who were in that cabin. They are safe. And the rest — well —" He cleared his throat. "Obviously God thinks we can manage without the rest." Gently shoving Aaron off his lap, the reverend stood up. "And now, I'm going outside to hitch up Rory and see if I can't drag some of the bigger timbers out of the rubble so we can see if there's anything else to be saved."

"Do you think it's cooled down enough?" Ellen asked.

"I think so. It's still hot in the very center, but we should be able to finish at least around the edges."

They worked feverishly for the rest of the day, hauling the few things they had managed to save from the burning cabin down to the church, cleaning and sorting, setting up a makeshift kitchen in one corner by the small stove meant to keep worshipers warm in the winter, using benches to create a cubicle for Meg and Aaron, one for Two Stars, one for Gen, one for the Reverend and Mrs. Dane.

At midday, Two Stars wobbled out onto the porch and sat in the sun, holding a piece of kindling in his left hand, trying to whittle with his right. When his right hand could not grip the knife, he gave up and sat leaning against the church, watching the family pick through the remains of the house.

"Do you think we can rebuild?" Ellen asked when they paused to rest and eat a cold lunch of water and stale bread.

The reverend shook his head. "With all the Dakota moving away to be closer to the agencies down south, this country is bound to be deserted. There is little possibility of a viable mission work here anymore." He took a drink of water before continuing. "Dr. Riggs spoke of starting a new boarding school near Cloudman's village. That would create three missions — Pajutazee near Akipa and John Otherday's villages, Hazelwood near Enehah and Running Walker's villages, and then a new mission — ours — near Cloudman and Simon

Anawangami's villages. Three missions to blanket the Upper Agency Indians with the gospel! Dr. Riggs thinks we could expect as many as thirty students as soon as we open. They even promised to loan us a teacher from Hazelwood until someone can be recruited from the east."

By the end of the day, it was apparent they could not stay at the ruined mission site for long. The heat of the fire had destroyed nearly everything, bursting crocks and jars and spewing their contents all over the cellar, reducing potatoes and other root crops to charred black balls.

"Thank God we still have the wagon," the reverend said over their supper of cornmeal mush and fresh milk. "We'll load up in the morning and head for Hazelwood."

"What about Two Stars?" Aaron blurted out.

From where he sat in the corner of the large room, Two Stars answered. "Two Stars will go north and find Standing Buffalo's people."

"Don't be absurd," Reverend Dane protested. "You are in no condition to go anywhere alone. You'll go with us to Hazelwood Mission. At least until you are stronger."

Rebellion rose in Two Stars's eyes, but Ellen erased it by pleading softly, "Please, Two Stars. Come. We'll get word to Gray Woman." She smiled at Two Stars. "She is very worried about you. Who better to care for a boy than his mother?"

Two Stars leaned his head back against the church wall. He finished eating his bowl of mush and drank an extra glass of fresh milk. When they left early the next day, he allowed the reverend to help him into the back of the wagon, where he sat alongside the meager supplies rescued from the fire. The reverend's children and Blue Eyes sat just behind the wagon seat, and he was relieved not to have their constant chatter buzzing in his ears. Meg's youthful laughter rang out as Koda, shining like a ghost in the predawn light, chased a rabbit down the hill and nearly turned a somersault to keep from falling into the river.

Two Stars turned away. He could not remember laughing for a very long time. How was it, he wondered, that he had come to be so somber? As a boy he was the jokester in the village, playing harmless pranks on his friends, hunting endlessly, riding horses, racing canoes across the lake, contemplating nothing more complex than the best way to trap a rabbit.

Things had begun to change when he had lived about twelve winters. That was the winter that Bad Eagle began to come home drunk with the trader's whiskey. If he had only stumbled in drunk and gone to sleep, Two Stars could have endured it. But whiskey transformed the once proud Dakota warrior into a reeling wife-beater. The night Two Stars placed himself between his mother and father and knocked his father out with a well-placed fist, things changed forever. He left his mother's tepee and went to find his best friend Otter. After that, Two Stars timed his moments at home with Bad Eagle's absence. He lurked in the shadows and made certain no real harm came to Gray Woman, but he refused to watch his father's decline.

Bad Eagle blamed the whites for all his troubles. When he was only ten, Two Stars was inclined to agree with Bad Eagle's simplistic excuse. If the whites had stayed away, there would have been no whiskey. But by the time he had lived eight more winters, Two Stars had learned that the problems facing the Dakota were many and complex. The government had promised to pay annual annuities to each of the Dakota. But when it came time to pay, the agents often gave money and food to only the farmer Indians. Thinking to encourage more Dakota to become farmers, they only created factions among the natives who began to fight and bicker among themselves. "Blanket" or "Annuity Indians," the ones who fought the idea of farming and clung to the old ways, called the farmers "Cut-Hairs," "Pantaloons," and "Dutchmen." They heckled Dakota who took jobs at the agencies and vandalized the farms of those who took up agriculture. Sometimes they did more than heckle.

Loitering with Red Thunder and Otter around various trading posts and agency Indians, Two Stars learned that the men in Washington who wrote the laws and the treaties and then sought to bind them around Dakota necks knew very little about how a Dakota man thought and lived. Most soldiers and agents seemed to think all Dakota thought and acted as one. This was because in the white world all men, even the greatest warriors, must bend to what the Great Father in Washington said. The whites didn't seem to realize that while Dakota men considered what their chief said carefully, if they did not agree, they were under no obligation to obey. Chief Little Crow could sign treaties and papers until there were enough to touch the sky, but respected Dakota warriors could ignore those papers and do as they pleased and still be honored.

Red Thunder and Otter said the only way to be true to the Dakota nation was to hate all whites. Red Thunder reserved his fiercest venom for the missionaries he saw as weak and without honor. He had heard one give a sermon once where he spoke of the words in a book as a sword. When Red Thunder told about it, he spat on the ground to show his contempt for men stupid enough to think the words in a book could protect them or fight for them.

The more he thought about the changes and opinions swirling through the Dakota nation, the more confused Two Stars became. Bad Eagle and Red Thunder and hundreds like them said whites were evil. Two Stars realized they were guilty of the very thing he hated — refusing to understand that men had minds and opinions that differed, regardless of their skin color. Obviously white people were not all the same. All traders were not thieves. Broken Pipe proved that. And the Danes had proven that all whites were not greedy land-grabbers. It was an unsettling realization, and it made him uncertain as to what he should do next.

His mind whirling, Two Stars turned to watch Lac Qui Parle disappear into the distance. As the sun rose in the sky, it glowed red like a piece of sacred pipestone nestled between the hills. Long ago, he and Otter had stolen Bad Eagle's canoe and headed off across the lake. They were in the exact center when a storm came up. Unwilling to bow to nature, they fought the wind until, their strength gone, they could only concentrate on keeping the canoe afloat. But in spite of their best efforts, the canoe capsized and both boys were flung into the water. They clung to the canoe and weathered the storm, and when the wind finally died down, Otter had earned his name by laughing at the wind and the lake and proclaiming himself master of the waters.

As Lac Qui Parle disappeared from sight, Two Stars thought that today, as he rode across the prairie in a white man's wagon, weak and helpless, he was like that canoe, caught in a storm of change, adrift on the water, not knowing whether he would survive the storm or drown in it.

# Nine

Be hospitable to another without grumbling.

— 1 PETER 4:9 (NKJV)

The only thing on Miss Jane Williams's mind was a cup of tea with lemon and honey and the opportunity to roll her stockings down and prop up her feet. She was headed home to the little cottage she shared with two other spinster teachers at the Hazelwood Mission, and appeared frustrated when a half dozen students surrounded her.

"*Now* what do you want?" Miss Jane growled.

But Rosalie, a tall, slender girl who had been at the school for nearly two years, knew better than to believe Miss Jane's gravelly complaint. Smiling, Rosalie tugged at Miss Jane's apron.

Miss Jane pushed the girl's hand away. "*Ihnuhan hecanon kin!*" she ordered. "Don't do that!"

Rosalie's friend Bessie tugged at her arm. "Let's go, Rosalie," she hissed, standing on tiptoe to whisper in her friend's ear. "Leave Miss Jane alone. She's tired." Bessie backed away, eyeing the regal Miss Jane carefully.

"Bessie!" Miss Jane's naturally loud voice made Bessie tremble. "What is nine times seven?"

Bessie stood still, telegraphing a silent plea for help to each pair of eyes that watched her. She was the newest student in the school, and learning the white man's way of counting was confusing. Bessie looked down, growing more and more nervous as she saw that Miss Jane had folded her arms and was tapping her toe.

"Six-three — no," Bessie said, correcting herself with a big smile. "Sixty-three. Nine times seven equals sixty-three."

"Exactly," Miss Jane said tersely. She reached behind the ever-present apron, into the deep pockets in her skirt, and withdrew a handful of nuts. "Excellent." Miss Jane eyed the rest of the girls through gold-rimmed glasses. "Bessie worked hard in arithmetic today. She deserves a reward."

As Bessie reached out and took a hazelnut, her eyes sought Miss Jane's face.

The blue eyes that had been so stern all day sparkled with warmth. Miss Jane asked each girl in the group a simple question and produced a reward from what seemed to be an eternal supply somewhere beneath the apron.

"I told you she wasn't really mean," Rosalie whispered, nudging her friend. "She just acts that way in class so the big boys don't try to take over." She nodded towards the teachers' cottage where Otter sat waiting on the porch. He had been especially willful that day, and Miss Jane had punished him by ordering him to cut some firewood for her. "Look at Otter. He knows where the ax is. But he's still trying to get out of work."

When each child had won a treat, they scampered off toward the dining hall, and Miss Jane continued along the well-beaten path to her cottage. When Otter stood up and met her gaze, he saw ice where the younger children had just seen the fire of friendship.

Miss Jane seemed to stretch herself to a greater height as she faced Otter. The ankle that had been aching furiously all day suddenly seemed worse. Miss Jane pressed her lips together firmly. Her nostrils flared as she stared Otter directly in the eyes. The boy, who was taller than most of his friends, found himself looking up at a woman. He had never been so close to the white teacher and had not realized she was so tall.

"It takes more than an overgrown Dakota boy to intimidate me, young man," Miss Jane said evenly. "I know what you're up to, Otter. You are determined you will not learn, and you are hoping to induce some of the other students to follow your rebellion. Well," Miss Jane said, "I won't tolerate it. You can't frighten me and you can't rule my class. If you don't want to learn, that's your business. But don't think for a moment I'm going to let your troublemaking steal opportunity from the others."

A rumble in the distance made Miss Jane glance over Otter's shoulder. Angry clouds were rising in the sky behind the Riggses' house. So *that* was why her ankle had been troubling her all day. Those clouds probably held rain. Movement along the trail that ran north and south along the western edge of the mission compound caught her eye. Otter turned around to see what she was looking at. A bedraggled bunch of white people in an old wagon were driving up to the Riggses' house. Resentment made Otter clench his teeth. *More white settlers to steal more Dakota land.*

But Miss Jane didn't see white settlers. She recognized the couple on the wagon seat. Without looking at Otter she said tersely, "We'll talk again. You know where the ax is. And see to it that the wood is stacked neatly beside the kitchen door this time." Ignoring her sore ankle, Miss Jane lifted her skirts and hurried towards the Riggses' house on the opposite side of the compound.

"Rosalie!" Bessie called from inside the girls' cottage. "Rosalie come quick! Someone's coming . . . and Miss Jane . . ." Rosalie hurried to her friend's side, and they watched through the window as Miss Jane lifted her skirts and ran towards the Riggses' house. Bessie and Rosalie looked at each other and giggled with delight. Old Miss Jane's stockings were *striped*. They were bright pink and red! Now, *there* was something to talk about!

Otter had no interest in Miss Jane's stockings. He was studying the newcomers. Whoever they were, they didn't have very much. He could tell they were tired from the way the man climbed down. When he took his hat off, Otter could see he was not as old as it seemed from the way he moved. The woman must be the white man's wife, the yellow-haired boy and redheaded girl his children.

A girl in the back of the wagon piqued his curiosity. She was Indian. But the way the young ones clung to her, it didn't seem she was their servant. From the greeting they were getting from the Riggses Otter could tell they had some connection with the missionaries. He turned and looked north. Newcomers to the area always came from the south, the direction of the Yellow Medicine Agency. Just as the Indian girl looked his way, Otter ducked behind the cabin. Peering around the corner he saw the whites helping someone out of the back of the wagon. He saw the white dog. And he knew.

For the rest of her life, Gen would remember her arrival at Hazelwood Mission. She had dozed off and was dreaming of Papa and Fort LaCroix, of speaking French and reciting Shakespeare, of new lives and wounded Indian braves when the reverend shouted, "Whoa!" The wagon stopped, and Gen woke up to a chorus of noise. At Renville she could sit on the porch and hear the flight of the geese overhead, the gentle *plip-plip* as ducks settled onto the surface of the river, the far-off bellow of a bull elk. But Hazelwood's sounds were all about humanity and progress. A blacksmith pounded his anvil, sawmill workers guided their blades through a log sending a high-pitched whine into the air, and children's laughter underscored everything.

The laughter made Gen sit up and peer over the edge of the wagon just in time to see a group of girls skitter out from behind one of the buildings and dash through the golden rays of the sun that poured through the open places in the storm clouds chasing toward them from the west. They charged up the hill behind a huge barn, ignoring the impending storm in favor of a few more moments of outdoor play. Gen glanced towards the three largest buildings. One of those buildings must be home to the girls.

She gazed across the pile of things in the wagon to where Two Stars half sat, half lay. His eyes were closed, and he had one hand on Koda's collar, holding the dog next to him. A gust of cool air ruffled the dark hair that spilled over his forehead. Gen could tell he was awake, but weariness and something else she could not decipher were etched into his face. When the reverend climbed down from the wagon seat, Koda moved as if to jump out of the wagon, but Two Stars's hand tensed up. Koda stayed. When someone called a greeting, Two Stars opened his eyes and looked at Gen. If she had not known better, she would have thought he looked a little afraid.

Voices sounded from the opposite side of the wagon, and Gen sat up. Her first impression of the Riggses' home was that missionary work only a long day's ride from Lac Qui Parle must be very different from what the Danes did. Instead of a crude log cabin, Dr. and Mrs. Riggs lived in a two-story frame house, with shutters at the windows and a yard filled with blooming flowers. Even more amazing than the house and the yard was the sparkling white slat-board fence around the yard.

Meg and Aaron got to their knees and peered over the side of the wagon as the reverend opened the yard gate and went up on the porch. Someone nearby said, "You poor dears." It seemed impossible that a voice so powerful could emanate from the slender woman peering at them through gold-rimmed glasses. She had copper-colored hair and a motherly smile that drew

Gen to her. "You poor, poor dears," she repeated.

A placid-looking woman who proved to be Mrs. Riggs appeared at the door of the house just at the moment a man the reverend greeted as Dr. Riggs came hurrying across from the sawmill. Suddenly everyone was talking at once. Gen heard Reverend Dane's voice say "fire" as he pointed to the charred belongings in the wagon. She heard her own name and nodded to Mrs. Riggs, who put her arm around Ellen's shoulders at the same time that she smiled at Meg and Aaron. And while everyone was clamoring to tell about the fire, the copper-haired woman who had called them "poor dears" was walking to the back of the wagon and holding out her hand, introducing herself as Miss Jane Williams to both Gen and Two Stars. She scratched Koda behind the ears and let down the backboard. When she saw how stiff Two Stars was and how he winced when he moved, she had the audacity to ask to see his shoulder and to tell Reverend Dane she was the mission nurse and she would see to Two Stars and she would be pleased to have the girl stay with her in the teachers' cottage.

Before Gen had time to realize that she

was "the girl" in question, Miss Jane was helping Two Stars out of the wagon and making her way towards a small clapboard cottage with a porch almost entirely obscured by a wild vine that crawled the length of the cottage porch and up over nearly half the roof.

Gen looked around uncertainly.

"Come inside with us, Miss LaCroix," Mrs. Riggs said. "Miss Jane will be along directly." She smiled, and her soft brown eyes crinkled at the edges. She headed for the house. "You must all be so hungry." She nodded at Meg and Aaron. "Don't be shy, you two. I've a big trunk of things that belonged to my own children. We'll find you some fresh clothes . . . and I suspect you'll find some other treasures inside that trunk."

Gen followed the family inside, pausing at the door long enough to turn around and see Miss Jane motion for Two Stars to sit down on the cottage porch. She saw him shake his head, but Miss Jane laid one hand on his arm and said something that resulted in Two Stars sitting down. Then Miss Jane patted Koda on the head and disappeared inside the cottage. Gen slipped into the Riggses' parlor and watched through the window as Miss Jane came back outside. She set a bowl down on the porch and whatever it held Koda found it delicious. Then she coaxed Two Stars inside.

While Dr. Riggs and the reverend hurried to get Rory unhitched and a tarpaulin pulled over the wagon before it rained, Mrs. Riggs, Gen, Ellen, and the children headed for the kitchen at the back of the house. As soon as the children had washed their hands and faces, Mrs. Riggs said to Aaron, "Young man, you take your sister upstairs to the second room on the right. That trunk I was talking about is just inside the door. It isn't locked. You have fun. We'll call you as soon as we have something ready to eat." She added, "And while you're upstairs, would you check and make sure all the windows are closed? From the sound of that thunder, we're in for some rain."

While Gen and Ellen ground coffee, built a fire in Mrs. Riggs's massive cookstove, and set the table, Mrs. Riggs let down the oven door and hoisted a huge iron pot up onto the stovetop. "Dr. Riggs teased me about making so much for the noon meal today. 'Mary,' he said, 'we'll be eating stew for a week.'" Mrs. Riggs smiled softly. "But the Lord knew we'd need a quick supper tonight."

Meg and Aaron clattered back downstairs just as Gen poured fresh milk into each of the five mugs at the table. Frowning slightly, Aaron asked, "Shouldn't we get Two Stars? He's hungry too."

"Miss Jane is seeing to Two Stars," Dr. Riggs explained as he and the reverend came in the back door. "She'll put some medicine on his shoulder and then take him over to the young men's residence hall. They'll have plenty for him to eat, and he can meet our other students." Seating himself at the table, he took a sip of coffee and leaned forward, stroking his bushy gray sideburns absentmindedly. "Tell us about the fire." When the reverend had finished, Dr. Riggs said, "You must stay with us while we write to the American Board. I think they are prepared to support the work up near Cloudman's village." He looked at Aaron. "This house has just been longing for children." He smiled at Meg. "And now we'll have some again." He stood up. The reverend followed his lead, and the men retired to the parlor together, leaving the women to tend to the children and the dishes.

Miss Jane appeared at the back door.

She stepped inside. "That boy's been shot," she said. "But it's healing nicely. You're a good nurse, Mrs. Dane." She motioned to Gen. "Come along, my dear. You're the first company we've had in ages and we're bored to distraction. The girls will be back any minute. Come tell us about yourself." She took Gen by the arm. "You're about Lizzie's size. We'll get you some new clothes —" A loud clap of thunder and a flash of lightning interrupted Miss Jane. "Let's go before the rain starts!" She pulled Gen towards the door just as raindrops the size of pebbles began to fall. Miss Jane said, "We'll have to run for it!" She glanced at Mrs. Riggs. "See you in the morning!"

The two went out onto the porch just as another bolt of lightning chased across the sky. Thunder crashed, and Gen and Miss Jane ran towards the cottage, arriving on the porch at the same moment the dark clouds kept their promise. They stood together on the porch watching the downpour while Miss Jane kept up a running commentary about life at the mission. "We have nearly thirty students this term. Every size, every age, and every possible opinion of the white man. Some already know English before they come to us. A few can even read a little. Everyone calls me Miss Jane." She sighed with mock sadness. "It's my curse in life and I must accept it. I shall forever be a Miss, I suppose . . . although I don't think there's anything particularly *amiss* about it." She grinned at Gen and headed inside.

Miss Jane lit the two oil lamps in the simply furnished parlor. "I've wanted to ask. Reverend Dane said your given name is LaCroix. Is that LaCroix . . . as in Etienne LaCroix?"

Gen didn't hide her amazement. "You have heard of my papa?"

The older woman put her hand on Gen's shoulder. "I've been here for twenty years, my dear. Your father has a very good reputation among the Lord's workers here." She headed for a narrow stairway on the opposite wall of the parlor, a stairway that appeared to have been some carpenter's afterthought rather than an integral part of the building plan. "If you'll give me a moment, we'll head back to the kitchen and have some tea." She bent down enough to peer out the window. "I suppose Lizzie and Belle will be late, now." She straightened up and adjusted her glasses. "Miss Huggins is just about your size." Miss Jane headed for the stairs. "Belle just put the buttons on a new dress last night. I'll just get it and be right down."

Gen protested. "Oh, please, don't — I wouldn't want to —"

"Lizzie won't mind," Miss Jane said firmly and continued up the stairs, calling behind her. "We've been teaching sewing classes all spring, and we each got two new dresses. Now who on earth needs *two* new dresses at once?"

She came back downstairs with a pale blue calico dress folded over one arm. Motioning for Gen to follow her, she headed to the back of the cottage. "You can change in Lizzie's room. She and Belle have both been gone to Chief Enehah's village all day. With the rain, they may decide to stay the night."

As she talked, Miss Jane led Gen through the front room of the cottage, across the corner of the kitchen, and into an adjoining room. "I'll be right back with some fresh water so you can get cleaned up."

"You don't have to go out in the rain for me," Gen protested. "I can get it. Just show me where —" But Miss Jane was already out the door, umbrella in hand. When she returned, she poured fresh water in the basin on a little stand in Lizzie's room then scurried off. She soon reappeared at the door and held out a bar of scented soap. "I'd say you deserve a special treat after all you've been through." She rummaged through a trunk in the corner of the room and produced a clean petticoat, which she spread on the bed with an apology, "I can't seem to locate any stockings. You could have a pair of mine, but I'm so much taller than you."

"It's all right," Gen said. "I hate stockings anyway." She held up the soap, inhaling an unfamiliar but delightful aroma. "What is it?" she asked.

"Lavender," Miss Jane said. "I'll see what I can do about shoes and stockings tomorrow." She handed Gen a linen towel and a comb and brush. As she left, she pulled a curtain across the doorway. Gen noticed it was made from a tattered quilt, sewn around a pole someone had fitted inside the doorway. From the other side of the quilt Miss Jane said, "I'll make us a cup of tea."

Peering into the mirror nailed to the wall above the washbasin, Gen let down her tangled hair, brushing at it halfheartedly. For once, she thought, she was grateful that her hair was so straight. At least there were no curls and waves to contend with.

Her arms were beginning to feel like lead. Although she wasn't really finished with her hair, Gen laid the brush aside and leaned closer to the mirror to inspect herself. Dark circles shadowed the places beneath each eye, and a line of soot ran along her hairline. Lifting her jaw and tilting her face away from the mirror, she inspected her neck, where dirt had collected in every crease. Even in the lamplight she could see a ring of filth around the dress collar. When she unbuttoned her cuffs she was appalled to see a ring of dirt encircling each wrist just above where her hands had been immersed in Mrs. Riggs's dishwater. Gen undressed, leaving her filthy clothing in a pile on the floor, slipping out of her shoes and standing barefooted in front of the washbasin.

Plunging her hands into the cool water, she looked into the mirror again and began to scrub at the dirt on her face. When at last it was clean, she closed her eyes, inhaling the delicious aroma of lavender. With a spurt of energy, she began scrubbing her body, not stopping until the water in the basin was gray. As she wrung out her washing cloth, she noticed with chagrin that a wide ring of dirt marked the waterline in the basin. She scrubbed at it, leaving the cloth floating in the dingy water.

After pulling Miss Huggins's clean petticoat over her head, Gen reached for her new dress and pulled it on with leaden arms. The minute the hem touched the floor, she leaned against the bed wearily. She looked at the bed longingly but told herself she must not sit down and wrinkle the blue-and-white quilt that served as a spread. But she was so tired. She gave a little hop and managed to perch on the edge of the mattress for what she told herself would be just a moment. She could hear Miss Jane humming as she moved about the kitchen. The storm mellowed, the rhythm of gentle rain forming a soothing accompaniment to Miss Jane's mellow voice. Gen had barely managed to button the last of the twenty-five tiny pearl buttons that marched down the front of the blue calico dress when she fell asleep, crashing sideways, her feet still dangling over the edge of the bed. Sometime later she was vaguely aware of her feet being lifted up onto the blue-and-white quilt, of being covered with a lightweight sheet that smelled of lavender. It was still raining. Gen pulled the sheet up under her chin and sighed.

# Ten

I will instruct you and teach you in the
  way you should go;
I will guide you with My eye.
  — PSALM 32:8 (NKJV)

Gen stretched lazily and let out a soft groan of pleasure. She sighed and turned on her side, breathing in an unfamiliar but pleasing scent. Her eyes flew open and focused on the "door" to her room. Then she realized she had slept the entire night away atop the blue-and-white quilt in Miss Huggins's room. Someone had covered her with a sweet-smelling sheet. She looked down and saw her shoes waiting on the floor, right where she could slide down the side of the unusually high bed and into them, which she did at once.

Someone had emptied the washbasin and brought in a pitcher of fresh water. She hurried to wash her face, suddenly aware of movement on the opposite side of the curtain. They weren't talking, but Gen could hear carefully softened footsteps and what sounded like a chair being picked up and then set down as quietly as possible. She smelled coffee. It was so unnaturally quiet that she could hear the stream of liquid hitting a cup. Her stomach growled. In the predawn light, she couldn't locate her hairpins. She pulled aside the quilted door just enough to be able to peek into the kitchen.

Miss Jane was standing at the stove, turning griddle cakes. Two other women sat at the table drinking coffee. One had outlandishly red hair and extremely pale skin blotched with small brown dots. "Good morning," she said, revealing two oversized teeth when she smiled. Gen had the fleeting image of a rabbit. "I'm Eliza Huggins, but call me Lizzie."

Gen hesitated. "I — I'm sorry about taking over your room." She stroked her long brown hair self-consciously. "And I can't seem to find my hairpins."

"Oh, don't worry about that," Miss Huggins said cheerily. "The room, I mean. My room has always been our official guest room." She nudged her companion. "Belle gives me a tiny corner of her mattress whenever we have company."

Belle regarded Miss Huggins with steely

gray eyes, then stood up to pour coffee, nodding towards the empty place at the table. Gen obeyed immediately. *Belle*. She could not imagine a woman more unlike her name. Thick-waisted and broad-shouldered, Belle had huge, masculine hands with broad palms and large knuckles. There was nothing feminine about her face, either. Thick, dark eyebrows floated in a straight line above her round gray eyes. The woman's wide mouth turned down slightly at the corners.

Gen concentrated on her coffee, trying to hide her amazement when Belle said in a soft, melodic voice, "I hope you're hungry. Jane always makes too much breakfast."

Pushing an errant strand of hair back from her face, Gen nodded before turning to Lizzie. "Thank you for the dress."

"You're welcome," Lizzie answered, blushing furiously. "You have amazing blue eyes. The dress makes them even more striking. I can help you with your hair after breakfast, if you'd like."

Miss Jane set a platter piled high with griddle cakes in the center of the table. With a "see what I mean" glance in Gen's direction, Belle helped herself, stabbing four griddle cakes with a fork and transferring them to her plate to be drowned in molasses. Before she took a bite, she offered grace for the four of them. She ate rapidly, excused herself, and with the explanation that she had promised to tutor Rosalie Feather in grammar, disappeared out the back door.

After breakfast Miss Huggins, who insisted again that Gen call her Lizzie, went into the little room to help Gen do up her hair. Opening the top drawer of her washstand, she produced an array of hairpins and more than one adornment that Gen had no idea how to use. "You have beautiful hair. I wish mine were straight like this and not so frizzy. And my goodness, it's so thick!" Lizzie brushed Gen's hair until it shone before showing her how to tie up a chignon in one easy twist.

"Will you be staying at Hazelwood?" Lizzie asked. "I'm only asking because I hope you will. We don't have many older Dakota girls. It would be so good for the students to have one of their own as a teacher."

"I couldn't teach," Gen said immediately. "I've only just finished the first books Mrs. Dane had."

"You could teach our primary class. They are just learning to read and write."

"I think," said Miss Jane from the doorway, "we had better leave the hiring of teachers to Dr. Riggs, Lizzie."

Lizzie blushed furiously and stammered, "Of course, Jane. I was just —"

"They are expecting you over at the main house, Miss LaCroix," Jane said, motioning for Gen to hurry. They went out the front door, pausing on the porch to admire the effects of the previous night's rain. Miss Jane inhaled deeply. "I just love the smell of things after a good rain. Look there." She nodded towards the open space between the cottage and the Riggs house. "It looks like God scattered silver plates on the ground." Looking over the compound where the morning light reflected off dozens of puddles scattered across the landscape, Gen had to agree.

"Those buildings there," Miss Jane said, pointing towards two large houses on the right, "are the girls' residences. The one on the opposite side of the church is the boys' hall."

"That's where you took Two Stars last night?" Gen asked.

Miss Jane nodded. "Robert Lawrence is staying there temporarily with the boys while we wait for the new schoolmaster from St. Louis. Robert had quite a reputation when the Lord snatched him. One of the worst troublemakers from Shakopee's band. It's been a blessing to have him for the older boys." Miss Jane sighed. "They hang in the balance, sometimes. Such troubled times for them." She shook her head sadly. She nodded towards Riggs House. "I don't see any signs of life yet." She motioned to a pair of rockers sitting on the porch. "Sit down, if you like." She opened the front door again. "I'll get us another cup of coffee while we wait."

While she waited for Miss Jane, Gen was once again struck by the contrast between Renville Mission and Hazelwood. She could see the mission coming to life, single figures coming out of doors and picking their way around puddles towards the church, towards the sawmill, towards other buildings she couldn't yet identify. Belle came out of the girls' residence, accompanied by a slender Dakota girl. They walked towards what Gen knew must be the school. In a blur of white, Koda shot out of the sawmill and tore around the back of the boys' residence hall. Gen realized that Two Stars must have come outside. She watched expectantly, but Two Stars didn't materialize and Koda didn't reappear.

Something moved near the porch railing,

and Gen was delighted to see a brilliantly colored hummingbird hovering near the porch ceiling, feeding on the bright orange flowers that hung in clusters along the vine that ran the length of the porch.

Miss Jane said quietly, "I see my little friend has joined us for breakfast." She moved slowly to the vacant rocker nearest the bird, handing Gen a hot cup of coffee as she went by. Instead of darting away, the tiny bird hovered as if inspecting Miss Jane and then continued making its way from one blossom to the next.

"What kind of flowers are they?" Gen asked quietly.

"I have no idea," Miss Jane said. "Something we found growing along a creek bank one day when we all went berrying." She chuckled. "I transplanted roots for five years running before it finally gave up and grew for me. And now it is taking its revenge by gobbling up our little cottage." Miss Jane leaned forward. "At last!" She nodded towards Riggs House.

Aaron had come out on the front porch and was sitting on the top step. While the women watched, he set something on the porch, and when he made a twisting motion with his hand, Gen realized he was playing with a top.

"There's the signal we needed," Miss Jane said, standing up. Lizzie came to the door and took their coffee cups, and Gen and Miss Jane started towards Riggs House, picking their way around the mud holes left by the rain.

The moment Aaron saw Gen, he flew down the steps and opened the yard gate, holding the top up for her inspection, bantering excitedly about his "new room" in the house and the trunk full of surprises. "Father says we may stay here for a few weeks. And then we'll go to our new home." He stopped abruptly and changed the subject. "It's much nicer here than at Renville. Don't you think?"

Gen nodded absentmindedly while she turned the top over in her hands. The front door to the main house opened, and Reverend Dane stepped over the threshold, followed by Dr. Riggs. The men tipped their hats and bowed to Gen. Dr. Riggs asked if she had been comfortable in the cottage, and Reverend Dane echoed concern. They headed for the sawmill with Aaron tagging along behind. Miss Jane excused herself and set off for one of the girls' residence halls.

Gen set the top on the porch just as Meg appeared to lead her inside and down the hall to the back of the house where Ellen and Mrs. Riggs were enjoying after-breakfast tea in a sunny little room that served as a private family parlor. Meg settled at her mother's feet and picked up a piece of cloth, explaining that she had to sew three tiny buttons along the back opening of a dress made to accompany a rag doll found in Mrs. Riggs's trunk.

The doll's face was muslin, its features drawn on with the kind of pen women used for signing their names on quilts. Someone had smudged the ink when they drew the doll's eyes, but Meg didn't seem to mind. Of all the things lost in the fire, Gen knew that Meg missed her doll the most. It had been a lovely china-headed doll, sent from the east by the grandmother she had never met. But even though it was a fine doll, it had never had a complete change of clothes like the rag doll.

Gen sat down opposite Ellen, listening politely while Ellen and Mrs. Riggs continued the conversation her arrival had interrupted. They spoke of Gray Woman and White Fawn, of Wing and others. "One by one, they've all disappeared," Ellen said with a sigh. She swallowed hard. Her eyes clouded with tears as she put one hand on

Meg's head and stroked her hair absent-mindedly. "Sometimes all I can think is that I want to go home. Or anywhere where failure doesn't scream at me everywhere I look."

Mrs. Riggs got up and walked across the room to a small shelf of books in the corner. She took what appeared to be a ledger book down, turned a few pages, and handed it to Ellen.

Ellen glanced down and then motioned to Gen. "Come and look." Gen complied, reading over Ellen's shoulder.

Joseph — Taken in at age seven. Remained three and a half years. Learned to read and speak English quite well.

Albert — A bright boy, but his father feared he would be poisoned and took him away.

Mary — Stayed for two years. Learned to read and write both English and Dakota. Considerable progress in Geography, Arithmetic, and English Grammar. Committed to memory the whole of the catechism in both languages.

Fanny — Died a Christian.

Susan — Talked English, read the New Testament and committed to memory a number of hymns. Murdered by Ojibways.

Emma — Taken home and not brought back. Confiding, willing, and obedient.

Harry — Has a fine mind but strongly disinclined to most kinds of manual labor.

Bessie — Placed in the family of Dr. Colburn.

Isaac Paul — Received into the boarding school, 1855. Taken away, 1856.

*"Gone . . . taken away . . . ,"* Ellen said aloud. She looked at Mrs. Riggs. "But taken away to *where?* And *why?*"

Mrs. Riggs smiled softly. "That *is* the question, isn't it? How we wish we knew." Her gentle expression clouded as she shook her head. "I still read that record over and over, praying for each name individually." She got up and went to the window, staring out as she talked. "After all these years, it is still very difficult to leave in God's hands the ones who left or were taken away. I have a little ceremony I perform in my mind, where I literally hold each name in the palm of my hand and lift it up to heaven. It helps me to remember that He knows where each one is . . . and that while *my* record book may be incomplete, *His* is not."

He was called Little Buffalo in the days when he rode a spotted pony and preyed on the Chippewa. He was small, even by Dakota standards, but he could inspire terror in the eyes of anyone he fought. He was savage and ruthless and without conscience. He had once slit the throat of a woman who came at him when he was raiding her camp. When she fell to her knees in the dust before him, blood spurting out onto his moccasins, Little Buffalo had laughed.

He was called Robert Lawrence now, and as he stood before the classroom of Dakota boys, he folded his arms to hide his nervousness. He had told Dr. Riggs he would help with classes until the new teacher arrived, but he had not expected the boys to be quite so old. He had pictured young ones looking up at him, respecting him as an elder, impressed that he knew the white man's writing. He had not expected the half dozen older boys in the back of the room who stared at him with eyes that dared him to teach them anything.

There was a new student named Two Stars. He had arrived only yesterday with the missionaries from the north. Apparently the missionaries had been taking care of the boy, who had appeared mysteriously in their barn one night after being shot. No one knew how. Then the missionaries had lost everything in a fire. Dr. Riggs said the Reverend Dane would be helping Robert with the new work near Cloudman's village. But they must wait until they no longer needed Robert to teach the boys. And until the Danes had had time to recover. Reverend Dane would be preaching this Sabbath, and Robert would have a chance to become better acquainted.

But today, and for many days to come, Robert must be a teacher. He surveyed the class. "Where is Otter today?" he said aloud. He noticed Two Stars jerk his head up and look around him with surprise.

"Who knows where the Otter goes," was the answer. "We haven't seen him since Miss Jane Williams sent him to cut firewood for her before the rain."

"And how is it that it takes Otter so many hours to cut a little firewood? He must not be very strong."

Another boy shrugged. "Otter is strong enough. When he wants to be. Maybe he decided cutting wood for a white woman isn't good work for a Dakota brave."

Robert said, "Too bad he does not see the need to be strong here." He pointed to his head and launched into the morning's lesson without another word about Otter. More than once his broad, work-worn hands lost their grip on the chalk and dropped it. Arithmetic had always been his worst subject, and when he stumbled on a problem and was corrected by one of his students, the older boys grinned at one another. Robert sent silent prayers to heaven, asking God to give him patience.

As the morning went on, he was drawn to the new boy. There was a light in Two Stars's eyes that told Robert the boy was intelligent. He said he had never been to school, but when another student struggled with an arithmetic problem, Two Stars seemed to have no trouble solving it. He could read English, and by day's end had memorized a short passage of Scripture in Dakota. And this, Robert could tell, was possible without Two Stars really having tried very much.

He could also tell from watching Two

Stars that the state of his injured arm and hand concerned him. Many times when Robert looked his way, Two Stars was rubbing his hand, massaging his arm, or simply resting one hand over the site of the gunshot wound. Robert wondered if some permanent muscle damage had been done. He hoped not. A Dakota boy with a crippled arm would have an especially difficult time of it. And times were already difficult enough for the Dakota.

Just before he dismissed his class for the noon meal, he went to the desk where Two Stars sat. Smiling, he nodded his head towards the door. "All day I have been watching a white dog just outside. He lets the other boys pet him, but he waits." When they headed outside Koda gave a soft yelp before bounding up and putting his paws on Two Stars's chest. Robert led Two Stars to the dining hall. Once again, Koda waited. And so it went throughout the day. Two Stars followed Robert Lawrence from the dormitory to the dining hall, from the dining hall to the school room, and always Koda waited.

Robert learned that the boy came from near Lac Qui Parle, that his father Bad Eagle and mother Gray Woman had moved, along with thousands of others, to

146

be closer to the Upper Agency. He learned that the boy had been injured and taken to Renville Mission and that he was grateful for the care he had received. But Robert learned more from what Two Stars did not say than from the words he spoke. There was something between the boy and his father. And however he'd been shot, it must have involved something unlawful, for when he spoke of it, Two Stars looked away nervously.

At the end of the long day, Robert asked Two Stars if he would like to work in the sawmill. "All the older students learn a trade. They attend classes in the morning and then work in the afternoon." Robert looked down at Two Stars's hand. "It might help bring the strength back."

Two Stars held up his hand and turned it over. For the first time, Robert saw the scar running from wrist to elbow. Two Stars reached down and patted Koda's head. "Our friendship began with blood. Sometimes I think Koda stays with me because he is sorry for this." He paused and then said, "If you think the work here would help, I will try it."

They went inside the sawmill and Robert showed Two Stars the machinery, explaining how it worked. They were standing beside a pile of logs waiting to be stripped of their bark when Robert said abruptly, "I understand the struggle inside you, my brother." Robert looked at Two Stars with a sad smile. "You have been taught that the way to prove your manhood is to kill a buffalo and fight the enemy. But the buffalo are gone from the reservation, and if you fight your enemies, the soldiers will come and take you to the white man's jail." He sighed. "It is a hard time to be Dakota." He put his hand on Two Stars's good shoulder and said quietly, "I was a great warrior in my time. My name was Little Buffalo." He waited for the impact to show on Two Stars's face.

Two Stars looked at him, his eyes wide with disbelief.

Robert smiled and nodded his head. "I know the stories they tell of me around the campfires. But what they do not tell you, Two Stars, is that the face of that woman I killed haunts my dreams. God has forgiven me. But I still live with bloody moccasins." He dropped his hand and headed for the door. "I hope you will come back to my class tomorrow." Patting Koda on the head, Robert left.

# Eleven

Ponder the path of your feet,
And let all your ways be established.
—— PROVERBS 4:26 (NKJV)


Otter had ducked into the mission sawmill just before Robert and Two Stars. When he heard Robert's voice outside, he hid behind a tall stack of logs. He was tired of pretending to want to learn so they would let him stay at the mission, but just when he thought he would return to Renville Mission and see if Two Stars could travel, Two Stars had arrived in a wagon with the whites. People said that the mission cabin was burned down and the missionaries would stay at Hazelwood now. From what Otter could tell, Two Stars was weak. They would have to steal another horse to get away.

Otter overheard Robert Lawrence's talk with Two Stars. After Robert left, the sawmill was quiet. Rain had brought a temporary halt to the building at the mission, and the students who usually ran the mill were at school, learning to talk the white man's talk. Otter was sick of white man's talk. He moved to the back of the mill where, reaching behind a small pile of oddly shaped logs, he withdrew a bottle. Removing the cork with his teeth, he took a drink, sputtering as the firewater chased down his throat, producing a warm glow in his midsection.

"They will make you leave if they catch you."

Otter peered at the slightly stooped figure of his friend standing in the doorway. He shrugged. "I am leaving anyway. I have had enough of sitting behind a desk looking at paper with chicken scratches they say is Dakota." He took another swallow of the liquor. "And I am finished with their church while they make speeches about the white man's God." He spat on the ground. "They say He let them kill Him by nailing Him to a tree. And He did nothing to fight back. What kind of god is that?"

Two Stars slid down the wall and sat beside Otter, wincing as his shoulder bumped into one of the logs.

Otter said, "You would have died before we got to Broken Pipe's fort. I had to leave you."

"Why did you come here?" Two Stars wanted to know. "I thought you would be at Broken Pipe's by now."

Otter shrugged. "Broken Pipe was gone. His gate was lashed shut. I went to Standing Buffalo's people. But there was sickness in the village." He spread his fingers and touched his cheeks. "The sickness with the red spots. Everyone was dying. Then someone was talking about the soldiers asking questions about stolen horses. I don't know if they meant the ones we took, but I had to leave that country. I thought that if I came to the missionaries and if I was a good Indian for a while, that would end the worry about soldiers." He leaned his head against the rough-hewn board wall behind him and looked over at Two Stars. "Now we can leave together."

"Where would you go?"

"Renville Mission," he answered quickly. "The barn is still there. The church is there." He snorted with derision. "That might not be enough for a white man and his family, but it is more than they give our people. We could live well. There are fish in the river. The whites have not yet chased all the game away from the woods up there."

Two Stars reached down and lifted his

right hand with his left, turning it so that it lay palm up on his leg. "This hand does not listen when I tell it to move." He showed Otter that he could barely move his thumb and the tips of his fingers. "That hand will not hunt. It will not fish. It cannot trap."

"Then we will ride farther to Broken Pipe's." Otter smiled with sudden inspiration. "He will share with us gladly if we take him news of his daughter."

Two Stars stood up. He reached for his friend's bottle, and while Otter shouted protests, upended it and poured the wine out. "Pretend to be good a little longer," he said.

Perhaps Papa had been right to send her away, after all. She didn't want to admit it — indeed she would not admit it right away when she saw him. Still, Gen thought, she was beginning to see what he meant when he said that the world was changing. Up north at Fort LaCroix things had been quiet and peaceful. Oh, she heard the Dakota who came to trade grumble about things from time to time, but she never gave it much thought. But since being at Renville and Hazelwood Missions, she saw what Papa meant.

Things with the Dakota seemed to be in turmoil all the time. And just when the missionaries thought things might settle for a while, a new president was elected and put new people over everything. Dr. Riggs tried to be kind, but it was obvious he thought Agent Galbraith was arrogant and stubborn. He knew almost nothing about the Dakota, and he drank. Gen had seen the damage liquor had done among the Dakota, and she had to agree that having an agent who drank didn't seem very wise.

As July approached, Gen began to watch the road, looking expectantly at anyone approaching her papa's size who came to the mission. He had often come down to the Upper Agency with other traders when the annuity was to be distributed. He never made any claims against the Dakota, but it was a good time to see old friends. But July 1 came and went and Etienne did not appear.

Amid her own disappointment, Gen learned from Miss Jane and Robert Lawrence and other teachers at the mission that the new agent was worse than they thought. Traders had demanded more than five thousand dollars in payment for damages done at a trading post near Big

Stone Lake out west, and the agent had deducted the money from the Dakota annuity. The Indians were outraged, and even the missionaries worried there might be serious trouble.

Miss Jane had snorted indignantly. "I know those two thieves. Neither one of them even owns a horse. Now tell me, how could they possibly haul away five thousand dollars worth of goods?! Those traders just used that as an excuse to steal Dakota annuity money."

The Dakota at the mission said that the blanket Indians came away from the annuity meeting so angry, they were threatening to do something terrible to the traders. Hearing that made Gen glad her papa wasn't there to be accused.

At Riggs House, the same incident brought more uncertainty. Dr. Riggs sighed and shook his head. "Just another in a long line of injustices done the people. Where will it end? Don't they know they are sitting on a virtual powder keg? The warriors aren't stupid. They know Fort Ridgely is underpopulated with soldiers. They know the war of rebellion back east is taking all the attention away from the west. They aren't blind, either. They can see that the area farms are increasingly populated by women and old men because the young men have gone off to fight." He shook his head and looked up at Reverend Dane. "I am beginning to think we are being premature to think we can sustain a new work, at least right now. We can't do without Robert Lawrence here until a new teacher arrives, and the situation is becoming increasingly unsettled. I don't know that I want the responsibility of sending a married man with young children to a new location right now."

"Did you hear me, Simon?" Ellen sat before a small mirror in their borrowed bedroom, combing her hair. She spun around on the covered barrel that served as a dressing table chair and faced her husband who stood beside the bed openmouthed, his thin legs sticking out from beneath his nightshirt. "I said we are going to be having another baby. At least I am fairly certain of it." The shimmering happiness she had been holding inside faltered. She lowered the brush, and her brows knit together slightly. "Aren't you — I mean, isn't it all right?" Her cheeks colored.

Simon cleared his throat and swallowed hard before sitting down on the edge of the bed. "Well of course it is, Ellen." He looked at his wife. "It's just that things were difficult before. With Meg and Aaron. And we're not exactly settled. And —" The agonies of fear he had endured during Ellen's two difficult pregnancies returned in a rush. Fear crawled down inside him and exited through his pores, making his skin feel cold. He turned to look at his wife, who misinterpreted his expression as disappointment.

"I know we thought our family was complete." Ellen fought back the tears that threatened to spill over.

"My dear." Simon went to his wife and put his hand on her shoulder and pulled her head towards him, patting her like a child. "I am only concerned for your health." He willed a shudder of dread away.

"It isn't the best timing, but —"

"Nonsense." Simon did his best to rise to the occasion. "The timing is perfect. Dr. Riggs has been reluctant to commit to a new work this year." He sighed. "You heard what he said this evening. He called the situation here a 'powder keg.' Now we have guidance on what we should do. I'll speak to Dr. Riggs tomorrow. Certainly he will agree that you have earned a rest."

Ellen looked up at her husband. "You

mean we could go home? To Leighton Hall? The children can really get to know their grandmother!" She barely took a breath before adding, "Gen could go with us! She could attend Miss Bartlett's!"

Simon frowned. "I don't think Miss LaCroix will want to leave Minnesota. Remember, dear, she didn't want to come to us in the first place. I admit that she seems to have found her place here at the mission. She has a bond with Miss Jane. But her concerns for her father grow daily. We cannot expect her to agree to be torn even farther away — and for a longer time."

"Perhaps someone could take word to Monsieur LaCroix. Oh, Simon!" Ellen's gray eyes lit with enthusiasm. "Two Stars would do it. He'd be glad for a reason to leave the mission. And after he brings Gen's father to visit, I'm certain she'd agree to go. He would *want* her to go!" Ellen laid down her brush. "This must be right, Simon. Why else would God have timed things this way? Bringing her just before the fire . . . and now, giving us the one thing that would make us go home . . . we would never have considered Miss Bartlett's before, Simon. It's one of the ways we can redeem the fire . . . can't you see? Our loss could result in Gen's getting a better education than even Monsieur LaCroix thought possible. And we've gotten a *baby*, Simon! A precious new life!"

Looking into his wife's gray eyes, Simon Dane saw only joy. It flowed out of her and into him and lit the fires of enthusiasm in his own fearful heart. Perhaps, he thought, Ellen was right. Perhaps this was the answer he had been praying for. With all the uncertainty in Minnesota with new agents and annuities, with conflicts with traders and hatred for the whites, with mutterings and failures — perhaps in it all, God had sent them Gen as a symbol of His promise for the future. They would go home and welcome a new baby and see Geneviève LaCroix become a young woman under the careful tutelage of Miss Bartlett. And if Two Stars agreed to try to locate Etienne LaCroix and get his blessing, Simon would have at least one small success in a long string of failures with Dakota men.

Robert Lawrence had already agreed to help with a new work. And he appeared to have interest in young Two Stars. Perhaps, Simon thought, this would be a new beginning. Perhaps when they returned to Minnesota, Robert Lawrence and Two Stars would be the nucleus of a ministry among a band of Dakota who would, at last, learn to accept his leadership.

Simon pulled Ellen up and into his arms. "I'll speak to Dr. Riggs tomorrow."

"And then I can tell Gen," Ellen said happily, nuzzling her husband's shoulder.

Gen stared at Ellen, dumbfounded. "But I don't *want* to go to New York."

They were sitting in Mrs. Riggs's family parlor. It was just Mrs. Riggs, Ellen, and Gen. Meg and Aaron had begun regularly attending classes with the mission children. Dr. Riggs and Reverend Dane had announced their intention to take a walk together and discuss mission business. Now Gen knew what at least part of that business was. The Danes were leaving. They would spend the rest of the summer and the winter at Ellen's mother's in New York, and come back next spring . . . and they wanted her to go with them.

"How can you even think I would leave when I haven't seen my papa in nearly three months now?"

"I know it's sudden, Gen," Ellen said quietly. "We didn't expect it, either." She paused and licked her lips nervously. "But I'm going to have a baby." Without waiting for Gen to react, she rushed ahead. "When I told Simon last evening, everything seemed to fall into place. We can go east for the children to meet their grandmother. And then I thought how they would miss you, Gen, and it just seemed logical to take you with us. And then the thought of Miss Barlett's came up —" Ellen paused and took a deep breath. "It just seems a perfect plan."

Gen stood up, half angry. "You sound just like my papa. He had a perfect plan too. To push me out of my home and send me off to a school I never cared about." She paused. "I've grown to like it — a little — but . . ." Her lower lip trembled and her eyes shone with angry tears. "Why is it everyone is always sending me away from where I want to be?! And how *could* you think I would go anywhere without seeing Papa?"

Gen sat down abruptly, her hands in her lap. She looked out the window. The sun was shining brightly. A flash of blue caught her eye. Dressed in a bright blue shirt, Two Stars was helping load a wagon with freshly milled boards. In the two weeks since he had quit going to classes and begun working there, his arm had grown stronger. Gen had heard Robert Lawrence say good things about Two Stars. She had noticed that he had cut his hair just enough to please the missionaries, but not enough to keep it from straying out from beneath the bandanna wrapped around his head. He had gained back some weight, and when Gen passed by the sawmill on some errand for Miss Jane or Mrs. Riggs, he would stop what he was doing and nod a greeting. Gen had begun to look forward to being sent on an errand that would take her past the sawmill. She studied her hands in her lap, and her cheeks colored. She might be blustering about her papa when she protested going east, but the truth was she was so angry with her father for abandoning her that she wasn't certain she even cared if he came. She was growing up and changing, just as Papa had wanted. And part of the growing and changing meant that while she missed her father, she had begun to think he had been right to send her away. She had begun to think that her future lay away from Fort LaCroix. She looked back out the window just in time to see Two Stars pick up a stick with his weak hand and toss it up the hill. Koda retrieved it, and Two Stars patted the dog's head, smiling. He had a nice smile.

For days he had been pulled first one

way, then the next, between Robert Lawrence and the mission and Otter and his
old life. Early that morning he'd had a
fight with Otter about Robert Lawrence.

"You don't know anything about him,"
Two Stars had said abruptly when Otter
made fun of the teacher's short stature.
"You sit in his class like a stone, and you
don't even hear what he has to say."

"I sit in his classes and I hear him say I
should be white," Otter said, spitting on
the ground. "That's all I need to hear."
Otter taunted his friend. "Don't tell me
you are going to follow that cut-hair and
become a farmer like the rest of those
know-nothings." Otter reached up and
tugged at Two Stars's hair. "If I didn't
know better, I would say you are already
becoming a cut-hair."

Two Stars ducked away from his friend.
He stared at the earth, trying to control the
rage and confusion bubbling inside him. "I
know I am going to work at the sawmill
today. When my arm is strong and my
hand can once again hold things, then I
will be able to decide. These people are
willing to help me, and I will take their
help." He walked away from Otter before
any more could be said.

He was tired of thinking in circles that

brought him to no answers, and he was tired of being caught between two opposing worlds. He was in no mood to talk to anyone about his future, and here, only a few hours after his fight with Otter, was Reverend Dane with a perfect plan.

If the missionaries had stayed away, he would have had time to think about Otter and make up his own mind. But Reverend Dane and Reverend Riggs interrupted his work at the sawmill and said just the wrong thing. "I hope you aren't listening to that boy's nonsense." Reverend Dane nodded toward Otter, who was ambling towards the mission garden.

"Otter is my friend," Two Stars said fervently. "He saved my life." He bent down and picked up the stick and tossed it for Koda to retrieve.

"We want you to stay here at Hazelwood. To become part of the community here."

For the past two weeks he had been listening to Robert Lawrence all day and to Otter all night. He had been pulled and shoved back and forth between the two until he could not sleep. And all the while he tried to make his wounded hand work, and it would not. Two Stars glared at Reverend Dane. "You want me to be white. You cannot help me." Two Stars wasn't certain he believed what he was saying, but he could not bring himself to agree with a scrawny white man like the reverend while the faces of Otter and Red Thunder and the warriors of the past battered his thoughts. He held his right hand out, palm down. "What you see before you can *never* be white. My skin is dark. My soul is Dakota. And so shall it be."

Reverend Dane cleared his throat nervously. "Robert Lawrence's skin is dark. And his soul is no less Dakota now than it was when he was called Little Buffalo. Just because he is a member of the alliance of farmer Indians does not mean he is less Dakota. You don't have to deny your people to become part of our family."

"Robert Lawrence told me about the lodge they call Hazelwood Republic. They promise faith in the white man's God. To send their children to the white man's schools. To obey the white man's laws." Two Stars's nostrils flared and his mouth turned down at the corners. His voice shook as he spat, "I will *die* before I ever become a white man." He turned and strode away from the reverend, up the hill behind the sawmill. Koda chased after him.

After an awkward silence, Reverend

Dane sighed and looked at Dr. Riggs. "Now you see what I have had to contend with up at Renville Mission."

"He is angry and defiant now," Dr. Riggs said gently. "But he has promise."

"Then why doesn't he accept the fact that the world is changing and his people must change with it or be destroyed?"

"They have already had to change so much," Dr. Riggs said, his voice warm with emotion. He put his hand on Simon's shoulder as they headed back to the house. "If you had seen this country when we first came back in '43 — the most beautiful country in all the land, many said. And now they have a strip of it only ten miles wide to call theirs. And that only at the whim of the government they see as always changing, never trustworthy. The game is nearly gone. The land is filling up with settlers who complain when they hunt on the very land their people have occupied for generations." As the men stepped up onto the porch, Dr. Riggs sighed. "We can hardly expect them to be grateful because we offer to teach them to speak the language of their enemies. A few acres of land and a wooden shack are small compensation for the loss of an entire way of life."

"Then what are we doing here?" Simon asked.

Dr. Riggs smiled. "Bringing them the words of life, my friend. The gospel of our Lord Jesus Christ. The only words that can change hearts and make life livable — for any man in any walk of life."

Reverend Dane shook his head. "My flock was not willing to hear what I had to say."

"Then perhaps you need to speak without words, Simon," Dr. Riggs said gently. At the reverend's look of confusion, Dr. Riggs smiled. "Just love them, brother. *Love them.*" He nodded up the hill in the direction Two Stars had fled. "Beginning with that young man." Together they went inside. "Unless Robert and I have both lost all ability to judge character, I'd say Two Stars is worthy of our best efforts." Dr. Riggs sighed. "But we must pray that God moves to separate him from Otter. That's a bad association by anyone's standard."

Reverend Dane had no opportunity to put Dr. Riggs's advice into practice with Two Stars. The night after Two Stars's defiant declaration, he took Koda and left for the north with Otter. Stopping at what was left of Renville Mission for a night, they went on to Fort LaCroix, where they found ample food to keep them satisfied and enough liquor to keep Otter happily drunk for most of the summer.

They also found Etienne LaCroix's decomposing body beneath a white antelope skin on his bed. Wrapping him in the skin, they buried him on the hillside near the trading post where a wooden cross marked the grave of Good Song Woman.

# Twelve

A man's heart plans his way,
But the LORD directs his steps.
        — PROVERBS 16:9 (NKJV)

Two Stars waded through ankle-deep mud to the gate that closed Fort LaCroix off from the rest of the world. Opening the gate, he peered out, swearing softly at the sodden landscape.

Otter shouted from the cabin doorway. "I thought we agreed no one should know we are here."

Two Stars closed the gate and slogged back to the cabin.

Otter sat down by the fireplace and uncorked a new bottle of wine. He held it out to his friend. "Drink. You pace like a wolf stalking its prey."

Two Stars reached for the bottle with his right hand. It had regained some strength, but when Otter let go of the bottle, it still slipped out of his hand. He caught it with his left, kicked a chair out from beneath the table and flopped down, taking a huge swig of wine.

"You are getting stronger." Otter tried to encourage his friend. He tossed him a ball they had made by wrapping a wad of paper with string.

Instead of trying to catch the ball, Two Stars took another drink. He felt restless, unsettled. Even though Broken Pipe and Good Song Woman were dead, even though Blue Eyes would probably never return to this place, Two Stars felt their spirits remained in the things they had left behind. What he observed about their family life made him feel like an intruder.

First, there was the book he found beside Broken Pipe's body. The sketches inside made it obvious that the drawing of Blue Eyes hanging beside the trader's bed had been drawn by Broken Pipe himself. The words in the book were French, but Two Stars didn't need words to read the family's life. He spent several evenings sitting just outside the cabin door, reading Broken Pipe's drawings. He saw Good Song Woman grow old, and Blue Eyes grow up. He smiled at one sketch of Blue Eyes frowning, her fists clenched, one foot raised off the floor. Two Stars could almost hear the little foot pound the floor . . . just as it had the night she had refused to leave him in the fire. She had spirit, Two Stars thought. And a temper. He liked her spirit . . . and he didn't mind the temper. A temper could be tamed, if it was handled the right way.

But more than just the book made Two Stars feel like he didn't belong at the trading post. Upstairs where Blue Eyes must have slept, things had been kept in order. Only a thin layer of dust had accumulated since Broken Pipe's death. The trader must have cleaned the room regularly until the sickness that killed him made it impossible for him to climb the ladder. Good Song Woman's grave was marked with a cross, and either Broken Pipe or Blue Eyes had planted wildflowers around it. Some of the things scattered on the trader's bed seemed to show that when he knew he was dying he wanted to be surrounded by reminders of his wife and daughter.

Two Stars wondered if Bad Eagle ever missed his son. Life had not always been unhappy for them. Before they moved near the agency, Bad Eagle had taught him to hunt and trap. But then came the times when Bad Eagle was always angry. And nearly always drunk.

Two Stars could remember innumerable times when Gray Woman had stood between him and his drunken father. More than once, she had felt blows intended for her son. She was always working — cooking, cleaning, fishing, gardening, drying food, decorating hides, making moccasins. When his father drank, she worked harder; when his father slept, she stayed awake; when his father stumbled off to the trader's, she went to the missionary's church. She never complained. And she stayed. In a society where the woman owned the tepee and could put her husband out at will, Gray Woman stayed. Two Stars realized it was probably because of him. All she had ever asked of him was that he come with her, away from the whiskey, away from Red Thunder, away from the ever-present sense of hopelessness that seemed to hang like a cloud in the air around the village. He should have gone to see her instead of leaving the mission.

Otter was drunk. He belched loudly and toppled over, giggling.

As soon as Otter slept, Two Stars rummaged in the storeroom until he had filled a box with bottles of firewater. Opening the cabin door, he hefted the box onto his hip and slogged through the mud towards the stable. Setting the box down, he took a bottle in his right hand. When it threatened to fall, he caught it, willing his hand to grip tighter. Then, with monumental effort, he pulled his wounded arm up and back until he could throw the bottle against the wall. Instead of breaking, the bottle landed in the mud a foot or so from the wall. Two Stars tried again. And again. And again. Finally, when the earth was stained red and brown and there was nothing left of Broken Pipe's saloon except a pile of broken glass, Two Stars called Koda to him and went back inside the cabin.

In the weeks since her arrival at Hazelwood, Gen and Miss Jane had become close. Miss Jane didn't find silence uncomfortable. She could wait indefinitely while Gen fought some inner struggle, and when Gen finally found words and opened the floodgates to let her feelings out, Miss Jane didn't offer platitudes or quote Bible verses. Somehow, with *this* missionary, it was all right to say exactly what one felt and thought. It was all right to indulge the emotions that raged inside, to shed tears and express frustration. And so it was only natural that Miss Jane eventually be the audience for Gen's tirade about being dragged east against her will.

"They expect me to be thrilled with the idea of leaving everything I've known . . . to just readjust and fall on my knees with gratitude!"

"Ellen isn't like that," Miss Jane said tersely.

Gen looked across the table where Miss Jane sat hemming a towel. She was stitching energetically, and she looked almost angry. "I appreciate our friendship, Gen, and I want you to be able to share with me, but don't be unfair to Ellen Dane. She's been through a lot, she isn't well —"

"I'm sorry," Gen said immediately. "I didn't mean Ellen. She *isn't* like that. It's the reverend." She blustered, "How could a man live among a people for ten years and know so little about them? He speaks their language, but he doesn't care about them. He's spent the summer helping Dr. Riggs take down their music, their folk tales, their customs — but it all goes into the ethnology book for the government. None of it goes into his heart. Everything he learns about the Dakota he lumps into some evil bundle — like a medicine bundle he wants to toss into the fire and destroy."

She shook her head. "It's no wonder Two Stars left. He didn't want to be a project for the reverend. And neither do I."

"Do you always call him 'the reverend'?" Miss Jane finished the hem, snipped the thread, and raised the needle to the lamp, squinting as she rethreaded it.

Gen thought for a moment. "I suppose I do. I'm always shocked when I hear Ellen call him 'Simon.' It seems inappropriate, somehow."

"Sad," Miss Jane murmured, "that he isn't more of a person to you." She counted out twelve white buttons and passed a girl's dress over to Gen. "We want to surprise Rosalie with that for her birthday next week. It only needs the buttons and it's finished."

Gen began to sew on buttons. "Well, I'm not a person to the reverend, either. Two Stars was his project. I'm his wife's — a half-breed Dakota girl he rescued from papism — or paganism. Take your pick. Someone he can take back east and show off. Like a hunting trophy." Miss Jane only nodded, and Gen took it as encouragement to continue. "Why is it they only see the *Dakota* in me? What about the *French* part? My French ancestors were building cathedrals before the reverend's wore shoes." Gen sighed. "But the reverend doesn't see that part of me. He only sees a poor Indian girl in need of the white man's help."

Miss Jane looked up from her work. "What if you *are* only a project to the reverend? Should that make you repeat Two Stars's mistake and run away from opportunity? Should it keep you from traveling and learning? Should it keep you from helping Mrs. Dane? Should it keep you from Meg and Aaron?" She got up and poured them both a cup of coffee. "I don't know Reverend Dane as well as you. Perhaps what you say about his opinion of the Dakota is true. However, it has been my experience that God often uses unlikely messengers to carry His will and His love to others."

The two women sat quietly for nearly half an hour before Gen asked, "What's it like back east?"

Miss Jane looked up quickly and then back to her work. "I'm not certain I'm the person to ask," she said. "I've been on the frontier for nearly a quarter of a century." She grinned at Gen. "That's longer than you've been alive."

"But surely you've visited your family," Gen protested.

Miss Jane shook her head. "No family to visit."

"None?" Gen said softly.

Miss Jane shook her head and began to describe traveling by riverboat and canal. She explained that fashions in the east were always ahead of the rest of the country, that people dressed and behaved much more formally than they did at the mission. Gen took some of what Miss Jane said about the cities under advisement. There could not, Gen thought, be buildings as tall as those Miss Jane described. And the notion of ten *thousand* people in only one place was totally incomprehensible.

Gen finished sewing on Rosalie's buttons and stared down at the table, thinking hard. Finally, she sighed, got up, rinsed her cup and saucer, and set them up on the shelf before heading for the little room behind the tattered quilt curtain. Pausing at the doorway, she asked, "Can you help me think of a way to thank Lizzie for the use of her room all these weeks?"

# Thirteen

It is good for me that I have been
    afflicted,
That I may learn Your statutes.
           — PSALM 199:71 (NKJV)

And now, Gen realized, she, like Mrs. Riggs, had her own list of names. Even though she was not a teacher, even though she had only helped Lizzie and Belle and Miss Jane for a few weeks, she would always wonder what happened to the one they called Joseph, who was really Good Fifth Son, and his sister Barbara, known by her people as Little One. Joseph had a round face and a space between his front teeth that made a soft whistling sound when he talked. Barbara was tiny and moved with quick, sure movements. She learned quickly and was fascinated by the line drawings in her grammar book. Both left before the end of July. Gen would always wonder where they were. There were others she would miss: the little girl who came to them with hair so matted they nearly had to shave her head; the boy who limped but whose smile could light up an entire room.

Perched on the rock ledge that jutted out beneath an ancient cottonwood tree, Gen watched the rush of activity at the mission below. Groups of students worked to bring in the last of the pumpkins and squash. The corn crop at the mission — and everywhere on the reservation — had been decimated by something the government farmer called cutworms. It would be a hard winter for the Dakota. Gen wondered about Two Stars, if he, too, would go hungry this winter.

It had been a difficult summer for the Danes, for as Ellen's waist thickened and her pregnancy progressed, she seemed to falter. She grew pale, and while she insisted that she felt much healthier than she ever had with Meg or Aaron, everyone worried. The reverend was anxious to get away, to get Ellen home to her mother and familiar surroundings and the well-known physician who was a close family friend.

While Gen contemplated their soon departure for the east, a wagon was coming up the road from the direction of the Lower Agency. Wagons had been coming and going all morning. They were building a new residence for the doctor at the

Lower Agency, and the sawmill was running from dawn until dusk. This wagon, however, had a passenger seated next to the Dakota driver. Something in the way he held himself attracted Gen's attention.

It was Two Stars. He followed the wagon driver inside the sawmill. Presently they reappeared, a stack of boards poised on their shoulders. Heaving the boards into the bed of the wagon they went back for another and another. Obviously Two Stars's hand and arm had finally returned to full strength.

Miss Jane came down the path that wound around the outer perimeter of the mission station, laughing about something that had happened in an earlier class. Settling beside Gen, she chattered away while Gen nodded and mumbled half-answers. ". . . and that is why they always sacrifice a Dakota girl in New York City every spring. I'm certain you can understand that, can't you?"

When Gen mumbled agreement, Miss Jane erupted with laughter. "He looks fully recovered, doesn't he?"

Gen blushed. "It's good to see that his arm and hand are all right."

"I see a lot more good than just his arm and hand," Miss Jane teased. When Gen looked surprised, she shook a finger at Gen. "And you are absolutely forbidden to ever tell anyone I said that." Miss Jane put her nose in the air and mimicked the agency doctor, who was known for his ridiculous claims of being British nobility. "Absolutely shocking behavior. Such an antique missionary noticing such things. Shocking, indeed." While Gen could not appreciate the accent, she did understand the body language. She smiled, wondering why her cheeks felt so warm.

Miss Jane nodded towards the wagon. "Isn't that Robert Lawrence with Two Stars? We haven't seen him since he got his farm down by Redwood Agency. He must be doing some of the work for Doctor Wakefield. He's a wonderful carpenter."

Aaron and Meg came out onto the porch at Riggs House. Aaron had grown at least three inches over the summer. He towered over his sister and seemed to take that as permission to exercise greater authority over her. Amazingly, Meg didn't seem to mind. They looked towards the wagon and ran to greet Two Stars. Aaron shook his hand. Two Stars patted Meg on the head and said something that made Meg point up the hill to where Gen and Miss Jane sat. Dr. Riggs came outside and shouted something. Robert Lawrence waved and drove the loaded wagon up to the main house. He went inside with Dr. Riggs, while Two Stars headed up the hill. He wore a red plaid shirt, open at the neck, the sleeves rolled up to his forearms. A dull metal cross dangled from one of the many strands of beads and shells around his neck. The ends of a brightly colored sash wrapped around his waist hung down his left side almost to his knee. Each leg was wrapped below the knee with more strands of beads decorated with fur and feathers.

"Your arm," Gen said awkwardly. "It's better."

He turned his hand palm up so she could see the neat scar running from wrist to elbow. "Mrs. Dane is a good seam-stress." He clenched and unclenched his fist. "It took most of the hot moons, but it finally remembered how to work."

"We worried about you," Miss Jane said. "It's good to know you fared well this summer. Did Otter go with you?"

Two Stars nodded.

"And you went — ?" she asked.

"— we went north."

"Did you see Papa?" Gen blurted out.

He nodded slowly.

Miss Jane watched Two Stars carefully.

When he did not offer more information about Etienne LaCroix, she said abruptly, "If you will excuse me, I have just remembered that I promised to help Mrs. Dane with Meg's new dress for the trip east." She smiled warmly at Two Stars. "I am glad to see you well, Two Stars. If you see Otter, please tell him that Miss Jane Williams asks for him and wishes he would return to the school."

Two Stars nodded. "I will tell him."

With a look of concern in Gen's direction, Miss Jane headed off down the hill towards the main house.

"You saw my father," Gen said. "Did he tell you why he hasn't come to visit? Is he coming to Hazelwood? Is he well?" She could not meet his gaze at first, but concentrated instead on the powerful forearms. Finally, she looked up at him. Something in his luminous dark eyes made her catch her breath. A flicker of anxiety gripped her. She laid a hand on his arm. "Papa is sick. That's it. He's very ill — did Otter stay with him? What is it, Two Stars? *Tell me!*"

"Broken Pipe is dead, Blue Eyes."

Gen caught her breath. A dull pain shot through her. "Dead? My papa can't be dead! He never gets sick. He nursed my mother's entire family when measles broke out in the camp. He took care of Mama too. Until she died. And he was never sick. Not one day."

Two Stars put one hand on each of her shoulders. He waited for Gen to look up at him. "When Otter and I left the mission, we went north to Fort LaCroix. We meant to give Broken Pipe news of his daughter and to ask to stay through the cold moons. But it seemed that Broken Pipe was not there. The gate was closed. Otter climbed over and let me in. When we went inside the cabin, we found him on his bed."

Gen shook her head. "It was someone else." She looked at him, pleading, "It could have been someone else?"

He took a deep breath. "It was Broken Pipe, Blue Eyes. Some of Good Song Woman's things were on the bed. Your picture was on the wall by his bed. He was wrapped in a white antelope skin."

*The white antelope skin.* The prize of Etienne LaCroix's hunting and trapping life. It had been tacked over his bed for years. He had always teased Gen that he would only take it down when it was time to make her husband a wedding shirt to match Good Song Woman's dress — the one Gen would wear for her own wedding day. *He wrapped himself in the antelope skin . . . he died alone . . . thinking of Mama . . . thinking of me.*

She began to tremble. For a moment, it seemed that she would not cry at all. She asked woodenly, "Did you bury him yourself?"

He nodded. "Next to Good Song Woman. I made a cross. Like the other one." He lowered his voice. "As much like it as I could. My hand was not working well yet."

Gen began to cry. When Two Stars wrapped his arms around her, she let herself be pulled in, crying against his chest until his shirt was damp with her tears. He smelled faintly of sweat and dust and a masculinity that reminded her of her father. Even when she was finished crying she was content to have him hold her. They sat down together, and it seemed only natural for Two Stars to keep his arm around her, for her to lean on his shoulder.

"Tell me everything," Gen asked. "I want to hear about everything." She didn't really care about Otter, but she was reluctant to let Two Stars go. As long as the man who had buried her father was close, she felt connected to home. They sat down, and Two Stars recounted the weeks at Fort LaCroix.

"After I broke all the bottles of firewater, Otter grew increasingly restless. We did not agree on many things. We shouted and fought." He hesitated. "So I came back. I followed Robert Lawrence down to the Lower Agency — he said he will teach me."

Two Stars touched the back of Gen's hand. "I am sorry about Broken Pipe, Blue Eyes. He was a good trader. If all the traders had been like him, things would be better for my people."

Gen nodded, croaking "thank you" as tears spilled down her cheeks again.

"What will you do?" he wanted to know.

"The reverend and Mrs. Dane will be leaving soon. There is another child coming. They will visit their family in New York and the reverend will speak for the mission. They have asked me to go with them to help with Aaron and Meg. Dr. Riggs says that I can go to Mrs. Dane's school. And then when they come back to start a new mission in Cloudman's village, I may help them."

He nodded slowly and got up. When she stood up beside him, they both looked down the hill towards the main house. Miss Jane was sitting on the front porch with Meg beside her. They waved.

Gen looked up at him. "Will you be leaving with Robert Lawrence, then?"

"Dr. Riggs has invited Robert and me to eat lunch with the missionaries. Then we will go."

They stood together awkwardly for a moment before starting down the path towards the wagon, Two Stars in the lead, Gen following.

# Fourteen

Blessed are those who mourn,
For they shall be comforted.
— MATTHEW 5:4 (NKJV)

The only way Gen knew to deal with grief
was to keep busy, and in the days following
Two Stars's revelation about Etienne, cir-
cumstances arose that kept Gen busy. Dr.
Wakefield examined Ellen and pronounced
her well enough to make the long journey
home, as long as she was not exhausted from
preparations for the trip. He recommended
that she rest every afternoon and forbade her
to lift anything heavier than a teacup. Mrs.
Riggs appointed herself Ellen's nurse and
Aaron appointed himself Meg's guardian
and performed the task quite well — with
Gen's tactful oversight.

Reverend Dane left the task of packing
in Gen's hands, spending hours each day
closeted with Dr. Riggs and various other
mission leaders, preparing talks to be given
back east and writing letters to various

churches and organizations where he would represent the Dakota Mission.

In the midst of the Danes' preparing to leave, Miss Jane came down with the ague and was confined to her bed. While Belle and Lizzie took on Miss Jane's teaching duties, Gen volunteered to keep house and cook for the four of them.

Surrounded by needs that she could meet, Gen learned that usefulness could be a tonic for grief. She learned that caring for others was a good way to care for herself. As she became more involved in mission life, her own grief began to heal. She thought less about the past and more about the future, and she wondered how Two Stars fared down south at the Redwood Agency.

The night before they were to leave, Gen lay in Lizzie Huggins's bed staring at the ceiling, unable to sleep. A full moon rose in the starlit sky, spilling through the window next to Gen's bed and throwing a square of blue-white light onto the rough pine board floor. Gen closed her eyes and listened to the night's music, wondering if she would be able to hear crickets and locusts at Leighton Hall in New York.

Slipping out of bed, she crept out to the front porch and sank into one of the rockers. The mission buildings were bathed in moonlight so brilliant that they cast shadows on the earth around them. She thought of Fort LaCroix: her mother teaching her to make coffee and corn bread; Papa showing her how to bully a half-wild horse into submission. She remembered watching her mother dye and weave porcupine quills, decorating a cap for Etienne, bending over beads so tiny Gen wondered how she could see to work with them. With the bittersweet memories came the realization that something had changed. The grief was still there, but it was no longer an uncontrollable monster that sent her running to her room to cry. Taking care of Miss Jane, overseeing the preparations for the trip east, growing closer to Meg and Aaron, had all combined to change her. Instead of focusing on the past, she was looking forward to the future both for the adventure of new experiences and the promise of education. It would be strange to sit among girls who had never seen an Indian, never walked the tall grass prairie, never heard wolves howling at the moon; girls who knew nothing of buffalo hunts and Indian agents, of annuity woes and cut-hairs; girls who wore fine dresses and feared the sun lest their skin grow dark like Gen's. It would be strange, but the thought no longer terrified her. Now the unknown future challenged and excited her.

She leaned her head against the chair back and closed her eyes.

Somewhere off to the left an owl hooted. Gen got up and perched on the porch railing, just as a rabbit emerged from a bunch of tall grass near the sawmill. She watched expectantly, waiting for the owl to swoop down, but instead of hunting, the owl hooted again. Frowning, Gen looked towards the line of trees running between the cottage and Riggs House.

"You are forgetting your Dakota ways, Blue Eyes. When the rabbit hopped away, you should have known the owl had only two legs." Two Stars stepped out of the shadows and walked up to the railing.

Gen hopped down and retorted, "I merely thought I had discovered a stupid owl. And what are you doing here?"

"Robert said that you were leaving tomorrow."

She nodded, grateful for the soft light that hid her glowing cheeks. How could he have known she was thinking of him? She thought that surely he could hear her heart beating through her nightgown. Her nightgown! She had forgotten! Instinctively she reached up to pull her wrapper closed. Two Stars grabbed her hand. Then, he separated the fingers of his free hand and combed through her long, dark hair. Gen held her breath as a new emotion traveled the length of her spine and settled in the pit of her stomach.

Two Stars stared down at her. "I am glad Otter left me in that barn." He swallowed, looking down at her hand in his. "How long will the Danes stay in New York?"

"Not even twelve moons," Gen said quickly. "They want to come back as soon as it is warm next year. To begin the new mission." Her voice trembled. She pulled her hand away. Two Stars came up on the porch. She asked abruptly, "Are you going to stay with Robert Lawrence?"

Two Stars nodded. "Robert is a good man." He looked up at the moon. "That is not so long . . . until the warm moons return." He looked back down at her and slipped his hand under her hair, caressing the back of her neck, willing her to look at him. He kissed her so quickly she had no time to respond. Then he reached up and took the string of beads from around his neck. Handing them to her, he said quietly, "Don't forget me, Blue Eyes."

He kissed her again, holding her face gently in his hands, looking into her eyes, smiling. And then he hopped off the porch and trotted away. He paused at the stand of trees at the edge of the compound and turned around just long enough to raise his hand.

The owl hooted. And Gen raised her hand in reply.

The Agency Road was little more than two wagon tracks winding across the hills, but it made the way easier. Gen sat with Meg and Aaron on a pile of comforters just behind the wagon seat as together they watched Hazelwood Mission grow smaller and smaller in the distance until it disappeared and the Dane's wagon was the only sign of civilization in a sea of prairie grass and goldenrod.

It seemed no time at all until the Upper Agency came into view. Located on a high hill west of the Yellow Medicine River, the agency boasted a dozen or so buildings, including an impressive brick structure that served as both warehouse and the agent's residence. Flags flying from every building made the complex look like a fort.

The travelers stopped at Doctor Wakefield's impressive two-story home for lunch. The doctor's wife, Sarah, provided Gen's first introduction to eastern life, for while she lived on the frontier, Mrs. Wakefield had kept her taste for eastern fashion. She entertained Mrs. Dane and Gen in a formal parlor furnished with shining walnut and mahogany tables laden with daguerreotypes, miniatures, and vases.

When Mrs. Wakefield excused herself to check on lunch, Ellen ran her hand over the green sofa fabric. "Damask," she murmured admiringly. Looking at Gen she shook her head in wonder. "I had no idea anyone on the frontier could live like this. How does she manage it?"

"I manage," Mrs. Wakefield said crisply from the door where she had overheard, "by keeping up my subscriptions to *Godey's* and *Harper's Weekly. Peterson's* and *Eclectic* come, too, although irregularly." Mrs. Wakefield settled her generous frame into a chair. "I told John when we came west there was no reason a family couldn't live comfortably."

The Dakota servant girl announced lunch. The Wakefield dining room held more wonders in store for the amazed travelers, including two birdcages, each housing three canaries. Meg was so entranced with the beautiful little yellow birds, she barely managed to eat her lunch.

"Do you think Grandmother would buy me a canary?" she asked her mother.

"I think, Miss Meg," the reverend interrupted, "that you should concentrate more on how *you* may please your *grandmother* than on how *she* might serve *you*."

Duly silenced, Meg took a small bite of lunch, while her eyes strayed back to the birds.

Mrs. Wakefield apologized for the simplicity of the meal. "If we had known you were coming sooner, I would have spread a proper luncheon."

She seemed sincere, but Gen could not imagine what might be missing from the dizzying array already on the table. They drank something called green tea and were served from a platter of meat including dried beef, codfish, sardines, and boiled pork.

For all her wealth, Mrs. Wakefield seemed genuinely interested in the Indians her husband was charged to serve. Her conversation showed uncommon understanding and sympathy for the Dakota. She treated her servant girl kindly, even helping her bring in some of the dishes. She seemed truly interested in Gen, and spoke of Etienne with unreserved admiration. When the travelers finally climbed into their wagon and headed south, Gen had the sensation of having been picked up by a whirlwind, tossed about gently, then deposited back into the real world of cabins and primitive living.

"When you return," Mrs. Wakefield said to her unexpectedly, "you must call on me. I know several women who would love to have you work for them." She patted Gen's arm and flashed a smile.

Just south of the Upper Agency, they descended into the Yellow Medicine River valley, crossing the river without mishap in spite of the fast-running waters that rushed and tumbled over boulders and rocks. When the team struggled to climb the steep hill on the other side of the river, Gen and the children climbed out of the wagon to walk. In spite of her husband's protests, Ellen insisted on joining them. She trudged along, her lips pressed together firmly, determination etched in the fine lines around her mouth.

When they crested the hill, she pointed to the tops of the agency buildings just visible in the distance. "You heard what Dr. Wakefield said, dear," she reminded her husband. "He said walking would be good for me." But she agreed to climb back into the wagon soon thereafter, and Gen noticed that her head rested on her husband's shoulder for much of the afternoon.

They gave a wide berth to the next three Indian villages because, according to the reverend, chiefs Red Middle Voice, Shakopee, and the Jug were known as "a rebellious lot of troublemakers."

"Robert Lawrence mentioned a few Dakota farmers near Rice Creek who might give us shelter for the night," he said. "We'll stay to the west of the villages and see if we can't locate one of the new farms."

By the time they stopped for the night, Ellen had to be helped down from the wagon. When her knees buckled, the reverend carried her inside the simple cabin of Robert Lawrence's friends, who insisted the entire family come inside and sleep. Meg, Aaron, and Gen shared a pallet beneath the kitchen table. The reverend and Ellen slept, fully clothed, atop the only bed in the small house. Their hosts slept in the barn.

The next day they had to cross the Redwood River. The children clung to Gen, their eyes wide with horror, as the reverend guided his team down the steep bank and into the water. When the horses hesitated the reverend stood up, lashing their broad rumps until, with one mighty lunge, they hauled the wagon up on the opposite shore.

The prairie between the Lower and Upper Agencies was covered with flowers of all descriptions. There was not a shrub or tree to be seen, and Gen thought the tall grass waving in the breeze made the entire area look like a vast green lake. The reverend drove carefully, trying to avoid the frequent sloughs that dotted the low ground, but in spite of his care they did get bogged down once, the wagon wheels held fast in the mud. Ellen and Meg were ordered to a comforter spread in the grass. The reverend removed his coat and rolled up his shirtsleeves. Together he and Gen and Aaron unloaded the wagon.

The reverend positioned himself behind one wheel. Leveraging a board beneath the wheel, he gave orders to Aaron. "Take the horses' nose straps and, when I give the signal, you pull with all your might." When he walked past Gen she heard him mutter "_____ annoyance" under his breath.

Gen could barely suppress a smile as she grabbed the board from the reverend. "Let me do this. You push."

The reverend gave the order, Aaron shouted and pulled, the horses strained, Gen leveraged, the reverend strained and pushed and finally, with an agonizingly slow, sucking sound, the wagon was freed from the bog.

"Ho, there!" Aaron ordered, blushing with pride when his father praised him.

Wearily, the mud-spattered group reloaded the wagon. Gen and Aaron decided to walk ahead of the wagon to keep an eye out for marshy ground.

They camped one night on the open prairie before topping the rise leading into Fort Ridgely, which Gen saw was not really a fort at all, but rather a loose collection of stone and log buildings clustered on a hilltop.

"Two days' hard ride in that direction," Reverend Dane said, "and we'll be at Fort Snelling." He smiled at Ellen. "Of course we shall not make it a hard ride, and it will take us more than two days, but soon we'll be on the steamboat and you can enjoy the rest of the trip home. The mission has good friends in Alton, Illinois, just upriver from St. Louis. We'll rest a few days there. And then . . ." He went on to describe the rest of the trip for Meg and Aaron, who heard little of what he said after he described the steamboat, for neither of them could grasp the concept of a boat large enough to haul hundreds of people down a river at once.

They rested in Alton as the reverend had planned. St. Louis proved that everything Miss Jane had told Gen about the east was true. Tall buildings, crowds of people in the streets, paved roads — all were true. Gen felt small and unimportant and displaced. She failed to laugh when Meg called a sandbar a sand-burr. And she barely ate her supper. Even the attention of an attractive gentleman who walked by and tipped his hat failed to cheer her.

That night when the family had gone to bed on board the steamship, Aaron peeked over the foot of the bed at Gen, who had insisted she sleep in the children's room.

"Geneviève," Aaron called.

Gen raised her head from the pillow. "Yes?"

"Do you miss your father very, very much?"

Gen stifled an unexpected sob. "I think it must be that he spoke of St. Louis. We talked of him bringing me to school here someday." She swallowed hard. "Yes, Aaron. I do miss him tonight. Very much."

It was quiet for so long she thought he

had fallen asleep. But then he said, "I just wanted you to know, Gen. Meg and I talked, and we decided. If it would make you feel better, we'll share our father with you."

Gen mumbled a reply, and Aaron slipped back beside his sister.

Meg whispered, "Did it help? Does she feel better?"

"She said she does," Aaron murmured. "But she's crying harder than ever."

# Fifteen

Choose for yourselves this day whom you will serve . . . But as for me and my house, we will serve the LORD.
— JOSHUA 24:15 (NKJV)

"Friend, I am no fool. I want a good life for my family. If there is a better way, I want to learn it. It seems to me that the Dakota who farm have found a better way." Robert Lawrence and Two Stars were sitting before the fire in Robert Lawrence's government-provided house. It had grown late as they talked, but Two Stars had shown unusual interest in the conversation, and Robert was content to talk the night through if Two Stars would listen.

He held his hands out before him. "My grandfather provided for his life by hunting in the Big Woods. If I provide with farming, where is the dishonor? It still comes from these hands."

"But the white government gives you the house and the tools."

Robert shrugged. "They lied to convince our chiefs to sign treaties so they could take all the land we used to hunt. Now they tell us to keep off that land and let the whites have it. If they are willing to give me a piece of what our grandfathers and their fathers had, I will take it. If I can live in peace and feed my children, then I am content." He leaned forward and stared into the fire. "When I was still Little Buffalo, I went to see my friend John Otherday. He was a great warrior, feared by many. But then he changed. He went to church and took up farming. One day I heard his wife read a story from the Bible. It told of a man named Daniel who was trapped with lions." Robert paused, watching the dying fire. Then he looked up at Two Stars. "Sometimes I feel like that man Daniel. But I think I have found a way to keep from being devoured."

Robert sat back. "Our Dakota brothers are like lions too. They hate the whites. They despise the traders. They growl and threaten. Then they wait for the annuity to be given out so their families may live. The traders take what should be theirs, and they are powerless to do anything about it. They bluster and think to count coup, but they do nothing. They cling to the old ways and speak of clearing the land of the whites, and all the while they are poor and miserable and hungry. To me, these men are pitiful. The Dakota who become farmers work hard. Their families are not hungry. And," Robert said solemnly, "they look at a man in the eyes and they are not ashamed."

More for the sake of argument than because he disagreed, Two Stars spoke up. "Otter says the whites are fighting with each other. He says the soldiers are going away to fight in that war. He says the north has lost many great battles, and that the south will win."

Robert waved his hand in the air with disgust. "And what if they do? Will the whites in the south suddenly come to love the Dakota and give their land back?" He laughed bitterly. "Who had the land in the *south* before the whites went there? Other native people! And what happened to them?" He shook his head. "It means nothing. They will never give it back. And when that war is over, more of them will come." He sighed. "There is nothing we can do about that. But there is something *I* can do. I can take the farm they offer me and the help they give and learn to live. I can love my family and my friends and learn to be happy here.

"Look around you, my friend. It is not a bad place to live. We have mills for wood and corn. We have a blacksmith and a carpenter. We have schools and churches and plowed land. Ninety more homes are going to be built this year. One could belong to you."

Two Stars sat back and shook his head. "I don't want to be a farmer."

"Then sit on your haunches and take what the Great Father in Washington hands out."

"I could go west," Two Stars said stubbornly. "The people still live well there."

"Then go," Robert said quietly. He looked at his friend. "You will be fighting the same battle in a few years. And then your children will fight it. And your children's children. Unless you take the land that is offered and learn a new meaning of what it is to be a Dakota man, you and your children will always be fighting."

Robert paused. "We all must decide for ourselves. I have decided. With God's help, I am going to take the land and grow a farm." He grinned suddenly, trying to defuse the growing argument. "— and if my childhood admirer, White Fawn, will have me, I am going to grow some children. Her worthless husband died last year. I have seen her twice, and she did not seem to mind when I smiled at her." He stood up and filled his mug with coffee. From beside the stove, he said, "You should come to church with me on the Sabbath." He sat back down. "I know you have been wondering about the missionaries' teachings."

Two Stars nodded. "I have been thinking about their God and that man Jesus." He paused, then added, "When some of the missionaries talk of Him —" He stopped again and shook his head. "Otter laughs about Him. He says we Dakota have nothing to say to the white man's God."

Robert thought for a moment before saying gently, "Did you ever think, Two Stars, that perhaps *God* has something to say to *you?*" He stood up and stretched. "I must be at the sawmill at dawn. There is a load of wood they want me to carry to Little Crow's village. Will you come?"

Two Stars nodded. When he stood up, the white dog that had spent the evening curled at his feet got up with him. They headed outside to sleep beneath the stars.

The making of Daniel Two Stars took most of that winter of 1861. He attended church with Robert Lawrence and listened to young Reverend John Williamson preach. He asked Robert questions, and on occasion he read the Bible for himself. He pondered and watched and worked. When the change to a farmer Indian seemed particularly offensive, when the old ways called him, he went to Otter and his friends, listening around campfires while they grumbled and plotted.

Many moons ago, they said, Inkpaduta had killed some whites down by Spirit Lake in Iowa. He had never been punished. Was that not proof that the whites were too preoccupied with their own war to care what happened in the Far West of Minnesota?

One of the half-breeds up at Yellow Medicine was recruiting other mixed-bloods to go fight that other war. Was that not proof that the whites were desperate for soldiers? The Great Father in Washington would send no soldiers to fight for Minnesota. Perhaps the time was coming when he would let it go.

Was it not true that in every white settlement they passed on their hunting trips they saw mostly women and children and old men?

Otter told Two Stars that to become a cut-hair was to be a traitor. "You see how it is. They get more food and clothing than we do. They get a cow and oxen, cookstoves and tubs, and buckets and churns. We are hungry. The cut-hairs have coffee and tea and salt. They have sugar, soap, molasses, rice — more than their brothers."

When Two Stars echoed Otter's ravings at Robert Lawrence's farm, Robert did not disagree. "But," he added, "all these things are available to Otter and his friends, if they will only listen and learn."

The turning point for Two Stars came late one night when he and Robert were sitting up playing cards. Koda got up and ran to the door, growling savagely. When Two Stars cracked the door open, it was pushed in by several Dakota braves painted for war. They dragged Robert and Two Stars outside and held them while they led Robert's oxen out of the barn and slaughtered them in the yard. Then they set the barn on fire. Not content with that, they beat Robert, warning him to return to his people or be killed.

Two Stars, they left alone. "You have not turned away from us yet," one of them hissed in Two Stars's ear while he struggled to get free and help Robert. The ones holding him knocked him to the ground.

"Let this be your warning." They jumped on their horses and disappeared into the night, filling the air with war cries.

Two Stars helped Robert inside and bound his wounds. He watched over him through the night and went the next day to the agent to report what had happened. When he came outside, Otter was leaning against the brick wall of the agent's house.

Two Stars glowered at him.

Otter smiled. "Was it *your* cut-hair's barn that lighted the sky last night with flames?"

Two Stars looked at him. "Is it *your* friends who show their bravery by holding men down so they cannot fight and destroying what they have worked to build?" He turned his back on Otter.

"Little Crow is forming a soldiers' lodge. You are still welcome," Otter called out.

Two Stars spun around. "I cannot come. I have a barn to build." He walked away from Otter and towards the sawmill, where the agent had said he would be loaned a wagon and given lumber. When he drove into Robert's yard, his friend was standing beside one of the dead oxen, knife in hand. He looked up as Two Stars jumped down from the wagon. "There's enough meat here to give an entire village a feast."

Two Stars jumped down, and together the men cut up Robert's oxen. They built fires to smoke the meat and spent hours slicing thin pieces to dry for jerky. When they had worked themselves nearly to the point of exhaustion, they dropped to the earth beside the house, leaning against the front wall in the shade.

Two Stars cleared his throat. "Could you go see the agent with me tomorrow?"

Robert looked at him, surprised. "About what? He will do nothing to the ones who did this. He gave me wood to build another barn. That is enough."

"I need someone to sign the paper that says I am a good Indian," Two Stars said. He nodded towards a ridge that ran between Robert's land and the river. "If you will say that I am a good Indian, the agent will give me that land."

# Sixteen

Who can find a virtuous wife?
For her worth is far above rubies.
                    — PROVERBS 31:10 (NKJV)

"The Prescotts sent a servant with a message
late last night," Ellen's mother lied over
breakfast, "that if the snow continued, you
must come and spend the day. They'll take
you to school and then Harry — that's William's older brother — will pick you all up
and take you coasting."

Aaron frowned suspiciously. William
Prescott was nice enough, but aside from
inviting the Dane children to a party
Christmas Eve, he had not shown much
interest in becoming friends with the missionary children from Minnesota. With a
glance up the stairs towards the room
where his mother lay, Aaron said, "I don't
want to go coasting today. Not when
Mother isn't feeling well."

Mrs. Leighton patted Aaron's hand.
"Nonsense. Your mother said to tell you to

go have some fun. And this evening when you get home you can come in and tell her all about it. She just needs some rest. And quiet." Mrs. Leighton glanced across the table at Meg, who was nibbling on a biscuit. "You are good children, but there is a certain amount of clatter and clamor with your comings and goings. A quiet day with no one about will be the best thing for her. The doctor agreed."

Meg and Aaron exchanged concerned glances.

"I didn't know the doctor was already here," Meg said, looking at Gen.

Gen, who had already argued more than once with Mrs. Leighton about "shielding the children," managed a little smile. She could almost feel Mrs. Leighton willing her to support the older woman's deceit. "Your father is being careful to give your mama the very best care," she said. "Do you remember back at the mission when we took care of Two Stars, how your mama asked you and Aaron to try and be quiet when he was very sick?"

Meg nodded.

"Well, it's the same with your mama right now. We all want to help her feel better, and sometimes being quiet helps sick people rest so they can get better."

211

Aaron's brown eyes focused on his plate while he thought. Presently he nodded. "All right." He looked at Meg. "If it helps Mama, then we'll do it."

"Don't act as though it's such a chore, Aaron," his grandmother scolded. "You said you loved coasting down the hill onto the river at the mission. Wait until you see the hill near Harry's house! On a good day you can slide all the way out onto the pond. Maybe they'll even have it cleared off so you can try ice skating!" Mrs. Leighton's false enthusiasm did not impress Aaron, who looked at Gen and then quickly away. He pushed himself away from the table. "When is Harry coming?"

"Any minute," Mrs. Leighton said.

"Well then," Aaron said, holding his hand out to his sister, "we'd better hurry."

The children went up the stairs to their room and descended again in minutes. They were bundled and ready when Harry arrived. Meg was already in the sleigh when Aaron turned back and grabbed Gen, hugging her fiercely. "Tell Mama we love her," he whispered. His eyes added a wordless *They aren't fooling me*. Gen pulled him close for another hug, whispering, "*Wakantanka ape ka wastedaka wo*. Hope in God and love Him." Aaron nodded and stumbled away. Climbing into the sleigh beside Meg, he waved at Gen before putting his arm around his sister. Just before the sleigh disappeared around a corner at the top of the hill, Gen saw Meg lean her head on her brother's shoulder.

That had been hours ago, long hours that Gen had spent standing or sitting just outside the Danes' bedroom door, listening to the murmurs on the other side, wincing at Ellen's piercing cries, waiting in case something might be needed. On the other side of the door, Mrs. Leighton and Reverend Dane, Doctor Princeton and his nurse, and most of all, Ellen, battled for a new life. The morning had passed. Glancing out the Palladian window on the stair landing to her left, Gen realized the clouds had cleared away. Sunlight shone on the dormant garden below, highlighting the contrast between glistening snow and black, barren tree branches. A dark splotch spread over the garden swing as the thin layer of snow along the top began to melt.

Gen smiled, remembering how, all last fall, Ellen had been waiting in the swing when Gen arrived home from another day at Miss Bartlett's. Eager to hear how the day's lessons went, encouraging Gen when other students displayed prejudice against their dark-skinned classmate, Ellen ignored her own waning health and thought only of her family. She lounged on the swing with Meg or Aaron, read them books, watched while they played, laughed at their anecdotes from school or church.

Seemingly unaware that her own life was being threatened by the life growing inside her, Ellen insisted that Simon keep to his speaking schedule. "The mission needs you more than I do. Mother and Gen are taking perfectly good care of me." When Simon hesitated, she pretended to be angry. "For heaven's sake, Simon, I don't need you moping around. You've never been a good nurse, and you and I both know it. Now get on with the work Dr. Riggs gave you to do!"

When winter arrived, Ellen held court in the parlor. And then, after Christmas, she was too weak to come downstairs. Still, she wanted her children around her. And she continued to summon Gen for a daily report on the happenings at Miss Bartlett's.

Valentine's Day was especially happy. They didn't say the words, but by their smiles and enthusiasm, the adults at the Leighton home communicated new hope to one another. Perhaps the rest prescribed by the doctor was all Ellen needed. The baby was due in April. That was only eight weeks away. Perhaps things would be all right after all. Their hopes were shattered a few days after the holiday, when Ellen woke in pain and suggested Simon might want to call the doctor.

Gen was brought back to the moment by the silence. It was unnaturally quiet on the other side of the Danes' bedroom door. A knot of fear gathered in the pit of her stomach. Whispers, an anguished "NO!" and Simon Dane ripped open the door and stumbled out. The long, thin hair atop his head had fallen forward over his bloodshot eyes. He wore no jacket, and the smell of the sweat that stained his day-old shirt permeated the air. He gave Gen one wild look of disbelief before opening his mouth to blubber something almost incomprehensible. It didn't matter. Gen knew what he meant. They were both gone. Not only would Meg and Aaron not have a new brother or sister, now they had no mother.

The reverend stumbled downstairs. Gen heard his footsteps retreat towards the keeping room. Through the Palladian window she could see him floundering through the snow down the pathway in the garden — coatless, hatless, oblivious to the cold.

As the silence in the house pressed down upon her, Gen slid down the wall, curling up like a child, her head on her knees. The door to her left opened again. This time it was Mrs. Leighton.

Gen stood up, clasping her hands in front of her. Mrs. Leighton took in a breath and let it out in a succession of short bursts that caught in her throat. She didn't even try to speak, pursing her lips and shaking her head as she extended a trembling hand to Gen.

Mrs. Leighton stared past Gen towards the window. It had begun to snow again. "They want —" Her voice broke. She closed her eyes and inhaled deeply. Clearing her throat she said, "They want to know which gown." Her gaze floated back from the window to Gen. She ignored the handkerchief held tightly in her free hand and let tears fall, oblivious to their course down her wrinkled cheek and off her jaw. "I don't think I can —"

"I'll do it," Gen said softly. She patted the elderly woman's hand. Her mind whirled, trying to remember all the gowns in Ellen's wardrobe. "The green one, I should think?"

Mrs. Leighton sighed with relief. "Yes. The green one."

"Don't worry over it. Please, Mrs. Leighton. I'll take care of it."

Gen looked past her towards the room. "Do you think it would be all right for me to go in now?"

Just then the nurse came to the door and motioned to her. She was a stern woman by nature, but not unkind. "Will you be all right, Mrs. Leighton?" she asked. "The doctor will be out directly. I'm going to the apothecary at once to mix some powders. They should help you feel better. You *and* the reverend, poor man."

"Someone has to tell the children," Mrs. Leighton said woodenly.

"Perhaps that is where the reverend went," Gen offered. "I saw him leave through the garden."

Mrs. Leighton shook her head. "No. I think not. He needs time to collect himself, poor dear."

"I can fetch them on the way back from the apothecary," the nurse offered.

Mrs. Leighton nodded. "Just don't tell them. Please." Her voice wavered. "I suppose I should be the one to tell them."

The nurse nodded and slipped down the stairs. Mrs. Leighton drew Gen closer and squeezed her hand. "Thank you, my dear," she managed as she dabbed at her cheeks with her handkerchief. "I don't think I could —"

"It's all right," Gen interrupted.

Mrs. Leighton released her and headed off down the hall towards her room at the end of the corridor, feeling her way, suddenly feeble. Gen knocked softly at the door. The doctor opened it and stood back. Looking past him, Gen could see Ellen. She lay beneath fresh sheets, her golden hair spread over a crisp linen pillowcase, the wide border of handmade lace along the edge of the sheet folded back just enough to reveal a tiny bundle, no bigger than the white-wrapped loaves of bread that came from the bakery every day. The sight of the tiny face barely peeping out of the bundle, seeming only to be asleep, brought Gen's tears.

The baby was a dark-haired boy with a perfect little pointed chin and a nose the size of the button on Gen's dress. His traumatic route into the world had misshapen his head so that it rose to an unnatural point at the crown, something that would have been normal within weeks of his birth — had he lived. Gen reached out and smoothed the dark hair up and over the little head, and as she did so, she wanted to wail a death song like the ones she had heard back home.

Her eyes went from the baby to Ellen's sweet face, drained of all color except for the sickly blue circles beneath her eyes. Gen smoothed the golden hair on the pillow.

She thought back over the day, her heart aching for Aaron, who was not fooled by his grandmother's ruse, and for the reverend, whose reaction had amazed both Mrs. Leighton and Gen. "I will not be shut out," he had said firmly that morning when the doctor and his nurse tried to keep him from the room.

First, he looked at Gen and said, "*Pray. If you have ever loved Mrs. Dane, and I know that you do, pray like you have never prayed in your life.*" And then he went into the room and sat down beside the bed and took Ellen's hand.

Just before Gen closed the door, she heard Ellen ask, "Did I hear Gen?" Gen had answered, "I'll be just outside, Ellen. Praying."

Ellen smiled with relief, closing her eyes momentarily. Another contraction began and she choked out the last words Gen would ever hear her friend say. "Take-care-of-my-children." As the contraction gripped her body, she arched her back and groaned, *"Please."* It seemed to take minutes for her to get the one word out.

"Don't worry about Meg and Aaron," Gen said quickly. "They're at the Prescotts'."

Reverend Dane stayed with his wife all day, anguishing as she struggled to give him another son. From her place in the hall outside, Gen heard him pray aloud. She noticed that the prayers were nothing like the ones he was known for. There was no formal language, no pretense. The words were simple and heartfelt and, Gen realized, more powerful, more moving than any she had ever heard.

Once, when Mrs. Leighton came out to get fresh water for the doctor, she muttered almost to herself, "He hasn't let go of her hand. Not once. I had no idea he was so devoted —"

As the day progressed and Ellen's condition declined, Gen heard the reverend try to sing a hymn, but in the middle of the chorus Ellen screamed with pain. The reverend broke off singing, yelling at the doctor, "Save my wife, you fool! Do you hear me? Don't you dare let this child take my wife!"

The doctor was unable to comply with the reverend's command. Not only did he lose the battle for the child, but in what seemed like an instant of time he lost the mother to postpartum hemorrhage.

And now the battle was over. Mother and child lay as if asleep, waiting to be dressed and displayed and sat up with and buried in the walled cemetery beside the church down the street. Gen laid her open hand on Ellen's forehead. She bent over and kissed the cold cheek, whispering as she did so, "If there is a heaven such as the Bible describes, dear friend, I know that you are in it."

The doctor cleared his throat. Gen took the hint. She was there to do a job. She scooped the little bundle up in her arms and gently laid it in the bassinet for which Ellen had made a new covering. ("It was mine," she had said. "I wished so to have it with me when Meg and Aaron were born.")

Gen retrieved Ellen's green dress, smiling sadly as she realized that she had chosen it impulsively, with the now meaningless thought that green made Ellen's eyes look especially lovely.

The undertaker came, placing mother and child in a dark, polished walnut coffin with a white satin lining. Mrs. Leighton's parlor was cleared of all furniture except chairs, and a seemingly endless parade of mourners paid their respects. There were distant relatives, townspeople, former students at Miss Bartlett's, even Miss Bartlett herself.

Gen was a distant observer of what she considered a ridiculous number of customs. There must be a black wreath on the front door. Every portrait in the house must be draped with black crepe, and mirrors must be covered with the stuff. The family would be dressed in black for the foreseeable future, except for Meg and Aaron, who must wear white, the appropriate color for children in mourning. Mrs. Leighton would veil her face whenever she went out in public for several months to come. The reverend would wear a wide, black armband for at least a year.

The undertaker provided several locks of Ellen's hair, which Mrs. Leighton had taken to a local hair artist who made something called mourning brooches, tiny glass-covered miniatures made by skillfully arranging strands of hair to look like urns of flowers. The reverend was given a watch fob created by a special method of braiding and knotting human hair. When he realized what it was, he literally shuddered.

Gen took it from him and laid it next to her own mourning brooch in a drawer. For Meg and Aaron, Mrs. Leighton ordered a recent photograph of their mother framed in a small shadow box. At the base of each photo would be a small cluster of flowers, fabricated entirely from Ellen's hair.

The family had to take turns sitting up in the parlor, placing glass jars filled with ice next to the body to enhance preservation. During the day, Reverend Dane spent hours standing beside the coffin, repeating almost the same phrase to everyone. "Thank you for coming." "How kind of you to come." "Thank you for coming." "How kind of you." When around people, including his children, he was remote. Whenever possible, he was absent.

When at last the service was concluded and Ellen and the baby were laid to rest in the cemetery, the crepe and the wreaths and the gloom in the house were not lifted. Servants crept through the halls on tiptoe, whispering as they went about their duties. Meals became contests of who could avoid speaking the longest.

Gen spent nearly every waking moment of the next few weeks with Aaron and Meg. They took long walks together. They sat in the parlor, reading books and poetry.

She told them stories. They spoke of Ellen and the baby. They cried together. And then, one day in March, Meg laughed aloud. She clapped her hand over her mouth and stared at Gen guiltily.

Gen smiled. "It's nice to see the old Meg."

Through necessity, Mrs. Leighton, who had held Gen at a very distinct arm's length upon her first arrival, forged a new relationship with her houseguest. "She's French, you know," Gen overheard her say to guests one afternoon. For Gen, it confirmed that the term she had spent at Miss Bartlett's had borne fruit, after all.

Reverend Dane fled into the ministry. He was gone for weeks at a time speaking at different churches on behalf of the Dakota Mission. When he was home he spent most days either locked in his room studying or walking the streets. He barely spoke to Aaron or Meg, and when he did, he was so deliberately formal it would have been comical if it were not so painful for the children.

Although Gen and Mrs. Leighton didn't discuss the reverend's behavior, Gen was grateful that the elderly woman went out of her way to spend time with the children, almost as if she were trying to make up for the reverend's failures. Both women clung to the hope that in time his grief would abate and he would become more of a father. Gen thought that between the two of them, the women were doing an excellent job of smoothing over the reverend's failings and sheltering Aaron and Meg from an even deeper sense of loss. She was wrong. A few weeks after Ellen died, a bowl of oatmeal revealed her error to both Gen and Mrs. Leighton.

Meg stared down at her breakfast and announced rather loudly that she despised oatmeal and would not eat it. When wheedling and bribery failed to break through her granddaughter's stubborn resolve, Mrs. Leighton asserted the authority she felt was rightly hers by virtue of the fact that Simon had abdicated his role. Entertaining and overseeing two active children had put a strain on Mrs. Leighton, and this morning that strain broke through her iron-willed patience.

"Margaret Marie Dane," Mrs. Leighton said sternly. "You will remain at this table until you have eaten the breakfast God provided. An unthankful attitude will not be tolerated in this house." She rang for the maid and directed that the table be cleared except for Miss Meg's bowl of oatmeal. Then, Mrs. Leighton headed for the stairs. Just as she reached the doorway to the foyer, a bowl of oatmeal sailed past her. It hit the wall where it broke into three pieces and fell on the Persian carpet with a dull thud. Clumps of oatmeal stuck to the blue-and-white silk wall covering. Warm milk and melted butter ran down the wall and pooled in the place between the Persian carpet and the broad cherry wood baseboard.

Gen jumped to her feet and cried out in disbelief, "Miss Meg!"

Mrs. Leighton whirled around, the two bright pink spots on her cheeks a testimony to the anger she was barely controlling. "Go to your room. The maid will bring you another bowl of oatmeal." Her eyes blazed with new color as she added, "You will stay in your room until the empty bowl appears on the floor outside your door, *and there had better not be one drop of oatmeal or milk or butter anywhere in that room but inside your stomach, young lady.*"

Meg burst into tears. She jumped up, shouting defiantly, "You're not my mother! You can't tell me what to do! I've been good all summer, and I'm tired of it! When my father comes down he'll tell you I don't have to eat oatmeal. I don't!" She shoved her chair back from the table. "Mother never made me eat oatmeal. And you can't, either!" Meg's round cheeks colored with the fury in her slight body. Even her red hair seemed to tremble with anger.

Mrs. Leighton clasped her hands before her and stepped towards Meg. Aaron jumped to his sister's side and put his hand on her shoulder. "Meg's right," he snapped, his eyes cold. "She doesn't like oatmeal, and Mother never made us eat it." His chin quavered slightly, but he had taken on the mantle of protector for Meg now, and he would not back down. "And as soon as Father comes downstairs, he will tell you so!"

The air in the room crackled with tension while the older woman calculated her next move. Gen watched breathlessly, not daring to intervene.

"You may go to your rooms while I discuss the matter with Miss LaCroix," Mrs. Leighton said crisply.

Meg and Aaron looked at Gen soberly as they left the room, hand in hand. Without a glance at their grandmother, they marched out of the dining room, across the foyer, and up the stairs.

The moment the children were out of

sight, Mrs. Leighton collapsed in a chair. "I can't *do* this," she half-sobbed into her handkerchief. She motioned for Gen to sit down opposite her. "It's too much. I can't be both mother and father to them." She looked up at Gen pitifully. "I'm not in the best of health myself, you know. I thought Simon would recover and — and —" She caught her breath, slowly regaining control. Finally, she inhaled sharply and regained her composure. "I know you are doing what you can, Gen. We both are. But these children obviously need their father." She allowed the frustration to sound in her voice as she concluded, "Simon has not always been the most affectionate of men, but I would never have believed that he would abandon them so completely. Something must be done. They are my grandchildren, and I love them, but I cannot raise them. I cannot."

Gen nodded in sympathy, not daring to express her own doubts as to whether it was even possible for the reverend to be the kind of father his children needed. "We'll think of something," she said hoarsely. She patted the back of Mrs. Leighton's hand. "I'll — I'll speak with the reverend." She expected Mrs. Leighton to gather herself and put Gen in her place. To her great disappointment the older woman nodded. "Thank you."

Gen got up to leave, hesitating once she reached the foyer of the great house. She looked up the stairs. The reverend was up there right now, "studying." She had only climbed three steps before she stopped. What could she possibly say to him that would make any difference at all? She needed to think. Maybe she would even pray. While she didn't have a close relationship with God, surely He would listen to something concerning Meg and Aaron. He had to know that she needed help. It wouldn't hurt to at least try to talk to Him about it.

Mrs. Leighton came out of the dining room followed by a servant bearing a tray with toast, tea, and Meg's favorite raspberry jam. She looked apologetically at Gen. "I suppose I'm spoiling them, but —"

"— I think they need a little spoiling right now, Mrs. Leighton," Gen said quietly. She reached for her bonnet and, tying it on, explained, "I'm going to take a walk and think. When I come back, hope I'll have something helpful to say to the reverend." She smiled nervously.

Mrs. Leighton nodded. "Good. You do that, dear. You know him so much better than I. You've seen him in better days. You'll know what to say." She hurried up the stairs. Gen heard her mutter to herself, "Oatmeal, indeed! Who cares if she eats *oatmeal*, for heaven's sake?!"

# Seventeen

Honor your father and your mother, that your days may be long upon the land which the LORD your God is giving you.

— EXODUS 20:12 (NKJV)

Like most other farmers throughout southwestern Minnesota in the fall of 1861, Robert Lawrence lost his corn crop to something the government farmer said was a cutworm. The winter was severe, and because of lost crops and more broken promises by the government, hunger took up residence among the Dakota, causing more unrest and hardship than ever before. However, enduring the hungry months together strengthened the bond between the farmer Indians and their missionaries.

Sharing simple meals and working together made Robert Lawrence and Two Stars friends as well. They raised a small cabin on Two Stars's land before the worst winter storms came. And then, some time after Christmas, Robert shared his Savior with Two Stars and found a ready heart. Two Stars cast his lot with Christ and selected the name Daniel. He began to think he could have a good life, even among the lions.

Otter could not name it, but it was not long after Daniel's conversion that he sensed a change in the tie between Two Stars and Robert Lawrence. He resented it, but he said nothing until one frigid night in the Hard Moon of January when he knocked at Two Stars's door and stumbled in, slightly drunk and half frozen, hoping his friend had something to eat. Daniel shared what little he had with his friend. Later that night, while they sat beside the fire and reminisced about their time at Broken Pipe's deserted fort, Daniel told Otter that he had made a pact with Jesus and asked to have his sins forgiven. "I have decided for myself, Otter. I want a better life, and the way to have it is to learn to farm. I don't want to fight with the whites. They saved me when I was wounded. They nursed me even when I hated them. They bring words of life from the book God wrote. I belong to God now, and I am going to try to live to please Him."

Otter raged against his friend's selection of a white name. He swore. He argued. When Daniel only smiled at his friend's protests, he bolted out the door.

In the Raccoon Moon, which the whites called February, Robert Lawrence finally went after White Fawn and the two children she had had by a worthless man who abandoned them and died in a stupid fight over gambling winnings. He went north from the Lower Agency, stopping at the Hazelwood Mission to visit, and then proceeded to Cloudman's village, which was the northernmost of the villages camped near the Upper Agency. When he returned with his bride, Robert told Daniel that Dr. Riggs said Blue Eyes was doing well at the school in the east. "White Fawn says Gray Woman is up at John Otherday's village," he added. "But things are no better with Bad Eagle."

The night was really no different from any other. Bad Eagle went to trader Myrick's for whiskey, spent the evening gambling with his cronies, drank himself into oblivion, and staggered home. Gray Woman had come to expect it. In fact, Gray Woman thought as she lay beside the fire listening to her drunken husband

233

snore, if it were not for their son Two Stars and his diplomacy with the traders, they would have starved long ago.

Her husband lay like a stone beneath the buffalo robe next to her. Gray Woman sighed, thinking back to the days when they had been young and in love, the days before the white men came with all their treaties and their land-grabbing, when Bad Eagle was an admired and feared warrior, when Two Stars was a boy just learning to hunt. They had camped beside the Talking Waters where game was abundant, and except for an occasional raid from the Chippewa, life had been peaceful and good.

Bad Eagle snorted in his sleep and leaned heavily against her. Gray Woman slipped from beneath the buffalo robe, dressed, and went outside. It was a clear night. All around them, dozens of tepees glowed, illuminated by the fires within.

A dog barked. Gray Woman jumped, rubbing her forearms nervously. The young men of the camp had been especially restless of late. Everyone was grumbling and unhappy. Like last year, there were rumors that the annuity would not come because of the war between the whites in the east. No one liked the new agent Galbraith. Gray Woman sighed. It was a hard time. The crops last year had failed. They were hungry. And she had heard nothing from her son. He was probably dead, she thought. Hopelessness settled over her. She crept back inside the tepee and slept.

The morning began like any other. Bad Eagle woke complaining that his head pounded, wanting something to eat, grumbling against his wife and the agent and anything else that came to mind. He got up wearily and trudged down to the river where he lay facedown, dunking his head in the icy water, trying to rouse himself.

While Bad Eagle was at the river, Gray Woman sat outside her tepee, enjoying the warmth of the sun while she tried to mend a worn moccasin.

"When I think of you, it is always like this. Working. Always working."

Gray Woman looked up, blocking the morning sun with her hand to her brow. What she saw made her leap off the earth and burst into tears of joy. She clutched Two Stars to her, hugging him fiercely, caressing his cheek, touching the gold earring dangling from one ear.

"I thought you were dead. Otter has not come back. Red Thunder is dead. I thought —"

Two Stars hugged his mother fiercely. "I should have come before now. I should have sent word. But I did not know where to find you until Robert Lawrence came for White Fawn. She knew where you were."

Gray Woman nodded. "I have moved three times, trying to find a place where Bad Eagle cannot drink." She shrugged. "He always finds bottles."

They settled beside the tepee and Two Stars told her of being shot, of the missionaries at Renville, of the fire, and last of Robert Lawrence. "I am called Daniel now, *Ina*. Daniel Two Stars. And I have a house near Redwood Agency. And a farm." He looked down at his hands. "Otter calls me 'cut-hair' now."

Gray Woman didn't seem concerned with the loss of Otter's friendship. She asked him, "Do you have a wife?"

He shook his head, smiling. "There is a place for you in my house, if you will take it."

Gray Woman hesitated. "Bad Eagle will not come."

"I will talk to him. Perhaps he will come."

There was no joy in the reunion between Bad Eagle and his son. Hearing that he called himself Daniel made the father angry. "Is your ancestor's name not enough for you? Two Stars was a great warrior."

"As was Daniel in the Bible. He was a warrior in prayer and in faith."

Bad Eagle snorted. "So my son not only takes handouts from the whites, he takes their name and their God." He shoved Daniel away from him. "Then he is not my son." He stumbled away up the river.

Daniel ran after him. "Come with me, my father. There is a place for you in my house."

Bad Eagle roared angrily, "There is no place for *you* in *my* house!" He waved his arm in the air. "Go! Take the old woman with you and go! If you love the whites so much, go among them." He spat on the ground. "You are dead to me." He stumbled up the river and out of sight.

"You cannot change Bad Eagle," Gray Woman said gently.

Daniel looked at her. "Will *you* come, *Ina?* Will you let me care for you?"

She smiled at him. "I think that you must let *me* care for *you* a little longer, my son. If you have no wife, who cooks for you? Who mends your moccasins?" She pointed to Daniel's feet, still clad in moccasins in spite of his having adopted white man's clothing from the ankles up.

He grinned and shrugged.

In what seemed like moments, Gray Woman's tepee was struck, her belongings piled atop the travois lashed to an ancient pony. Daniel convinced her to ride his horse while he walked alongside the travois. And so it was, that Daniel Two Stars's house acquired an addition in the form of his mother's tepee. Gray Woman was reunited with her friend White Fawn. And Bad Eagle, who would not listen and would not come, drank so much one night that he fell unconscious into the river and drowned.

In the Moon in which the Geese Lay Eggs, Robert Lawrence and Daniel Two Stars went to look over Robert's fields to plan how much they would plow up and what they would plant. When they headed back toward the house, a child darted out from behind Robert's new barn and wrapped herself around Daniel's legs. Laughing, Daniel picked her up.

"Where is Koda?" she demanded.

Daniel whistled and Koda appeared, streaking across a plowed field. Screeching to a halt at his master's feet, the white dog licked the little girl's toes. She howled with delight and, when Daniel deposited her on the ground, fiercely embraced the dog. Together, they ran toward the house where White Fawn waited to feed them lunch. White Fawn, who had taken the name Nancy for herself, waved at Daniel and called out that he should eat with them.

Not until he entered Robert's cabin did Daniel see that there were other visitors for lunch. Gray Woman sat at the table, smiling innocently. Beside her sat a pretty young Dakota girl Daniel had seen in church.

"I invited Rebecca to eat with us," Gray Woman said. "She wants to learn how to bead in the old way. We will work on something together after we eat." Gray Woman reached across to tug on Daniel's necklaces. "Take that one off," his mother said. "Let her see how you did it."

Daniel pulled the simply decorated string over his head and handed it to the girl, who blushed.

After lunch, Daniel and Robert went outside. They were hitching up Robert's new team of horses to take them to the blacksmith at the agency when Robert burst out laughing. " 'She wants to learn the old way to bead . . . here, Daniel, show her your necklace.' " Robert teased him halfway to the agency.

Finally, Daniel shrugged. "You had a mother. You know how it is. Or were you found beneath a rock and raised by the medicine man?"

"I had a mother," Robert said. "But I made certain she knew that I would be picking my own wife."

Daniel nodded agreement. "And I will pick mine."

# Eighteen

Have mercy on me, O LORD, for I
   am in trouble;
My eye wastes away with grief,
Yes, my soul and my body!
          — PSALM 31:9 (NKJV)

Gen headed up the lane from Mrs.
Leighton's house in the direction of the cemetery. Spring rains had melted the last vestiges of a light snow and washed the cobblestone road clean. In the distance Gen could hear the rhythmic approach of a regiment of soldiers, who presently rounded a corner and passed by, singing about "killing Johnny Reb." Gen stopped to watch them. She had grown up among a warrior people, and since most of the whites she first knew were missionaries, she had had the impression that the whites were different from the Dakota — more peaceful. It had been a shock to learn that war dominated their lives even more than it did the Dakota's. Since she had come east the subject of war was

never far from anyone's mind. Even with Ellen's death, they were not insulated. Most of the men who came to the funeral were dressed in blue uniforms. The sinking of two Union ships by the Confederate ironclad *Merrimac* had sent shock waves all the way into New York. Now there were more troops marching in the streets. Gen sighed.

When the familiar brick wall of the churchyard came into view, she decided to pay a visit to Ellen's grave. Her mother had once told her that the spirits of the dead hovered over their burial place until they were no longer needed. It surely couldn't hurt to have Ellen's help with the reverend.

Just inside the churchyard gate, Gen stopped and tilted her head. Someone was in the burial yard crying. A man. She hesitated, thinking she should leave the mourner to his solitary grief.

Peeking inside the gate, Gen looked across the graveyard towards the back wall where a massive stone bier topped by two marble angels flanked Ellen's simple marker. The reverend's back was to her as he stood looking down at the dark mound of earth in the row of graves along the back wall of the cemetery.

He was sobbing. "Can you ever forgive me, Ellen. I didn't — know how much — I didn't know —" He choked back sobs, then looked towards the sky. "My God in heaven, tell her I loved her. Tell her I loved her — so much!" His shoulders shook with sobs. He took a scrap of white cloth out of his hat and mopped his face, then moved towards the head of the grave where he knelt beside the newly placed tombstone. He traced the outline of a carved hand pointing up. Then he leaned his head against the marker, muttering to himself. He slumped over, his head in his hands.

Swallowing hard, Gen made her way up the grassy path towards Ellen's grave. She cast a brief thought to the sky, hoping that God would somehow help her, even though she had had little time to think what she might say. When she reached Ellen's grave, she crouched down beside the reverend and put a hand on his shoulder.

"Go away." The voice was filled with bitterness. "Whoever you are, go away and leave me in peace."

Gen gulped. "But, Reverend . . . you have no peace." She forced resolve into her voice. "And I will not go. Not until we talk." She backed away from him and settled on a stone bench.

He jerked his head up. Seeing Gen, he sat on the damp earth, his back to her, once again mopping his face with the white cloth. After a moment, he stuffed the cloth back in his hat, clamped his hat on his head, and moved to the bench beside Gen.

It seemed like an eternity before he said, "I'm useless without her." He laughed tragically. "And the joke is on me. I didn't know how much I needed her until she was gone." He stifled a sob and turned his face away. "We should willingly give our loved ones to God." He leaned over, resting his elbows on his knees, studying the ground. "Why am I so earthly minded — so *weak?*"

Gen looked at him oddly. "I don't think it *is* weakness, Reverend. I think it's just being human." She paused, biting her lip while she thought. "My father was the strongest man I ever knew. When my mother died, he tried to hide his grief, thinking to save me from pain. I did the same thing. It only made things worse for both of us. But the night he held me and literally howled with grief — that was the night when things started to get better. It drew us closer. It made us need each other even more."

The reverend looked at her with such pain in his eyes that she wanted to reach out and comfort him. But she held back, concentrating instead on Meg and Aaron.

"Your children need you, Reverend Dane."

He shook his head. "I can be of no use to them now. Not until I can control myself."

"If you share your grief with them —"

"— it will frighten them to think their father has lost control."

Gen shook her head. "No, it frightens them to think you have abandoned them." She pressed on. "They have lost their mother, and their father pretends they do not exist. What could be more frightening to a child than to lose *both* parents?"

He listened without looking at her, reaching down and picking up a fallen leaf. "I preached a sermon on leaves once." He laughed sadly. "I think it was one of my better efforts, actually. All about how the beautiful color only comes with dying, how the Christian life is perfected through the process of dying to self. I recall using several illustrations about those whose physical death yielded beauty in the lives of others. It was quite dramatic." He paused before concluding slowly, "And completely meaningless. I didn't have one shred of understanding of anything I said." He shook his head. "No wonder the Dakota people hated me. Even savages know when they are listening to empty words."

"Then *do* something to give those words life. Find some way to let Ellen's death count for something besides sadness and loss."

He shook his head sadly. "I wouldn't know how to begin."

"Begin with Aaron and Meg," Gen said quickly. "Just *love* them, Reverend Dane."

A glimmer of hope flickered in his eyes. "Do you think they could forgive me?"

"I think they would throw themselves at you and overwhelm you with joy."

The reverend sighed. "Meg has Ellen's eyes — don't you think?"

"Almost exactly."

He sucked in air. "It makes it — harder — somehow."

Gen nodded. "I know. Papa said the same thing when my mother died. He said every time he looked at me, he thought of her. But he said that in time, it made him feel like he hadn't lost her, after all."

The reverend sighed. "Your father didn't push you away, did he?"

Gen smiled. "Only for a little while. Then we cried together."

"And seeing your father cry didn't lower your opinion of him — make you think he was weak?"

Gen shook her head. "It drew us closer. I

saw that Papa was hurting, too. That he was human. It made me love him even more."

He looked down at her with new understanding. "When your father died —" He patted her hand awkwardly and looked away. "Please forgive me for being so unfeeling." He sighed. "I have spent years and years of my life trying to minister to people without really caring for them. Dr. Riggs tried to tell me once. He said I should simply love the Dakota people, and they would respond. But I didn't believe him. I did not think I could serve if I got caught up in the emotion." He shook his head sadly. "What I failed to realize was that unless the shepherd loves his sheep, he is worthless to them." He smiled sadly. "I have been a noisy gong and a clanging cymbal for all of my life as a pastor." He shook his head. "And in many ways, I was a worthless husband. And now I'm failing Ellen's children." He sighed. "I suppose I must try to remedy that. I owe it to Ellen."

The reverend mopped his face again. Taking a deep breath, he stood up, extending his arm to Gen. She took it, and they left the cemetery together. They had walked nearly halfway to the Leightons' when the reverend asked, "May I ask whatever made you come looking for me? Or was this encounter a heavenly coincidence?"

"Oatmeal," Gen said abruptly. "Meg wouldn't eat her oatmeal this morning."

He looked at her quizzically. "Meg despises oatmeal. Ellen never made her eat it."

"That's exactly what Meg said — just before she tossed the bowl against the wall."

The reverend stopped and looked down at Gen. "Meg did that?"

Gen nodded. "And then she delivered a sermon on the fact that her father would back her up." She briefly recounted the morning's events, finishing just as they reached the Leightons'.

When the reverend hung his hat by the door, he turned to Gen. "Thank you, dear girl, for speaking so openly." He looked up the stairs. "It isn't going to be easy to change the habits of a lifetime."

Gen smiled. "Meg and Aaron will help. I expect you won't find it quite so difficult as you think."

# *Nineteen*

> I will instruct you and teach you in the
> way you should go.
> — PSALM 32:8 (NKJV)

"It isn't working," Reverend Dane said one morning. Meg and Aaron had just left for school, and the reverend came back into the breakfast room after collecting dutifully proffered good-byes from his children. He ran his hand through his thinning hair and sat down. "They don't believe the change in their father." He sighed and stirred his coffee. "And I don't blame them. I'm awkward and ill at ease with them." He looked across the table at Gen and Mrs. Leighton. "I love them. But I don't know how to show them. They've held me at arm's length for so long — because I demanded it — I don't think the barriers will ever come down."

Mrs. Leighton reached over to pat him on the shoulder. "Give it time, Simon. There isn't a child alive who can resist love. You just keep showing them you love them. You'll get better at it."

Reverend Dane persisted in his awkward attempts with his children until one Saturday morning he came downstairs and looked outside to see Meg and Aaron crouched down in the garden, peering at something in the grass. He went to the back door and called out, "What's so interesting out there?"

Aaron looked at Meg with now familiar suspicion. *When's he going to stop trying to be nice and just be himself?* "Nothing, Father," he called back. "We're just watching some old spider."

"What kind of spider?" the reverend asked, coming down the path.

"I dunno'," Aaron said.

"A big fat one," Meg offered, smiling up at him. She pointed to where a black and orange spider hung on a lacy web between two rosebushes.

"That's *argiope aurantia*," the reverend said, crouching down beside them. He smiled at Meg. "Orange garden spider to *you*, little miss."

Meg lost her balance and lurched back against her father. The unsuspecting reverend toppled over on his back, landing in a patch of mud.

Meg's eyes widened. She leaped up. "I'm sorry, Father," she whispered, horrified. "I — I was afraid it was going to get on me —"

The reverend smiled while he brushed himself off. "Are you all right, Miss Meg? Did I land on you?"

Meg shook her head.

"Look — there's another one," the reverend said, pointing to a second spider. He sat in the path, not offering to get up. Aaron was standing by uncertainly when the reverend patted the earth beside him. "Sit down, Son. I've something to tell you. You, too, Meg." They sat down, their hands folded politely.

The reverend hesitated. This wasn't working at all. They were sitting like two royal attendants waiting to do the master's bidding. Ah, well. He would press on.

"When I was about your age, Aaron," the reverend began, "there was a boy named William in my school. I hated William. He was always making fun of my glasses, or my long neck, or my ears, or something. But I knew a secret about William. *He was terrified of spiders.* One day at recess, I saw a spider just like that one crawling along the fence around the schoolyard." Reverend Dane smiled. ". . . I let it crawl up on my finger at recess."

Meg shuddered.

"And I took it into the schoolroom —"

"— and you put it in William's desk!" Aaron said triumphantly. Then, shocked by his enjoyment of a prank, he looked uncertainly at his father. "Right?"

The reverend nodded. "Right."

"Then what happened?" Meg wanted to know.

"When William opened his desk to get his geography book out after lunch, there was the spider. He screamed and ran out of the room. I walked over and rescued the spider and threw it out the window. And the teacher knew right then who had put the spider in William's desk in the first place." The reverend grinned. "I guess I looked pretty smug."

"Did you get punished?" Aaron wanted to know.

The reverend nodded. "The worst paddling of my life. And then when I got home my father gave me another one. And I went to bed without supper and had to stay after school for a week."

Aaron stifled a smile. "Was it worth it?"

The reverend nodded solemnly. "Yes. It was." He jabbed Aaron in the ribs. "But don't *you* ever use that as an excuse to put a spider in anyone's desk."

Aaron dodged his father's finger and clutched his side, giggling. The reverend jabbed him again. And then, before either he or Aaron quite knew how it happened, the reverend and his son were wrestling playfully. And then he was giving Meg a horseback ride around the grape arbor.

As time went on, the Reverend Simon Dane found it increasingly easy to succumb to the charms of his daughter and the love of his son. He looked at them both and saw Ellen, and while it caused him pain for a moment . . . joy came in the morning. It would not happen overnight, but the seed had been sown that, if watered, could transform even a noisy gong and a clanging cymbal like the Reverend Simon Dane into a beloved father — and the shepherd of a flock. There were still hints of the old reverend in his formal speech patterns with adults, in his hesitancy with new people, in his dealings with servants. And yet even in those moments there was new warmth in his eyes and sincere feeling behind his greetings and questions. The unthawing of the Reverend Simon Dane was permanent. The metamorphosis had begun.

*May 1, 1862*
*Hazelwood Mission Station*
*Upper Sioux Agency*
*Minnesota*

*Dear Brother,*
*I regret to say that our beloved Dakota are having a very hard time of it. Last summer's crop was nearly a total loss. Were it not for the stores shared out of the agency warehouse, and the natural custom among the people to share whatever they have with their brothers, starvation would be widespread. Thanks be to God who provides adequately for His workers even in the midst of drought and depredation. We are amply supplied and share as we can with those who seek our help.*
*The hostilities between our farmer Indians and those who persist in their nomadic ways have worsened. A group of them broke into Robert Lawrence's home near the Lower Agency late last year, terrorizing Robert and young Two Stars, who had come to investigate the life of a "cut-hair," as he put it. The brigands killed Robert's oxen and burned his barn, but, thanks be to God, did not seriously harm the men. We have had further evidence of our God's working in mysterious ways, as the incident seemed to be the turning point for Two Stars. He helped Robert build a new*

*barn and surprised everyone by settling on the farm next to Robert's. He has been joined by his mother Gray Woman, and we have been gratified to have him take the name of Daniel and to see God's salvation poured out on another life.*

*The unrest among the blanket Indians seems to be growing. The new agent, Thomas Galbraith, may be part of the increasing problems. You know with what difficulty he managed to pay the expected annuity last year. He has done little since to encourage the Dakota to trust him.*

*As the War of the Rebellion wears on, we see its effects even here in the Far West. It has not gone unnoticed by the more warlike faction of Dakota that our men are leaving to fight the south. They cannot but realize that many farms are now left in the hands of women and the elderly. It is rumored that southern rebels are among us, inciting further expectations of victory should violence erupt. While I have no personal knowledge of this, I suspect it may be true.*

*It does not help that because of last year's difficulties, rumors are already abounding that this year's annuity will be delayed — or perhaps not come at all — because of the war. With the hunger about us, such an event would give rise to the deepest kind of tragedy.*

*You have helped us a great deal by impressing upon your listeners the need for every kind of assistance they can give. We have thousands of hungry Dakota who want for the smallest bit of bread. Your analogy of sending barrels of flour to help us impart the Bread of Life to the Dakota nation is a good one, for the people desperately need both kinds of bread.*

*We continue in faith and love with the brethren, heartened by our small victories and trusting God to accomplish His purposes among us. I believe you will be likewise heartened upon your return. There is a small flock awaiting the beginning of the work near Cloudman's village up north. We will have a small home ready by the time you return. The people wish to build a church as soon as possible.*

*As to your enquiry on Miss LaCroix's behalf, Miss Jane Williams informs me that the Hazelwood teachers are anxious to have their sister back with them. She will be a welcome help. Her devotion to your children is certainly to be admired. I would ask, however, that you take measures to ensure that her devotion to Christ is strong, for as you know, dear brother, without that, her usefulness to the work will be limited.*

*Your letters warm our hearts and fill us*

*with anticipation of your return. Thank you for your kind words as to my encouragement in your life. We rejoice that you have been enabled to triumph over your loss and trust that it will, as you have said, be used of God to make you more fit to serve His kingdom among the Dakota.*

*As to your concerns about traveling alone with Miss LaCroix, I have arranged for you to journey to Alton, Illinois, with a group from the American Board. Reverend Samuel Whitney will be contacting you soon regarding the details. He is a dear brother in Christ and you will find him a sympathetic and wise companion. I think his wife, Nina, is a former classmate of yours. She will be a willing confidante for Miss LaCroix.*

*I will join you in Alton, for I have business in St. Louis regarding the printing of a new hymnbook for the mission. If my journey goes as hoped, I should arrive in Alton no later than June 15. I believe your itinerary should bring you to that city within a few days of my arrival, and I shall be content to await you so that we complete the journey home together.*

*Looking forward to our meeting, I remain your servant for the eternal good of the kingdom,*

*Stephen Riggs*

"I have news from Minnesota," Simon said at the breakfast table one Sabbath morning. Unfolding Dr. Riggs's letter, he read aloud, judiciously editing out Dr. Riggs's references to unrest.

From the far end of the table, Mrs. Leighton dabbed at her eyes with the corner of her napkin. She pointed to Aaron and Meg. "You must promise to write your old grand-mama every week."

Meg frowned. "But I don't write good yet, Grand-mama."

"That's all right," Aaron said. "You can tell me what you want to say, I'll write it down, and Gen can check it." He looked across the table at Gen. "Isn't that right, Gen? . . . GEN!"

Gen looked up, startled. "Oh, yes, of course, Aaron." She glanced at Mrs. Leighton and smiled. "I'll see to it." *Whatever am I seeing to?* she wondered. "We'll talk about it more later, Aaron. Eat your breakfast."

"I ate it already," Aaron said impatiently.

Gen looked at Aaron's empty plate. "Good boy. Now take your sister upstairs and get ready for church."

"But we're ready," Meg said, looking confused. "You helped us get ready earlier, remember?"

"But you have neglected to bring your Bibles downstairs," Simon said. "And I wish to read a passage together before we go to the service."

Aaron started to protest, but something in his father's eyes warned him. Nodding, he and Meg excused themselves and headed for the library to retrieve their Bibles.

Simon frowned. He had not expected the mention of Two Stars, who was calling himself Daniel, to distract Geneviève to this extent. Perhaps it was not that, he thought, sipping his coffee. Perhaps it was simply the excitement of returning to Minnesota after months away. He set his coffee cup down, looking at Gen's plate and saying gently, "You haven't eaten anything, Geneviève. Are you feeling well?"

Gen blushed. "I'm fine. Just — excited — I guess. About the letter. We actually have a date for going home." She took a deep breath, looking in Mrs. Leighton's direction as she said, "Please don't think I haven't appreciated you, Mrs. Leighton. It's just that —"

Mrs. Leighton waved her hand in the air. "Not at all, Geneviève. Not at all. The ties to home are the strongest ties in the world. I understand completely." She reached across the table and patted Gen's hand. "I shall miss you." She looked down the table at Simon. "I shall miss all of you." Her chin wavered as her gaze went to Ellen's empty chair. She took a deep breath. "But perhaps you will come again to visit. And" — she raised her eyebrows at Simon — "I shall expect Aaron and Meg when they are ready for higher learning. That has been settled to your satisfaction, Simon?"

Simon smiled at his mother-in-law warmly. "It has. And I thank you for your generosity, Mother Leighton."

Aaron and Meg returned with their Bibles.

"I — I need to fix my hair before the services," Gen said abruptly. Without waiting to be excused, she fled the room and hurried upstairs to her room. Closing the door behind her, she walked across the Persian carpet to look at herself in the mirror. *Blue Eyes*. Reaching up, she pulled a narrow string of beads out from beneath her collar, fingering the dull metal cross that hung between two bright blue beads. She went to the window, pulling aside the lace panel that obscured the street. *Daniel Two Stars*. She whispered it several times and decided he had chosen a good name. She could tell that Simon had not read every word of the letter. She wondered if it said anything else about Daniel, if he had edited out the one thing she cared most about. Except for one very formal letter to the reverend expressing sympathy after Ellen's death, she had heard nothing from him. Of course it wouldn't have been proper for him to write. Robert Lawrence would have made certain Two Stars knew that. Still, Gen thought as she ran her fingers up and down the rows of beads, she wished she knew more.

She had thought about Two Stars more often than she would admit to anyone . . . even herself. And she realized that if she tried, she could probably sketch a portrait of him as exacting as any her papa had ever drawn. She would draw hair flowing over his shirt collar like a lion's mane, a mouth that turned down slightly at the corners, kind eyes. He moved with certainty and grace, but she'd never seen him strut like Red Thunder. And while he was physically strong and she had seen him tremble with rage, she knew he could be gentle too. If what the reverend's letter said was true about him, if he really had become a farmer, then Two Stars — Daniel — had begun to overcome the warrior within.

Looking to the cobblestone street below, Gen saw families headed up the hill towards the church. Simon was preaching today . . . a farewell sermon. From the number of families headed in that direction, he would have a good-sized congregation.

"Gen?" Aaron knocked at the door. "Father says we should be going."

Gen dropped the curtain and turned away from the window. "I'll be right down," she answered. Tucking the beaded necklace back beneath her collar, Gen grabbed her Bible and headed for the door. She had learned to pour tea at Miss Bartlett's, she could stitch samplers and set a table, but as Gen headed down the broad, winding staircase towards Simon and the children, she realized that she would never really belong anywhere but on the prairie, among the Dakota people of her mother.

*He has a farm. He has a house. I wonder . . . will he have a wife?*

# Twenty

Now set your heart and your soul to
seek the LORD your God.
— 1 CHRONICLES 22:19 (NKJV)

"We had hoped for better times with the new
administration, but things have declined
even more since President Lincoln's election." Missionary Amos Hendricks sat on
the deck of the steamship *Annabelle* with
Simon. They were taking on passengers at
St. Louis in preparation for the final journey
north to Fort Snelling. He shook his head
sadly. "As you've heard from Dr. Riggs, the
harvest last fall was almost nonexistent. And
still Agent Galbraith refuses to open the
storehouse and share provisions until the
July annuity arrives." Amos shrugged. "Congress doesn't seem to understand the
pressing situation in Minnesota." He
paused. "I suppose it's hard to focus on the
frontier when the war goes on and on."

Simon interjected, "But surely someone
in Washington can be made to see how

desperate the needs are."

Amos shrugged. "They know. I don't think they care. Thousands have no way to eat unless they beg or steal. Seeing droves of 'white warriors' leaving to serve with the Union army has fueled the idea of using force to open the warehouse." He set his glass of water down. "Before I left, one old brigand even threatened me. He's called the Singer, and for a while he helped me with translating some of the hymns. Then he took to edifying me with long harangues about his being a leading man and my using too much firewood. He had style, though. No begging like a humble suppliant. Acted like he had a right to the wood and that I had received it through his generosity." Amos chuckled. "I had to yield after a while. I made him a present of an old flintlock rifle."

"Do you think that was wise," Simon asked, "with the atmosphere so tense?"

Amos shrugged. "The Singer blusters, but he wouldn't hurt us. I showed him his name in the hymnbook and told him everyone would know of his talent. He was immensely pleased. When I go back with a printed book, he will be even more delighted."

Gen walked up with Meg and Aaron.

Amos jumped up, bowing low and motioning for Gen to take his seat.

"Thank you, Mr. Hendricks," she said. "But Meg and Aaron have a few lessons to complete before supper."

She looked at Simon. "Is there any hope of shoving off yet today?"

Simon shook his head. "Perhaps tomorrow."

Gen sighed.

Simon tried to cheer her. "We can walk on the wharf this evening if you like."

"Perhaps," Gen said halfheartedly. Nodding at Amos, she herded the children before her and headed for their room.

Amos dropped back into his seat and picked up the conversation. "Daniel Two Stars —"

At the sound of Daniel's name, Simon noticed Gen stop short. She tried to camouflage her interest by pretending to have dropped something on deck, but it was obvious to Simon what she was really doing. He was surprised at how much her interest in Two Stars bothered him. He forced himself to concentrate on what Hendricks was saying.

"— and others have maintained their relationships in the other camps. So we have a solid and true group of Dakota friends. I have full confidence they will let us know if there is any real danger. In the direst of needs, we can always send the women and children to Fort Ridgely. I wouldn't worry, Reverend Dane."

When they finally reached Alton, Illinois, the travelers were guests of friends of the Dakota Mission who lived in a large brick house on a hill overlooking the Mississippi River.

Gen was sitting on the back porch fanning herself one sweltering afternoon when Nina plopped next to her. "Lemonade?" she asked, shoving a glass in Gen's hand without waiting for a reply. She held the glass up to her forehead. "I know he *looks* like Reverend Simon Dane," she said abruptly, "but he's definitely an impostor." She nudged Gen. "Who is he, really?"

Gen frowned. "I'm afraid I don't know what you mean."

"Of course you do," Nina said impatiently. "*This* Reverend Dane — the one who reads to Meg and plays catch with Aaron — has nothing in common with the Simon Dane I went to school with."

Gen raised her eyebrows. "You knew Simon?"

Nina nodded vigorously. "I did. He was

sullen. Not exceptionally bright. Argumentative. Overly religious. None of us liked him. None of us could believe Ellen Leighton chose him. Never were two people more unsuited to one another. What's happened?"

Gen shook her head. Nina Whitney had to be the most irritating woman on earth. She had lustrous blonde hair that was never out of place and a melodious voice that captivated every man she spoke to. Her small dark eyes snapped with energy and took in everything around her. She watched people intently and had a maddening ability to understand the mood that lay beneath every expression. Had she been inclined to gossip and vacuous conversation, Nina Whitney could have been the belle of every ball she attended. But Nina was irritatingly pious. Nothing discouraged her. Nothing worried her. When they were delayed in St. Louis, Nina had quoted something about God's working everything out to the good of those He loved. When they finally reached Alton and discovered Dr. Riggs had not yet arrived, she had taken it in stride — and quoted more Bible verses. And when Reverend Riggs finally did get to Alton — two weeks late — Nina had greeted him as if he were right on time. She assured him they had enjoyed the unexpected rest, and was so jolly that Gen wanted to strangle her.

Did she mention the stifling heat that drove them out into the yard to try to sleep? Did she mind being accosted by mosquitoes the size of hummingbirds? Did she fret over the steamship captain's announcement that traffic on the river was at a standstill because of the drought's exposing too many sandbars? Not Nina. Gen had been around missionaries for nearly two years now, and she knew they took their religion personally. But when Nina told Gen she was praying that God would move the sandbars, Gen nearly laughed out loud. She had never met anyone who took her religion to the point of the ridiculous. And now Nina was calling Simon overly religious — and asking personal questions. Gen smiled politely and ignored the question, taking the one precious piece of ice out of her glass of lemonade and running it across the back of her neck.

"Did I say something amusing?" Nina asked.

Gen shook her head. "No. It's just ironic to hear you — the woman who prays that God will move sandbars — calling someone else overly religious."

Nina was quiet for long enough that Gen thought she had successfully silenced the other woman's questions. But presently Nina said quietly, "What I meant was, when I knew him before, there was something — artificial — about Simon. Stiff. Almost inhuman. He's different now. It's as if he's finally taken all the knowledge stuffed in his head . . . and moved it down to his heart where it can do some good." She murmured, "I never thought I'd live to see the day when I thought Simon Dane would be thought of as a potentially good husband." She looked sideways at Gen. "I'm surprised he hasn't approached *you*, Miss LaCroix."

"About what?" Gen asked innocently.

"About being his wife, of course — and mother to Aaron and Meg. You already fill the latter role quite nicely." At Gen's look of horror, Nina said, "Don't be so naive. I've seen the way Simon looks at you. He's seen you grow and develop into a charming young woman. Why, just last week Mr. Whitney officiated at the marriage of a settler and his housekeeper. The wife was killed in a farming accident the week before. With four children under the age of ten, the man had to do something."

Gen shuddered. "That's — repulsive.

How could he even ask? And how could she accept?"

"God enables us to do what we must, even when we think we cannot." Nina smiled. "The Lord's ways are mysterious. That is one thing we can depend upon. He works in ways we do not understand."

"Well," Gen retorted, "if that is the kind of thing the Lord requires of the people who know Him personally, I'm glad I have kept my distance."

"What do you mean — kept your distance?" Nina asked quickly. "Don't you — don't you *know* Christ?"

Gen swallowed the last of her lemonade and set the glass down on the stairs. She looked at Nina, her blue eyes flashing with anger. "What kind of question is that? I grew up listening to my father read the Scriptures to me — both in French *and* English. And since being with the mission I've learned to recite the catechism — in *three* languages. Ask me anything you want, Mrs. Whitney. I know all the answers." She stood up. "I thought I was doing a fairly decent job of things. The children seem happy, the reverend doesn't have any complaints. What exactly have I done to make you think I'm not a Christian?"

Nina's dark eyes blinked rapidly. She

reached out and put her hand on Gen's arm. "Please, Miss LaCroix. Don't take offense. I didn't mean it that way at all. Of course you're a good person. Anyone can see that. It's just that — well, it doesn't matter if you can recite the entire *Bible* in three languages." She swallowed and tapped her temple with her finger. "There has to be a transfer of information from here . . ." — she moved her hand down to the place over her heart — ". . . to here."

Meg and Aaron came running up the street alongside a huge iron hoop. Aaron had kept the hoop upright for nearly a block and a half through the center of town, and they shouted for Gen to watch. She waved. Relieved for an excuse to escape Nina's prodding questions, she excused herself and set off across the lawn. When the hoop finally crashed over and the children ran to the house for lemonade, Gen headed towards the city park, more disturbed by her conversation with Nina Whitney than she wanted to admit. The business about making religion personal nagged at her. She wondered if that really was at the heart of Simon's change. And while Nina's cheerful reliance on God irritated her sometimes, she had to admit that she secretly admired the woman's resilience. It made her think of Miss Jane back at the mission. And Mrs. Riggs. They weren't as vocal about it as Nina, but Gen had heard them pray, and she knew they didn't hesitate to ask God about everyday matters.

Gen had rounded the park and headed back for the house before she let herself consider the other part of her conversation with Nina. Simon had changed, and most of it was for the good. But some of the changes worried her. He had asked her to call him by his given name. He had begun to call her Gen. Occasionally he even called her Geneviève — with the French pronunciation and a strange smile on his lips. Gen took a deep breath and rubbed her arms briskly. It suddenly occurred to her that while his transformation in regard to his children was completely wonderful, perhaps Simon was relaxing just a bit too much in his relationship with his children's governess.

Gen wondered what she would do if Two Stars was involved in the kind of Christianity Nina Whitney espoused. She couldn't imagine a young Dakota warrior praying about the details of his life the way Nina Whitney did. Still, Gen thought as she stared down the street towards the river, she almost wished she *did* believe that God would move sandbars for people like her . . . because she was having a hard time waiting to get home. And if she thought God cared, she might just ask Him to keep Daniel Two Stars occupied with farming and away from other girls, at least until she had a chance to see him again.

# Twenty-one

If they say, "Come with us,
Let us lie in wait to shed blood . . .
My son, do not walk in the way with
   them,
Keep your foot from their path;
For their feet run to evil,
And they make haste to shed blood.
        — PROVERBS 1:11, 15–16 (NKJV)

It had been the worst hunting trip in recent memory. For five days Otter and four other half-starved braves had scoured the Big Woods without success. Their pemmican was gone, and as they walked along the trail on the way back to camp, their stomachs rumbled with hunger. Ahead of them was Robinson Jones's combination post office, lodging place, store, and homestead. Seeing the Jones place, the hunters realized they were in what the whites called Meeker County, where many new settlers were taking up claims, thinning the woods even more, chasing the game away, complaining when the Dakota left the reservation.

As the five men filed along Robinson Jones's fence, a hen rose from a bunch of grass and waddled across the clearing, clucking loudly. Looking down, Otter smiled. He scooped up the hen's eggs.

"Don't take those," Brown Wing protested. "They belong to that white man. If he sees us, we will get into trouble."

Otter was furious. He threw the eggs to the ground. "Coward! Look at you! Look at all of us — half-starved, yet afraid to take so much as an egg from a white man!"

"Who do you call a coward?" Brown Wing shot back. He gestured so violently that the eagle feathers in his hair shook. "I am no coward!" He stepped over the homesteader's fence. "And to prove it, I will go to that house and shoot the white man who lives there." He sneered at Otter. "Are you brave enough to go with me?"

Otter met the challenge. "I will go. We will see who is the coward among us." He looked behind him where their two companions stood.

"We will go," Breaking Up and Killing Ghost said. "We will be brave too."

When the five young men went inside Robinson Jones's store, they were loud and boisterous, each one trying to outdo the other in impressing Jones and frightening the girl who was minding the cash register. But Jones was not easily frightened, and when he realized the braves weren't serious customers, he picked up his rifle and headed out the door, telling the girl behind the counter he was going across the road to the neighbor's, where his wife had gone to pay a visit.

The Dakota braves went outside where Otter taunted Brown Wing. "I thought you were going to kill a white man today."

Brown Wing threw the challenge back in his face. "Follow me and see what I will do."

They crossed the road and followed Jones to his neighbor's, suggesting a game of target practice with the white men. Otter set a block of wood atop a tree stump and backed away. Brown Wing fired. The white men took turns. But the Indians all reloaded their rifles after each shot. The whites didn't. And so, when the Dakota finally made good their promises to one another to kill a white man, the whites proved to be easy prey. Before they had finished firing, the Indians had killed three of the men and one woman. When they ran off, they passed Jones's store. The girl from behind the counter had heard the gunshots and come to the door. When the braves ran past, one of them stopped long enough to kill her, then ran to catch up with his friends.

When the realization of what they had done sank in, the braves were terrified. They had killed whites. Worse, they had killed women. The entire world would come against them, and punishment would be swift and sure. Stealing some horses, they raced for their village on Rice Creek.

Whatever they thought might be the consequences of their attack, the Dakota braves could not have anticipated the magnitude of what they had begun. Before it was finished, there would not be a house or a store or a living white person in ten Minnesota counties that remained untouched. Nearly three hundred women and children would be held in captivity, hundreds (some would say thousands) would die, and nearly forty thousand settlers would abandon their holdings in the state.

It was August 17, 1862. The day after Christmas in that same year, thirty-eight Dakota Sioux men would die in the largest mass execution ever held in the United States. Among those hanged was an innocent man who had risked his life many times to protect his white friends. The missionary who served as interpreter at the trials would write about it in his memoirs, calling the innocent man's death "an unfortunate accident."

August 17, and still there was no word. Reverend Dane had been expected since late June, and still he had not come. Daniel took another nail from between his lips, set it in place and pounded it in with three strikes.

"And you say you aren't a carpenter," Robert Lawrence shouted from the road. He pulled his team up and climbed down, standing back to observe the progress on the new church being built near the Lower Agency.

Young Reverend John Williamson came around the corner. "I'm glad to see you, Robert." He shook Robert's hand briskly. "We'll have our first service soon. I hope you'll come."

Robert nodded.

Williamson turned to go, but hesitated. "I thought you might want to know, I ran into some missionaries from the Upper Agency yesterday. One was Reverend Dane, I believe he said his name was. Apparently he was here for a few years, then left last year for a trip east. He was traveling with Dr. Riggs. I think they are beginning a new work up near Cloudman's village for the American Board. Do you know him?"

Daniel nearly swallowed the nails in his mouth. "Are they still here?"

Williamson shook his head. "Said they would be leaving for the Upper Agency this morning right after breakfast —" He was speaking to Daniel's back.

"How kind of you, Daniel," Mrs. Wakefield said. "Reverend Dane will be so touched when he hears you came to welcome him back. But they left for the Upper Agency this morning right after breakfast." Daniel lingered on the first step, his hat in his hands. Mrs. Wakefield smiled. "Dr. Wakefield and I had a good visit with the reverend. He has changed in the last year. And for the better. He's quite eager to begin his new work."

Daniel nodded and said something noncommittal.

Mrs. Wakefield finally put him out of his misery. "Miss LaCroix was with them, of course. She seems very interested in what's been happening in their absence. She even inquired about *you*." She cleared her throat. "A very caring young woman. An excellent addition to the mission, don't you think?"

*She had asked about him.* "Yes, ma'am. I think so." Daniel put his hat back on his head, barely resisting the urge to leap on his horse and charge away at top speed.

Mrs. Wakefield chuckled. "I'd invite you to stay for supper, Daniel, but I think there's something else on your mind." She waved him off the porch. "Go along, young man. Never let it be said that Mrs. Wakefield stood in the way of young love. If you ride all night, perhaps you'll catch up with them."

Flashing a smile, Daniel jumped down off the porch. He was in the saddle with one leap, never touching the stirrups until the horse had already moved out. Without turning around, he raised his hand to Mrs. Wakefield. He rode home and grabbed his bedroll. Gray Woman packed his saddlebags with food. Slipping his rifle into its scabbard, he leaped back up into the saddle and headed north.

Gray Woman waved good-bye happily. Perhaps she would finally get a daughter-in-law.

As his horse cleared the first rise and began the descent into the valley beyond, Daniel planned the next day. He would not, of course, be so bold as to sit beside Blue Eyes during the service. No, he decided, he would linger until it was almost too late, and then slip in and sit on one of the back pews where he could see her. Then he could get used to her presence before actually having to speak to her. He was nervous, and observing her for a while might help him get hold of himself. What had the year done to change her? Did she still have his necklace? Would she even care to see his small cabin, the beginning of his farm? Until he knew if God had a future for them together, he must be very, very careful.

*But she asked about me . . .*

It was growing dark before he crossed the Redwood River. He stopped to water and rest his horse and to stretch his legs. He thought about his farm, about the new mission Reverend Dane would begin. He hoped that Dr. Williamson was right and that Reverend Dane had changed. He needed to change or he would never be fit for missionary work. He wondered if Reverend Dane had learned to see past dark skin and accept Dakota as his equals in Christ.

His thinking was circular, always coming back to Blue Eyes. Should he tell her that every night he had looked up at the moon and thought of her and wondered if she was watching it? He had wanted to know if she ever thought of him. He had wanted to write. But when he mentioned it to Miss Jane up at Hazelwood, Miss Jane had shaken her head. "It simply is not done, Daniel. You aren't betrothed. Reverend Dane would be very upset, and Geneviève might be cast in a bad light."

His horse stumbled. Gathering itself and proceeding up the trail, the horse suddenly jerked its head sideways, pricking its ears and slowing down to listen. Daniel pulled him to a halt and listened, too, his eyes closed, his head down. Far, far in the distance, so far that it was almost indiscernible, came the steady throb of a drumbeat. Daniel listened for a few more moments before deciding it was coming from the direction of Red Middle Voice's village on Rice Creek.

Dread clutched at his midsection. Red Middle Voice's camp was populated with some of the more violent members of the tribe. Otter lived there now and had joined a recently created soldiers' lodge. More than likely he and his friends had been to the trader's and acquired a barrel of whiskey. But he had to be sure. He headed in the direction of the drumbeat. The closer he got to the village, the clearer the sound. Soon, the air was punctuated by war cries.

The braves who had burned Robert's barn and threatened him were from Red Middle Voice's camp. He realized that if they saw him and if trouble really was brewing, he could be killed as a spy. At the edge of the camp, he removed his hat and shirt. He had made another necklace identical to the one he hoped Blue Eyes wore. He pulled it over his head. Stuffing his shirt and the beads into his hat, he hid the bundle behind a tree. Rifle in hand, he walked towards the center of camp. From the fringe of the gathered crowd, Daniel saw Red Middle Voice and his best warriors riding slowly through the camp, their faces and bodies painted, their horses decorated for war.

No one paid any attention to Daniel as he slipped away, weaving in and out of tepees until he found one painted with a distinctive design that told everyone who passed that this was the home of Wing. Daniel noticed that the American flag Wing usually flew from a pole beside her tent was absent. He ducked and went inside unannounced.

When she saw Daniel, Wing raised her hands to her face and began to wail. Words tumbled out in a jumble as she lamented having parted from Gray Woman and the missionaries. She recounted what had happened, how young fools had begun by stealing eggs and ended by killing white women and children. "I heard them come riding in. They were shouting, 'There is war with the whites and we have begun it.'" She wailed, "What has our nation become when young braves *boast* of killing women and children?"

"Where are they going?" Daniel asked.

"To Shakopee's village," Wing said. "They know they cannot fight alone. All the chiefs and warriors must fight or they will never succeed."

Daniel shook his head. "They will not succeed, whether they all fight or not." A flicker of hope shone in his eyes. "Perhaps they will go on to Little Crow. He will tell them they are fools."

Daniel put his hand on Wing's shoulder. "We must warn our friends." He was thinking aloud. "The people at the agency have time to get away if they hurry."

Wing nodded. "A few of the men have already gone to them. And one went to the fort to bring the soldiers."

Daniel slipped out of the tepee and across camp. Grabbing his shirt and hat, he dressed, leaped up on his horse, and headed after Red Middle Voice and his warriors.

What he saw from the edge of the woods near Shakopee's camp filled Daniel with dread. More braves were painted for war, piercing the night air with war chants and an occasional shot from a rifle. When they began chanting the familiar name *Taoyateduta,* Daniel headed south. As he had hoped, they were headed to see Chief Little Crow.

If anyone could calm the warriors down, it was Little Crow, who had been to the capital city of the United States twice, who knew the power of the whites, who favored negotiation. A gifted orator, Chief Little Crow had recently cut his hair and begun to dress like a white man. He had even attended Dr. Williamson's church on occasion.

Little Crow's plain board house was located on the bluffs two miles above the Lower Agency. Two stories high, it was still not large enough to house the chief's four wives and seven children. Several tepees pitched near it helped alleviate the crowding, and it was inside one of these tepees that the confrontation between Little Crow and the two other chiefs took place.

Emotions were running high as the warriors bent on war approached Little Crow's camp. Red Middle Voice spoke first, followed by Shakopee, who reminded his listeners what the now despised trader Andrew Myrick had said. When the July annuity payment was delayed, the traders had had a meeting at which they agreed they would not extend any more credit to Indians until the annuity funds had been received and all the traders paid. When one interpreter expressed concern that starvation might set in, trader Myrick had snapped, "As far as I am concerned, if they are hungry let them eat grass!" When Shakopee quoted the despised trader, the air was filled with whoops and gunfire.

After Shakopee's speech, Wabasha, Big Eagle, and Traveling Hail each spoke. With each tirade it seemed to Daniel that the hatred in the air grew thicker until it hung above Little Crow's camp like a brooding thundercloud. The young warriors gathered around, shouting and demanding white blood. The annuity had not come. Perhaps the war among the whites would keep it from coming at all. They would starve waiting for the Great Father in

Washington to think of his children in the west. And even if the annuity came, the traders like Myrick and the others would only come forward and claim it. They would starve anyway. The time had come, they shouted. The time had come to kill everyone and take back the lands they had lost. They were ready to fight as brothers, to drive the white men from their lands or to die. It was a good day to die.

As the mood escalated and the chiefs talked, the moon crossed the sky and at last, Little Crow, the one they respected most, rose to speak. A gifted showman, Little Crow had, at some time during the night, blackened his face as a sign of mourning. He was reluctant to fight, he informed the crowd. But the voice of reason only enraged the crowd more. Someone wearing an eagle headdress accused the chief of cowardice.

Little Crow grabbed his taunter's headdress and threw it to the ground. "Do you see the scalp-locks of your enemies hanging there on the lodge-pole of my tepee?" he retorted. "And do you remember when I covered your back like a she-bear covers her cubs when you ran from your enemies?" The crowd quieted as Little Crow continued. "You may kill one white man — two — ten — and ten times ten will come to kill you. Count your fingers all day long, and white men with guns in their hands will come faster than you can count."

Someone reminded the chief that many of the white men from the area were away fighting the other war. Little Crow laughed derisively. "Yes, they fight among themselves. But if you strike at them they will all turn on you and devour you and your women and little children just as the locusts in their time fall on the trees and devour all the leaves in one day. You are little children. Fools. You will die like the rabbits when the hungry wolves hunt them in the Hard Moon."

For a brief second, Daniel thought that perhaps Little Crow would succeed in averting disaster. But then, to his horror, the chief abruptly concluded his speech. "*Ta-o-ya-te-du-ta* is not a coward. He will die with you."

The air in the camp exploded with bloodthirsty chants. "Kill the whites!" the warriors screamed. "Kill the whites!"

Daniel slipped out of the maddened crowd and mounted his horse. Just as he was about to leave, someone grabbed his leg. "Where are you going?" Otter shouted, saturating the air with the smell of liquor. He nearly pulled Daniel off his horse.

Daniel leaned down. "I have to get these white men's clothes off if I am to join you. And I want to paint my horse for battle." He leaned over and in a conspiratorial stage whisper, he lied, "I have everything ready in a cache between here and the agency. I'll wait for you near the broken tree." Mentioning the tree convinced Otter. It was an ancient tree, almost a sacred object to the Dakota.

Otter narrowed his eyes momentarily. Daniel met his gaze and did not waver. Finally, Otter released him. "Go then. I will look for you."

Daniel raced towards home, his mind whirling between Little Crow's village to the Lower Agency, from the agency to Fort Ridgely, from the fort to the farmer Indians, and then north to Hazelwood Station . . . and Blue Eyes. If the soldiers didn't act quickly, the entire Dakota nation would be torn apart as each man was forced to choose a side and act with it, either attacking or defending a way of life, a family, a friend.

Gray Woman's old friend Wing had said that messengers had slipped away to warn people at the Lower Agency and to summon help from Fort Ridgely. Daniel wondered if the messengers would be able to make the soldiers believe them. No whites really thought the Dakota would dare to challenge the powerful government. Daniel had not wanted to believe it, either. But he had seen the fires of rebellion lit in the camps of the most warlike chiefs, and he was terrified at what might happen when the sun rose and the warriors went out to reclaim their lands.

He did not know how far the fires of hatred would burn, but he knew that he must run ahead of them, first to protect his mother and Robert Lawrence's family, and then north to Hazelwood Station and Blue Eyes. He urged his horse forward, clearing a small stream, tearing up the incline on the other side, hunching down over his horse's mane, kicking the animal's sides, urging him to run faster, ever faster.

# Twenty-two

Teach me Your way, O LORD,
And lead me in a smooth path,
  because of my enemies.
            — PSALM 27:11 (NKJV)

Daniel jerked his horse to a rearing halt outside James Anderson's trading post just as a covered wagon of immigrants pulled into the yard. A pale, frightened woman poked her head out from the wagon box.

"Trouble at the agency!" Daniel shouted. "Head back across the river. Fast as you can go!"

The woman's eyes widened. She looked at the driver uncertainly. "Jeremiah?"

The bearded driver retorted, "We can't leave. I haven't filed my claim yet."

Anderson hurried outside. "You're frightening these folks, Two Stars." He spit a stream of tobacco juice at a wildflower nosing its way through the trampled earth. With a nod at the woman in the wagon he explained, "Our blanket Indians cause a stir once in a while, dance around a few fires, let out a few war whoops. Never amounts to anything."

Daniel could barely manage to keep himself from jumping down and grabbing the trader by the throat. "Look!" He pointed in the direction of the agency where a tower of smoke rose in the sky.

Anderson frowned.

The woman turned even paler and clutched her husband's shoulder.

"New Ulm," the young homesteader stammered, "we'll go to New Ulm."

"Too far," Daniel said. His horse whirled around. "Head for Fort Ridgely. Tell them what is happening. Warn everyone you know!" He sped out of the farmyard, heading for home.

"If it's so dangerous, why isn't *he* heading for the fort?" the homesteader asked Anderson.

The trader shook his head. "Can't say."

Jeremiah hesitated. "Do you think we should do what he said? Should we head for Fort Ridgely? How far is it?"

Anderson scratched his beard. "Time you get to the ferry, fourteen, maybe fifteen miles."

"It's so far, Jeremiah," the woman

whined. "We just got here. It can't be that bad, can it?"

Anderson studied the sky. It *was* a lot of smoke. "Don't know what to think," he said honestly, "but I can tell you one thing. I'm not leaving my store for a bunch of marauding troublemakers to destroy." He closed the shutters over the one window in the cabin. "Got a cellar we can hide in, if it comes to that. Never showed it to anyone. Hidden under a wagon in the barn out back." He looked up at young Jeremiah. "You and the missus want to take your chances with me, I expect we could all three fit down there. Don't expect we'll need it. But we can use it. If we have to."

Jeremiah's wife disappeared inside the wagon, emerging at the back and hopping down without her husband's assistance.

Jeremiah looked at Anderson. "Guess we're staying."

Anderson assumed that in the unlikely event there really *was* serious trouble they would have time to make it to the barn and his secret hiding place. He would be proven wrong.

Daniel was off his horse before it came to a complete stop outside his cabin. He charged into the little house, then into

Gray Woman's tepee. She was gone. Peering down the hill across the valley, he thought he could see a thin column of smoke rising from Robert Lawrence's chimney. Gray Woman was probably there.

His horse was trembling with exhaustion. Foam dripped from the bit in its mouth, sweat crusted its shoulders and ran down its legs. Taking a deep breath, Daniel closed his eyes. He must water his horse and let the animal cool down, or he would soon be on foot. He walked the animal around for what felt like hours, until the creature stopped gasping for breath and shaking. Only then did he raise a bucket of cold water from the well and let the animal drink. He jerked the bucket away long before the horse was satisfied and walked it around for another few minutes before giving it another drink. Finally, he left the horse standing by the well and hurried inside his house.

Rummaging around in his room he located an old parfleche made of dried-out skins. Flipping it open, he dumped the contents on his bed, smiling grimly at sight of the long blue sash he used to wear around his waist. He tied it there again, and then, as in the old days when he was a young man aspiring to be a warrior, he tucked jerky and ammunition into the sash. He headed for the door, pausing to look back at the crudely furnished one-room cabin. Perhaps the warriors would take out their anger on the agency buildings and leave the outlying farms alone. Perhaps the soldiers would arrive and put an end to the violence before it reached this far. He hoped so. As he climbed into the saddle and headed for Robert Lawrence's farm just a mile down into the valley, Daniel allowed himself one more look back at his little cabin flanked by his mother's tepee.

"What do you *mean* they are burning the agency?" Nancy Lawrence put her hand to her throat. "Robert is at the agency." She looked at Daniel, her eyes wide with fear. "He went to have the stallion shod." Her voice trailed off and she reached for Gray Woman. She took a deep breath and steadied herself as Clara darted out of the barn and ran up.

"What's wrong?" the little girl wanted to know. She studied the adult faces around her, frowning.

"There's some trouble at the agency," Daniel said quietly, trying to make his voice sound unconcerned. "It's probably nothing," he lied. He dismounted.

Gray Woman interrupted. "Clara," she said softly. "I think if you check in the barn and off that way" — she pointed to a field that stretched away from the barn and up over a hill — "you'll find that old hen of yours has been laying eggs and hiding her nest. Why don't you go see?" When Clara had trotted off, Gray Woman peered at her son. "It is bad."

He nodded. "Very bad. You might not be safe here. They are very angry with the farmers. I don't know what they will do, but I have to warn our friends."

"You should not look like a farmer if you are going to help our people," Nancy interjected. She motioned towards the house. "Robert kept some things from the old life. We have war paint."

Gray Woman helped Daniel apply the paint, two blue streaks of lightning on each cheek and down his bare back, white spots on his chest. Nancy used the rest of the white paint to create a series of crescent shapes across the dark bay horse's rump.

When they had finished transforming Daniel from a farmer into a warrior, they headed inside the house, where Nancy tucked more food in the sash at Daniel's waist. "Robert rode the stallion to the agency. He left the mare at home. She's due to foal any day." She hesitated, looking at Daniel. "Do you think we dare have her pull a travois?"

Daniel grinned. "She's an Indian pony. She's used to hard work." He ran to the barn and returned with the little pony, who was indeed almost as wide as she was tall. She submitted patiently while Gray Woman created a travois, weaving two long poles through a leather strap laid across her withers. Clara came back, having found the old hen's nest and a half dozen eggs. Nancy handed her a small basket and sent her to get hay from the barn to protect the eggs. "Too bad that old hen is so clever," Nancy said while she rummaged in her kitchen for provisions. "We could catch her and have chicken stew around the campfire tonight."

Finally, the travois was laden with supplies. "Go north," Daniel said. "But go a long way to the west first, so you stay away from the agency. Keep to yourselves. Go around all the settlements. If anyone asks you what you are doing," Daniel said, looking at Gray Woman, "pretend you don't know anything about the trouble. Tell them you are going to visit your son in Standing Buffalo's village up at Lac Qui

Parle." He smiled at his mother. "It won't be a lie. I will come to you soon." He tied a lariat around Koda's neck and handed the end to Clara. "Keep Koda with you."

Gray Woman put her hands on her son's shoulders. Closing her eyes, she prayed aloud, "Make Two Stars strong, his horse swift. Keep our little pony's feet sure, and open the way to Standing Buffalo's camp for us." Her voice trembled as she added, "And keep my boy safe, dear God, from all who would harm him. He only wants to help the ones who are Your children. Let him help them." Gray Woman stood for a moment looking up into her son's face. Then she turned away abruptly and, taking up the pony's halter, began the journey north.

Daniel leaped up on his horse's back. "*Ina,* don't go back to my farm." Gray Woman grumbled, "You think I am such an old woman I have no mind left? You said to hurry. Where is the 'stop at the farm' in the word *hurry?*" She waved towards the hill. "You have work to do. Go. Find Robert Lawrence. Warn your friends. And come to us at Lac Qui Parle."

When he reached the top of the first hill, Daniel pulled his horse up and looked back at the fields he and Robert Lawrence had plowed together. The corn stood tall and straight, ready to be harvested. A pumpkin patch near the barn glowed orange on the hillside. The smoke still wafted from Robert's chimney. And in the distance, three small figures followed a travois towards the north and what Daniel desperately prayed was a safe place.

Daniel approached the Lower Agency warily. Guns were going off everywhere. Two buildings were already on fire. Someone had broken into the warehouse, and a group of Dakota were dragging things outside, breaking open crates and kegs, shouting to their friends, displaying what they found.

It looked like they had killed every white man at the agency. Two bodies lay just outside Forbes's store. Sliding off his horse and tying him to a tree, Daniel looked up just in time to see Otter stumble through the doorway, a keg on his shoulders. He tripped over one of the bodies and nearly fell. The keg dropped to the ground and burst, spilling cornmeal on the ground.

Desperate to find Robert, Daniel let out a high-pitched war cry and charged from behind the tree, firing his rifle in the air.

"My brother!" Otter cried out, running

to meet him. "I waited for you by the ancient tree. Where were you?"

"They have broken into the warehouse!" Daniel waved his rifle towards the building and headed that way. Otter caught up with him, but then Daniel managed to lag behind just enough that as soon as Otter disappeared inside the warehouse, he could run back to the store. He checked the two bodies with a trembling hand, and thanked God when he recognized neither face.

Just inside the door of Forbes's store, he screamed Robert's name. A brave who had been rifling through the back room came out and grinned at him. He had found a gallon jar of kerosene and was pouring it behind him as he walked. Grabbing matches off the counter, he lit one and flicked it on the floor, yelping wildly as the flame crawled across the floor and towards the stairs.

"One of them is up there," he said happily. "I shot him. He is not dead." He looked at the fire and grabbed Daniel by the arm. "But he will be!"

Daniel jerked away from the other brave and leaped over the flames and to the stairs. He charged up them, calling out, "Robert! Robert Lawrence!"

"Here," came a weak voice. "Here on the bed."

Daniel ran down the hall to a room at the back of the store. Robert had been shot in the belly and lay on the bed, bleeding.

"We have to get you out of here," Daniel said. "They have set fire downstairs."

"Go," Robert panted. "Save yourself. I am dying."

Daniel looked at the wound. "You are not dying," he insisted. "The bullet only sliced you open. There is much blood, but we can sew it up. I am going to get you out of here." He ran to the window and looked out. The entire agency grounds were swarming with Indians, some on foot, some on horseback. A white man charged out of the warehouse a short distance away. A brave on horseback chased him down and buried an ax in his skull. Daniel flinched and turned away from the window.

Pulling Robert off the bed, he hauled him onto his shoulders and charged down the stairs, through the flames, and out the front door, where he stumbled over a body and into Otter.

Before Otter had a chance to speak, Daniel glared at him. "This man is my friend. If you had killed him before I got here, that would be one thing, but he is not dead, and I am going to take care of him."

He didn't stop moving, striding across the compound, daring anyone to stop him. To his amazement, no one did. No one even seemed to notice him until he helped Robert up on his horse and began to lead it towards the trees where his own mount waited. They passed the body of the trader named Myrick. The one who had said the starving Indians could eat grass was dead, his own mouth stuffed with bloodstained grass.

"You can't take my horse!" A brave so thin his arms waved like a scarecrow's brandished a tomahawk at Daniel's head.

Daniel dodged the tomahawk and threatened the brave with his rifle. He nodded towards Robert, who sat, hunched over, clinging to the saddle horn. "This is Little Buffalo. He is hurt. He cannot walk. I am taking him to his wife. The horse is Little Buffalo's. Not yours." Daniel pressed the barrel of his rifle against the brave's midsection.

The brave stared at Daniel for a moment. He looked down at the rifle and up at Robert. Regret shone on his face as, with one last admiring look at the stallion, he raised his hands and backed away.

His heart pounding furiously, praying that his shaking knees would hold him up and that the other brave was not watching, Daniel continued toward the spot where his own horse stood tied to a bush. He clambered up on his horse and leaned over to ask Robert, "Can you ride? I sent Nancy, the girls, and Gray Woman north. They can't have gotten too far. I'll try to find them."

Taking Robert's grunt for an answer, Daniel moved slowly up a hill, relieved when they reached the crest and he knew they were hidden from view. He rode southwest thinking that eventually he would intersect the trail left by the travois. When the sounds from the agency were finally muffled by distance, Daniel stopped long enough to take the blue sash from around his waist. He wrapped it around Robert's bleeding abdomen with trembling hands, hoping that by tying it to the saddle horn he could keep Robert in the saddle while he tried to find Nancy and Gray Woman's trail.

He leaned his head against his horse's neck, swallowing hard, trying to calm down. The carnage at the Lower Agency had been worse than he expected. He thought the war party would break into the warehouse and then, content with that store of food and goods, return to Little

Crow's village and await the soldiers. He had believed Little Crow would bargain for peace by turning over the criminals who had killed the whites. Obviously he was wrong. The war party was committed to wage a complete effort against the whites. They were killing everyone they saw who was not Dakota. Daniel had even recognized some farmer half-breeds among the dead at the agency.

He had heard cries of "Attack the Fort!" If they were planning to attack Fort Ridgely, towns to the south would be targets as well. They had probably already sent riders north to take the news of war to the seven chiefs whose villages were near the Upper Agency. John Otherday and Little Paul would try to defend the Hazelwood missionaries. But what if the Danes were already working near Cloudman's village? Who would warn them? Who could protect them?

Robert's head bowed lower and lower until it rested on his horse's neck. He began to slip to one side. Daniel finally had to ride behind Robert, steadying his friend with his legs while he guided the stallion and led his own exhausted horse.

*Show me the way, Lord, show me the way, help me to find Nancy, show me the way.*

Daniel said the prayer over and over until he was speaking it in rhythm with the horses' plodding feet. He had just begun to think he would have to backtrack all the way to his farm and pick up the trail there, when he heard Koda bark. It took all his willpower not to urge the stallion to a lope. Finally, when the sun was high overhead and Robert had long since lost consciousness, Daniel slipped off the stallion, untied his friend, and lowered him to the ground next to the travois.

Nancy bent low over her husband, crying softly, examining the wound. She sent Clara to a nearby brook for water and tore clean strips of cloth from her petticoat while Gray Woman and Daniel unloaded the travois to make room for Robert.

"The stallion won't pull the travois," Daniel said. He nodded towards the pony. "She'll have to do it."

"We can tie the food in blankets and put them over Robert's saddle," Gray Woman said.

"I've always been afraid of that horse," Nancy said uncertainly, eyeing the stallion. "I don't think he'll stand for bundles flopping against his sides."

Gray Woman went to the horse's head and took hold of the stallion's bridle. The horse snorted and tossed its head, trying to pull free, but Gray Woman didn't let go. As she spoke softly in Dakota, the animal quieted. Gray Woman reached up and stroked the horse's forehead, pulled gently on its forelock, and finally, kissed its muzzle. She looked at her son. "It will be all right now. He will take the bundles." She took one bundle and slung it over the stallion's saddle and, to Daniel's amazement, the animal only nodded its head and looked at Gray Woman as if to say, "Where's the other one?"

Gray Woman looked at her son. "You don't know everything about your old mother, do you?" She looked at Robert, frowning slightly. "We need whiskey to cleanse the wound. Thread for sewing. You must go back to the agency."

"Go back?!" Daniel looked at her, dumbfounded.

Gray Woman nodded. "You must go back and get what we need to care for Robert, unless you can find a homestead where they will give you what is needed. Or can you bring us the doctor?"

"Everyone at the agency is dead, *Ina*. I don't know where the doctor is. They are taking the women and children captive. We must get away. I can't go back there. I have to go north and warn the others."

"And you will. After you get what we need for your friend." Gray Woman nodded. "Wait until it is dark. Your horse will be rested then. You can ride back to your farm and bring me what is needed." She picked up the stallion's reins and began to walk away. The horse followed, head down, with all the complacency of a packhorse.

Clara had tied Koda's rope to a travois pole and sat next to Robert, moistening his lips with a cloth dipped in water. Nancy whispered to her husband, picked up the little mare's lead, and headed after Gray Woman and the stallion.

Looking north again, Daniel sighed. Finally he mounted his horse and rode up beside Gray Woman. "Keep going north, *Ina*. As God protects me, I will be back before the moon is up." Without waiting for a reply, he nudged his horse into a lope and headed back south. He avoided the agency, going instead to James Anderson's trading post. He found whiskey, a needle, thread . . . and three bodies down in Anderson's "secret" hiding place, burned beyond recognition.

# Twenty-three

If your enemy is hungry,
   give him bread to eat;
And if he is thirsty,
   give him water to drink.
            — PROVERBS 25:21 (NKJV)

"But you can't miss the service," Gen insisted. She wrapped a loaf of bread and tucked it in the small basket sitting on the kitchen table. "Nearly all the church members in the area are coming to celebrate your new beginning. They'll be so disappointed if they don't get to see you. It's bad enough that Amos hasn't arrived yet with the new hymnals. You can't deprive them of the chance to meet the new — and improved — Reverend Simon Dane. It will be a Sabbath to remember." Gen smiled convincingly. "Please, Simon. You must go. As soon as Amos arrives with the new hymnals, we'll all come down to Hazelwood and join you. I hate missing the service, but at least this way everyone can congratulate you on the success of the new mission station." She went on. "There's so much to be grateful for, Simon. Just think! You've barely begun and already there's a need for a school." She wheedled, "It's only one night. We're surrounded by friendly Indians, and you said yourself that Amos is one of the most reliable young men you know. He'll be here. Or he'll send word of what's happened. We'll tuck a few of the new hymnals behind the pulpit up at the new church, and then we'll ride directly to Hazelwood and join you all."

While her argument was reasonable, Gen hid the real reason for her wanting to stay behind while Simon attended the Sabbath celebration at the Hazelwood Mission church. When Amos Hendricks had left the group of travelers at the Lower Agency, he had said he was taking a detour, hoping to convince Daniel Two Stars to come up and help build the new school near Cloudman's village. Gen couldn't quite say why, but she much preferred a reunion with Daniel *minus* Simon.

Simon reached for the lunch basket. "All right," he relented. "I suppose you're right. The Riggses have gone to a great deal of trouble to arrange this celebration. And it *is* only one night." He headed outside to hitch up Rory. "But you must promise me that you will come along in the morning, whether Amos arrives or not."

"Of course," Miss Jane said briskly. When Simon had gone outside, she looked at Gen, shaking her head. "*Men.* Why do they have to be so stubborn? As if hundreds of women haven't been left alone on the frontier for weeks at a time while their husbands went off to the gold fields or wherever else. You'd think we were helpless ninnies."

As soon as Simon had left, Miss Jane organized an expedition for herself and Meg and Aaron. "We're going to see if we can find any late chokecherries. If not, there should be elderberries." She didn't invite Gen. "We'll be back in plenty of time to help with supper for Mr. Hendricks . . . and Two Stars. You don't mind entertaining the gentlemen alone for a few minutes, do you Gen?" Miss Jane winked.

It was a perfect plan. Except for one thing. Even as Miss Jane was convincing Simon to leave the women and his children behind to meet Amos and Two Stars, Amos Hendricks was driving up to Two Stars's farm, puzzling over the deserted house. As Simon drove off to keep his appointment with the believers at Hazelwood

Mission, Amos was discovering Robert Lawrence's empty barn and deserted home. And by nightfall, when Gen and Miss Jane sat listening for the approach of a wagon, Amos Hendricks lay dead on the road to the Lower Agency, his crate of new hymnals lying next to him on the ground, his wagon taken by one of the many war parties fanning out from the Lower Agency in all directions, killing every white person they met.

Miss Jane felt a hand on her shoulder. She grabbed the intruder's wrist.

"Shh — be still. I am a friend."

Her heart pounding, Miss Jane lay still in the dark. The intruder was so close she could feel his breath on her cheek as he spoke. "Big trouble coming. Tomorrow warriors kill all whites. Go, now, before too late. Tell no one I warned you or I, too, will die."

A shadowy figure climbed out the bedroom window. Miss Jane jumped up and looked out just in time to see a flash of white as the Indian jumped on his horse and fled. The distinctive mark on the horse's rump let Miss Jane know who had warned her. She had better believe the warning. She went to the room where Gen lay sleeping, Meg curled up next to her.

Miss Jane woke up Gen and, putting her finger to her lips, motioned for her to follow. In the kitchen, with the lamp turned low, the women talked.

"We can't wait for Amos now. We must get back to the mission. Dr. Riggs will know what to do. We should all be together."

Gen agreed and woke Meg and Aaron. They dressed quickly, threw two loaves of bread and a crock of butter in a sack, hitched up the horse, and were on the road before dawn.

"What about Father?" Meg worried aloud as the new little church at Cloudman's village disappeared from sight.

"He'll be waiting for us at Hazelwood Mission." Gen put her arm around Meg. "Don't worry. We'll all be together soon. It isn't far."

Gen scanned the fields and valleys along the road suspiciously. If only she felt as confident as she sounded.

*Over the earth I come*
*Over the earth I come*
*A soldier I come*
*Over the earth I am a ghost*

312

The singing drifted up the hill. Gen and Miss Jane heard it before they saw the war party. Miss Jane looked at Gen, frowning. At that moment the singing stopped, loud whoops rang out, and several mounted warriors tore up the hill behind them. Aaron and Meg, who had settled in the wagon bed, scampered up behind the seat and hunkered down in a corner, clutching one another, terrified.

As one brave grabbed the team's bridles and pulled them to a halt, another rode up and snatched Gen's hat off. Putting it on, he marched his horse around the wagon, singing at the top of his lungs. A third rushed up, gun in hand, brandishing a tomahawk.

Miss Jane stood up. She towered over the Indians on horseback. "What do you think you are doing? I know you, Otter!"

The tomahawk poised in midair, Otter blinked with surprise.

"You were my student at Hazelwood. What is this nonsense all about?"

Gen stood up beside her. "You are Two Stars's friend," she said quickly. "You brought him to us at Renville. We cared for him. Why are you trying to frighten us?"

The war party grew quiet, milling around uncertainly. Gen reached behind

313

her and tugged on Aaron's hair. "Come up here with me," she said under her breath. "Be brave and move quickly."

Aaron and Meg scrambled over the wagon seat.

One of the braves moved closer, leering at Meg. "I have not won a red scalp yet today," he said.

Gen hid her trembling hands by moving Meg in front of her and putting her hands on the little girl's shoulders. "And you think to win eagle feathers by killing a defenseless child?" Her blue eyes flashed with what she hoped the braves would interpret as anger and bravery. *Oh God . . . help us!*

"She helped your friend Two Stars," Miss Jane reminded Otter again. "These are the children of the woman who saved him. Will you repay the woman Two Stars called Mother-one by killing us? *You* are the ones who will be killed if you do this cowardly thing!"

A scarecrow-thin brave shouted back, "If we are killed, that will be all right. The whites are trying to starve us to death to get rid of us. Better to be shot and to die as becomes a Sioux rather than be starved to death."

"If you are starving," Miss Jane said quickly, "let us feed you. Take us back to the house. We have food there."

Gen spoke up. "We will both cook for you. But do not treat your friends this way."

Miss Jane looked at Otter again. "You know me, Otter. Have I ever been unkind to you? I have done all I can to help you. To help your people. Is this how you repay us?"

Gen noticed that Miss Jane's hands were beginning to tremble. She grabbed the reins out of her hands and sat down. "If we are going," she said abruptly, "then let us go. The sun is getting hot. Your horses will be wanting water." She nodded towards Aaron and Meg. "They can draw from the well at the cabin while we cook for you."

The mention of food seemed to be having its effect. One of the quieter braves rubbed his stomach. He leaned over and whispered something in Otter's ear. Otter nodded. "We will go. If we like what you feed us, we will not kill you. You can stay with us and cook for us while we fight." Brandishing his tomahawk again, Otter grabbed the team's harness and turned them back in the direction of the cabin.

With whoops and cries, the war party urged the team forward. Meg and Aaron tumbled into the back of the wagon, clinging to the sides of the wagon box, terrified, as Gen drove the team in a mad charge alongside the war party. Miss Jane clung to the seat, her face a mask of grim determination.

At dawn the next morning the war party ransacked the little house, piling food, bedding, and anything else they thought valuable into the back of the wagon. Otter hoisted Gen's little trunk onto his shoulder and took it outside. When she saw him aim a rifle at the brass lock, she ran up to him, pulling her mother's necklace from beneath her collar, begging, "Don't break it. Please. Here." She handed him the key.

Otter grabbed it, but not before he had noticed Gen's other necklace. He reached out and grabbed the cross dangling between two bright blue beads. Turning it over, he smiled enough to reveal a row of half-rotten teeth. "And I thought Two Stars left Fort LaCroix because of the white man's God." He lifted Gen's chin and ran his dirty finger along her jawline. "When I saw him last he was at the Lower Agency with us. He was painted for war." He leaned over and whispered in Gen's ear, "And he didn't seem to be thinking so much about God then, either."

Gen jerked her chin away.

Otter opened the little trunk, disappointed to find it held nothing more than a Dakota woman's wedding garments, one of them half-destroyed by some animal. He tossed the key into the trunk and, slamming the lid shut, hoisted it into the wagon. Handing his pony's reins to Aaron, Otter directed the boy to sit in the back of the wagon. "Don't let my pony go, or I will have to shoot you." Climbing onto the wagon seat, he picked up the reins and lashed the horses forward. With whoops and yells, the war party chased up the trail towards Rice Creek.

They headed south, stopping at other homesteads, gleaning whatever might have been left by other marauding parties and piling food and goods into the wagon until, by the time they reached the Upper Agency, Miss Jane and Meg were crammed into a small space right behind the wagon seat, barely able to move. Otter had demanded that Gen ride next to him on the wagon seat. Aaron still crouched in the back, hanging onto Otter's pony for all he was worth.

Gen's first sight of the Upper Agency made her clutch Meg to her and hide her face against her skirt. "Stay close, baby," she said grimly. "Don't look." She called to Aaron, "Close your eyes." He obeyed, leaning his head against a pile of quilts and clothing next to him.

They drove past Mrs. Wakefield's beautiful home. The door was open, the windows up, Mrs. Wakefield's lace panels dangling in the wind. Gen wondered what had happened to the easily frightened doctor's wife and her Dakota servant girl.

That night Gen and Miss Jane formulated a survival plan. "Otter seems to have some idea of repaying us for taking care of Two Stars. We must use it at every opportunity," Miss Jane said. She added, "Your wearing that necklace may prove to be our salvation."

Gen nodded agreement. "I'll be the best squaw Otter has ever known, if it will keep those two safe." She motioned to where Aaron and Meg lay, seemingly asleep.

Miss Jane hugged her. "As will I. We must give them no reason to be displeased with us. No complaining, no asking to go home."

"Are we going to die?" Aaron whispered.

Gen shook her head. "If they planned to kill us, we would be dead." She patted the boy's thin shoulders.

Meg woke, rubbing her eyes and begging, "Can't we go home now?" She began to cry. "I want to go home. These men aren't nice."

Miss Jane pulled Meg into her lap. "Don't cry, baby. We must be good. We must be quiet, and cook for Otter, and carry wood, and do whatever we can to show them we all can be helpful. If we are useful, they will keep us." Miss Jane didn't say what she was thinking. *If we prove useful, perhaps they will keep us alive.*

# Twenty-four

Bless those who persecute you;
    bless and do not curse.
          — ROMANS 12:14 (NKJV)

"I must start back. Something has happened or they would have been here long ago." Looking decidedly undignified, the Reverend Simon Dane was pacing back and forth on the front porch of the main house at Hazelwood Mission, his thin hair falling in his face, his collar unbuttoned. "Gen promised me they would start for the mission this morning — with or without Hendricks. They should have been here hours ago."

Dr. Riggs tried to reassure him. "Perhaps Amos arrived so late they decided to wait and start tomorrow morning."

"But if the rumors are true and there has been trouble to the south —" Simon ran his hands over his hair, unsuccessfully trying to smooth it back.

"If there had been trouble, we would know it. Our friends would warn us." Dr.

Riggs put his hand on Simon's shoulder. "I understand you are worried, Simon. But God watches when we cannot. And it does no good to pace back and forth on the front porch. Come in and have some supper." When Simon still hesitated, Dr. Riggs promised, "If they have not arrived by the time we eat, I will come with you myself."

Dr. and Mrs. Riggs, Simon Dane, Eliza Huggins, and Isabelle Stanford had just bowed their heads over the evening meal when someone charged onto the porch. Before Mrs. Riggs could get up to open the door, the visitor burst into the room.

Daniel Two Stars, shirtless and painted for war, choked out, "The lower Indians have destroyed the agency. They are killing all the whites —" He stopped short, looking around the table. "Where is Blue Eyes?" He looked at Simon. "Your children?"

"At the new mission near Cloudman's village," Simon choked out. "Surely — surely trouble can't have spread that far. Not in only one day."

Dr. Riggs got up and headed for the door. "There is probably no need for alarm, but we should ride out and check on them."

Two more Dakota rode into the yard. Looking through the window, Dr. Riggs said, "That's John Otherday and Little Paul. They'll know what's happening." The entire group followed Dr. Riggs out onto the porch.

"I have been at councils all day," John said. "The white men at the Lower Agency have been killed. The women and children are captives of Little Crow. Soldiers coming from Fort Ridgely were trapped at the Redwood Ferry near the Lower Agency and killed. The trouble will come here. You must leave."

"I'm not going anywhere without my children!" Simon half-shouted. He pleaded with Daniel. "We must find them!"

Otherday put his hand on Simon's sleeve. "You cannot go, my brother," he said. "When they see your white skin they will kill you." He pointed at Daniel. "He can walk among them. Let him go."

"I don't care what happens to me!" Simon shouted. "I can't let my children be —" He stopped abruptly and sank down on the steps. "I can't let anything happen to Geneviève! She's all I have!"

Little Paul spoke up. "Reverend Dane, you must listen to Otherday. There are Dakota friendlies walking among the warriors, but they cannot risk showing their friendship by traveling with a white man." He nodded at Daniel. "Two Stars can go. You must stay. You cannot help your children by being stupid."

Daniel crouched down in front of Simon. Looking up at him, he said quietly, "I will not rest until I have found your children. I swear it." He added, "Pray for me," and was gone before Simon could reply.

More Dakota began arriving, slipping into the boarding school, leaving with their children.

A government teacher from a village nearby came walking in. "A group of warriors stopped me and took my horses and wagon." He wiped his forehead with a trembling hand. "I can't figure why they didn't kill me."

A dozen Dakota neighbors rode up armed with rifles and farm tools. "We will guard you while you pack, but you must go now, Dr. Riggs." They gathered on the porch. Someone led in prayer. They sang a favorite hymn, "God Is the Refuge of His Saints."

With tears in her eyes, Mary Riggs gathered a few provisions and prepared to abandon the work of a lifetime.

John Otherday departed for the deserted

Upper Agency where he would spend the night guarding sixty-two white refugees collected from the area inside one of the brick buildings.

Near midnight, Little Paul said, "We must change our citizen's clothing and dress like Indians, or none of us will be safe." He pleaded with Dr. Riggs. "Please. The warriors will kill us to get possession of your women. They want captives. You must go."

The Riggs family, along with Simon, Lizzie, Belle, and several other mission workers, trudged to the Minnesota River where they waded halfway across to an island and formed a makeshift camp.

After questioning some of his Dakota friends, Dr. Riggs shook his head. "I can hardly believe it. Surely it cannot continue." He looked at Simon kindly. "The chiefs will get hold of the warriors and reason with them. It cannot be as bad as we think. They'll never allow a repeat of what's happened at the Lower Agency. When daylight comes, I will go to the Upper Agency and check things out." He smiled. "Why, in the morning Two Stars will probably appear with Miss LaCroix and Miss Jane and your children in tow, and we'll all go home, laughing about our night on the island."

"Do you really believe that?" Simon asked.

Dr. Riggs smiled and did not answer.

In the morning Dr. Riggs shook Simon awake. "Please keep everyone here while I make my way to the agency to see what is happening."

During an agonizing wait, the family huddled together, exhausted, frightened, confused. Simon led them in prayer, but even to him the words he spoke sounded hollow. Reverend Riggs returned, describing chaos at the agency. The Dakota had been so absorbed in looting agency buildings that they didn't take notice when John Otherday and his charges filed away towards the river crossing a mile north. Dr. Riggs took a deep breath. "We must pray for their safety, and, I think, we must leave as soon as possible. Andrew Hunter, the boy who worked for Dr. Wakefield, and some young folks have come away from the agency with two teams. They have a few provisions and the doctor's cattle with them. If we wade the rest of the way across the river, Andrew said he will drive one of his wagons up to meet us."

The little party of refugees grabbed up their pathetic bundles and waded across the river. As they emerged from a ravine,

Andrew Hunter appeared on the prairie ahead of them driving a wagon.

"We need another wagon," Dr. Riggs said, frowning. "The women and children cannot travel quickly enough on foot."

Simon stepped forward. "I'll do it." Without waiting for a reply, he plunged back through the tall grass towards the river, slid down a bluff, waded across, and climbed up the other side, his heart pounding. It seemed that a warrior lurked behind every bush and tree. But the landscape was quiet and he arrived at the deserted mission, panting. Just as he came around the corner of the school, a lone Indian came out of the stable leading Rory.

Gulping, Simon charged up. "Hold on there," he shouted rudely. "That's my horse and I need him!"

The Indian looked startled.

Simon noticed with great relief that the Indian was unarmed. Drawing himself as tall as possible, he repeated loudly, "He's my horse, and I mean to have him back." Simon jerked the reins out of the Indian's hand, expecting to be attacked, wondering if he could bring himself to punch a man in the face. The Indian just looked at him, dumbfounded. Finally he shrugged, backed away, and headed toward the sawmill muttering to himself about the crazy white man.

Shaking all over, Simon managed to hitch Rory to a light wagon and drive the rig back across the river, his cheeks red with the excitement of what he had done. He felt heroic. He liked the feeling. Piling the new wagon full of children, the group of refugees trudged east all day, staying as far north of the river as possible, watching smoke rise from various locations across the river, listening to distant gunfire, amazed that no one had discovered their flight and come to stop them.

Moving. Always moving. Groups of captives were dragged from camp to camp and left for days at a time while war parties combed the landscape, raiding individual homesteads, bringing back plunder and new captives, celebrating victories with dances and feasts. Every night, Gen and Miss Jane and the children stayed in a different tepee or house, lying awake listening to drumbeats and war cries. For hours at a time they clung to one another, listening to muffled screams as other women were visited by their captors and forced to submit to unwanted attentions.

One night they were herded upstairs to

sleep on the second level of a looted house. Forbidden to light a lamp, sweltering in the intense August heat, nauseated by the smells of unwashed bodies, Gen sought comfort in trying to learn something about the silent group she knew shared the darkness.

"I am Geneviève LaCroix from Cloudman's village," Gen said. "I have with me Miss Jane Williams of Hazelwood Mission and the children of one of the missionaries. Who else is here?"

Women's voices called out until Gen guessed she was in the company of nearly twenty others.

"What's to happen to us?" one cried softly.

Another woman with a thick German accent spoke up, lamenting the loss of her feather beds.

"But your family," Miss Jane asked. "Is your family all right?"

"*Ach,*" the woman replied. "Dead. They killed *mein mann.*" And then she went back to lamenting the five feather beds.

Another jabbered loudly, ending her senseless speech with the eerie crooning of "home, home, home." Gen stumbled towards the voice, intending to comfort the woman, but at Gen's touch she shrieked even louder, flailing the air with her arms and backing away. Gen called for Miss Jane and stumbled back towards the sound of her voice, crying softly. "Poor thing. Her mind is gone."

Meg clutched Gen's skirt tightly. "Don't you go away again. Don't." Gen reassured her, and they waited out the night while braves charged past the house, whooping and firing guns.

In the morning, Otter came for them. He had emptied their wagon and invited them for a ride, seeming to take pride in displaying his personal captives to everyone they passed.

"I am taking you to Little Crow's," Otter said bluntly. "We will attack and take the town of New Ulm soon. Then Fort Ridgely. When we have destroyed the fort, the Dakota will rule the entire river valley."

But the warriors failed to overrun the city of New Ulm. Otter came back, surly and half drunk. He slapped Gen across the face when she didn't move quickly enough to please him. Meg began to cry. Miss Jane grabbed the girl and smothered her sobs against her, trying her best to mollify Otter. "She is only tired, Otter. But you must be tired too. Here —" Miss Jane motioned to a pile of comforters. "Rest while we get you some stew." She moved towards the door, dragging Meg and Aaron outside with her.

Otter flopped down where Miss Jane had pointed and waited, leering at Gen. When she moved towards the door he motioned. "Come here, half-breed." Gen stood still, her heart pounding.

Just when Otter started to get up, a disturbance outside distracted him. He shook his fist in her face as he headed outside.

Meg came back inside with Miss Jane and Aaron. Gen held out her arms and Meg ran to her. Aaron stared at Gen's bruised face for a moment. He made a fist and pounded it into his open palm. "I'm going to kill him if he touches you again," he muttered.

"No, Aaron," Gen insisted. "As long as we are with Otter, we must try to appear that we are pleased. We must make him think that we have confidence in him. He will learn to love us if we treat him well. Our way of living until we are rescued is to serve Otter. Never give him a cross look. If he tells you about something terrible he has done, you must laugh and say, 'I wish I was a man, I would help you.' "

Aaron looked horrified. "You want me to *lie?*"

"I want you to *live*," Gen said abruptly. She looked at Miss Jane, pleading.

"We will pray that you do not have to lie, Aaron," Miss Jane said. She pursed her lips together and inhaled sharply before continuing. "But these are terrible times for us, and I think God would understand if we — pretend — so that Meg is kept as safe — and as innocent — as possible." Miss Jane looked meaningfully at Aaron. "Do you understand what I am saying, Aaron?"

The boy nodded reluctantly.

Life took on a surreal monotony. Goods taken from the homesteads all across the countryside were brought in by the wagonload and piled up beside tepees and houses in every village. Terrified women and children were added to the group of captives almost daily until an entire village of whites appeared among the Dakota. Because of the plunder no one lacked food. Women captives were kept busy feeding their Dakota masters, mending clothing, harvesting deserted homestead gardens, working from dawn until sundown.

Miss Jane and Gen, Meg and Aaron did their best to convince Otter they were worth keeping alive. To prove their admiration for their captors, they begged for moccasins and braided their hair. Gen dried meat and made jerky for Otter to carry in the sash around his waist when he went into battle. Miss Jane and Meg braided ribbons for the horses' manes and tails. Aaron brushed Otter's horse until he shone, and then painted big, colored splotches on his sides, preparing him for battle. Their efforts were rewarded. Otter was pleased. He stopped threatening to harm them, even smiling at Aaron and Meg.

Aaron looked at Gen when Otter rode away on his war horse. "Every time I painted a spot I prayed God would make it a good target for a soldier's bullet."

Fort Ridgely was attacked. The soldiers kept Little Crow and his four hundred warriors at bay with less than a hundred men. When it was over Otter muttered, "If the Dakota had just a few of those big guns like they have at the fort, they could rule the nation."

When a second attempt to take Fort Ridgely failed, the Dakota turned their attentions back to New Ulm. During the second battle, rumors flew among those left behind. One of the squaws ran to tell Gen and the others to pack up. "If they lose the battle, they will come back and kill you as revenge on the white men." She smiled wickedly. "But don't worry about the children. We will keep them. The Great Father will pay much money for them."

When the old hag departed, Aaron grabbed up a knife. His eyes glowing with hatred, he said to Gen, "If they hurt you I'll kill Meg first and then myself. I will! I swear it!" He began to cry. When Gen tried to comfort him, he pushed her away. "Stop it! I'm not a baby!" He pushed the tepee flap aside and went outside. It was raining, but he paid no attention to the rain, climbing up in a tree and looking off into the distance.

# Twenty-five

Do not fear therefore; you are of more value than many sparrows.
— LUKE 12:7 (NKJV)

While Otter kept Gen and Simon Dane's children in Little Crow's camp, Simon and the forty-odd refugees from Hazelwood Mission were thirty miles north, stumbling across the prairie towards the presumed safety of Fort Ridgely. To reach the fort, they would have to walk thirty miles to the southeast, in a line parallel to the Dakota villages dotting the opposite bank of the river. Even if they managed to get past the Lower Agency safely, they would still have another dozen miles to travel before reaching the fort.

No one in the group knew the territory off the reservation. The wagons bogged down over and over again in sloughs hidden in the tall prairie grass. Staying out of sight of the river, they used surveyor's stakes as a guide. No one dared start a fire at night for fear of attracting attention from across the river. When darkness crept over the landscape, the refugees huddled together and waited for daylight, too afraid to sleep even with lookouts posted.

On the second day it began to rain. The wagons had to be unloaded and pried loose from the mud time and time again. Having run out of cooked food, the group nibbled on raw grain and stale bread until one day they came to an abandoned homestead where ripe tomatoes weighed down a row of vines in a weedy garden plot. They feasted on tomatoes and dug up potatoes with their bare hands, crying with joy over the find.

Of the forty refugees, only a dozen were men capable of making any kind of defense. No one mentioned their pathetic arsenal of ancient rifles and one pistol until the second morning. They had just floundered across Sacred Heart Creek and were nearly opposite Red Middle Voice's camp, halfway to the Lower Agency, when Jonas Wright caught up with Dr. Riggs.

"Could you hit anything with that?" he asked, nodding at the rifle Dr. Riggs carried more as a walking stick than as a weapon.

Dr. Riggs raised the rifle and looked

down the barrel. He shook his head. "I don't think I could bring myself to even pull the trigger."

"You may have to," the man said, nodding toward the horizon where two Dakota had just appeared on horseback.

Everyone seemed to see the Indians at once. With frightened whispers, the women and children scrambled atop the two wagons while the men formed a ragged wall of defense around them.

"Don't stop," Dr. Riggs said quietly to the group. "We must continue on and appear to be unconcerned." He glanced at Simon, who held one of the teams. "Press on," he said firmly, and muttering under his breath so that only Simon could hear, he added, "and pray."

After a tense few moments, the Dakota disappeared from sight and were never seen again.

A day later the refugees were still miles from the fort when the thunder of artillery boomed across the landscape. The men exchanged concerned glances. Were the Dakota attacking Fort Ridgely? What if it had fallen? Were the two Dakota they had seen earlier reconnoitering from the fort, or did they leave to join their friends in making an attack?

Simon dropped back from his place at Rory's head and walked beside Dr. Riggs. "Can the fort put up a strong defense against a war party?" he asked. "If the northern villages have joined the warriors, wouldn't they be able to mount hundreds?"

Dr. Riggs nodded. "Yes. And the last time I was through Fort Ridgely, the quartermaster told me they had been reduced to less than a hundred men."

Simon frowned. "Could a hundred men defend the fort if all the chiefs unite against them?"

Dr. Riggs looked around him. "We'll give them twelve more men to fight."

"— and three dozen more mouths to feed," Simon said under his breath.

"Troops will be coming from Fort Snelling," Dr. Riggs replied. "The fort is still our best hope."

As darkness came on and the sounds of battle waned, they began to hope that perhaps the fort was safe and would take them in. But then they topped a rise and saw the light from what could only be smoldering buildings. Rockets flashed in the night sky.

"Distress signals," Simon whispered to himself.

Bolstered by his success at retrieving

Rory and the much needed wagon, Simon volunteered to approach the fort under cover of darkness. It seemed like hours before he managed to creep near. When one of the pickets fired at him, he waved his handkerchief, thankful that the rain had stopped, praying the white handkerchief could be seen in the moonlight.

He stumbled ahead and finally came face-to-face with a surly officer who shook his head at the prospect of taking in more refugees. "The hospital is full, we've over two hundred already packed into the barracks. I don't know where we'll put you." He spat tobacco juice and scratched his nose. "But if you can't go on, then I suppose you must come in. Your chances of getting here without running into a bunch of marauders are slim. And I can't spare a man to come after you. We're stretched to the limit, and until reinforcements come" — he lowered his voice — "*unless* reinforcements come soon, we'll likely be overrun." He turned to go. "I'll inform the watch not to shoot." He strode away, leaving Simon standing alone in front of the officers' quarters.

Simon stared after the officer, realizing he had just been told that they would all likely be dead in the next twenty-four hours. He looked around him. He knew deep ravines ran along three sides of the table, providing easy cover for attacking the Indians. Most of the log outbuildings had been set afire, although the rain had prevented a total conflagration. The officer had said that ammunition was in short supply. How were they feeding the refugees they already had? Simon turned away and, skirting along the back of the guardhouse, made for the hills where the refugees waited.

"If you aren't going in, you're fools," one of the men half-shouted when Simon expressed his doubts about the fort. "I've come this far with you, but I won't go another step."

"You can't leave. You'll give us away," Dr. Riggs said. "God only knows why we haven't been discovered already."

"Well, I'm going," the man said. Three of his friends joined him.

Simon grabbed an old pistol from one of the wagons and, cocking the revolver, said steadily, "I am a man of God, and I do not want to do this, but if you take one step away from this group, I will shoot you dead." He stared at the four men unwaveringly. "You cannot abandon these women and children who depend on your protection. We are only twelve men. We must stay together until morning. When we are farther away from danger, you can do what you want. But we need every able-bodied man here to help get us across the stream ahead and up on the prairie beyond."

Dr. Riggs looked on, dumbfounded. Simon kept the pistol pointed at the men. Finally, one of them cleared his throat. "What's a few more hours, Jacob?" he said to his companion. "Let's see them across the stream."

The tension in the air melted as the four men began to help move the wagons out. Somewhere in the distance dogs barked. An eerily human cry was heard. Everyone held their breath, expecting an attack to materialize. But the travelers moved on, unaware that all around them Dakota were watching — Dakota who had, for some reason, decided to let their old missionaries and their friends pass by.

Sunrise found the group trudging past the beleaguered Fort Ridgely, headed for the little village of St. Peter, another thirty miles east. The four rebels left the party as agreed. Simon watched them disappear into a little wood a mile away. And then they heard gunfire. Everyone exchanged glances and trudged on, coming at last to the road that led to St. Peter. In the distance to the south they could see smoke rising from burning houses. They passed a dead body bloating in the afternoon sun. After a brief argument, they agreed to stop and bury the man. Simon and two others covered their noses with kerchiefs and dug a grave after gingerly searching through pockets in a vain attempt to identify the dead man.

In the middle of the afternoon they passed another deserted house, dishes set on the table for a meal, clothes hanging on a line between the house and the well. Simon found himself praying for the owner of the dishes, wondering if she was in Gen's company, if she had children, if right at that moment she was suffering from hunger. The cellar yielded cream and butter. Corn and potatoes grew in the garden. The refugees ate, more tears of thankfulness streaming down their faces.

For the first time in his life Simon neglected to keep the Sabbath rest. With a prayer for God's forgiveness of their sin, the party agreed to keep going. They finally entered St. Peter, where a hotel keeper recognized Dr. Riggs and caused quite a ruckus welcoming them into town.

"You've been reported dead, Dr. Riggs," he said, astonished, looking over the party. "All of you." He waved the group into his hotel, directing that they be provided free room and board for as long as they required it.

Simon met Dr. Riggs in the hotel dining room later that day. "You understand, of course, that I must go back," Simon said. He looked away, struggling to keep back tears. "I'll attach myself as chaplain if whoever is in charge will have me."

"Two Stars will do what he can," Dr. Riggs said quietly. "You must not lose heart, Simon."

Simon cleared his throat. "I am grateful to you, Dr. Riggs, for all you have done. Your patience over the years when I was little more than a prideful fool — your unwavering example."

Mr. Shaw of the hotel brought a telegram to Dr. Riggs. As he read it, his blue eyes filled with tears. He handed it to Simon. "When all is lost, God gives us tender mercies. Read it, Simon. See how much we are loved by our co-laborers — even when they think we are dead."

Simon read, "Get the bodies at any cost." *Yes*, he thought, *I know exactly how they feel.*

Daniel Two Stars slid off his horse and sat beside the stream, looking at his reflection in the water. Rumors abounded about the missionaries from Cloudman's village. They had escaped over the river. They were all killed when they camped near Hawk Creek. They were with a group of captives near Chief Mankato's camp. They had fled north to Lac Qui Parle, where Standing Buffalo's people had taken them in. Rumors abounded, but none of them had proven true.

Thousands of warring Dakota were combing the countryside, murdering settlers, looting homesteads, skirmishing with small detachments of soldiers sent out from Fort Ridgely. They had taken hundreds of captives and were constantly moving from place to place. Daniel had promised himself and God that he would protect Meg and Aaron, Blue Eyes, and Miss Jane with his life, and he would do it. But he could not find them. He had been looking for nearly two weeks, and he could not find them.

He crouched low over the stream and stared down at his reflection, angry tears dripping off his chin and rippling the water.

Scooping up a handful of water, he doused his face before leaping back on his horse and heading north. One of the more recent rumors was that all eight Lower Agency villages were moving northward to camp together up near the deserted Hazelwood Mission. There were still Indians who favored peace in the midst of the warriors, and he had heard they were getting stronger. If they really did camp together, perhaps he could learn more.

He would keep looking. Someone must know what happened to them. If they did not remember Blue Eyes, surely they would remember Miss Jane. There were many half-breeds with blue eyes, many blond-headed children like Aaron. But it was not every day the Dakota saw a white child with hair as red as Meg's. And no one would forget a woman nearly six feet tall. If they were still alive someone, somewhere, must know what had happened.

*If you know when a sparrow falls, then you know where they are.* Daniel spread his arms wide and looked up at the sky, crying aloud, "If You know where they are, then why do You not take me to that place?!"

One of the rumors Daniel Two Stars heard was true. After failing to take either

Fort Ridgely or New Ulm, the warriors decided to move north and camp near the Hazelwood Mission. Little Crow knew soldiers were coming. In his heart he knew he commanded a defeated army. But he had promised to die with his warriors, and he would keep his promise. If they could convince Chief Standing Buffalo up near Lac Qui Parle to join the fight, defeat could be delayed. He might even journey farther to other bands and other tribes to raise support.

Gen would bear scars from the trek north for the rest of her life. At first Otter kept them off the road, driving them like cattle through the tallest and thickest brush, not allowing them to part the berry bushes, cruelly ordering them to tear through them. "Stay close, Meg," Gen whispered, grabbing the child's arms and wrapping them around her waist. Aaron followed suit behind Miss Jane, and together they trudged along while thorns tore at their skirts and scratched their bare feet and arms. The women tried to cover Meg's and Aaron's arms with their own, but their poor attempts at protection did little to help. By day's end, the children's arms were running with blood, and they were all close to tears from exhaustion.

A kind old woman called them into her tepee that night. When Otter protested, she badgered him into submission. Once inside the tepee, the old woman said, "I am Mother Friend. My son is a farmer Indian, and I will do what I can to help you. We are going north now. The peaceful Indians have come together and will try to make their own camp away from the war party. You will be well cared for. You will see." She produced new moccasins for Aaron and Meg, and helped wash and bind their scratches.

"That Otter is a bad man," the old woman said, shaking her head. "You are lucky you are not dead already."

The next morning they were allowed to stay with Mother Friend and the procession on the road. As far as Gen could see, coaches, ox carts, chaises, baker's carts, and peddler's wagons, laden with plunder, moved along the road. Braves rode by dressed in every imaginable bit of finery, much of it worn in odd ways — a white crepe shawl wound around a head, gold watches tied around an ankle. Native women dressed in silk ball gowns. Most unexpected of all, United States flags adorned many wagons and teams.

The noise was deafening. Children cried,

mules brayed, dogs yelped, and all the while warriors ran up and down alongside the procession, trying to keep order, singing "Hi, Hi!" over and over again.

Gen and the children trotted along beside the road through prairie grass, which was five feet high in places. More than once, Gen stepped on a snake.

When they stopped for lunch, Mother Friend found them. Noticing that Gen was limping, she demanded to be shown. Gen lifted her raw foot. The skin was nearly gone from a long patch along one side. Mother Friend found Otter and berated him, insisting that Gen and the children be allowed to ride atop one of the loaded wagons. Otter argued, brandishing his rifle. "If they cannot keep up, then I will shoot them."

Mother Friend shook her fist at him. "The soldiers are coming. What do you think they will do if they find this young girl and these two children dead on the side of the road? How many Dakota women and children will they kill as their revenge?!"

Otter considered, and then jerked Gen up beside him and deposited her atop a barrel in the back of a baker's wagon. "Go on," he shouted to Meg and Aaron. "See if

you can catch her!" He laughed uproari-
ously when Meg fell trying to climb into
the moving wagon. Miss Jane lifted Meg
up on the wagon and then helped Aaron
aboard. Otter prodded Miss Jane with his
war spear. "You walk," he said. "You are as
strong as a buffalo. No reason to tire out
the horses for you."

Reaching the Upper Agency meant a
steep climb. They had marched for hours
without so much as a drink of water. Miss
Jane straggled behind, her face running
with sweat. When she stumbled and fell,
Otter prodded her up. He laughed. "White
woman got a dirty face."

"You leave her alone!" Aaron shouted,
jumping down from the wagon. He lifted
Miss Jane's arm and put it on his shoulder.
"I'll help you, Miss Jane. We'll climb the
hill together."

Otter stared at Aaron. "You are a brave
little white boy, Aaron Dane. Be careful
that your bravery does not get you killed."
He rode away, whistling.

Passing through the abandoned Upper
Agency this time nearly broke their hearts.
Dr. Wakefield's fine house had been
burned to the ground. Broken dressers and
pitchers, mirrors and every imaginable
item lay around the yard. Miss Jane

pointed to several copies of *Peterson's Magazine* as they filed by.

Word was passed down the procession that Chief Red Iron from up north had stopped them, telling Little Crow that his Sioux must camp where they were told. Hundreds of Red Iron's warriors had refused to have anything to do with the war, and now Red Iron was determined to protect his people from any military retaliation.

Mother Friend insisted that Otter give her charge of his captives and let them camp with the growing peace party. Otter put on a show of reluctance, but at last he gave in and rode away.

"What's happening, Mother Friend?" Miss Jane wanted to know. She nodded towards the opposite side of the creek, where Otter had joined a group of warriors milling about while their women erected a separate village of tepees.

Mother Friend shrugged. "All Dakota do not agree with what has happened." She motioned for them to sit down.

Meg climbed into Miss Jane's lap, while Aaron leaned against a pile of quilts and stared into the fire, looking quickly over his shoulder every time a warrior broke out in song or fired his rifle. Gen sat cross-legged, listening intently.

When they were settled, Mother Friend leaned forward and spoke quietly, her eyes watching to guard against being overheard. "All Dakota do not agree, but we do not know what to do. Secret messengers have been sent to Colonel Sibley. He is bringing soldiers to end the fight. Messengers have told him he must hurry, that the friendly Indians are still here and we are doing what we can, but he must come soon." She grinned at them. "At first I did not know there were so many Dakota like me who wanted to help the whites. I did what I could, without speaking of it to others."

"Like making Otter let Gen ride in a wagon," Aaron said.

Mother Friend nodded. "When I saw there were many friendlies among us, I knew I could make Otter give you up." She waved around her at the village that was springing up on the prairie. "We are going to keep the captives we have and take care of them. Our leading men are going to try to convince the warriors in the other camp to give up the rest of the captives to us. The government will be pleased to see we have protected you." Mother Friend looked at them, hope glimmering in her eyes. "Perhaps they will even give us our farms back." She looked at Miss Jane. "Do you think so?"

Miss Jane nodded. "My government is fair. I am certain they will reward those of you who were kind and wanted no part of the bloodshed." Miss Jane reached out and patted the back of Mother Friend's aged hand. "I will speak for you. So will many others."

From across the creek came loud singing and more gunfire. Mother Friend sighed and shook her head. "The soldiers must hurry. We want to protect you, but we are only human." She stood up. "You must sleep now." She raised her hand, extending one finger to emphasize a warning. "Do not stand up inside the tepee. If the fire glows, if the bad Indians see you move . . ." She held up an imaginary rifle and pulled the trigger.

Gen sat by Mother Friend's campfire looking up at the moon. When Miss Jane came out of the tepee and sat next to her, she jumped.

"I couldn't sleep, either," Miss Jane said. She rubbed the back of her neck. "It's too hot."

Gen sighed. "How long has it been since they took us? I can't even remember."

"I'm not sure," Miss Jane replied. "A lifetime." She looked around her at the other tepees. "I never thought it would come to this. I never believed anything like this could happen."

Gen rested her forehead on one hand. She closed her eyes. "I just want it to be *over*," she whispered hoarsely. "I'm beginning to feel like that poor creature in the attic that night . . . the one who sat keening the word *home* over and over again." Tears began to slide down her cheeks. She reached up and touched the necklace around her neck. "Except that I don't even know where *home* is anymore."

Miss Jane put her scarred hand over Gen's. "We've made it this far. Aaron and Meg need us. We can't give up."

Gen wrapped her arms around her knees and wept, smothering the sounds of her sobs in her skirts lest she wake the children. After a few moments, she raised her head and wiped her face on her sleeve. "At first I was terrified they would kill us. I'm beginning to wish they had." She began to cry again. "I don't think I can be brave much longer . . . but I don't want Aaron and Meg to see me like this." After crying quietly for a while, she wiped her face again. "Tell me something. Where does

God fit in to all this?" She waved her hand around her. "How do you reconcile a loving God with violated women and tortured children? Is He asleep? Is He powerless? Doesn't He *care?* None of it makes sense."

"Dear Gen," Miss Jane said softly. "Don't blame God for man's sin. Men can always choose a better way." She took Gen's hand. "I don't understand about all of this, Gen. But I know that God sees and knows. I know He loves me. And somehow, He is going to work this out for my good."

"You sound just like Nina Whitney," Gen whispered. "When she said that it made me angry."

"Does it make you angry to hear *me* say it?" Miss Jane asked.

Gen shook her head. "No. It just makes me sad."

"Why?"

"Because I don't believe it. I want to. But I can't."

"Faith to believe comes from God, Gen," Miss Jane said.

"And why, then, doesn't God give me faith to believe what I wish I could believe?"

"Ask Him," Miss Jane urged. "Ask Him to show you Himself."

"And if I ask, will He answer all my questions?"

Miss Jane shook her head. "Probably not. He still hasn't answered all of mine. But that's where faith comes in. It helps you live in that space between what you understand . . . and what you don't."

Gen smiled sadly. "Ellen said exactly that to me once." She looked around her. "It looks like I'm in that space . . ." Her chin trembled. "But I don't have the faith." She looked at Miss Jane, her eyes filling with tears.

Miss Jane put her arms around Gen. "Dearest Lord in heaven," she whispered, "You see us here by the campfire outside Mother Friend's tepee. Thank You for Mother Friend. Thank You that Meg and Aaron are safe tonight, that they are sleeping, that they have come so far through dangerous places. Thank You that we have enough to eat. And thank You, dearest Father, for protecting us" — Miss Jane's voice wavered — "for protecting us as women." She stopped for a moment. "And now, Lord, I ask You to come to my friend Geneviève LaCroix, who knows the catechism in three languages . . . but who does not know You as her Friend, dear Father. Forgive me, Lord, for not knowing.

Forgive me for taking it for granted that Gen knows You. Help her tonight and tomorrow, Lord, to look around her and see evidence of Your love for her. Help her to know the meaning of that cross that Two Stars added to the beadwork around her neck. May she know Christ, and His redeeming love, and may the peace that passes understanding reign in her heart. Amen."

Gen cried on Miss Jane's shoulder for a long time before finally pushing away. "Thank you," she finally said. She got up and went back inside the tepee, leaving Miss Jane alone by the fire . . . to watch, and wait, and pray.

# Twenty-six

Indeed I Myself will search for My sheep and seek them out . . . and deliver them from all the places where they were scattered on a cloudy and dark day.

— EZEKIEL 34:11–12 (NKJV)

The morning after Miss Jane prayed that Gen would see God working, warrior Indians charged into the peaceful camp on horseback, yelling and firing guns. Peeking out of Mother Friend's tepee, Gen saw Otter newly adorned with an eagle headdress, freshly painted, and looking especially threatening.

The warriors demanded that the camps be united and all captives kept together. After what seemed like hours of haggling the warriors left, but not without threats that they would be back the next day with reinforcements to force compliance. Gen was filled with dread. Mother Friend had said the warrior Indians had threatened to kill all the captives. What if they gained advantage over the peaceful Sioux?

As soon as the mounted warriors left, runners went to nearby camps and houses, summoning help from northern farmer Indians. In a short while several hundred charged into camp, ready to fight. Armed with every conceivable weapon from rifles to pitchforks, they stood guard while a huge tepee was erected in the center of the camp. "We will have our own soldiers' lodge now," Mother Friend explained. "We will choose leaders for the Peace Party, and the warriors will have to listen to what we say."

In the confusion, two orphaned children standing outside a tepee across the way began to cry. Miss Jane exclaimed, "Dear Lord in heaven, that's Timothy and Rebecca Sutton! Their parents homesteaded just a few miles from here. They attended church at the mission!" Hurrying over to them, Miss Jane knelt down and wrapped her arms around them. Timothy, who Gen guessed could not have been three years old, grabbed Miss Jane's skirt. A Dakota woman charged up, arguing adamantly with Miss Jane, who gestured energetically for a few moments. Finally, Miss Jane hurried back to Gen. "It seems the

Dakota are vying for the right to say they protected white children. Fallen Moon won't let me bring them here. Will you be all right if I stay with them tonight?"

"But —" Gen protested. "I — we — we need you here!" She looked across the clearing to the forlorn twins. Finally she relented. "Of course you should go to them." She sounded more certain than she felt.

Miss Jane hugged her, whispering, "Trust *God,* Gen. He's always near." She hurried back to the two orphans, turning just long enough to blow a kiss in Meg's direction before disappearing inside a tepee.

Mother Friend led Gen and the children to an abandoned two-room cabin in a little clearing near the encampment.

"You stay here tonight. Tomorrow I will bring more whites to stay with you." When Gen mentioned Miss Jane and the twins, the old woman nodded. "I know them. Fallen Moon can be difficult. I will see what I can do." She smiled, revealing the space between her upper teeth. "We have decided we are not going to let Little Crow cause any more trouble for us. We have our own soldiers' lodge now, and we will keep you safe until they come. Rest." She grinned. "Tonight, no one can see you inside my tepee to shoot you."

Mother Friend helped them get settled inside the cabin. That evening the old woman fed them until Gen thought Meg and Aaron would burst. She patted Meg's red hair and gave Aaron a pocketknife and a compass.

"Whose do you suppose they really were?" Aaron said bitterly after Mother Friend left.

"Some little boy who is very glad to share them with such a brave young man as you," Gen said.

Hours after Mother Friend tried to reassure them, Gen lay staring up at the cabin ceiling, listening. Meg was sleeping soundly, emitting a softly whistling snore with every breath. Aaron lay beside her, muttering in his sleep. Gen tried to pray, wondering what horrors haunted the youngster's dreams. Tears slipped from the corners of her eyes, wetting the hair at her temples.

She had nearly dozed off when the sound of singing made her turn her head towards the window. Someone was drunk again, apparently stumbling toward the cabin, his voice becoming louder as he approached. When she recognized the voice, her body stiffened with fear. She made a fist with each hand, grasping the sides of her skirt.

Otter didn't knock. He flung the door of the cabin open and stood in the doorway. Moonlight spilled onto his shoulders, and from the bed Gen could see him stagger and then lean heavily against the door frame. He was wearing his eagle feathers, and as he raised one hand to steady himself, moonlight glinted off the blade of a huge knife clutched in one fist.

"Where is Blue Eyes?" he called out softly.

Otter was rarely loud and boisterous when he drank. Unlike the others in his lodge, as he grew more and more drunk, he grew quiet. Quiet and deadly. Gen tried to calm herself with the thought that at least he wouldn't wake the children with some wild, drunken display. Perhaps, if she didn't answer he would leave.

Meg snuffled softly in her sleep. When Gen turned to look at her, Aaron curled one arm protectively across his sister's sleeping form.

"Oh, Blue Eyes," Otter sang softly, "you must come to me. I have missed you today. You will be my wife before the dawn . . ." He paused momentarily before adding,

". . . or you will die." He headed towards the bedroom.

Gen leaped out of bed and hurried into the main room.

At sight of her, Otter smiled. His heavy eyelids were half closed, and he tilted his head back to look at her. His upper lip curled back to reveal the blackened space where two rotten teeth had been pulled out.

Gen raised her finger to her lips and hissed, "Don't wake the children!" She backed away from him, her hands behind her, desperately groping for the iron poker she had seen hanging beside the fireplace.

Otter laughed quietly. "I have no use for children. I have come for a wife." He stepped towards her. "And tonight, I think, I will have one." He reached out and grabbed her by the wrist, pulling her close.

She fought against the nausea that overwhelmed her at the stench of his unwashed body and the liquor he had consumed. Turning her head away from him, she struggled silently, gasping for air.

He pulled her closer and pressed the cool blade of his knife against the base of her neck. "If you make a sound, I will go in that other room and kill those two children." He inhaled sharply, twisting her arm behind her back. "And then I will come back to you. You cannot escape me."

Aaron called out from the other room. "Gen?"

"It's all right." She forced her voice to be calm. "I'm just out here. Don't wake your sister. Go back to sleep. If we move camp tomorrow, it will be another big day for us. You need to rest." She turned toward Otter and whispered, "Take me outside. Please. I won't fight if you just let the children sleep."

Otter hesitated. Then, miraculously, he agreed. "All right. Outside then. In the moonlight." He moved towards the door, dragging Gen with him.

All around them tepees glowed like lanterns, the cooking fires inside them burning low. Otter dragged Gen across the open space between the cabin and a small stand of trees, ensuring her cooperation with the tip of the knife.

The moon disappeared behind a cloud, and Otter stumbled. In an instant, Gen pulled away from him, lifted her skirts, and dashed across the compound towards the soldiers' lodge and the huge fire where earlier in the night the men had danced.

The fire had died down, and she leaped over the coals, praying that in his drunken state Otter would be unable to follow. He stumbled through the coals and let out a screech of pain just as another brave leaped out of the darkness and grabbed Gen.

The new tormentor wrapped his arm around her waist like a vise, refusing to let go. She wriggled and squirmed, clawing at his face and neck. He ducked away and pinned her arms to her sides. Wrapping one arm around her, he hoisted her onto his hip like a sack of potatoes. She quickly realized she was helpless, and stopped fighting. As Otter stumbled around the fire, swearing, her captor set Gen down.

She realized who it was. She wanted to cry with relief as he placed himself between her and Otter. "I have come a long way to find this woman and her children. Why do you treat her this way?" He added convincingly, "I want this woman. I want the children."

Scorching his moccasins had sobered Otter. He stood upright, brandishing his knife. "If she is to be your wife, then make it so. Otherwise, I claim her." He added, "I don't care about the children. You can have them."

Daniel pulled Gen to his side, holding her fiercely. She clung to him, stumbling along beside him as he began to walk towards the cabin. Otter limped after them, finally sitting down on a stump a few feet from the cabin and watching as Daniel pulled Gen inside.

Gen collapsed against him just inside the door. He held her close, not saying anything for a long while. Finally, he whispered, "I thought I would never find you."

"We waited for Amos Hendricks at the cottage. They said you were coming to help build the new church. I —" She gasped for breath and lay her two open palms against his chest. "I wanted to see you. Without — without Simon — there." Her voice trailed off. "Someone came in the middle of the night. They warned Miss Jane and we left right away — and then —"

Daniel placed his hand over her mouth. "— And then you were taken. And I have been looking for you ever since." He held her close. "Is Miss Jane all right? Where are the children?"

"Meg and Aaron are asleep in there." She nodded towards the bedroom. "Miss Jane went with two other orphaned children last night. We were hoping she could move here tomorrow —" She stopped abruptly. "Simon?"

Daniel shook his head. "I don't know. I went to the mission to warn them. John Otherday and many others were trying to convince them to get away. I don't know what happened." He looked at her, touching her cheek. "I left to find you."

He traced the contours of her face and stroked her temples.

Otter stumbled to the door. "I have called you brother. I have given you a woman you said you wanted. Did you lie?"

Trembling with fear, Gen wrapped her arms around Daniel's neck, hiding her face against his chest. He lifted her off the ground and carried her to the corner of the room where a moth-eaten buffalo robe lay on the floor. Standing with Gen in his arms, Daniel asked half angrily, "Are you going to watch?"

Otter peered at him. "No, my brother. But I may be back to make certain that you are not lying to me." He stumbled outside. Daniel followed him to the door, his heart sinking when he saw that Otter had once again seated himself on the ground and was leaning against the stump.

Daniel crossed the room and lay down beside Gen. She turned away from him, trembling, feeling her skin go cold and hot. Her stomach was churning. Just when she thought she might get up, Otter stumbled into the room.

At the sound of his first step, Daniel reached out and, grabbing Gen by the waist, pulled her towards him. He curled himself around her and lifted his head just enough to make it seem that they were in an embrace. Groaning with feigned frustration, he rolled over.

"What is it now, Otter?"

Gen didn't dare turn over to look at him, but she could feel Otter's eyes boring into her back as he took in the scene before him. She sat up abruptly and grabbed Daniel from behind, pulling him towards her, kissing his earlobe.

Otter chuckled wickedly. "And I thought you were a virtuous maiden, a missionary's housekeeper." He headed outside, pausing at the doorway to say something vile about what he thought was ahead for Daniel.

When he was gone, Gen leaned against the wall, trembling. Daniel crept to the door and looked outside. When he was satisfied that Otter was really gone, he crossed the room to sit down beside her.

"It's all right now," he said softly, touching her shoulder.

She knew she should get up, but she could not will herself to move. What was wrong with her? The danger was past. Why, then, was she shaking so? She felt foolish, and tried to push herself upright, but then everything went bright white. She sank back down, shaking so hard her teeth chattered. She began to cry quietly, and the more she tried to stop, the harder she cried.

Daniel pulled her close, smoothing her hair, rubbing her back. "It's all right," he said over and over. "I'm here. I won't leave you. You are safe now."

She looked up at him dumbly, tears streaming from her eyes. He wiped them away with his finger.

When Gen woke up she was curled up on the buffalo robe, her head on Daniel's lap. His hand was on her waist, his breathing even as he slept propped up against the wall. She closed her eyes momentarily. He smelled of wood smoke and sweat, and she was not offended.

"Two Stars!" Aaron almost shouted from the doorway. He looked happy, but halfway across the room he glanced at Gen and hesitated. Meg appeared in the doorway behind him, smiling shyly.

"When did you come? Why are you here?" Aaron asked.

Daniel stood up. "Otter came after Gen last night. He was going to take her away. God brought me just in time to stop him." He extended his hand to Gen and pulled her up beside him.

Aaron looked at Gen. Complete understanding shone in his eyes. He drew the corners of his mouth down in an exaggerated frown. It was an expression Gen had come to recognize, to despair of, to wonder how to eradicate.

"Does that mean you are one of the friendlies?" he asked abruptly.

Daniel nodded. He looked down at Gen. "I have a farm down by the Lower Agency." He shrugged. "At least I had one when this started. Only God knows what will become of it now."

"But you haven't done anything wrong," Aaron said. He eyed Daniel's war paint pointedly. "Have you?"

Daniel shook his head. "I have tried to stay away from the trouble." He held out his arms. "This paint kept me alive. It made me look like one of them." He nodded towards the door. "My horse is painted too."

"I painted Otter's horse before the battles at New Ulm," Aaron said. He held his hands out. "Big white circles like this." He looked at Daniel. "Targets."

Meg eyed him carefully. "You look like one of the bad Indians."

Daniel nodded. "I know. But I'm not."

"How can we be sure?"

Daniel thought for a moment. Then, he reached for a string of beads around his neck. Taking it off, he held it out to her. "Do you see that?" He pointed to the cross.

Meg nodded, still rooted to her place by the door.

"What is it?"

"A cross."

"What does it mean?"

"You tell me what it means," she said solemnly.

"It means that I love Jesus. I prayed and asked Him to help me find you. To help keep you safe so I can take you back to your father."

Meg considered. Finally, she smiled. "I prayed too. I asked Jesus to send someone to take us all home." She looked Daniel up and down. "But I didn't ask for anybody painted with *blue stripes*."

# Twenty-seven

He preserves the souls of His saints;
He delivers them out of the hand of the
  wicked.
> — PSALM 97:10 (NKJV)

With Daniel's presence and Mother Friend's
pledge, Gen thought they might finally be
safe. But then the Peace Party braves threatened the warriors and demanded the release
of all the white captives to them. The ten-
uous relationship between the two camps
collapsed. There were speeches and argu-
ments, threats and promises. Once again the
warriors danced around fires, boasting of
terrible atrocities, shouting for more war,
acting out the murders they had already
committed and threatening to kill all the
captives.

Sibley had sixteen hundred men at Fort
Ridgely, but they moved like old women,
taking five days to cross the distance a Dakota could cover in one morning. It became a joke in camp. "White men don't

think very much of women and children or they would march faster."

Runners reported a defeat of a small detail of soldiers at Birch Creek. Colonel Sibley wrote a letter to Little Crow and had it left in a cigar box staked there. It promised fair treatment if only the white captives would be released unharmed, and invited Little Crow to send someone to meet him. "Only have them come on the road with a white flag."

Rumors were constantly circulating. One evening criers marched through camp with the message, "White women to be killed now very soon. They eat too much. We are going away, and they cannot travel. They had better die at once." Another night the criers said all the half-breeds would be killed.

Camps were parted and re-created as the friendly Indians attempted to once and for all gather all the white captives to them in an attempt to provide some kind of protection. "It hurts my heart," Little Paul, one of the leading men, was heard to say, "to see how they suffer."

One day when things were especially uncertain, Daniel ordered Gen, Meg, and Aaron to hide beneath the bed in the cabin. He grabbed his rifle and sat in the doorway for hours while mounted warriors milled about yelling and firing their rifles into the air.

It was after sundown before they felt it was safe to come out from underneath the bed. As he dusted them off, Daniel tried to make jokes with Meg and Aaron, but Gen saw that his eyes did not laugh. Later, after Meg and Aaron fell asleep, they sat outside together.

"Look at that." Gen pointed to the hundreds of tepees fanning out as far as they could see. "Tonight it looks so peaceful. Who would guess that just across the creek are hundreds of Dakota warriors." She shivered. "They want to kill us, don't they?"

Daniel was quiet for a long time. "Little Paul and the other head men in the Peace Party are well respected. Here is what Little Paul said today." He quoted the chief almost verbatim:

You think you are brave because you have killed a lot of defenseless women and children. You are cowards.

If these prisoners were only men, instead of women and children, it would be all right, but it is hard that this terrible suffering should be brought upon women and children. It makes my heart hot to think of it.

You think to get me and my people to help you in this work? No! Never! You will never get our help!

These prisoners will have to be given back to their people, and the sooner you do it the better it will be for you.

Daniel added, "We are working hard for the captives. We have nearly half of them with us now in this camp." He lowered his voice. "But if we try to take them by force, they will certainly be killed. We must be patient."

"Miss Jane is still over there," Gen whispered, nodding toward the lower camp. "Could you stop it — if they were intent on killing the captives? What could you do?"

"I promised Simon Dane I would protect you and his children with my life. I will keep that promise."

"But Miss Jane —"

Daniel raked his hands through his hair and stood up. "I cannot save them all!" He didn't raise his voice, but she could hear him shouting, nonetheless. He strode away.

For all his reassurances to Gen, Daniel

Two Stars spent that night praying for God to tell him what to do. Blue Eyes had little understanding of just how precarious their lives were. At any moment, if the warriors desired, they could mount a party five times the size of the Peace Party, slaughter everyone, and make their escape into the west or up north. He had seen Otter nearby many times in the last few days, watching Blue Eyes, looking to see if Daniel was in sight. When he saw Daniel, he usually made some gesture that communicated anger or disdain and walked away laughing.

Whoever this General Sibley was, he knew nothing about fighting Indians. He moved like a plodding mule, making enough noise to tell the whole countryside he was coming. He had already sent one small group out ahead of his train, and they had been stupid enough to camp where they were easy prey to the Sioux. He had by now received several messages urging him to hurry, and still he moved like a snail. Everyday Daniel awoke worried about what Little Crow and his warriors might do.

On September 8 the camp was moved again, farther north, near Red Iron's village of Sissetons. Red Iron and his warriors ordered Little Crow to keep out of Sisseton country. "You commenced the outbreak," they said, "and you must do the fighting in your country. We do not want you here to excite our young men and get us into trouble."

Camp was set up, fires built, dancing and singing and feasting commenced. A group of dancers hung a war trophy — long red whiskers — on a pole in the middle of a ring. To the steady drumbeat of their musicians they danced for hours, reenacting what they had done to the settlers. Once again, the captives went into hiding inside friendly tepees.

The next day, Little Crow's warriors dragged six friendlies into camp. They had left with some captive women and children, but had been discovered. There was such an outcry between the opposing camps that Daniel positioned himself across the opening to the tepee the entire night, a loaded rifle at his side.

After that, things became more peaceful for a while. Small groups of warriors went out on individual warring parties, but the majority of the Indians had settled down to playing cards and hunting while Little Crow and Sibley communicated through runners. Fallen Moon still refused to let

Miss Jane bring her charges to Mother Friend, so Mother Friend and Gen worked alone, drying corn and potatoes, cutting and drying beef, laying in stock for the winter.

They roasted potatoes in the fire at night and read books aloud to friendly Dakota who found them among the plunder from homesteads and wanted to hear white words. One night a woman she had met earlier while digging potatoes at an abandoned homestead brought a Bible and asked Gen to read. Because she did not know where else to turn, she fumbled until she found Psalm 23.

The LORD is my Shepherd; I shall not want . . . Yea, though I walk through the valley of the shadow of death, I will fear no evil . . .

The woman nodded. Then she surprised Gen by saying, "Put your trust in God. Never forget that He has the power to save, and feel as if His eye is upon you, His arms around you, and all will be well."

Gen nodded as if she agreed, but she lay awake that night, contemplating the irony of a girl schooled by missionaries being comforted by a full-blood Dakota who obviously believed more strongly in the God of the Bible than she did. For the first time she obeyed Miss Jane, praying, *Lord, where are You? Help me. Please take all those facts in my head and move them into my heart.*

Someone loomed over him in the darkness. He tried to leap up, but a knee shoved him to the earth, knocking the breath out of him. Otter covered Daniel's mouth with a dirty hand and leaned down, staring him in the face. He pressed the blade of his knife to Daniel's throat.

"Little Crow is leading his warriors against Sibley's soldiers at Wood Lake. When he comes back, he is going to kill everyone in the friendly camp. Then he will escape to the north."

At the question in Daniel's eyes, Otter said, "I like killing whites. It is so easy. If it were only the captives, I would not mind. But I don't want to kill my brother. Take your half-breed wife and those children and get away from this place." He disappeared as suddenly as he had come.

Daniel sat looking after Otter. He reached up and touched his neck where the knife had drawn blood. He sat for a while, looking around him at the peaceful camp. Clouds were gathering in the sky above. He closed his eyes. *Dear God, we are going into the valley of the shadow of death tonight. Go with us.*

"Blue Eyes," Daniel whispered in her ear. "We are going."

Gen woke with a start. "What?"

"We are going. Tonight. Little Crow is going to fight Sibley somewhere near Wood Lake. When he comes back he means to kill everyone in the friendly camp."

"How do you know that?"

"Otter told me."

"Otter?" Gen sat up.

Daniel nodded. "He has warned me as a brother. When he comes back he will kill me as an enemy." He shook his head. "I never thought my own people would kill me."

Gen woke Mother Friend. When the old woman realized what was happening, she began to cry, but she didn't try to stop them. Instead, she rose quickly and began shoving loaves of bread, dried beef, and raw potatoes into a flour sack.

When at last they were ready to go, Mother Friend kissed Aaron and Meg on the cheek. "Always remember your old Mother Friend," she said to each one. She handed Gen the flour sack and patted her hand.

"If you see Miss Jane —" Gen began.

"I will help her just as I have helped you."

Daniel knelt down, ordering Aaron to climb onto his back. He looked at Gen. "Can you carry Meg? It's not far. Two tracks are easier to hide." Gen handed the sack of food to Aaron and bent down for Meg to scramble onto her back. They crept out of the tent and ran quickly towards the woods. Mother Friend scurried after them, erasing their tracks with a branch.

Once in the woods, they set the children down.

"Why can't we take your horse?" Aaron asked.

"As long as the horse is outside the tepee, they assume the warrior is within." He ordered, "Follow me like good Dakota," meaning that they should walk single-file. He led them in a contorted path along the edge of the woods. It began to rain, a gentle drizzle that barely moistened the earth but still obliterated their trail.

When they reached a creek bank, Daniel had them wait while he slid down to find a hiding place. When he came for them they waded into the creek and plodded along until they came to a place where the earth had been worn away, carving a deep niche in the muddy bank. Daniel motioned for Gen to climb up onto the ledge. She obeyed, shuddering when she reached the ledge, and tree roots dangling from above touched her head and shoulders. From below, Daniel shoved Meg and Aaron up to her. Then he climbed after them.

"I have a canoe hidden nearby," he whispered. "You are safe here as long as you stay quiet. No one from above can see you, and I will be back soon." Without waiting for an answer, he slid down the bank. After a hasty attempt to disguise the tracks up the incline he disappeared from sight.

It began to rain again, harder. The wind blew, lashing at the tree roots, sending showers of mud and filth down from above. Before long, they were in the midst of a terrible thunderstorm, lightning flashing, rain and mud washing down the side of the hill. They unrolled a blanket and tried to huddle under it, but in minutes they were thoroughly soaked. Meg began to cry. She didn't make a sound, but Gen could feel her shoulders shaking. She patted her head and held her close. Aaron sat beside them like a stone, his forehead on his knees.

The storm passed, but there was no sign

of Daniel. A limb cracked overhead and Gen jumped and looked up, certain they had been discovered.

"Is that wolves coming after us?" Aaron whispered in her ear.

Something was just above them on the cliff, sniffing their scent.

The moon came up, peeking behind a cloud, painting the sky with soft, golden light. Above it one bright star hung along the rim of the halo of light around the moon. The shadows of the bare tree branches were cast across the creek. They drew back farther into the niche below the bank, shivering with cold, wrapped in the sodden blanket.

"Where is Daniel?" Meg whispered. "He said he was coming back for us."

"He will," Gen said. "But we must wait. And be very, very quiet."

Aaron lifted his forehead off his knees. "What if he doesn't come back?" he wanted to know.

"He's coming back," Gen said. *Please, God, bring Daniel back.*

Aaron looked doubtful.

She opened the sack of food and broke off a piece of bread for each of them. After they ate, she whispered, "Try to sleep if you can," realizing as she said it how silly it must sound. They were covered with mud, shivering with cold, and terrified. Who, she thought, could sleep? But to her amazement, Meg put her head in her lap and dozed off.

The moon began to sink in the sky, low enough that the tree branches formed a curtain of black lace across its face. Aaron nodded to the east where a faint pink blush appeared in the sky. "He isn't coming back," he said. "It's been too long."

"He will come," Gen insisted.

"I'm thirsty. Can't I just get a drink from the creek and climb back up?"

Gen shook her head. "You'll leave a trail that will give us away." She pressed her finger to her lips. Her knees were beginning to ache. She couldn't feel her feet anymore. But if she stretched her legs out, someone might see them. She kept her legs drawn up beneath her skirt.

Meg woke up, rubbing her eyes and whimpering about the mosquitoes.

The moon sank behind the horizon, turning golden, then orange. The halo around it receded and gave way to morning light until it was little more than an orange ball hanging against a dark gray sky. The eastern sky turned deep pink, then an ever-widening arc of light blue spread over the canopy of the sky.

Dawn, and no Daniel.

A sound from above them. Footsteps. Voices. Gen clutched the children to her.

Morning light sparkled on the surface of the water. A splashing sound, and then he appeared, wading through the water, looking above them, a worried look on his face. He scrambled up the bank and reached for Meg. "Some hostiles camped just above you last night. I saw their campfire." He looked at Aaron. "If you had not been brave, you would have been discovered. If you were my son, Aaron, I would give you an eagle feather for this night."

Aaron looked at Gen guiltily, then slid down the bank behind Daniel.

They waited below for Gen, but when she tried to straighten her legs out, she couldn't. She bit her lip and looked at Daniel, tears in her eyes. She shook her head.

He climbed back up beside her.

"They won't move," she said, pounding her thighs with her fists. "I lost feeling hours ago. They just won't move." She began to cry quietly.

Aaron climbed up beside Daniel and they worked together until, finally, they were able to straighten her legs out.

"Keep rubbing," Daniel ordered Aaron. "We'll bring the canoe." He slid down to the creek again and lifted Meg onto his back. Presently they came floating down the creek in the canoe. Daniel pulled it to shore and motioned for Aaron. "Just keep it from floating away." He climbed up after Gen and half-carried her down, lifted her into the canoe, and with Aaron's help, shoved off.

They had only paddled a short distance when Daniel turned the canoe into an inlet and waded ashore. "Better we travel at night," he said. And so they sat huddled together, shivering in the cold, waiting for night to fall. Gen told every story her father had ever told. They recited the catechism, they sang hymns. They slept.

And Daniel prayed. "Oh God, these are Your children. You love them. So do we. Show us the way we should go to take these children home. Be with us in our secret wanderings. Make the eyes of any hostile Dakota look another way." He squeezed Gen's hand. "Help us find peace."

A cold north wind began to blow, but they dared not build a fire. They traveled all night until finally they came to Lac Qui

Parle and the old mission station. The barn had been burned, but the adobe-brick church stood firm. Daniel hid the canoe in a thicket of bushes that hung out over the water. They had just begun to stumble up the path when a blur of white shot out from behind the church and charged down the hill toward them. It was Koda, welcoming his family home.

# Twenty-eight

Faith is the substance of things hoped
for, the evidence of things not seen.
— HEBREWS 11:1 (NKJV)

"Daniel," Aaron whispered, touching his
shoulder. "Daniel, wake up. There's
someone outside!"

Koda began to bark, frantically scratch-
ing at the church door.

Daniel motioned to Gen, who led the
children to the front of the church where
they hunkered down behind the pump
organ. Daniel crept to the door, pressing
his ear to the wood for a moment before
slowly pulling it open to look outside.

Peering over the top of the organ, Gen
saw him relax. He looked over his shoulder
and winked at her. "Meg. Aaron," he
called. They popped up beside Gen. "God
has brought breakfast." He swung the door
wide, and there stood a brown bull, pawing
at the dirt.

Ignoring Daniel's order to stay put,

Koda tore after the bull. When the animal lowered its head and charged, Koda dodged, nipping at the bull's hocks as it lumbered past, spinning away just in time to escape. The creature rolled its eyes and tossed its head.

"Koda!" Daniel yelled. "No! Come!"

Koda was having entirely too much fun to heed the command. He crouched in the path, haunches in the air, wagging his tail and barking.

"He thinks it's a game," Aaron said.

"I hope his game doesn't lose our supper," Daniel muttered. He grabbed his rifle and took aim at the bull, but not in time to prevent Koda from giving chase. This time Koda miscalculated, and with one thrust of its head, the bull speared the dog's body in midair. Koda let out one high-pitched yelp and plummeted to the earth. Daniel took aim and fired. The bull staggered briefly, then lumbered a short distance up the hill and crashed on its side.

The minute the bull toppled over, Meg and Aaron ran to Koda. They knelt in the dirt and stared unbelieving at the still mound of white fur. Aaron reached out and stroked the dog's head. Daniel stood motionless just outside the church door, rifle in hand. "Stupid dog," he said, swearing under his breath.

"He was trying to protect us, Daniel," Gen said.

Daniel looked down at Gen, his eyes smoldering with anger. He looked towards the river, pressing his lips together, lifting his chin. Finally, he took a deep breath, pulled his knife, and headed up the hill. "I have a bull to slaughter," he choked out. He waved in the direction of the children. "Help them bury the dog. Then see if you can get a fire started. We'll roast some of the meat before we leave tonight."

"What about the smoke — won't it be — dangerous?" Gen sputtered the question when Daniel glared at her.

"We'll take the chance," he said tersely.

While Daniel sliced meat off the dead bull's carcass, Gen and the children dug a grave and buried Koda. They fashioned a small cross out of two sticks tied together with twisted prairie grass.

"We ought to pray," Meg insisted. "People always pray at funerals."

Aaron said a prayer, thanking God for sending Koda to protect Daniel, ". . . 'cause we need him, Lord, to take us back to Father." They spent the rest of the day roasting the beef Daniel had cut off the bull and hauled down the hill.

"Can't we stay another day and cook more?" Gen asked. "It's a shame to just leave it."

Daniel shook his head and nodded towards the horizon. "Every wolf for miles around is probably already hiding in the grass out there, just waiting for our cooking fire to go out. Starving homesteaders' dogs will come too. We don't want to be here when they all arrive." He grimaced. "They might decide the bull isn't enough. And I have only three more shells for the rifle." Wiping the knife blade on his pant leg and sticking the weapon back in its holder at his waist, he picked up his rifle and headed for the river. "Get things ready. I'll be back for you."

Gen found him near sundown, sitting by the water's edge, leaning against a tree with his eyes closed.

"Where are the children?" he asked, without moving or opening his eyes.

"They're safe. Inside the church. We bundled as much meat as we can carry in the blanket. We can go as soon as it's dark."

He opened his eyes and leaned forward, his elbows on his knees. "I have to go find

Gray Woman. Robert and Nancy. I have to know why Koda was here and not with them."

"He probably just chewed the rope and came back to his old home," Gen said quietly. "It doesn't mean anything bad happened." She put her hand on his shoulder.

"Do you think Miss Jane will be safe?"

"She won't blame you, Daniel. You said it yourself. You can't save everyone."

He snorted as he scraped a spot of dried blood off his pant leg. "I haven't proven yet that I can save anyone." He looked up at the sky and shook his head. "I never thought my own people would turn against me. They may have killed Robert and his family. Even Gray Woman. And you —" He took her hand and pulled it towards him, touching the scars and scratches on her forearms. "— you will never be the same. Meg and Aaron — all the children in that camp — never the same." He paused. "When I was a boy, I was taught that if I could hunt well and provide for my family, if I could fight the enemy and defend them, I was a man." He shook his head. "My own people have become my enemies. I fight my brothers. And I have no family." He turned away and bowed his head. "Leave me alone for a while longer, Blue Eyes. Please."

Gen crept back up the hill towards the church. *Please, God. Help us.* She tried to remember what Miss Jane had said that night by the campfire . . . something, anything that might help Two Stars. All she could remember was Miss Jane praying — beginning her prayer by thanking God. It had seemed absurd to Gen at the time, but now she realized it had lifted her thoughts away from herself, away from hideous reality and towards the God who was supposed to be able to handle things — the one Miss Jane said loved them and would work things out for their good.

Gen tried to think of signs that God loved her. She looked back towards the river. *Thank You, God, for sending Daniel.* She thought about the night waiting along the creek bank. *Thank You that we were not discovered . . . that we have come this far . . . that we have enough to eat . . .* Gen was almost at the church when Daniel caught up with her.

"We should get the children," he said. "It will be dark soon." He headed past her up the hill.

Gen followed Daniel up the path, wishing she could help him. *You do it, God. You help him. Give him some of that peace that Miss Jane said You give Your followers.*

*He already has faith in You . . . he knows Your love . . . he has mine, if he wants it . . . I think he needs hope, God. Maybe we both do.*

That night it got cold enough for the grass along the water's edge to frost over. Daniel had to get out of the boat and wade in icy water several times, pushing the canoe off one shoal after another. Once they nearly upset in a shallow rapids. Again, Daniel climbed out and pushed the canoe to shore. Gen and the children disembarked, Aaron and Daniel carrying the canoe over a mile along the shore until they passed the rapids. By morning, when they floated into some tall grass and took cover in a thicket of plum bushes, Daniel was half sick.

"I'll be all right, Blue Eyes." He forced a smile. "Just let me rest."

The children fell asleep, and Gen managed to nap between trips to the river to get Daniel fresh water in a gourd they had ripped off a tangle of vines at the mission. *What are we going to do if he gets sick, God? What are we going to do?* It was more a worry than prayer, and yet by nightfall Daniel was feeling better.

When they came ashore the next morning to rest, they spotted a house on the ridge just above them. Gen asked, "Do we dare check up there for supplies?"

Daniel flattened down an area in the center of a tall stand of elderberry bushes and ordered Gen and Meg and Aaron to settle there while he investigated. "If you hear *anything*, if you see *anything*, don't try to warn me. And don't come up the hill." He crouched down and looked soberly at Gen. "You stay put. No matter what." He nodded towards Aaron and Meg. "For their sake, you stay. After dark, get in the canoe and go on down stream. It isn't that far to the fort. You can do it. Promise me." When Gen reluctantly nodded agreement, he slipped out of the hiding place and headed up the hill, pausing often to look around him, giving special attention to Chief Shakopee's old campsite across the river in the distance.

Gen pushed aside a few branches and focused on the homestead, trying to see if Daniel made it. *Keep him safe, God. Please.*

The house seemed deserted. Daniel crept around the perimeter of the clearing and headed for the barn, which proved to be empty except for a few broken tools and some half-rotten harnesses tossed in one corner. The wind had shifted when he came out of the barn, and a familiar stench filled him with dread. He didn't want to look, but he had begun his inspection and he must finish. Just around the corner of the barn, beside a half-cut pile of firewood, lay a farmer, his head nearly severed from his body. Whoever had done it hadn't even bothered to take the ax they had used. Shuddering, gulping in fresh air to keep from vomiting, Daniel backed away from the body and turned his attention towards the house.

He stepped across the threshold, listening intently. The interior had been sacked, jars broken, pillows ripped open, feathers shaken out, everything destroyed. He picked his way through the debris, hoping to find clean clothes for Aaron and Meg, something for Gen, perhaps dry clothes for himself. Lifting a blanket tossed in a corner he was greeted by the sight of a small child and what must have been its mother. The woman had curled herself in a fetal position around her child before being stabbed in the back and scalped.

Turning away, Daniel staggered outside and slumped down on the porch, his head in his hands. *It's too much, God. I can't take any more of this.* He tried to inhale, but the breath wouldn't come. When it did, the stench of decaying bodies filled his nostrils again, and he leaned over the edge of the porch, retching. He plodded back to the barn and found a shovel tossed into the corner with some rotten harness and frayed rope. He began to dig on the opposite side of the house, away from the wind. When he was finished, he went back inside and, taking a deep breath, bent down to pick up the dead child. Except the child wasn't dead. At the touch of Daniel's hand, a bloody leg moved, the head turned, and bright blue eyes were staring up at him.

With an exclamation that was half sob, half sigh, Daniel jumped back. The baby sat up and crawled towards him, smiling. While Daniel stood, immobile, the child sat down at his feet and held up both hands, begging to be held. Taking the child into his arms, Daniel examined it. It must have survived by picking its way through the broken crockery and bowls and scavenging whatever bits of food it could find. Its hair was matted and stringy, its face and legs scratched and smudged with bits of dried food. The rag tied around its middle was filthy, both inside and out. The child smelled . . . and Daniel thought he had never seen anything so beautiful.

With the blonde-haired child in his arms, he charged outside and down the path. His eyes shone with tears as he crept into the hiding place with the baby.

"But why didn't they kill him — her — it?" Gen wondered aloud.

Daniel shook his head. "Only God knows." *God knows.* He sat wordlessly for a moment before clearing his throat and saying, "I dug a grave. For her — his —"

Aaron checked. "Her," he said, and they all laughed nervously.

"I dug a grave for her parents."

"Let me come with you," Gen said. "Now we need diapers. Anything will do — rags — whatever I can find."

Daniel shook his head. "No, Blue Eyes. Let me do it. I'll bring back whatever you need." He hesitated, then added, "You don't want to see."

"No," Gen agreed. "I don't. But I won't let you do it alone. I'm coming." She turned towards Aaron. "Watch the baby. If she cries, let her suck on your knuckle." She held up her hand and demonstrated, "Bend your finger like this. I'm going to help Daniel bury the poor child's parents. We'll see what we can find to help us with our journey. Remember. Don't make a sound."

They climbed the hill together. Gen gave one sharp exclamation when they stepped inside the cabin. She covered her mouth and ran outside, giving up the little she had eaten that day. Then, breathing through her mouth, she went to work helping Daniel, trying not to look at the bodies they must handle. They nestled the couple together in one grave. Gen blinked back tears as she helped cover the bodies with earth.

Back inside the house, they found a few bits of cloth Gen could use for diapers, but little else to help them on their way. There was nothing to give a hint of who the couple might be.

"I can look for surveyor's stakes before the sun goes down," Daniel said. "If we get the marks, Reverend Dane might be able to find out something at the surveyor's office."

They found a half-empty bottle of ink in a drawer, but no pen. A foray to the barn yielded a handful of turkey feathers. The woman had tacked several layers of newspaper over the boards in a lean-to at the back of the house. Pulling a sheet of newsprint off the wall, Gen sat down and scratched in the margin, *I am Geneviève LaCroix. I have been captive and was rescued by Daniel Two Stars, who is taking me and the children of Reverend Simon Dane to Fort Ridgely. We found these people dead and have buried them. Their female child was unharmed and we have her.*

They tacked Gen's note to the cabin door and headed back down the hill. The sun set before Daniel could locate the surveyor's stakes that might be a clue to the couple's identity. The baby slept the night away in the bottom of the canoe.

"She never cries," Meg observed the next day.

"She learned it does no good to cry," Daniel said quietly.

They floated by Redwood Ferry, silent as they thought of the soldiers from Fort Ridgely who had been overwhelmed and killed there in a surprise attack when they tried to get across to defend the Lower Agency. They had not gone far when they heard the booming of cannon from the direction of the fort.

Meg looked at Daniel, her eyes wide, asking with a trembling voice, "Is that Indians?"

He shook his head. "No, Miss Meg. We are far away from the Indians who want to fight now. And Indians don't have cannon.

Those are the soldiers at Fort Ridgely. And soon you will be safe."

They came ashore in the middle of the night, at the foot of the hills that would lead them up to the fort and to safety. When they stepped ashore, Gen blinked away tears of relief.

Once the children were asleep, Daniel sat down and put his arm around her.

"In the morning," he said, "you must be sure to have Aaron wave one of the white rags when you get near the fort. They will send some soldiers out to meet you." He added, "Be sure you tell them that Daniel Two Stars helped you. Make them write it down. Make sure they know I am a good Indian."

Gen swallowed hard. "You really are going back."

He nodded. "I must find Gray Woman. And Robert and his family. I have to know."

She grabbed his arm. "I don't want you to go! Please stay with us. Where it's safe. You've done enough. Stay with *me*. You — you said you can't save everyone."

He smiled, reaching out to touch the sleeping baby's yellow hair. "But I saved one — two — three — four." He pointed to the children one by one, and then to

Gen, touching her cheek gently. "I have lived among the lions for a long time, Blue Eyes. And I have not been devoured yet." He looked away and said quietly, "There is something I must ask you. When I was leaving to come to find you, Reverend Dane said something. He was talking about you, and he said, 'I can't lose her — she is all I have.' " He cleared his throat nervously. "What did he mean?"

Gen closed her eyes and shook her head. "I don't know. Maybe — maybe he cares too much for me." She rushed to explain. "I respect him. I never thought I would say it, but Ellen's death — changed him. For the better. But, Daniel, I don't love him."

He waited a moment before bending down and touching her lips lightly with his own. He pulled her close, holding her so tightly she could feel the row of beads that hung around his neck pressing into her chest. He stroked her hair, whispering in Dakota.

Tears slipped down her cheeks. "I don't want you to go. I don't know what I'll do if anything happens to you." She wrapped her arms around his neck.

He rested his chin atop her head, inhaling deeply. "I had almost lost hope of ever having a life, Blue Eyes. But yesterday — yesterday God gave it back again." He smiled at her and nodded. "We must not lose hope, Blue Eyes. God will bring us together again. And when He does . . ." He kissed her again, more fiercely this time. "I love you with my whole heart," he said. "In all my wanderings, it will be your eyes that follow me. Do not let any other man take your heart." He disappeared into the shadows.

# Twenty-nine

You shall love your neighbor as yourself.
— ROMANS 13:9 (NKJV)

He was trying to learn to love them. The
Lord knew how hard it was, what with his
natural tendency to vanity and self-righ-
teousness. It was hard to live among the un-
educated, coarse soldiers gathered at Fort
Ridgely and not feel defiled. Still, Simon
thought, he had made progress. He rolled up
his sleeves and helped anywhere they would
have him. He gave up his vanity about his re-
ceding hairline and had the post barber crop
his hair short, revealing an almost bald head.
His skin had weathered until he was almost
as dark as the Dakota. He was surprised to
find that physical labor agreed with him. Not
that it kept his mind off Meg and Aaron and
Gen. But it kept him sane.

On August 29 Sibley's troops arrived.
The fort and the surrounding countryside
swelled to a teeming community of nearly
two thousand. When the danger of an at-

tack on the fort was past, displaced home-steaders were moved to St. Peter. Simon helped move them, driving a wagon back and forth, smiling to himself when no one seemed to suspect that he was a preacher. Everywhere he watched for bright blue eyes and blond- or redheaded children.

On September 15, Sibley received a message from the peaceful chiefs up north. Its contents sent a chill through Simon Dane. *If your troops do not reach here till the last of the week, it may be too late. The warrior bands have already held two councils about killing off the captives.*

Simon stood on the parade grounds late one night, looking north, praying desperately. When a violent thunderstorm blew over the tent where he slept, he sought refuge with the fort doctor, whose wife had become a local hero by commandeering a small cannon and saving the hospital from a Sioux attack. He could not know that as he listened to the thunder roll, his children were hiding along a creek waiting for Daniel Two Stars to rescue them.

When, on September 18, Colonel Sibley finally gave the order to march, his troops were enlarged by a few citizen soldiers. One of them was really a missionary who had talked long and hard to convince his companions to let him come along.

"You know how to shoot that thing?" someone asked, nodding at the rifle in a scabbard behind Simon's saddle.

Simon nodded. "Sergeant Brady has been good enough to let me take target practice with him." He demonstrated his skill by pointing to a broken-down wagon in the distance. When a crock sitting on the wagon seat shattered, the doubter nodded and stuck out his hand. "Welcome to the army, Parson."

He was learning an entirely new aspect of trusting God. He had no choice. Sibley moved with all the speed of a snail. Simon had traveled the road from the fort to the Upper Agency hundreds of times. What took a missionary driving a wagon one day took trained military men four days.

They camped near Wood Lake. When the men of Company G of the Third Minnesota grew dissatisfied with rations, they decided to do some scavenging in the surrounding territory. Thus were Little Crow's warriors discovered — by accident. Because of the premature discovery, more than half of Little Crow's warriors never got in the fight. The military considered the Battle of Wood Lake a victory.

After the battle, Simon stumbled upon a

wounded Dakota crawling through the bushes. He had been shot through the lungs. Simon convinced his weapons instructor, Sergeant Brady, to help him carry the warrior to one of their tents. Once the brave was inside, Simon gave him a drink of water. "Do you know of a half-breed named Geneviève LaCroix?" he asked. "She and my children were taken weeks ago." The man coughed, yelping with pain.

"Are you cold, my brother?" Simon asked. When the brave jerked his chin up in a half-nod, Simon covered him with an army blanket. "Do you know the God who loves all men?" he asked gently.

The brave frowned. "Who are you?" he asked in Dakota.

"Your people call me Many Words," Simon said. "I was the missionary at Renville. Can I pray for you?"

The brave turned his face away. Simon prayed anyway, simple words that spoke of God's love and forgiveness.

When the brave died, Simon sat back. "I wish I knew his name," he said to no one in particular.

"Why?" Brady muttered. "One less bad Indian. Good riddance."

One of the Peace Party chiefs, Wabasha,

sent someone to tell Sibley that the warriors were all gone and the captives were safe in the friendlies' camp. "The road is safe," the chief said. "But you must hurry. Little Crow may return and kill us all." Still Sibley waited, taking four days to travel north to Lac Qui Parle, a journey that Simon had often made in half a day.

Finally, they arrived. With drums beating and fifes playing, the army marched to within five hundred yards of the friendlies' camp. They also aimed howitzers at the camp where the captives waited with the Dakota who had risked their own lives to protect them. White flags of truce were everywhere. Bits of white cloth decorated wagon wheels and bridles. American flags flew above dozens of tepees.

Sibley and his aides marched to the center of the friendlies' camp and called the chiefs to meet with him. He demanded that the captives be released. Little Paul stepped forward.

"I take your hand as a child takes the hand of his father," he said. "My hand is not bad. With a clean hand I take your hand. I have regarded all white people as my friends. This is a good work we do today, whereof I am glad. Yes, before the great God, I am glad."

The captives stumbled towards the soldiers, some weeping, some shuffling along, expressionless.

Simon ran through the crowd, not caring if he looked like a fool. "Geneviève! Meg! Aaron!" he called over and over again, peering into faces. He saw indifference and despair, smiles and tears, but he did not see the faces he longed for.

"Reverend Dane!" Miss Jane was striding towards him, looking ridiculous in a dress at least two sizes too small for her. She clutched a child by each hand, but let go long enough to engulf him in a hug.

"Meg? Aaron?" he barked out, terror rising in his throat when Miss Jane shook her head.

"Daniel Two Stars protected them as long as he felt it was safe to stay here. But when Little Crow left for Wood Lake, the rumor spread that when he returned he would kill everyone in the friendly camp. Mother Friend — that is the Dakota woman who kept Geneviève and the children the entire time — Mother Friend said she helped them get away. Daniel had a canoe," Miss Jane reassured him. "By now they are probably safe at Fort Ridgely, waiting for you."

Simon rallied. He looked down at Miss Jane's charges.

Miss Jane smiled. "This is Rebecca and Timothy Sutton. Their parents came to settle near Hazelwood shortly after you and Mrs. Dane left for the east. Wonderful Christian couple."

Rebecca spoke up. "The Indians didn't hurt us. But we didn't have good things to eat like Mama made us. And sometimes we got cold sleeping on the ground. The Indians killed Papa on his birthday. Mama had a cake for him, and when he sat down to eat it, they came and called him outside. And they killed him."

Simon knelt down beside the child. "Your papa is in heaven this very moment, Rebecca, and he is happy that you have had Miss Jane to watch out for you."

Rebecca looked up at Miss Jane. She frowned. "Who's going to take care of me and Timothy now?" she demanded.

"You'll stay with Miss Jane for a while longer yet," Simon said. "Is that all right with you, Rebecca? Timothy?"

Timothy was sucking his thumb, but he nodded. Rebecca looked at Timothy. "He don't talk much. He lets me talk for him. He got real scared when they shot Papa. Papa's blood got on his shirt." She looked soberly at Simon. "I was scared too. But Mama told me to be brave just before the Indians shot her."

Sibley made no secret of the fact that he intended to hang every Indian found guilty of a crime. His general agreed. *It is my purpose to utterly exterminate the Sioux,* he wrote. *They are to be treated as maniacs or wild beasts.*

Dr. Riggs had returned to serve the Dakota nation after taking his charges to safety. Sibley charged him with the task of interviewing the captives and reporting crimes against them. But soon the plan changed. Every man was to be taken before the commission and tried. If he was innocent, it would be discovered. If he was not, he would be hanged. For the Dakota, a new rule prevailed: they were guilty until proven innocent. After all, one reporter wrote, *The fact they were Indians, raised the moral certainty that, as soon as the first murder was committed, all the young men were impelled by the sight of blood and plunder . . . to become participants in the same class of acts.*

"Go and find your family," Dr. Riggs said. "When you know they are safe, there will still be work to do."

Simon went.

# Thirty

Blessed are you when they revile and persecute you, and say all kinds of evil against you falsely for My sake.
— MATTHEW 5:11 (NKJV)

"Fiends!" the crowd screamed. "Murderers!" Someone threw a brick. It glanced off Daniel's head. He staggered and fell. The crowd would have been on him if a soldier hadn't charged up and ordered them back.

"They killed my family!" a woman shrieked, shaking her fist at the soldier. "How *dare* you defend them?!" She screamed curses at the soldier, turning her rage against the military charged with protecting their Sioux prisoners.

Someone helped Daniel up and he staggered on, trying to stay near enough to a mounted soldier to prevent another mishap.

Daniel Two Stars was part of a train of Dakota Sioux being moved downriver to Mankato. The men had been tricked into giving up their rifles — not that they would have done any good against the howling mob. But if he could get away, Daniel thought he could have used his gun to hunt up a decent meal. He tried to close out the sound of the mob, remembering how easily the soldiers had fooled them back at Red Iron's camp. They were invited to be counted so the overdue annuity could be distributed to the friendlies. It seemed reasonable that they would be rewarded for protecting the captives. So the men walked through a doorway and laid down their weapons — and were immediately chained together in pairs.

After weeks near Red Iron's camp, renamed Camp Release, with provisions running dangerously low and no end in sight for the trials, everyone had been moved to the Lower Agency where the trials were finished at the rate of forty a day.

Every one of the friendlies was considered guilty of something. Unless someone stepped forward to defend them. Thank God Miss Jane was there for him. He trudged through St. Peter, head down, trying to close out the screaming mob by remembering the good things that had happened.

It had looked bad for him at first.

Someone identified him as a friend of Otter. Another one said he was present at the Battle of Birch Coulie. "I heard him say he killed one," a woman said.

Daniel looked at Dr. Riggs, pleading for a chance to speak.

"I was a friend of Otter. He warned me of Little Crow's plan to attack the friend-lies. That is when I took Reverend Dane's children and went away. I took them to Fort Ridgely. I was never at Birch Coulie, until we floated by it in our canoe. I buried a white settler and his wife, and I saved their child. She is with Geneviève LaCroix at Fort Ridgely. We left a note on the cabin door where we found the child. As for someone hearing me say I killed one, I cannot think what that would be. Unless they heard me speak of how I killed a cow at old Renville Mission." He spoke in short bursts, waiting for Dr. Riggs to translate for the commission of five who sat at a table across from him. The commissioners stared at him with cold eyes.

Things were looking bad until Miss Jane strode up. "Captain," she addressed one of the commissioners. "If you hang this man, I will shoot you myself!"

Accustomed to hearing the complaints of traumatized victims, the commissioners sat speechless while Miss Jane rained down a diatribe upon them the likes of which they had never heard. Even Daniel looked surprised by the outburst.

"You've let all the guilty Dakota get away, and now you are trying to find someone to punish. It's a disgrace!"

"Madame —" One of the commissioners started to speak.

"Don't you 'Madame' me, young man!" Miss Jane said. "I've spent the past few weeks of my life waiting while your crack troops wore themselves out marching five miles a day! Oh, yes," Miss Jane said, her voice dripping with sarcasm, "I forgot. You had to wait for the great Indian fighter General Sibley to capture all the bad Indians before you could take care of us. How clever of him to manage to capture the men who had been sitting on the prairie waiting, sending runners to urge him to hurry! What glory and honor is due to the great general!" She put her hand on Daniel's shoulder. "While your brave soldiers were lounging at Fort Ridgely, this young man lay across a cabin door with a rifle in his hand to protect white captives! While your brave soldiers were taking their little stroll across the prairie, he was finding a canoe and risking his life to get a woman and two children to safety!"

She cast a withering glance at the commission. "I give no praise to Sibley. I don't owe him any praise. The praise and thanks in my heart go to this young man . . . and to John Otherday and Paul Mazakutemane and Simon Anawangami, and dozens of Dakota like them who risked their lives, day after day, trying to save as many of us as they could! The only evidence you have against Daniel Two Stars is that he was *there*. Well *I* was there too. Perhaps you should hang me!"

Miss Jane finished, her eyes blazing, her chest heaving with anger.

The commissioners looked at one another nervously. Dr. Riggs bowed his head, and coughed a few times, trying to hide a smile.

After a few uneasy moments, one of the commissioners stood up. "The prisoner is innocent."

And now, in the cold of approaching Minnesota winter, while the Great Father in Washington decided what to do about the three hundred Sioux General Sibley insisted must be executed for war crimes, Daniel and over two hundred other innocent men were being moved to Mankato where it would be easier to feed them.

They must trudge past abandoned homesteads and burned barns, past fresh graves and battlefields. What had once been the most beautiful land in the world to them was a wasteland from which it appeared they were to be exiled forever.

And as before, just when Daniel was tempted to give up hope, God provided a glimpse of His love. Someone called his name. He glanced behind him and there, hobbling along in the crowd of prisoners, was Robert Lawrence.

"I forbid you to go. There is no possible way you can accomplish anything on behalf of Daniel Two Stars by getting trampled by a howling mob." Simon slammed his fist down on the desk before him. "Dr. Riggs has assured me that Daniel is in no danger. The military are guarding the prisoners —" Miss Jane snorted softly, but Simon ignored her, repeating, "The military is guarding the prisoners and as soon as they are settled up at Fort Snelling I will go there myself and do whatever is necessary to get him freed." He gentled his voice. "Please, Geneviève. Trust me. Nothing will happen to Two Stars. It's just that with the atmosphere as it is now, we can't exactly bring a Dakota friend home for dinner. Surely you can see how impossible that would be. We must wait and let God work things out."

Gen looked unconvinced.

Miss Jane sighed. "Reverend Dane is probably right, Gen. We must be patient. God will work things out for everyone's good. You must trust Him."

After Miss Jane and the Sutton children were brought in on a wagon filled with captives, the missionaries had been given the use of a small cottage behind the hotel in St. Peter until the mission board reassigned Simon. Simon slept in the hotel, but conducted his business from the cottage where Gen and Miss Jane spent their days recovering and caring for the children.

Gen walked to the window and looked up the street. Just up that hill a few blocks away, he was probably passing by. *At this very moment, if I ran up the hill* — Gen's thoughts were interrupted as a horse flew up the street, its rider hatless, screaming epithets about the dirty Sioux. She shivered and stepped away from the window, crossing the room to add a log to the fire. *Does he even have a blanket to protect him from the cold?*

The silence in the small parlor was

416

broken when Aaron came in carrying the baby. Meg was not far behind, excited to tell them that Baby could stand up by herself for nearly an entire minute.

Gen forced a smile and held out her arms to take the baby. "Have you heard anything at all?" she asked Simon.

He shook his head. "Not yet. But we'll keep looking. There must be some family. Somewhere."

"What if we don't find anyone?" Aaron asked.

"Then we'll keep her," Meg said abruptly. "She'll be our sister!"

Simon got up and crossed the room to where Gen sat with the child. He stroked the blonde hair and smiled, looking down at Gen. "What do you think, Mademoiselle LaCroix? Shall we give our little gift from God a name?"

"She has a name," Gen said abruptly, nuzzling the baby's cheek. At Simon's look of surprise, she said, "She appeared just when Two Stars and I had given up hope." She lifted her blue eyes to Simon's. "We'll call her Hope."

Simon cleared his throat. "Well, then, that's settled."

The day after Christmas Gen tried to

keep busy. They were hanging thirty-nine Dakota down in Mankato. She and Miss Jane began an orgy of baking, kneading bread dough, stirring up cookies. Meg had just put the last lump of cookie dough on a tray when Aaron came in with the newspaper, his face white. Trembling, he held the paper out to Gen.

"They have a list —" His voice broke. Tears gathered in his eyes. He pointed to the list. "A list of the —" He held it up to Gen.

Gen read . . . grabbed the paper. "NO!" She looked at Miss Jane wildly, then ran to the door, grabbed her cloak and bonnet, and tore out the backdoor towards the barn.

"Run for your father, Aaron," Miss Jane said. "He's gone to the telegraph office. You must hurry. Tell him they've listed Two Stars among the men to be hanged. Run quickly!"

Aaron ran out the door without taking time to get his coat. Gen flew by him astride Rory. Wild-eyed, crying, she lashed the horse into a run and headed south for Mankato.

"But they can't hang Daniel," Meg said, frowning. She looked at Miss Jane, confused. "Can they?"

"We must pray to God that they cannot, dear child," Miss Jane said. She closed her eyes. *It cannot be our Daniel. It's a mistake, dear Lord. Let it be a mistake.*

*Too late . . . God . . . dear God . . . I'm too late.*

Flinging herself down from her horse, Gen shoved and pushed her way through the unheeding crowd. From somewhere up ahead she could hear the death song. The men's voices floated across the crowd as Gen clawed at the back of a man who blocked her way. "Please . . . let me pass . . . let me pass."

The man turned around half angrily, but at sight of the diminutive girl, he smiled. "Want to get a better view, miss? Here . . ." He grabbed her by the shoulders and propelled her forward into the teeming crowd of onlookers. She was lost in a sea of sweating bodies and dust, and for a moment she thought she might faint. Still, she pressed forward, feeling as though she were caught in a dream where every movement took unbelievable effort, every whispered word had to be shouted.

Before she managed to claw her way to the front of the crowd, the order was given. Gen's screamed protest was drowned out by the strange sound that went up from the crowd. Not a cheer, really . . . but a collective sigh of satisfaction followed by mutterings from the men around her.

No one noticed Gen. No one saw her face go white as she collapsed in a heap. Someone helped her up. She pulled away and stumbled to the edge of a boardwalk and sat down. It was a long time before she could bear to look up. When she finally did, they were cutting the bodies down. The faces were hidden by sacks that had covered the heads of each one of the thirty-eight condemned men. Some of the bodies had already been put into a wagon. There was no way to know if one of them hid *his* face.

Someone walked by muttering about Dakota women. Only he did not say "women."

Gen lifted her face from her hands. People were walking by, looking at her oddly. A small group gathered around her.

"How dare you show your face —" Someone shoved her from behind.

A buggy moved slowly through the crowd.

"Geneviève." Simon climbed down from the buggy. "Come home, Geneviève." He climbed down and moved through the crowd.

"Half-breed." Someone spat on her.

Simon stood over her. "This young woman is nurse to my children. She risked her life keeping them safe during the recent horrors, and I'll thank you to show her the respect she has earned." He bent down and helped her up. The crowd melted away.

"You foolish, foolish child," Simon said, tucking a horsehair lap robe around Gen's legs. "What did you think to do?"

Gen put her hands up to her face. She shook her head and burst into tears.

"It was a mistake, dear girl," Simon said gently. "It had to be a mistake. I'm taking you home. And then I shall look into the matter. You know how easy it is to confuse Dakota names. Dr. Riggs would never let such a thing happen." He tied Rory to the buggy and turned up the road for St. Peter.

Back in St. Peter it took all of Gen's energy just to climb down from Simon's buggy, to walk to the house, to drink the tea Miss Jane offered. She felt ancient. Every movement took more effort than it was worth. Miss Jane finally led her to her room, suggesting that she nap. Later that night, Miss Jane found Gen curled up on the bed, still fully clothed. She helped her undress and pulled a nightrobe over her head, clucking and fussing over her as if she were a child.

The change in Gen over the next few days frightened Simon. She reminded him of some of the women who had been terribly abused as captives. Even when they told their stories, they seemed oddly disconnected from reality. They could speak of unspeakable things with no display of emotion at all. It was as if the awful things they described had happened to someone else — someone they didn't even know. It seemed that the vibrant Gen he knew had withdrawn into some inner world where he couldn't follow. She read to Meg, she helped Miss Jane prepare meals. She did laundry and tended the fires in the small house. She did everything that was asked of her. But she never initiated activity or conversation. What hurt Simon the most was that she never smiled.

Love for Gen made Simon keep looking for a man he thought dead. When he learned the Dakota bodies had been exhumed from their mass grave for study by local physicians, he slogged from physician to physician, trying to find someone to verify the identity of one Daniel Two Stars.

"He had a scar from here" — Simon pointed to his elbow — "to here," he said, indicating his wrist. "And an old gunshot wound through the right shoulder."

Dr. Robert Mayo shook his head. "I claimed Cut Nose. Identity was certain. I don't recall seeing another body with those scars. Don't know who would have taken it."

"He wore a beaded necklace with a cross woven in," Simon said.

"None of the executed wore any decoration at all," the doctor said. "I heard most of them took such things off and gave them away to family that morning." The doctor nodded. "You might try to find his family. They're probably up at Fort Snelling with the rest of the peaceful Indians."

Finally Simon wrote to Dr. Riggs. When the letter came, he didn't have the heart to share it with Gen. *It does appear that a mistake was made,* Dr. Riggs wrote.

# Thirty-one

Even so then, at this present time there is a remnant according to the election of grace.

— ROMANS 11:5 (NKJV)

Rising from her bed and pulling on her wrapper, Gen padded down the hallway, past Miss Jane and the Sutton children's room, past the stairway to the garret where Aaron and Meg slept, into the kitchen where Simon sat hunched over the table, his reading glasses perched on the end of his nose. She watched him for a moment, saw him rub his neck and then sit up straight, taking his glasses off to rest them on the table, closing his eyes wearily as he leaned back in the chair and rubbed his neck.

"Don't waste your time on it anymore, Simon," Gen said from the doorway. She went to the stove and stirred up the fire and set the pot of cold coffee back over the burner. "You've done all you could. Dr. Riggs would have written us by now if he'd

424

been able to find anything. It isn't right for me to take any more of his time."

Simon cleared his throat nervously. "Actually, Gen, I've heard from Dr. Riggs."

Gen sat down abruptly opposite Simon. She stared at him and then closed her eyes and sighed.

"I didn't have the heart to tell you yet. I thought I should wait —"

"He's dead. The newspaper wasn't a mistake." Gen reached up to touch the beaded necklace hanging around her neck.

Simon reached over and took Gen's hand. He held it fast while he said, " 'It appears a mistake was made.' That's all Dr. Riggs said. That — and, of course, offering his sympathies. He — he feels responsible since he was involved in numbering the prisoners."

Gen pulled her hand away and, putting her elbows on the table, rested her forehead on her hands. "Does he know what happened to Gray Woman or the Lawrences?" She kept her voice even, emotionless.

"That's what I'm working on tonight," Simon said quietly. "I've written letters to John Williamson at the prison camp up at Fort Snelling to ask him about them. They have about sixteen hundred inside the stockade now. With their homes destroyed and no place to go, the Dakota came in willingly. At least they won't starve or freeze to death." Simon rubbed his arms and flexed his fingers against the chilled air in the kitchen. "It may take some time, but John's dependable. If our friends are there, John will find them."

The coffee was boiling, and Gen got up and poured them each a cup.

While she worked, Simon added, "I'm putting a notice in several of the surrounding newspapers about Hope. And I'll do the same in the St. Louis newspaper to see if we can't locate Rebecca and Timothy's relatives. Miss Jane remembered their parents speaking of an aunt in St. Louis, but she couldn't recall a name."

"You're a good man, Simon," Gen said quietly. She set her coffee cup down and stood up. "I — I just wanted you to know you can stop —" She gripped the back of the chair before her and waited to control her voice. "You can stop all the questions about Two Stars." She set her empty coffee cup on the counter and headed back to bed.

Settling beneath the pile of comforters, she laid her head on the pillow. *Now. Stop mucking around in self-pity, Miss LaCroix.* She closed her eyes. Sometime during the night, her hand closed around Daniel Two Stars's beaded necklace. When she woke the next morning, her pillow was damp with tears she didn't recall shedding.

She had ordered herself to go on with her life. And there were days when she thought she had. But then she would awaken in the middle of the night crying. One day on the way home from market she passed a pile of spoiled meat outside a hotel. The smell brought back visions from the summer before that made her physically ill. She ran home, barely making it to the outhouse before her body was wracked with dry heaves. She hurried inside and rushed to do a long list of chores.

"Gen," Miss Jane said, taking the dust cloth out of her hand later that afternoon. "You've already dusted this room today. Before you went out. Remember?"

Had it not been for the children, she was convinced she would have gone mad. Aaron had begun to smile again. Not the full-blown, childish smile from before the outbreak, but a wiser, sadder smile. Still, Gen thought, it was a sign he would be all right.

Meg was beginning to show a penchant

for reading that threatened to challenge even their host's substantial library. Miss Jane taught the children, but Gen sat in on most sessions, and it kept her mind occupied.

Rebecca and Timothy Sutton were more of a challenge. At times Rebecca woke screaming for Miss Jane. She was pale and nervous and couldn't bear to have Timothy out of her sight. Timothy still hadn't spoken a word, but Gen noticed he sucked his thumb less and seemed to take more interest in his surroundings.

"Give them time," Miss Jane said confidently. "Time and love." For a spinster who had once joked about not wanting children of her own, Miss Jane seemed to step into the role of surrogate mother with amazing ease.

And then there was Hope, the baby who had forgotten how to cry, who gave love without measure, and served as living proof that there had been a man named Daniel Two Stars who had, indeed, been a hero.

"I declare," Miss Jane said one day during school when Gen sat dandling Hope on her knee. "That child adores you."

"And I adore her," Gen said, kissing the

fringe of curls along Hope's hairline. "Who could resist those blue eyes?"

Hope reached up and patted Gen's cheeks with two pudgy hands, chortling happily.

Gen said softly, "I hope no one ever surfaces to claim her."

From where she sat at the table copying a composition, Meg said, "We claimed her. She's ours. Two Stars rescued her and we love her and we named her and that's that."

"We still must make certain," Miss Jane said gently.

Gen agreed. "Simon said he'll try to find the homestead in the spring and look again for the surveyor's stakes. Perhaps that will end the matter." *Please . . . God.* Gen could not think that after taking Two Stars, God would require Hope. Surely there was a limit to what He demanded.

Gen had begun to think she was over the worst of her struggle when one day she thought she saw Daniel. A crowd had gathered outside the newspaper office to read a list of orphaned children residing in St. Peter and one of them, about Daniel's height, with shaggy dark hair and a bright red plaid shirt, stood with his back to her. She walked towards the man, her heart pounding, her cheeks flushing with emotions — only to have her hopes dashed. The man was not even Dakota.

Hurrying back to the missionaries' rented house, Gen crept down the hall, grateful that Miss Jane had taken the children out for the day. She crawled into bed, fully clothed, trembling. *What's wrong with me? . . . I'm acting like the only person in history who's had to face the death of someone they loved . . . this is ridiculous. I'm the one who scolded Simon for letting Ellen's death ruin his life . . . and here I am, doing the same thing . . .* A loud bang sounded out in the street, broke through Gen's logic, made her scream, sent her back to the day when thirty-eight trap doors banging open meant the end of the Minnesota Sioux Uprising.

Simon found her crouched between the bed and the wall, her hands clapped over her ears. "It's nothing, Gen," he said gently. "Just a barrel that fell off a wagon. You are safe." He knelt before her, pulling her hands away from her ears and taking them in his own. "Remember where you are, Gen. You are in St. Peter with Miss Jane and the Sutton children. With Meg and Aaron and Hope — and me. You are safe, Gen." He coaxed her to lie down.

Covering her with a quilt, he left just long enough to retrieve a kitchen chair and to sit down beside her.

Gen began to cry. "I'm so stupid," she muttered. "I'm acting like I'm the only one something bad ever happened to."

"You've had a great shock," Simon soothed. "And many losses in your young life. It's only natural to be melancholy." He patted her hand. "I'm going to make you some tea."

"You don't have to be my nursemaid, Simon."

From the doorway he said firmly, "I am not your nursemaid, Gen. I'm your friend."

When he returned, tea in hand, Gen sat up. "That's kind of you, Simon, but —"

"Drink your tea, Gen. Stop trying to ignore your emotions."

Gen jerked her head up and met his gaze.

He smiled, almost embarrassed. "I don't suppose you ever expected to hear Simon Dane say *that*, did you?" He forced her to sit back on the bed, propped up with pillows. When he put the cup of tea in her hands, Gen drank it like an obedient child.

Simon sat beside the bed in a rocker. "There is a time for everything, Gen.

There *is* a time to mourn. I seem to remember someone telling me once that it's all right to cry when a loved one is gone . . . and we miss them." He left the room again and returned with his Bible. "After that day in the cemetery back in New York," he said, "I began to read the Psalms every day. They seemed to provide words for things I didn't know how to say. Things I was feeling, but I just couldn't express. One day," he said, opening his Bible near the middle, "I ran across this verse: *'Thou tellest my wanderings: put thou my tears into thy bottle: are they not in thy book? When I cry unto thee, then shall mine enemies turn back: this I know; for God is for me . . . In God have I put my trust: I will not be afraid what man can do unto me.'* " Simon raised his eyes to look at Gen. "It's a beautiful illustration, don't you think? God — the almighty God of the universe . . . cares enough about *me* that He keeps even my tears in a bottle." He leaned forward and laid the open Bible in Gen's lap. "God sees your tears, Gen. He sees your heart. And He cares for you." He took her empty teacup and turned to go. At the doorway he turned back and said softly, "You have questions, Gen. Try reading the answer book."

"Aaron," Simon said one morning at breakfast, "I've been asked to help with distributing some of the funds that our friends back east are sending to assist the refugees returning to their farms. I'd like it very much if you would come with me." He looked around the table. "We'll be moving up to St. Anthony where my old friends, the Whitneys, are coordinating the relief effort. They have a large and comfortable home and they've invited us to stay with them." He looked at Meg. "The Whitneys have a new baby, Meg. Now you'll have *two* babies to play with!"

"What about Miss Jane, and 'Becca and Tim?" Meg wanted to know.

"We can't do without Miss Jane," Simon said. "She'll come with us?" He put the question in his eyes, relieved when Miss Jane nodded firmly from her place at the opposite end of the table.

And so they went, gliding in a sleigh over snow-covered roads and across drifts until they topped a rise and looked below them to a level plain where hundreds of canvas tents had been pitched inside a high board fence. Soldiers patrolled the perimeter.

"Are those the bad Indians?" Meg said, wrinkling her nose against the stench that floated up the hill.

"No," Simon said. "Those are the friendlies. The guilty Dakota are in a prison camp down by Mankato."

"But if those are friendly Indians," Aaron asked, "why are they kept inside the fence?"

"Because the government cannot decide what to do with them," Simon said quietly.

"They should let them go home," Aaron said abruptly.

Simon shook his head. "I don't think that's possible anymore, Aaron. People are too unforgiving. To them, all Indians are evil."

Aaron looked at Gen. "Then they don't understand very much about Indians."

Gen turned her face away from the camp and closed her eyes. *Oh that I had wings like a dove! For then would I fly away, and be at rest . . .*

"I wonder if Mother Friend is down there," Miss Jane murmured.

"I hope she died," Gen said without opening her eyes. "Better to be dead than to live in that place."

Simon cleared his throat. "John Williamson writes that there has been a revival in the camp. Some of the former church leaders began meeting for prayer . . . and

434

before long so many came they had to begin meeting in a garret above the warehouse. It's amazing how God always saves a remnant for Himself . . . and then uses that faithful remnant to bring in the harvest." They glided out of sight of the prison camp and turned on the road for St. Anthony.

St. Anthony had begun as one cabin near picturesque falls on the river ten miles above St. Paul. By 1863, it had become a bustling city of five thousand standing across the river from a new village of several hundred named Minneapolis. The population of the area was growing and had swelled in the last few months as thousands of refugees from the southeastern part of the state fled their homes.

"Welcome, welcome!" Nina Whitney greeted her guests enthusiastically. "It's drafty," she said, waving her hand around her as the travelers came inside, "but we feel blessed to have so much room." She smiled warmly at Miss Jane. "Perhaps the Lord has a boarding school in mind, after all."

Cloaks were removed and hung up, overshoes set by the fireplace to dry, the children admired, Hope roundly kissed, and everyone herded towards the kitchen for "fresh milk — can you believe it? We have our own cow!" and cookies. When everyone was settled around the vast kitchen table, Nina announced with a smile and a wink, "You haven't seen the baby!" She hurried off and returned with the baby and someone she referred to as "Nurse." But "Nurse" proved to be two people . . . and with whoops of joy, Belle and Lizzie swept into the room.

When the chaos from Nina's carefully planned surprise finally resolved, Simon and Samuel Whitney excused themselves to plan Simon's first relief trip. As Simon left the room, he leaned over and whispered to Gen, "You see, my dear . . . God always preserves a remnant."

That evening, while the gentlemen planned the future, the women tended to the children. Once the little ones were asleep, the women sat in the kitchen drinking tea. Belle and Lizzie recounted their harrowing escape with the Hazelwood missionaries. Gen smiled at Aaron and Meg as they all heard how Simon had recovered Rory and a wagon. She felt proud for them when Lizzie said it was Simon who went to Fort Ridgely in the dark of night, "and we didn't know if he was headed for warring Sioux or soldiers." And when Lizzie described the reverend shoving a pistol in a man's face and making him stay and help them, Gen decided there was more to Simon Dane than she had thought.

"But we endured nothing compared to you," Lizzie finally said, looking at Gen and Miss Jane, who shrugged and remained quiet for an uncomfortable silence until Miss Jane finally cleared her throat to mention Mother Friend's kindness. Gen mentioned finding Hope . . . in a deserted cabin. Neither woman could put words to their time among the Dakota. Neither wanted to.

Finally Nina Whitney said softly, "To think Samuel and I were safe here in St. Anthony, while our friends were going through —" She shuddered. "Thanks be to God it's over." Nina led the way upstairs where Miss Jane would have a room with the Sutton children, Aaron would bunk with his father, and Gen would share with Hope and Meg. When she said good night to Gen, Nina grabbed her hand and squeezed it. "I've never stopped praying for you, Geneviève." She winked. "Not since the day God moved those sandbars."

# Thirty-two

God, my maker, who giveth songs in the night.

— JOB 35:10 (KJV)

"But Simon," Gen said softly. "I don't love you. Not in that way."

How grateful she was that the children were asleep and the other adults had gone for a stroll. Simon had asked her to stay behind, "to discuss something about the children." When Miss Jane and Nina Whitney exchanged knowing glances, Gen had felt a familiar tightening in her chest, thinking God was about to admit more emotional pain into her life. Her mind had sorted through a list of possibilities before she decided that Simon must have learned something about Hope's family. And it wasn't good news. Good news could have been shared with everyone.

Instead, Simon had led her into the parlor and asked her to sit with him. And then, in a halting voice, he had proposed marriage. Gen looked into the dying fire, hating the idea of hurting Simon. When she raised her objection, she put one hand on his arm, trying to soften the blow. When she finally gathered courage to look up at him, nothing but kindness shone in his eyes.

He put his hand over hers. "I'm not a fool, Gen, to think that such a thing would happen." He swallowed hard. "But we have become friends — close friends — in these months since the uprising — haven't we?"

Gen nodded.

"I can't imagine life without you. Meg and Aaron would be devastated. And we must keep Hope at all costs. If we marry, the authorities cannot decline to let us keep her no matter where the board might send me next." He released her hand and shifted on the divan so he was facing her. "I cannot shake the deep conviction that we have been called, somehow, to Hope. And she to us." He stood up and crossed the room, standing beside one of the windows that framed the fireplace. "I don't mean to use the children as a weapon, Gen. Or as a means to a selfish end. Really, I don't. I have prayed about this for weeks, and I truly think that you belong with us. You cannot deny that the bonds that were

439

formed between you and the children during the outbreak are strong." He looked at the ceiling. "And I will not deny that the feelings I have for you are much stronger than friendship." His cheeks colored a little as his eyes met hers. "But I promise you on the Word of God that if you agree to marry me I will never violate your trust. I will never demand anything that you do not give willingly." He looked away momentarily, and then back again and swallowed hard. When Gen still didn't speak, he added, "If in your heart you must decline, I understand." He shrugged. "Surely you can see that I had to do my utmost to keep my little family intact. You *are* part of this family, you know. The family that is in here." He tapped his chest.

"But you don't know that the board will want you to leave St. Anthony," Gen said, her voice wavering. "With Miss Jane and Belle and Lizzie reunited, Nina said they might begin their boarding school after all." She pleaded, "You could go anywhere, Simon. And the children could stay here. Safe. With me."

Sighing, Simon turned away and pulled the curtain aside, staring down into the street below. "It's all right, Geneviève. I understand." After a moment he murmured, "A scrawny old preacher isn't much of a replacement for a Dakota warrior, is he?" Without looking at her again, he said, "I won't bring it up again. I'm sorry if I've upset you." He started to leave, but hesitated just long enough to say, "I know, Geneviève, what it means to lose the love of one's life."

He crossed to the door, but Gen ran after him, touching his arm, looking up at him with tears shining in her eyes. "Never, never apologize for loving someone, Simon."

"I wasn't apologizing for loving you, Geneviève. I was only apologizing for being so presumptuous as to think that you might feel — well — something that could make marriage at least acceptable, if not entirely desirable — for the sake of the children."

Gen asked nervously, "Can you give me time — time to consider?"

"My dear," Simon said warmly, kissing her hand. "If there is one glimmer of hope that you will say yes to my absurd proposal, take a lifetime." He squeezed her hand and released it. "I'll still be waiting when you decide."

From behind the emotional wall she had erected around herself, Gen watched. She enjoyed working alongside Belle and Lizzie again. She strengthened her friendship with Miss Jane. And she was surprised to find that Nina Whitney's close walk with God no longer irritated her.

Timothy Sutton stopped sucking his thumb. One morning when Miss Jane handed him a bowl of warm cereal, he looked up at her and said, "T'ank you, Aunt Janie." Miss Jane cleared her throat and put her hand over her mouth. "You're welcome, Timothy," she said with a trembling voice.

Rebecca Sutton stopped having nightmares.

Meg began to refer to Hope as her sister.

Hope took her first steps.

Aaron forged a relationship with his father that bordered on hero worship. On their mission to take relief to the white victims of the outbreak, they were gone for days at a time, during which Aaron kept a journal that he shared with Gen. When they were at home, he was always quick with a hug for Gen.

"Promise me something," she said to him one evening after supper.

"Sure, Gen. What?"

"Promise me you will never grow too old to give hugs."

Aaron laughed and hugged her again.

He had recovered, Gen thought. And by some miracle he had retained his mother's sensitivity. *Thank You, Lord.*

One day early in April when she whispered those words, Gen was brought up short, realizing that she had taken to doing that quite often — saying little things to God throughout the day as if she were communicating with a friend. No lightning had flashed, no thunder had rolled, but Gen realized that at last God had answered her prayer and given her faith. She discovered that when she read the Psalms, the words weren't stopping in her head. They were going into her heart. *The sorrows of death compassed me . . . in my distress I called upon the Lord, and cried unto my God: he heard my voice out of his temple, and my cry came before him, even into his ears . . . He sent from above, he drew me out of many waters . . . He brought me forth.*

The words held new meaning, and life held new promise. Gen still cried. She still mourned. But she no longer felt as if she was lost in that space between what she could and could not understand. She had seen God's love in the lives of her friends, she had felt His presence when she cried out to Him, and she was content to leave the unanswered questions with Him, until He should decide to answer them. And if He never did, she would rely on His love.

She touched the cross that hung around her neck often, newly aware of its meaning, comforted by the ultimate symbol of God's love for her. God was not a capricious dictator who sat back and enjoyed watching His creatures squirm. He had penetrated their existence with Himself . . . He had come down and dwelt among them . . . and He had let them kill Him. He had been willing to live among the lions and let them devour Him. Slowly, over time, the knowledge of God's never-failing love became enough for Gen. She remained in the gap between understanding and unanswered questions, finally at rest in the everlasting arms.

"We drove all the way to Glencoe on Monday," Aaron reported one evening. "When we drove up, Mr. Rediger was just leaning against the porch railing — almost like he was in shock. But Father and I soon had things right for them. We cleaned out the house first. Built a big bonfire of everything that was destroyed. Then Mr. Rediger chopped wood while Father and I cleaned out the barn.

"And you should have seen Mrs. Rediger's face when Father handed her ten dollars from the Friends to restock her kitchen! You would have thought we gave her the moon. Father read the Scriptures with them too. And he prayed. And then we sang some hymns. They wanted us to stay, but we had to get on our way. We had another family to help."

Gen listened, inwardly shaking her head with surprise. *Simon Dane chopping wood? Cleaning out a barn?*

Aaron said that at one house they churned butter and kneaded bread dough for a crazy woman who couldn't seem to remember how. "And when we left," Aaron said proudly, "she kissed Father on the cheek and said what a good man he was." He frowned momentarily. "I don't know about that family. They might not make it." His face brightened. "But we did what we could."

Simon would never be a handsome man, but something new in his face commanded attention. Gen decided it was his eyes. They seemed warmer, kinder. The cold superiority was gone. The time outdoors tanned and weathered the complexion that had always had the translucent quality of a scholar. His hands, once so soft they were almost feminine, had become calloused and weather-worn. *If only Ellen were here to see it,* Gen thought. She began to miss Aaron and Simon when they were gone.

*Perhaps it's a blessing that Daniel didn't live to see this,* Gen thought as she pored over the newspaper. The governor said the Sioux must either be exterminated or driven forever from the state. Someone proposed shipping them to an island and leaving them to fend for themselves. Sibley suggested a reservation in the Dakota Territory . . . where they would be surrounded by troops and reduced to slavery. And their old agent Galbraith was quoted: "They must be whipped and coerced into obedience . . . many will be killed; more must perish from famine and exposure, the more desperate will flee and seek refuge on the plains or in the mountains . . . a very small reservation should suffice for them."

In February all treaties between the United States government and the Sioux nation had been abrogated. Dakota annuity monies would be used to set up a fund to reimburse the uprising's white victims. Dakota land would be put up for sale. Realizing that if Daniel were alive he would be homeless, Gen took comfort in the notion that he was safe from harm.

But God saved His remnant and sent revival to Mankato and Fort Snelling. The local newspaper screamed "Awful Sacrilege." *God was mocked,* one journalist wrote, *and his religion burlesqued by the solemn farce of administering the sacred ordinances of baptism and confirmation to a horde of the treacherous fiends at Fort Snelling.*

Simon reported that Reverend Hinman was beaten unconscious when some white men forced themselves into the stockade and attacked him. No one who showed the Sioux any kindness was spared verbal abuse and threats. But the missionaries endured.

After a long, miserable winter in Mankato, convicted Dakota prisoners were being sent to prison in Iowa. Simon read a letter from John Williamson reporting that three hundred Dakota had died during the winter inside the board fence at Fort Snelling. They were being sent to a new reservation in Dakota Territory — someplace called Crow Creek — banned forever from their beloved Minnesota.

Gen experienced the hatred for the Sioux firsthand one warm spring Sabbath when she and Simon and the Whitneys walked to church together. They were headed inside when Gen heard someone in a group gathered at the foot of the stairs say, "They should have been exterminated when Sibley had the chance. Now our money goes to house and feed them."

Simon stopped short, and the Whitneys followed his lead.

"They'll be gone soon enough," another man offered. "Although they won't say when. They're still afraid of a mob scene."

"Someone said many of them have become Christians," a female voice offered.

"And they'd become Satan-worshipers tomorrow if they thought that would gain them advantage," was the curt reply. "You can't trust them."

"Mrs. Wakefield said they treated her kindly," the female voice said.

The man snorted. "Mrs. Wakefield? Mrs. *Wakefield?!* We all know what *she* did to protect herself! She *married* one of them — helped him make ammunition — laughed when he described his awful deeds."

"She was terrified," Gen said, her blue eyes flashing. "Her hair turned white practically overnight. The man who protected her was a good man. He never took advantage of her. And he risked his life many times to keep her safe."

The man turned on her. "On what possible grounds can you defend those murdering savages?"

Gen lifted her chin and stared at him. "On the grounds that I was there. On the grounds that I saw Mrs. Wakefield. I knew her protector. He was a friend of mine."

The man's face grew red. He swore and took a step towards Gen. Simon placed himself between them. "This young woman protected my children during the uprising. And I will thank you to apologize to her."

The other man scowled. Simon didn't move. People standing around the two men looked at one another nervously. Finally, the stranger blinked and took a step back. He bowed awkwardly. "My apologies to the lady if I upset her. I lost my brother and his wife in the outbreak." He swore again.

"You might find it of interest to learn that I would have lost my children," Simon said, "had it not been for a full-blooded Dakota named Daniel Two Stars — may God rest his soul." Simon added, "What's going on in this state is a travesty. The very men who protected our wives and children are languishing in prison . . . while the guilty have disappeared into the countryside."

"And I suppose you're just the man to

catch them," someone said as the crowd melted away. Simon cleared his throat. He looked at the Whitneys and said, "I hope you won't mind, but I don't think I wish to worship alongside those — men."

Samuel nodded. "I quite agree."

Gen squeezed Simon's arm.

"Delivering the relief funds has been important work. But my heart is with the Dakota." Simon smiled and shook his head. "Imagine that, Geneviève. After all these years in the ministry, I have finally received a calling." The missionaries had just gathered for breakfast when Simon announced that he intended to drive down to Fort Snelling, to witness the transfer of the Dakota prisoners to the steamship that would take them to their reservation in Dakota Territory, to provide whatever support he could in preparation for returning to a ministry among them.

"I don't see what good your being there will do," Gen protested. "They are expecting a crowd . . . and there may be violence."

"But John thought that if their old missionaries turned out in force, perhaps that would be a mitigating presence against the mob."

"You might be hurt!" Gen lifted her hand to her throat. "Simon, you can't take the risk."

"They wouldn't dare hurt a woman," Miss Jane interrupted. "Take us with you, Reverend Dane." Belle and Lizzie nodded emphatically. "Yes. Take us."

"Absolutely out of the question," Simon said, shaking his head.

"If you won't take us," Miss Jane said evenly, "I shall rent a carriage and drive myself. Someone has to stand for reason and right. Someone has to show the Dakota there are still sane white people who know they aren't all guilty. With all due respect, Reverend Dane," Miss Jane concluded, staring over her gold-rimmed glasses, "you are neither my husband nor my pastor, so I don't have to submit to you. I'm going."

"Don't split theological hairs to get your way, Miss Jane!" Simon said quickly.

But Miss Jane was getting up, prepared to head out the door for her own carriage. "All right, Miss Jane, all right!" Simon finally relented. "At least if you're with Reverend Whitney and myself, I'll have some control over the situation."

"But they can't be serious," Gen whispered, looking down the hill towards the river. "That steamer can't possibly hold everyone." They were sitting in a carriage, overlooking the dismal scene. Soldiers were everywhere, some holding back an angry crowd of townspeople, others on horseback patrolling along the line of bedraggled prisoners filing out of the enclosure and down the hill towards the river.

Simon shrugged. "I heard yesterday was worse. They jammed nearly eight hundred aboard the *Davenport*."

Gen closed her eyes. *Dear God . . . have mercy.*

"Company G of the Tenth Minnesota will be this group's escort." Simon and Samuel climbed down from the carriage. "You women stay here. And pray for our brothers and sisters."

Gen watched the Dakota file along the path to the river, and her eyes filled with tears. They were woefully thin. Simon had said hundreds had died over the winter. Her heart burned to think of the way Mother Friend had fed Aaron and Meg, insisting they share in the bounty of the "bad Indians'" plunder. And now, the same women who had taken such good care of white children had spent the winter watching their own children die for want of food and proper care. Gen raised the question *why* to God.

"If we're to be any encouragement at all, we must get closer," Miss Jane said, preparing to climb down from the carriage. "Where we can pray or sing or at least smile at them."

Gen and Lizzie followed close behind their tall friend, jostling their way through a silent, brooding crowd of onlookers, finally managing to reach the front.

"Whoa, miss," a soldier said, holding out his arm to stop Miss Jane. "We don't want any trouble."

The Dakota filed past, silent, sending fearful glances towards the onlookers. One little girl stumbled and fell and was snatched up by an old woman — it was Mother Friend! Miss Jane and Gen struggled to get past the soldier. "Mother Friend! Mother Friend!" they called out frantically in Dakota. The old woman paused and looked back, unbelieving. She squinted against the setting sun, her eyes filled with tears.

"You cannot pass," the soldier said firmly, grabbing Miss Jane's arm.

"Get out of my way, young man," Miss Jane said tersely. "That woman saved my life." She tried to shoulder her way past, but the soldier would not give way.

"With all due respect, ma'am," he muttered under his breath. "You're going to get yourself — and maybe me — killed if you don't stand back. You'd best save your reunions with old friends for another day." He didn't move, but he looked meaningfully at Miss Jane and around at the crowd. Miss Jane glanced behind her. Hatred and anger were so evident in the faces around her it sent a chill up her spine. She cleared her throat and relented. Together, she and the others headed back to Simon's carriage. They watched the last of the Dakota file on board the steamer just as dusk approached. A whistle blew, the paddle wheel slapped the water, and the boat pulled into the middle of the river.

And then, music. Softly, so quietly that only a missionary could recognize the words, the familiar tune wafted across the water and up the hill . . .

*Jesus Christ, nitowashti kin,*
*Woptecashna mayaqu.*
*Jesus Christ, thy loving kindness*
*Boundlessly thou givest me.*

"And they *sang*, Nina," Gen said, her voice breaking. "They *sang*."

While the men conducted a meeting encouraging church leaders to help the Dakota Mission, Nina and Gen sat on the old house's substantial back porch, watching the sun set. Inside, Miss Jane and Belle were doing dishes. Lizzie had herded the children upstairs for bedtime stories and prayers.

Listening to Gen describe the scene at Fort Snelling, Nina wiped tears off her cheeks, shaking her head. "I wish I had been there with you." She laid her hand across her expanding abdomen. Samuel had forbidden her to go because of the coming child and, unlike Gen and Miss Jane, Nina had obeyed.

"Simon wants us to follow them to the reservation. He feels a calling to them." Gen shook her head. "What could *I* teach *them?* They have faith a thousand times stronger than mine."

"Perhaps," Nina said gently, "that is exactly why you should go." She smiled softly.

Gen looked up. "Simon wants me — that is, he thinks we should marry." She smiled. "You weren't as crazy as I thought when you mentioned the possibility back in Alton last summer."

Nina looked at Gen closely. "But you

don't love Simon. Not that way." It was a statement, not a question.

Gen shook her head. "I respect him, though. And he has been a good friend."

"Successful marriages have been built on less."

"It isn't very — romantic."

"It doesn't have to be. To be right."

Gen reached up and touched the necklace hanging around her neck. "Pray for me, Nina," she said softly. "I want to do something useful with my life. But I'm afraid."

"I told you, Gen . . . I haven't stopped praying. Not since the day I asked God to move those sandbars."

Bidding Nina good night, Gen headed upstairs. Meg was asleep, snoring softly, her arm draped across Hope. Kissing them both on the cheek, Gen began to unbutton her blouse. She went to the dresser and looked at herself in the mirror. What was it Mrs. Riggs had said? . . . *I just picture myself placing the name of each child in these hands, and then I lift it up to God.* Gen closed her eyes. Lifting her chin, she held her hands palm out and waited. Presently, she took a deep breath and glanced back in the mirror as she took the beaded necklace from around her neck. She traced the edge of the cross with her finger. Then, opening the dresser drawer, she unfolded a lace-edged handkerchief, wrapped the beads in it, and laid it away in the drawer.

She raised her eyes to the mirror again. Then she went back outside and to the end of the hall, where she sat down on the top step, listening for Simon's return.

*But this one thing I do, forgetting those things which are behind, and reaching forth unto those things which are before, I press toward the mark for the prize of the high calling of God in Christ Jesus.*
*— Philippians 3:13–14*

# About the Author

Stephanie Grace Whitson grew up in southern Illinois where her mother taught her to love books and reading. Before beginning a career as a full time homemaker and home-schooling mother of four, Stephanie's job titles included high school French teacher, medical secretary, and publications secretary. Home schooling resulted in the creation of a home-based inspirational gifts company known as Prairie Pieceworks, Inc., which marketed a line of bears featuring Stephanie's original inspirational poetry. As an avid quilter, she was also involved in quilt pattern and sewing-related jewelry design.

When Thomas Nelson offered Stephanie a contract for her first series, Prairie Pieceworks's gift line was licensed to David C. Cook Communications and is now available through the "Best to You" mail-order catalog.

Today, Stephanie and her family live in southeast Nebraska where Stephanie pursues a full-time writing ministry from her home studio. She is the author of seven books, including the bestselling Prairie

Winds Series: *Walks the Fire*, *Soaring Eagle*, and *Red Bird*; as well as the Keepsake Legacies Series: *Sarah's Patchwork*, *Karyn's Memory Box*, and *Nora's Ribbon of Memories*. She accepts a limited number of speaking engagements each year and, along with her family, is active in her local Bible-teaching church. In 1998 she and Robert celebrated their silver wedding anniversary.

Stephanie can be reached at the following address:

Stephanie Grace Whitson
3800 Old Cheney Road #101-178
Lincoln, NE 68516
or
www.stephaniegracewhitson.com